MW01113450

Samhain Secrets

Irish Horse Productions Anthology

Published by Irish Horse Productions

Copyright © 2019 Irish Horse Productions/J.A. Cummings

This book contains works of fiction. Names, characters, places, and incidents are either the products of the authors' imaginations or are used fictitiously, and any resemblance to actual persons, living or dead, events, or locales is entirely coincidental.

Cover Design, 2019 Cathy Walker
Published by Irish Horse Productions
Edited by J.A. Cummings

Without limiting the rights under copyright reserved above, no part of this publication may be reproduced, stored in or introduced into a retrieval system, or transmitted, in any form, or by any means (electronic, mechanical, photocopying, recording, or otherwise), without the prior written permission of both the copyright owner and the above publisher of this book.

Table of Contents

Vanishing Act 1

Rocking Chair 21

The Grim Pumpkin 26

Keeping Dark Customs 38

    October 31st – Thomas 39

    October 31st – Nikki 42

    November 1st, Early – Nikki 47

    November 1st, Evening – Nikki 54

    November 1st, Evening – Thomas 63

Goth 'n Roll Salem 66

Balancing the Scales 84

Skull Games 101

Masks 104

Second Times 127

Act of God 165

The Keeper's Gift 177

Halloween's Amongst Us 188

Home for the Holidays 192

The Rap of Nails on Glass 206

It Came from the Film Can! 211

Reminders 229

A Haunted Affair 233

Ritual 239

Coach 248

The Photo 262

Candy Snatchers 269

Samhain Night **274**

Bits and Pieces **295**

    Emanuel 296

    Jude 302

    Gabriel 304

Changelings **306**

    Arietta 307

    Tilani 316

Frankenstein Escapes **326**

    Chapter I..327

    Chapter II...335

    Chapter III..346

Smoke and Mirrors **349**

The Halloween from Hell **372**

The Twins **386**

    Part I..387

    Part II...390

    Part III...393

    Part IV...397

Rotten Eggs **400**

Running with the Devil **411**

The Crimes of Colleen O'Byrnes **430**

When Sith Arrives **459**

Hugging Red Maggie **475**

Vanishing Act
by Andra Dill

Kayla stepped out of her car and goggled at the spectacle before her. She couldn't make out a stitch of grass for all the Halloween decorations crammed together on the postage-stamp-sized lawn. A bilious green ghoul whipped back and forth next to a monstrous, grinning jack-o-lantern.

Near the driveway, a trio of smiling witches gathered around a cauldron. 'The Monster Mash,' blaring from a speaker mounted by the garage door, competed with the whine of fans from the various inflatables. Flapping ghosts hung from orang-leafed maple trees and plastic skeletons lounged around a graveyard of Styrofoam tombstones.

Her son, Hunter, would love it. The green ghoul in particular would intrigue his cat nature. He'd find it endlessly amusing to stalk and attack the erratically moving inflatable. She scanned the other homes on the block. Based on the almost Scrooge-like lack of festive adornment, Kayla imagined the neighbors were less pleased.

She turned to watch the shapeshifter prowling toward her. Bronze skin covered sleek, lean muscle; Mateo Silva moved with a wolf's easy grace. Beneath the bright afternoon sun, his deep, brown eyes almost looked as black as his hair.

"Somehow, I don't think those are the ghosts your client is having trouble with." Kayla tilted her head in the direction of the flapping ghosts.

"Wait until you see the inside." Mateo winked at her. When he'd called asking Kayla to consult on a case involving a ghost, her mind had veered off-course, musing over ghosts and spirits. She *might* not have caught everything he'd said.

As owner of Silva Investigations, he had a slew of first-rate investigators – her sister, Bree, among them – ready to take on any assignment. None of them had Kayla's ability to sense magi. Her talent, rare for a shapeshifter, had landed her a job at the University in the Magical Antiquities Department. She hoped he wanted her to assess magic-infused objects, since ghosts weren't in her repertoire.

"I know you asked for a consultation, but fair warning: I've never seen a ghost, nor do I know much about them." She tucked her phone into the back pocket of her jeans and shut her car door. "Remember, I'm a lynx shifter, not a witch."

"I already talked to a Necromancer. I wanted her help communicating with the ghost, but she's out of town for a while. My client is anxious to get this resolved. So, I need your take on some magician's props." Mateo walked alongside her toward the Halloween-on-steroids house.

"You suspect that some of them have been spelled?"

A cool breeze sent dried leaves scuttling down the street and tousled her long, sable-brown hair. Her shoulders stiffened when her phone chimed, but she made no move to check it.

"This case is an unusual one." He scrubbed at his clean-shaven jaw. The citrus and peppery scent of his aftershave pierced the brisk autumn air. "My client believes her dearly departed husband is stealing from her, and she wants the stolen property returned."

Kayla's amber eyes widened in surprise. "You're kidding, right? I mean, ghosts are incorporeal; they can't *steal*. Can they?"

He shrugged one shoulder. "Mrs. Abernathy swears her husband's ghost is the culprit. From what she tells me, he was a relatively successful magician. All the items missing are his old props."

"Is your client human? Witch? Shifter?"

"She's straight-up human."

"So, you want to know if any of his things have witch-magic in them?" She eyed the wart-nosed crones huddled around the cauldron.

"That, and to check the rest of the house. Priya, the Necromancer I consulted, said that ghosts can move things – push them, pull them short distances… She doesn't personally know of a case where they transported an item from one location to another."

They climbed the porch steps.

"She's read an account of a witch's ghost who was purported to do just that, but she doesn't trust the source. After we talked, I wondered if maybe the objects were spelled in a way that could transport them. Maybe they're hidden in another room in the house." He rapped his knuckles on the Grim Reaper door cover. "It's probably a long shot, but I thought if there were any hidden magic items in this house, you'd be able to find them."

"I'm happy to help."

Kayla heard approaching footsteps within the house, then several clicks as multiple deadbolt locks were turned. The front door opened, and a pale, round-faced woman with an equally round body, flyaway gray hair, and oversized red-framed glasses peered up at them.

"Mrs. Abernathy, I've brought my associate, Kayla Byrne."

"Of course, Mr. Silva." She stepped back and gestured for them to enter. "Come in, please." Once they'd gone past her, she shut the door and relocked every deadbolt.

An overabundance of furniture and even more Halloween decorations made the small living room look cramped. The cloying aroma of pumpkin spice permeated the room. Kayla hadn't experienced claustrophobia before – in her lynx form, she'd been in plenty of tight spots, but this packed space made her long for the outdoors.

"Would either of you care for coffee or hot tea?"

They both declined.

"Mrs. Abernathy, would it be possible for me to see your husband's magician props first?" Kayla asked.

"Of course. Follow me." She led them through the cluttered living and dining rooms to the basement steps. "I've been reorganizing downstairs, so don't mind the mess." She flipped the light switch, then clutched the handrail in a death-grip as she descended the stairs.

"Mrs. Abernathy, I'm sure you're tired of repeating your story, but I'd like to hear what happened," Kayla said.

"Call me Myra, please. The first time Jerry appeared – Jerry's my husband." She shook her head. "Was. He's been gone almost two years now."

Kayla understood the verb tense mix-up. She'd been a widow a little longer than Myra Abernathy, but she still caught herself using 'is' instead of 'was' when talking about David.

"I've kept all his things down here since he passed," Myra continued. "Wasn't sure what to do with most of it, really. I just couldn't bear to part with anything that reminded me of Jerry. Anyway, Harold – he's my boyfriend – encouraged me to clean out my basement. I'm a bit of a pack-rat, as you can see."

That was an understatement. Kayla sucked in a breath and regretted it as several dank, moist scents assailed her sensitive nose. Mismatched chairs, end tables, dressers, two couches, and a folded-up ping-pong table crowded what she took for a TV room, even though she couldn't see a single TV. Several mattresses and box springs were propped against dark wood paneling. A battalion of cobwebs clung to most everything. Piles of newspapers, books, cardboard boxes, and plastic bins – a thick layer of dust covering all of them – took up the remaining floor space.

Mateo rested his hand on the small of Kayla's back when she would have bolted back up the stairs. He nudged her gently, and they followed in Myra's wake.

"Harold was going through Jerry's boxes. He's a magician, too. Harold isn't as talented as Jerry, of course. It's more of a hobby for him. Anyway, we were looking through the boxes when Jerry appeared." She stopped walking and patted her ample bosom. "Scared the wits right out of me."

"What did he look like?" Kayla asked.

"Pretty much like he did just before he passed but fainter. All see-through and wavery," she said, wiggling her fingers.

"You told me that Harold couldn't see him." Mateo prompted, his large, warm hand still resting against Kayla's back.

"No, he claimed he couldn't." Mrs. Abernathy resumed walking, taking them into the laundry room. The space had fewer cobwebs but was just as crowded.

"Wow!" Mateo made a beeline for a six-foot-tall, wooden cabinet adorned with stars and malevolently smiling demons. "A devil's torture chamber."

Magi sputtered from the apparatus like a malfunctioning neon sign. The erratic flow of magic was something Kayla had never encountered. Curious, she sidled close and brushed her fingers over the dark wood. The effect persisted. A dozen questions swirled through her mind. She'd love to get the cabinet over to the University to further study.

"I've always wanted to see one of these close up. May I open it?" Mateo asked Myra.

"Sure, just flip this back and this." Myra released two locking mechanisms, then helped him pull the box apart. Dozens of embedded spikes filled the interior.

The expression of rapt joy on Mateo's face was one Kayla had seen numerous times on her Hunter's face. Boys and their toys. She rolled her eyes, then leaned forward to whisper, "This has been spelled."

"I saw Jerry right over there." Myra pointed to a workbench with six blue, plastic tubs atop it. "I had Jerry's cape in my hands, and he… he appeared in front of me, just like someone turning on a light. One second, it's dark; the next, it's light. Pop!"

Lured by a feathery buzz of magic, Kayla edged forward. "What did Jerry do?"

"He touched his cape, shook his head, then he touched my lips." Her voice hitched on the last words. "Then he vanished."

"May I?" Kayla asked, tapping her fingers against the only tub that emitted a magical resonance.

"Go ahead." Mrs. Abernathy lifted her glasses and swiped at her eyes. "The cape disappeared that night."

Kayla pulled the container out and lowered it to the floor. She knelt and rummaged through it, pushing aside playing cards, scarves, and interlocking gold hoops. Her phone chimed, and she blew out an exasperated breath.

"I thought maybe Harold had taken it, but he swore he didn't." Myra reached into the bin and pulled out a shimmery silver veil. "Then a couple days later, I was down here alone, and I was holding Jerry's favorite top hat. He popped in again, and he did the same thing as before. He touched the hat, shook his head, then touched my lips. Then poof! He vanished. I checked first thing the next morning, and sure enough, he'd stolen the hat. I wasn't sure what to do, so I called the police."

Magic nipped at Kayla's fingers when she touched a thin, black, rectangular box. The magic spooling out from it felt like an inquisitive kitten that played coy, wanting to be petted, then arbitrarily repaying the affection with a sharp-toothed bite. When she lifted it, something shifted and thudded inside the box. She removed the lid.

"A Ouija board. I had one of those as a kid." Mateo chuckled, scooping up a wooden planchette. "Well, my best friend did. No way my Mom would have let me have one. She'd have skinned me alive if she knew I ever played with one."

The idea of contacting spirits made Kayla skittery. "Here, hold this for me, would you?" She thrust the Ouija board at Mateo, who accepted it.

"I don't remember Jerry using that." Myra squinted at the game board.

"Myra, was your husband a witch, by any chance?" Mateo asked.

"His mother claimed that her grandfather was one, but no one knows for sure."

A tendril of magic that had been masked by the board's magic drew Kayla back to the tub. She dug down through the remaining layers until she touched a folded, dingy white jacket with buckles. The magic woven into the garment flickered like an expiring florescent lightbulb. She lifted it up out of the container, shaking it out. The garment's sleeves unfurled and spilled to the floor.

"A straight jacket?" Kayla glanced at Mateo and mouthed, "Magic," casting her eyes from the Ouija board to the jacket.

He nodded in acknowledgment.

"Jerry would have his assistant buckle and tie him into it. She'd lower a black curtain down but not all the way. The audience could see him from the shins down. A little razzmatazz. Then, as she raised the curtain, his legs would vanish, and the straight jacket would fall to the floor. Got the audience on their feet, applauding every time." Myra held out her hands, and Kayla placed the jacket into them. The older woman hugged it to her chest and smiled.

A translucent older man, wearing jeans and a Grateful Dead t-shirt, manifested before Myra.

Kayla took an involuntary step back, hissing out a breath. Mateo stiffened; his growl rumbled like a distant thunder.

As they watched, the ghost, plumper than his wife but appearing rather spry, placed two gnarled fingers on the jacket. He shook his nearly bald head, then leaned forward to press a fleeting kiss on his wife's lips. Then the ghost winked out of existence.

Adrenaline coursed through Kayla; her heart pounded like she'd been running for her life. A ghost. She'd seen an honest-to-goodness ghosts. She wiped her palms on her jeans, then froze. Glancing down, she saw, to her embarrassment, that her claws had extended and were snagged on the denim. She folder her arms across her abdomen, hiding her claws until they'd shifted back to unthreatening fingers.

Mrs. Abernathy touched her lips as a tear slid down her wrinkled cheek. "He's never done that before."

"Myra." Mateo laid his hand gently on the older woman's shoulder. "Would you mind if Kayla checked through the rest of your home?"

She waved her hand distractedly. "Go on up."

The search for other magic items came up a bust.

Relieved to be out in the open, Kayla restrained herself from doing cartwheels all the way to their vehicles. Behind her came the sound of Mrs. Abernathy relocking all the deadbolts.

"I can't believe that woman wouldn't let me take those spelled props back to my offices for safe-keeping," Mateo snarled, dragging his hand through his thick hair.

"I can't believe you talked her into giving up the Ouija board." She rested her hip against Mateo's black SUV. "You saw the ghost, right?"

"Yeah. A freakin' ghost." He blew out a breath, sounding more like an exasperated horse than a wolf. "What did you get off the props?"

"The cabinet and jacket's magic are flicker-y. Both vacillate erratically from a low-level thrum to a medium surge of power, then crash. A different spell's binding the board. It feels, um, friendly, but it could take a chomp out of you if it doesn't like you." She laughed nervously. "Sounds weird, right? I can't tell you what spells have been cast on them. We could always run over to the University and do some research."

"I've got an idea. If it doesn't pan out, I'll take you up on that offer."

"What's your idea?"

"Do you have anything pressing to do? Pick up Hunter? Get back to the University?" he asked.

"No. Why?"

Mateo clicked his fob to unlock the SUV's doors. "I want to go to the cemetery. It's only a couple miles from here." He opened the back door and set the box on the floor. "I'd like to talk to Jerry."

"What?" Kayla frowned as she opened the passenger door. "How? I thought your Necromancer was out of town?"

He slid behind the wheel and buckled his seatbelt. "The Ouija board, of course."

Unease slithered down her spine. Seeing a ghost was one thing. Talking to one through a magicked board... well, she'd pass on that experience. "You're kidding, right?" A nervous laugh jittered out of her. "That board's been spelled. I'm a little freaked out that you want to use it without having it examined. What if it is more than a communication device? What if it opens... I don't know... a portal or something?"

"Come on, where's your sense of adventure?" He wiggled his dark brows at her; his finger hovered over the ignition button, waiting for her to decide.

"I'm out of my mind," she muttered, settling into the leather passenger seat. "For the record, using *that* board to communicate to a ghost *in a cemetery* is—" Her phone chimed again, and she muttered, "Oh, for the Lady's sake."

Mateo pulled away from the curb. "What's up with you ignoring your texts?"

"Hunter can't make up his mind on whether he wants to wear Aunt Bree's store-bough Spiderman costume trick-or-treating or Granma's handmade Teenage Ninja Turtle costume. They keep texting me to see if Hunter's decided yet." Kayla twisted sideways, jerked the phone out of her hip pocket, and swiped the screen.

"Which one?" Mateo asked.

"Which one what?" She didn't look up from deleting half a dozen text messages.

"Which Ninja turtle?"

"The blue masked guy."

"Ah, Leonardo."

Grinning, Kayla glanced over at him. "You know which one is which?"

"Sure."

Kayla stifled a laugh. She turned her attention to the passing houses, letting the sedate – by Myra's standards – yet creative Halloween yard displays distract her from her worries about using the Ouija board.

Cedars, oaks, and junipers bordered St. John's Lutheran Cemetery. Mateo drove past the first driveway that led to the original cemetery with its bleached stones and elements-blurred engravings. He turned into the second driveway. They both remained silent as they passed rose, gray, and black granite headstones decorated with autumn-toned silk flowers.

"Myra said Jerry is the fourth down from that mausoleum." Driving at a snail's pace, Mateo turned left at the World War II obelisk. He pulled slightly off the gravel drive and parked just past the mausoleum.

Kayla took a few steps from the car and stretched. "I think you should do a solo run with the Ouija board. If things go wonky, I can save your hide." She grimaced hearing the uncertainty in her voice over that last statement.

"Don't be a spoilsport. It's better with two."

The sweet, crisp scent from the junipers blended with the pleasant spice of the cedars. She inhaled deeply, enjoying the mingled fragrances. A familiar quivering magic whispered behind her. It emanated from the pale gray mausoleum. Kayla pivoted, changing course.

"Hey, it's this way," Mateo said, pointing to a rose-colored headstone engraved with 'Abernathy.'

"There's something magic in there, and it feels like the magic at Myra's house," she called over her shoulder.

Four neo-classical Greek pillars adorned the front of the mausoleum. Three steps led up to a barred entrance door. Kayla frowned when she saw there were several impressive locks on the door as well, not something she'd seen before on a mausoleum. If she were a betting woman, she'd put her money on the family interred within being related to lock-loving Myra.

Pine needles crunched beneath her boots as she walked around the building. Sparrows zipped from tree to tree, chirping to each other. Perched high on the back wall, she found a broken-out window, also barred.

"Do you think you can get in there?" Mateo stood next to her, arms crossed over his chest, assessing the window.

As a lynx, she could easily slip through the bars. Kayla studied the building, then turned slowly, examining the surrounding area. "It's what? About six feet, maybe a little more, to the ledge? I can jump that high, no problem."

"I could boost you up."

She rolled her amber eyes. "I'm going to change by the car. Stay here."

"I won't peek."

She elbowed him in his well-muscled gut, then stalked over to the SUV. Kayla undressed, laying her folded clothes on the car's backseat. She felt the warm, pleasant tingle of magic as she shifted. A minute later, she stretched, kneading her claws against the earth.

A squirrel chittered out an alarm as she strolled back to Mateo. Her black tufted ears twitched, and her stomach growled. As if he'd heard, the squirrel scrambled higher into the tree, protesting all the way.

"Your pelt is the same golden-brown as your skin." Mateo crouched down as she approached. "I thought you'd be buff-colored like Hunter."

She rubbed her whiskers against him, allowing him to stroke her coat.

"Beautiful."

Her ears switched back and forth, then she shook herself. Mateo stood and gestured toward the window.

"Go for it."

Kayla padded over to the granite building. She hunkered down, her muscles coiled tight, then she sprang up. Her front claws hooked into the window ledge. The bars brushed against her flanks as she vaulted through the window. She landed on a stone bench set below the window.

Dried leaves and twigs were scattered over the stone floor. A velvet cape, black magician's hat, and a slender black and white wand lay against the base of a crypt. Kayla prowled around the magicked items. The wand puzzled her. It gave off the same magical signature of the other two, but Myra hadn't mentioned it. Not that it mattered. She needed to figure out how to get all three out of the mausoleum.

She set her teeth on the top hat's rim and picked it up. It whacked her in the chest. Experimentally, she took a few step backwards. The hat scuffed against the floor. Releasing her hold on the top hat, she sat back on her haunches.

To get everything out, her best bet would be to change back and toss everything out to Mateo, then change back to lynx and get herself out of the mausoleum. Easy-peasy. The warm tingle lasted well over a minute this time.

"Mateo!" she called out.

A moment of silence, then a surprised, "Yeah?"

"I'm going to bundle everything up and toss it out to you." After she heard Mateo war-whoop, she crossed the cold, stone floor. She went down on one knee and slipped the wand inside the hat.

"Toss away, Kayla. You solved the case."

"Do I get a bonus?" She swaddled the cape around the top hat.

"I'll buy you a beer."

She barked out a laugh as she stepped up on the stone bench. "Here it comes." Kayla wedged the cape through the bars, pushing it forward until it slipped from her fingers.

"Got it."

"I'll be out in just a bit." When she called on her magic, it roiled through her, feeling more like the pinpricks of a numbed foot awakening. She didn't think she'd done this many fast shifts since she was a kid. The prickly sensation enveloped her legs and continued after she'd completed the transformation. She hissed, shaking her paws.

Her agility hadn't been affected by the closely spaced changes. She easily cleared the window and loped past Mateo. The annoying pins-and-needles faded slowly, finally clearing when she arrived at the car.

"What the—" Mateo's voice boomed out.

Startled, she whirled: teeth bared and claws out, ready to attack.

He stood, arms empty, his face dark with rage. "Jerry!" he bellowed.

Kayla yowled, then stalked back to the mausoleum. Mateo was close on her bobbed tail.

That damned ghost better not have another hiding place! She sagged in relief when she felt the sputtering magic. Another yowl, then she head-butted Mateo's leg.

"He put them back in there?"

She meowed, then trotted to the back of the building.

"Wait, Kayla. Wait. He'll just do it again. Change back. We need to talk to him.

Her shoulders tensed. Every shapeshifter learned from a young age that their magic had its limits. If she shifted too often, her magic would deplete. With her luck, she'd end up being a lynx, waiting for her magic to replenish.

She really didn't want to mess around with that blasted board, but the idea of trick-or-treating with Hunter in her lynx form... he'd love it, but she doubted her human neighbors would be amused. *Damned ghost.* Resigned, she headed back to the SUV and the clothes that she had stashed there.

"Grab the blanket out of the back, will you? I'll wait for you at Jerry's grave."

The fourth change took nearly five minutes, and her whole body felt like fire ants were feasting on her. She grumbled, threatening Jerry's ghost with all manner of violence as she slipped back into her clothes. She pulled a large, two-sided fleece blanket from the trunk, then jogged to the gravesite.

"Do you know how to do this?" she asked as he spread the blanket over the grave.

"Haven't you ever played with a Ouija board before?"

"Played?" Her eyebrows winged up. She'd never been tempted to talk with the dead and certainly wouldn't consider it play. "No."

"I don't know if there's a proper technique or ceremony or anything. We just messed around when we were kids. We'd ask if the spirits would talk to us, then started asking questions. My buddy made the planchette move."

"How do you know he moved it?" She sat cross-legged on the blanket, rubbing at the residual spikey sensation in her quads.

"Because he'd always ask which girl liked him, and there is no way Lila Owens like him."

"For the record—"

Mateo waved her off. "I know, bad idea." He shrugged. "But let's give it a go. Put your fingers on the planchette." He placed his fingertips on it. "Like this."

Kayla hesitated, looking to the descending sun. Not that daylight, or the lack of it, had any effect on witch-magic, but she felt marginally better that sunset was a few hours off yet. She gently laid her fingers on the pale wood. Magic stroked her fingertips and tickled her palms.

"Whoa. Do you feel that?" His eyes flared wide in astonishment. "Something is... petting me. I didn't feel anything until you touched the planchette. You feel it, right?"

Unable to speak for fear her voice would shake, Kayla clenched her jaw and managed a nod.

Mateo cleared his throat, rolled his shoulders a few times, then said, "Jerry Abernathy. Are you there?"

Only the wind, whispering through the evergreens, answered. The birds had fallen silent, along with the aggrieved squirrel. Magic continued to swirl playfully over Kayla's fingers and hands.

"Jerry. We know you're here."

The scent of moldering leaves infiltrated the fragrant cedar and juniper. Kayla's fingers trembled on the motionless, heart-shaped device. Her arm muscles bunched, twinging from nerves and anticipation.

"Jerry. Dude—"

The planchette glided to YES.

Slack-jawed, Kayla looked over to Mateo, who had a cat-ate-the-canary smile spread over his handsome face.

"Jerry. Your wife wants your props back. She—"

The planchette zipped to NO.

"Why?" Kayla surprised herself by asking. She'd had no intention of participating in this foolishness. A rough-tongued lick of magic across her palm made her squirm. She watched as the planchette moved laboriously over the board.

H-A-R-O-L-D

"I don't think he wants Harold to have them," Kayla whispered.

"Myra keeps everything. You know that. There's no way she'd give him any of your things, Jerry," Mateo said.

W-A-N-D

"What wand?" he asked.

"It was in the mausoleum with the other things," she explained. "Myra didn't mention the wand. What do you want to bet Harold took it without her knowing?"

YES, came the rapid reply.

"Well, if we tell her Harold—" He didn't get a chance to finish his sentence. The little plank of wood flew to NO.

"Don't just say no; hear me out." Mateo's voice took on a peeved tone.

Somehow, Kayla doubted that stubborn Jerry would listen to reason. "Did you cast the spells on your props?" she blurted out.

YES

Interesting. "You're a witch?"

M-A-G-I-C-I-A-N

"I've never felt magic like yours before. My boss, Gabriel, would be fascinated by it." Mateo nudged her knee – whether in encouragement or to get her to stop talking, she didn't know. She kept her eyes locked on the planchette. "Would you consider donating your treasures to the Magical Antiquities Department? It would be a coup. Gabriel will undoubtedly want to write a paper or two on your abilities, both as a magician and as a spell-caster." She sucked in a long breath, then forged ahead when the wood remained motionless. "You would leave a mark in the witch world."

P-A-P-E-R

"Um-hmm. Annals of Esoteric Spells, for sure."

"And best of all," Mateo cut in, "if you gift them all to the University, Harold will never get a single one."

M-Y-R-A

"I'll talk to her. Let her know that it's what you want, Jerry. Kayla will help, won't you?"

"If we tell her he's just going to keep taking them, that might work." The sensation of tiny claws scratching against her fingers startled Kayla. "Hey, cut that out."

"What?" Mateo asked as the planchette spelled out the exact same question.

"Sorry. The board's getting a little… frisky."

L-O-V-E-M-Y-R-A

"She knows you do. I'll tell her again, though. I promise," said Kayla.

The planchette glided off the board.

Kayla stood up. "I'll go get everything out of the mausoleum. Hey, if I can't change back, will you call Bree? I'll need her to take Hunter trick-or-treating."

"I don't think you'll have to shift." Mateo pointed behind her.

Turning, she saw the bundled-up velvet cape. She scooped it up, unwrapping it to make sure the wand and top hat were there as well.

"Thanks, Jerry!" She gathered everything up. "Let's get out of here."

Mateo folded up the fleece blanket, then put the Ouija board back into its box. "You will help me convince Myra, right?" Idly, he stroked the Ouija board before closing the lid.

"I will. If you give that—" she inclined her head toward the box— "to Gabriel to analyze."

"Oh, I thought I'd keep it. You said it wasn't Jerry's magic, and Myra didn't recall seeing it before."

"I'm not sure that's a good idea. It was friendly this time, but I don't trust it." She headed toward the SUV.

"But it's an amazing tool."

"Yeah. No."

"Come on, Kayla." He opened the rear passenger door, tossed in the blanket, and set the Ouija on top of it.

Kayla hopped into her seat, holding the magician's props on her lap. "*IF* Gabriel clears it, you can have it back."

Mateo rubbed his hands together gleefully. "Excellent." He closed the back door, then Kayla's door.

Boys and their toys.

Her phone chimed as Mateo slid behind the wheel.

"After we drop everything off, I'd like to see which costume Hunter picks," he said.

"If you come over, you realize Hunter will insist you go trick-or-treating."

"Sounds like fun." He punched the ignition.

Kayla peeked into the backseat; the Ouija's magic batted at her. "All right, but first we stop at the University."

When not daydreaming about plot lines and characters, Andra practices yoga, reads voraciously, and drinks too much coffee. She loves road trips and going off on wild tangents. Andra writes in multiple genres—including but not limited to—urban fantasy, steamy romance, paranormal romance, and horror. Follow her on Twitter @aedill, on Instagram at andradillauthor, and at:

www.facebook.com/andradillauthor

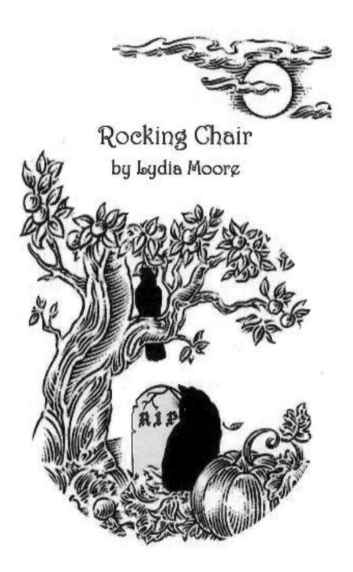

Rocking Chair
by Lydia Moore

They say ancestors come to visit on Halloween night. I never believed it until that October we moved to the house by the sea.

I was 17 then, planning to graduate from high school next spring. Dad was promoted at work, so my parents decided to move to the bigger and older house.

The house was really stunning, a beautiful Victorian-style set on a hillside practically on the beach. When we arrived in late summer, my two younger siblings and I spent days exploring the many rooms. Because I was the oldest, mom told me that I could pick any upstairs room for my bedroom, and there was a beautiful one that faced the ocean. That was my choice.

Summer ended all too soon, and we headed back to school. One night I was up late studying for a math exam and I heard a creaking sound coming from overhead in the attic. At first, I thought it was just the house settling or the wind causing the boards to groan, but it seemed to be steady. My heart beat a little faster, and I said to myself, "Don't be stupid. It's probably just the wind pushing something on the roof." I went back to my books and ignored it.

One night later, I heard it again. I resolved to check it out the next day, so I went up into the attic in the morning. Sunlight streamed into the attic space from the window that faced the sea. Dust motes floated in the air. There were several boxes to one side, and a small end table and a rocking chair by the window. Nothing seemed to be loosened up here – nothing to make that creaking sound. And nothing appeared to have been disturbed, as a fine layer of dust covered everything.

I told my parents about the sound at breakfast, and my theory of something on the roof scraping. "Well, I hope not," Dad replied. "We had the roof replaced before we moved in. But I'll check it out later today."

So, he did, and he couldn't find anything wrong. "Maybe you just dreamed you heard it," was his final answer.

But, that night, I heard it again. I wasn't dreaming and I wasn't imagining the sound. I figured that it simply HAD to be coming from the attic. I decided to "stake it out" the next night.

Armed with a flashlight, I went into the attic about an hour before I had heard the creaking sound the previous nights. I settled in near the door and waited. At the appointed hour, I felt a very cold brush of air go by me. Then as I stared, the rocking chair started moving a rhythmic back-and-forth. My heart pounded hard and I slowly got up and walked toward the moving chair. As I reached out to touch it, it suddenly stopped, and the attic fell silent.

Frightened, I quickly left the attic and retreated to the safety of my room. It took me quite a while to calm down and fall asleep.

In the cold light of day, I felt a bit foolish for being afraid. If this was a ghost, maybe I could find out more about it. I searched the internet and the local library for information on who had lived in the house by the sea. I discovered that there was a man in a nearby nursing home who had lived in the house for most of his life. So, I went to see him.

Mr. Thompson was talkative and witty. When I asked about living in the house by the sea, he became very animated, "Oh, yes, I spent many happy years there with my family. I married and moved out, but my sister and her husband stayed and raised their own family at the house. Did you know that my sister was an author? She wrote several books for children."

I asked him if he remembered anything significant about a rocking chair. He looked surprised. "Why did you ask me that? My sister loved to rock in her rocking chair and tell stories to her children and grandchildren!"

"I asked because I found an old rocking chair in the attic. It must have been hers," I said. I thanked him and promised to visit again, before I headed home.

Halloween was only a few days away, and I had decided to see if the ghost would appear. Every night from midnight to one o'clock or so, I could hear the creaking rocking chair in my bedroom. But now, instead of being afraid, I was curious.

On Halloween eve, I took a candle and a small plate of cookies to the attic. I set the lit candle and plate on the end table, and I waited. At midnight, I felt the brush of cold air move past me and then, I saw her! She was an older woman who was smiling and talking, but she made no sound. She sat in the rocking chair and started rocking back and forth. I swear I could see the forms of several children sitting at her feet, watching her.

As if on cue, at one o'clock, the candle went out and the chair stopped. She and the children had vanished.

When I picked up the plate, the cookies were gone.

SAMHAIN SECRETS

Lydia Moore has a background in journalism, technical writing, and editing. This is her first effort writing fiction. She loves mysteries, science fiction, and fantasy. She lives in Ohio with her husband, Larry, and their cat, Mimsy.

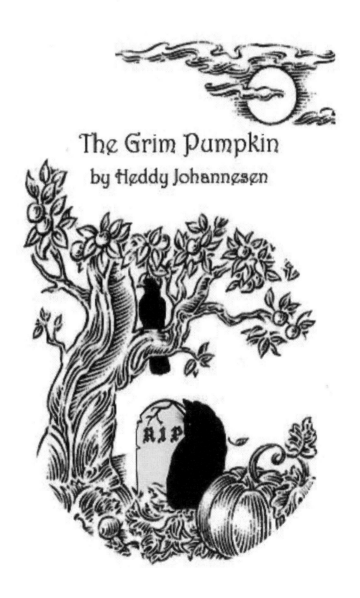

The Grim Pumpkin
by Heddy Johannesen

The child stole away from his mother's side. The yard beckoned him. The air was fragrant with the scent of mock orange blossoms. He giggled with delight and ran past the chipped, white picket fence. The dim yard whispered secrets to him.

The large pumpkin leaves unfurled themselves. The boy extended his small hand out to the pumpkin. His feet stung from the cold. He looked around for his mother, who was nowhere in sight. The yard was cloaked in darkness.

He turned to run when something snatched his ankle and pierced the young flesh. The boy shrieked as the night closed in around him.

"It's harvest time, Samuel," Liz, his wiry mother said as she swayed back and forth on the worn rocking chair.

Samuel slouched and silently watched the anchorman on the television screen drone on about next week's weather forecast.

"You know what that means? We'll sell some of our veggies to the locals. We'll save some to keep for the winter." Her dark curls blew in the late autumn breeze. "Samuel," she repeated to get his attention.

A beetle crawled along the floor and disappeared under the floorboards. Samuel wished he could vanish, too.

"Hon, go to the garden and get beans, basil, parsley, and carrots, okay? Check on the pumpkins."

Samuel stood in the garden. What did his mom ask him to get? Oh, yeah. He remembered now. He gathered carrots and beans and set those aside. They smelled earthy. He looked next for the basil and parsley. He left the rest to die back into the earth.

Samuel strode over to the pumpkin patch. The crescent moon shone. He stood before the ripe, round pumpkins and kicked aside a few dead mice.

The pumpkin vines sucked the essence out of the other withered plants. He shifted from foot to foot, rubbing his sweaty hands on his pants. He wished she didn't make him check on the pumpkins. He broke out in a sweat.

He carried the newspapers and wooden boards under his arm. He held his breath as he placed them under the pumpkins, then jumped away as if dodging a rabid dog.

He sighed, exasperated. His legs were shredded. His socks were soaked. Blood stained the lower hem of his bell bottoms. His hands were a mass of scars and blood stains.

The vines were hungry. They needed a blood offering.

He turned back. *Damn pumpkins, he thought. Nearly ate me alive.*

He wheezed and puffed by the time he returned to the kitchen.

Liz was sampling the spaghetti sauce when he walked in. "Look at you; what a mess."

"It's not my fault," he said. His mother gave him an annoyed look and waved him away.

"Go put on clean clothes before you sit down to dinner," she said. He stomped out of the kitchen, leaving a trail of muddy footprints behind him.

After dinner, Liz and Samuel flipped idly through the channels.

"I don't like those pumpkins, Mom. They try to eat me alive." Samuel wrapped a frayed blue blanket around him for warmth.

She shook her head. "No, they don't."

Samuel stared harder. "Yes, they do. Look at my legs." He rolled up the cuff of his jeans to reveal the red scars on his calves. Liz rose from the chair.

She returned a moment later with gauze, cold water, and a bowl. She soaked the cloth in cold water and dabbed at the blood. Blood stained the cloth. She wrapped the gauze around his leg and smiled up at him.

"Better?" she asked.

He flinched in pain. "Yeah, thanks."

"I'm sorry, my son," Liz said. He smiled back half-heartedly. Liz sat down, and they returned to the show they were watching "You know why I do what I do. It's not only for me." She stared harder at Samuel.

He averted his gaze.

"They will never understand us." She let out a hard sigh.

Samuel stared at the TV.

"Don't worry; the pumpkins don't want you."

Samuel nodded absently. He thought about Jessica, the prettiest girl in his algebra class.

Samuel awoke. He didn't remember falling asleep. Light shone through his bedroom window. The screaming kettle whistle was followed by the irresistible scent of bacon and eggs. He stumbled into the warm kitchen.

Samuel entered the classroom at Salem High School. He found his seat and sat down, casting nervous glances around the room. Most students ignored him, their faces buried in the comic books hidden in their binders, but a few students glared at him. He turned his attention to what the teacher wrote on the chalkboard. His face grew hot.

The teacher cleared his throat and gestured to the chalkboard.

"Today, we're going to discuss the Salem Witch Trials. It happened right here in our own town, in 1692. The Puritans believed the victims were real witches, due to hysterical accounts from local girls. The victims were unfairly tried and sentenced to die; for example, Giles Corey, who was pressed to death for refusing to admit or deny guilt, or Rebecca Nurse, who was hanged. They were regular people like you and me."

At that, Tommy cast Samuel a nasty look.

Jessica flashed Samuel a secret, sympathetic smile and then opened her textbook and pretended to be studying. Samuel gazed at her with interest. *Isn't she dating Tommy? Why did she smile at me like that?*

A crumpled white paper ball flew at Samuel's head. Samuel dodged it, knocking the books off his desk. He knelt to retrieve them.

"I saw that, Tommy. If you don't stop it, you will face detention. And on the most popular day of the year, the other kids will be at costume parties long before you've cleaned all the chalkboards." The teacher's frown deepened.

Tommy slumped in his chair as the teacher continued.

"It was believed witches worshipped the Devil, went to midnight Sabbaths, and ate children—"

"Not true!" Samuel blurted out loud. Heads turned.

"Care to tell us more about it, Samuel?" the teacher asked.

Samuel took a deep breath. "What does 'pressed to death' mean?" The students laughed. The teacher silenced them with a frosty glare.

"Many stones were placed on Giles Corey's body. The stones crushed him to death."

Samuel tried to remember what his momma told him. He heard her lyrical voice in his head.

"The ancient Celts celebrated a festival called Samhain, which meant summer's end. At the time, they feasted and drank wine and slaughtered some of their animals. They purified the animals with flame, and they held bonfires."

"I think you're confusing it with All Hallows Eve," Tommy snapped at him. Several students voiced their agreement.

"I am not," Samuel defended what his mother had told him.

"McCormack! You're facing detention tonight. That's the third outburst from you. One more, and it will be a week's detention. Understand?"

Tommy scowled at Samuel.

Samuel stared out the window. His face turned scarlet red. Before long, the school bell rang.

The muddy leaves crunched beneath Samuel's feet. He heard footsteps behind him. When Jessica called out his name, he turned.

"Hey, Jessica," Samuel said.

Her blond hair blew in her face. Her lips were the color of ripe peaches. Her cornflower blue eyes met his.

"Hi, Samuel," she said. "Uh, don't take everything Tommy says too personally. I wouldn't if I were you. He's mean to everyone."

"Why do you like him?" he asked and then regretted it. "Never mind."

"Sometimes, I don't know. Are you excited about Halloween?" She shouldered her backpack and looked down for a second.

"Yeah, I guess."

"Maybe I'll bring my younger sister over for some candy." She looked back at the school parking lot. Tommy leaned against his car, watching them.

"Uh—I…" His face clouded over. *Oh, no. The pumpkins*, he thought.

"Jessica!" Tommy marched up to them. Samuel's expression changed to fear. "What are you doing? Stay away from this weirdo."

"I mean, yeah, that'd be great." He looked to Tommy, then back to her.

"Okay, I have to go. Great talking to you," she said. Tommy glared at him and put his arm around Jessica, and they climbed into his Seville.

Samuel rushed home, hoping he wasn't followed.

The kitchen smelled good. Liz looked up from the magazine she was reading. Samuel eyed the pile of candy in the large bowl by the front door.

"Don't spoil your appetite, Samuel. That's for the trick-or-treaters. Yes, there's candy for you, too."

Samuel brightened. They sat down to eat dinner. Both knew there would be no trick-or-treating revelers, but Liz left candy out, anyway. Samuel would eat it all and get cavities, as it had been every year.

When they were done, they went outside to the backyard. Samuel walked with bated breath to the pumpkin patch. The moon glowed on the garden. Leaves rustled.

He let out a deep breath. Liz held a boline, a sickle-shaped knife, in one hand and examined the pumpkins. She savored their scent and stroked the hard rind of their skins. She stepped around them, careful not to sever the leafy green stems. The rind was hard as bone. The pumpkin hummed under her touch, ready for harvest. She smiled to herself.

Samuel shivered with fear. The vine fell to the soil with a heavy thump.

"Want to carve this one?" she asked. He nodded.

"Are you angry at me, Momma?" His voice sounded small.

She shook her head full of perfect dark curls as she moved on to another pumpkin. "No, Samuel. I love you. Don't talk to them. I know you want to, but trust me; it would be better to avoid them."

She cut the pumpkin from the vine using the boline and carried it into the kitchen. Liz spread newspaper on the countertop. They roasted the seeds and emptied the pulp into the compost.

They carved triangle eyes and a wide, jeering smile into the larger pumpkin. Liz set a candle inside, and they put it out on the front porch. They placed the smaller pumpkin at the window ledge to ward evil spirits from their home.

Liz pressed the buttons on the console television, flipping through the channels. Samuel sat on the couch. He popped a candy into his mouth.

"Mom, I have to tell you something." He asked her to turn off the television.

"What's wrong, Samuel?" She sat beside him on the sofa.

"It's about this girl—"

"Oh, I see… you met a girl." Her voice became strained.

Samuel clenched his fists. Tears threatened to flow. His chest tightened.

"Mom, she's dating someone else. She doesn't like me." Samuel's shoulders slumped.

"Then what is it?" She waited.

"I don't want her to get hurt." He waited for her response. "You know what I mean."

She pursed her lips. For long moments, she remained silent. Her shoulders tensed.

They heard the screech of tires and peered out the window. Someone climbed out of a car, whooping and hollering.

Liz hissed. "It's those rowdy kids again, I'll bet you anything. Put Grandfather Pumpkin out on the front porch." Liz cast a knowing glance at Samuel. She put out a hand to stop him and then left the house.

Samuel pressed his ear to the door. He heard angry voices, one male, and recognized the other as his mother's. She hollered at the guy to leave. Samuel ducked out to the back deck.

Samuel entered the pumpkin patch. He'd hauled the rusty wheelbarrow out to the patch. He held a white votive candle and a boline in his hands. He looked around to make sure no one saw him.

The moon shone over the garden. He lit the candle and pushed it into the soil. He stabbed his finger using the boline. He offered a drop of his blood to Grandfather Pumpkin. He wrapped a tissue over the wound. It would heal.

The vines hissed and twisted. Samuel inhaled the earthy scent. The vines crawled to the back deck. They slapped the windowpanes. A great moan emanated from Grandfather Pumpkin. *Soon.*

Samuel raised his other hand. The vines retreated to the shadows. The wide leaves pounded the earth and churned the soil. *It hungered.*

He hauled Grandfather Pumpkin, vines and all, in the wheelbarrow to the front porch, struggling with the effort.

Tommy McCormack marched up the porch.

Liz rested a hand on her hip. Her mouth was a thin line.

"Hello, ma'am. It's October 31st, and the police are watching you. My brother was the kid that went missing last year. He was last seen near this house. The police might not have found any evidence, but whatever you did, I'll find out." He met her gaze with defiance.

Samuel lunged at him with his fist extended. Tommy stepped back and smirked. Samuel peered harder. Was Jessica in the car? He sensed Grandfather Pumpkin's thirst. Fear gripped him.

"Look at you." Tommy smirked. "Coward."

"What are you doing here?" Liz snapped. "Did you come to start trouble?"

His eyes widened in surprise. "Me, trouble? I thought you would be—"

"I can call the police on you, too. Just know that. Now leave."

"Yeah, sure. I'm leaving." His gaze shifted to the massive cucurbit next to him. Samuel's chest pounded with anger.

Tommy marveled at Grandfather Pumpkin's impressive size and the knotted features resembling a face. The memory of his baby brother brought him back to the present. He ripped the pumpkin vines apart.

"You can't hide from me. I know the truth. I know what happened to my brother. It's time to pay the reaper."

Tommy tore at the long vines. He kicked Grandfather Pumpkin against the house. He hopped on one foot, holding his sneakered toes in pain.

"I hate you! I hate you! You will pay for what you've done. That darn squash is hard as rock."

"What's wrong with you? Would you please just calm down?" Liz yelled.

A vine snaked round his ankle. Tommy yelled in shock. He tugged his leg free. The vine hissed with fury.

The huge leaves slapped the walls of the house. The vines caught his limbs and squeezed. The thorns tore at his legs and arms. He screamed. Pain shot up his limbs. He tore at the vines. Blood stained his hands and arms. He stared around in confusion and scrambled to his feet. He fled to the car as Grandfather Pumpkin seemed to come alive, his knots taking on the features of an old man.

Jessica got out of the car, dressed as a pirate. There was an expression of worry on her face as her little sister peered out from the backseat.

"Tommy, stop it. Let's just go home," she begged.

A vine snaked out and snatched her ankle. She screamed and stared at Samuel in shock.

Samuel rushed up to her. He tugged her free and raised his hand to the vines. "Jessica, run. Run!"

Samuel cast nervous glances at Tommy and Jessica. She climbed inside the car with her sister and shut the door. Tommy remained where he was and balled his hand into a fist.

Liz and Samuel glanced at each other. Liz huffed and steered Samuel into the house, then locked it. Samuel protested, but his mother ignored him.

Tommy left with Jessica. Samuel heard the tires squeal out on the pavement. He hadn't expected to see him again that night, but an hour later, he returned. Samuel peeked out the window. He didn't see Jessica or her sister anywhere and let out a sigh of relief that was short-lived, as several boys appeared in the distance. Tommy hadn't returned alone.

Grandfather Pumpkin's two evil eyes scowled at Tommy and his friends with hate. The tiny nose arched between the eyes. Blood ooze down the face. The flesh dripped down from the mouth, revealing smelly, stringy pulp. The mouth curved back on both sides, displaying two rows of chiseled fangs. The green root lay motionless on the porch.

Tommy eyed the moldy, glowing thing. His hand caressed several eggs. He stared at the pumpkin in terror. He swallowed hard and glanced to see if his friends had caught up with him. They tossed toilet paper and eggs at a neighboring house. Their Converse sneakers shuffled on the damp, autumn leaves.

"Hey guys, check this out," said Tommy. "Egg it or what?" His best friends, Brian and Johnny, came to a dead stop.

"Who carved the freak pumpkin? Looks like no one's home." Johnny peered in the bleak windows.

"Who cares?" Tommy scowled. Fire flickered off the pumpkin as Tommy approached it. He wound the toilet paper in his hand and drew his other arm back to throw the eggs. The pumpkin grimaced at the boys, as if daring them.

Tommy threw the eggs. They landed with a sickening splat and dripped down the house. He threw toilet paper and tossed his head back and laughed. The others joined him.

"Look at that pumpkin. It's kind of cool," Brian said. Wind blew the crisp leaves on the porch. The bare tree boughs creaked as crows screeched at the moon.

Brian waved his hand in front of Tommy, but Tommy's gaze remained fixed on the pumpkin as he sauntered up the steps. A spider crawled down the slimy pumpkin's face.

"Tommy?" Johnny joined his side. "Earth to Tommy." Brian and Johnny glanced at each other.

"Let's get out of here," Johnny said. "We might get caught."

Brian checked over his shoulder and waved his hand. "Tommy? C'mon, bud."

Tommy was unable to tear his gaze away from Grandfather Pumpkin's now-apparent face. Tendrils of the slimy pulp tugged on his arms and legs. The pumpkin's maw widened. The root snatched Tommy's leg and wound around his ankles. Tommy screamed. Brian grabbed Tommy by the arm.

"Help him, Brian!" Johnny yelled. His eyes widened in fear.

Grandfather Pumpkin devoured Tommy whole. A horrible, gurgling sound roared in the night. A terrible scream was heard from the pumpkin's bowels.

Johnny ran for his life. Brian stood on the sidewalk, crying. He had one last egg. He dodged the root's vicious grasp. Brian fired. The egg cracked and spread on the pumpkin. He glanced at it one last time and ran home.

Samuel stood in the pumpkin patch with a burning matchstick in his hand. The pumpkin vines hissed and tangled into each other. Jessica stood on the back deck, waiting. Samuel threw the match onto the vines.

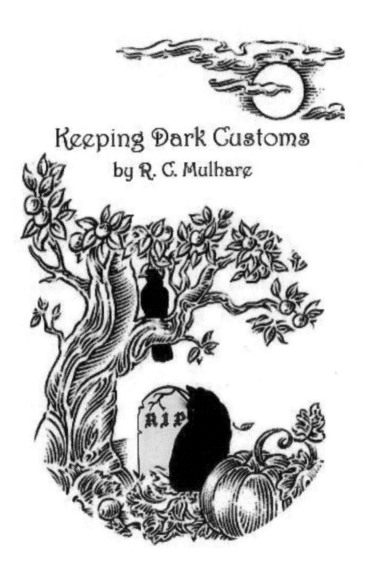

Keeping Dark Customs
by R. C. Mulhare

SAMHAIN SECRETS

October 31st – Thomas

"I don't know why you had to change the night of trick-or-treating. What are the kids gonna do tonight?" my daughter, Nikki, asked on Halloween night as she cleared the supper dishes, loading them into the dishwasher.

"The town council decided it was easier on the parents and you kids, with Halloween on a school night," I said. I'm one of those councilors, which made this conversation more difficult. "Besides, you and Jared seemed to have fun Sunday night."

"Jared had fun, but he's still too little to really get it. There's more to trick-or-treating than candy and costumes. It's the night itself. Having it any night but *the* night isn't the same." Since her mother's passing, she'd grown more serious in a wise-beyond-her-years way. "It's like… those douches who set off fireworks when it isn't the Fourth of July. The day itself makes it special. The darkness and mystery really make it."

"We only made the change because we wanted to keep you safe—"

Wrong words to say. She glared. "Safer? Don't start wrapping us kids in bubble wrap. Even getting out of bed can be dangerous. What are you going to do next, make us wear padded space suits to keep us from getting ouchies or sickies?"

I had to de-escalate this. "We had the best intentions."

"You know what people say about good intentions. You could start a whole construction company to Old Scratch's gates with them." She poured dish washing liquid into the reservoir, banging the door shut and turning it on before stalking upstairs to her room, ending the conversation by slamming her door.

I went to tuck in Jared, finding him on the floor of his room, his army men ranged before him all draped in Kleenex.

"What's this? Halloween at Fort Montgomery?" I asked.

"They're fighting monsters, and they're dressed as ghosts 'cause monsters are afraid of ghosts," he said.

"Now why are monsters afraid of ghosts?"

He bundled his toys into their bin. "'Cause ghosts can go through walls and monsters can't."

I chuckled at his cleverness. "That makes sense."

When I tucked him in, he insisted on a scary story. I tried changing his mind but eventually agreed on *The Witch Who Was Afraid of Witches*, Nikki's old favorite and a spooky but charming tale for the season.

Once I put on the nightlight and put out the room light, he settled down. I went to Nikki's room to see if she'd cooled off. She perched on the tall stool before her standing computer desk, wearing a witch hat as she video-chatted with someone. "No admittance."

"Just wanted to know if you'd like to watch a scary movie with me."

"What? Ootsy Tootsy Puppy's Not So Spooky Halloween?"

"I thought we'd watch Night of the Living Dead. Always got a shiver from me."

"Good taste but not this time." Her chat friend popped on screen wearing a pair of bunny ears, hooting at me.

"Who's that?"

"Tyler in Colorado. He thinks you're the number one boring dad in Massachusetts, if not the country. You know why."

"He's entitled to his opinion. There's always next year." I retreated, avoiding further confrontation.

Something thumped the front door as I came downstairs. I ran to find the cause of the noise.

On the doorstep lay a smashed jack-o-lantern with my name on it. Three hooting teenagers ran down the walk to a battered sedan idling at the curb, jumping in and speeding off before I got the license plate. I turned to go inside and call the police, alerting them to the troublemakers.

Footsteps click on the flagstones behind me. "Sorry, but there's no candy here. Trick-or-treating was Sunday night."

"Trick or treeeeat," said a high-pitched rasping sound.

I turned. A bed sheet ghost about four feet tall stood before me, a plastic pumpkin over its head as if they'd cut the bottom out of a light-up decoration and put it on. Its sheeted hands clasped a pumpkin treat pail.

"I told you, no treats. No tricks either. Sorry."

The figure held out the pail. "*Trick* or treeeeat." Something in the voice prickled the hairs on the back of my neck. I looked to the house, then looked back. "If I give you a treat, will you go away?"

"Treeeeat?" the thing said, hopeful.

I ran inside, hunting up the first sweet thing in the kitchen cabinet, a baking chocolate block left over from a school baking project. I contemplated staying in the kitchen and waiting for the kid to get bored and move on. I glanced at the monitor for the doorbell camera, sitting on the kitchen counter, hoping to watch them retreat. But the kid still stood there, staring at the door, not moving. For all I knew, the kid had friends hiding nearby who might get antsy.

Going back out, I dropped the bar into the pumpkin-ghost's bucket. "Okay, there you go. Happy Halloween. What are you supposed to be, the Great Pumpkin?"

The figure said nothing but reached into the bucket, taking out the block. It looked at me.

I noticed the figure's face. Or lack thereof. No eyes looked through the triangles cut into the plastic pumpkin. Only a flickering light shone behind them.

Vines sprouted from under the sheet and out of the bucket, whipping out to catch my wrists and ankles. "Let me go! I have a family to take care of! They need me!"

The jack-o-lantern only grinned broader, the light glowing brighter within. "Trick or treeeeat," it said, hungry now.

And the vines pulled me into the treat bucket. The opening swallowed me whole.

October 31st – Nikki

I decided, after a little while, I'd treated dad too harshly. I signed off Skype and went downstairs to see if he'd put the movie on and tell him I felt sorry.

The DVD lay on the coffee table, but he hadn't put the TV on. I started toward the kitchen. Sensing a draft, I headed for the front door. It stood ajar. I looked out into the night. Maybe some errant trick-or-treaters had shown up despite the obvious. We hadn't any porch light on, and Dad hadn't felt like decorating the yard, so the only orange lights or ghosts or light-up jack-o-lanterns we had lurked in my window and Jared's.

No sign of Dad. No trick-or-treaters, except a few at well-lit houses nearby, and that one down the street behind the huge pine trees with the four thousand plastic jack-o-lanterns. I thought I'd heard a car tear away earlier, probably Ryan McIlhenny and his goofy friends.

"Dad?" I called.

No answer.

I hit his number in my phone. From his study off the living room, I heard his phone ring on its charger. It didn't pick up, even after several rings.

I shut the door, locking it behind me. I looked in the guest room, where he'd often slept since Mom's death. No sign of him there. Scared now, I ran for the house phone, dialing 9-1-1.

"911, what is your emergency?"

"This is Nikki Ross. My dad, Thomas Ross... he's disappeared."

"Disappeared? Are you sure he didn't step out to run some errands?"

"No, he was going to watch some scary movies, and I'd gone down to join him. A car buzzed the house earlier. He's the guy who got in the vote to move trick-or-treating to Sunday."

"And that's important?"

"A lot of families got mad at him, even if they went along with it."

The line rustled. "I'm going to send a car around to check on your house. Have you looked everywhere? Does he have a workshop he'd be working in?"

"He's a copyright lawyer with a home office. He's not exactly St. Joseph the Carpenter."

A few minutes later, red and blue flashed in the front windows. I went to the front door to answer. Someone knocked. "East Manuxet Police," a woman's voice called out. "You okay in there?" I shuffled the door open.

Corinne Denehy, my best friend Colleen's aunt, stood on our stoop, accompanied by a male cop with the name "Strickland" on a tag pinned to his winter-weight jacket.

"I think someone took our dad." I described what had happened up to that point.

"Just to eliminate any possibilities, may we have a look around and make sure he's not somewhere around here?" Corinne asked.

"I'm sure he isn't here," I said.

"You check the backyard?" Officer Strickland asked.

"No, I didn't," I replied, partly feeling like an idiot for not checking and partly feeling like they stalled me.

"I'll take a look for you, if you'd rather I did," Strickland said.

"Yeah, okay," I said, and he, taking a big flashlight from his belt and clicking it on, went around the side of the house.

"You and your dad and Jared doing all right?" Corinne asked.

"Yeah, Dad has his good days and his less good ones. I think he's being overprotective, and that's why he voted that way about trick-or-treating."

Corinne glanced away. "This is one of those questions I have to ask when something like this happens, but your dad doesn't have any firearms, does he?"

I shook my head. "None besides the Ruger his grandfather brought home from Germany, but as far as I know, it's in the safe deposit box at the Manuxet Five Cents Savings."

She asked me more questions like this: if Dad had started drinking more, if we had a place he might have gone to stay unannounced... I told her Dad didn't drink much to start with and, if anything, he drank less now, and the cottage in Tamworth, New Hampshire, which he'd inherited, he'd sold to help pay for Mom's cancer treatments.

"You think maybe that's why he vanished? He called us about some angry messages. He didn't tell you anything about them?" Corinne asked.

"No, he's been really careful with us. Jared hasn't gotten it entirely through his head that Mom isn't coming home, that part of her is in the cemetery and we'll see her in heaven someday if we live as good a life as we can."

"I don't want you to worry too much, but your dad came to us with a few really angry, threatening letters, that something bad would happen to him because of how he voted. One really weird one warned him that changing the night of trick-or-treating could wake up something from the darkness. It sounded like it came from someone really disturbed, so we held onto the letters to send them up to the FBI, in case things got worse."

I looked away, feeling really small, wishing Dad would walk up the driveway, safe and sound. As pissed as I'd felt earlier, I wanted to hug him and never let him go, but I still wanted to snap at him for not telling me. I got not letting Jared know, but I could handle it.

"You okay?"

I looked back to Corinne. "Yes. No. I don't know. I wish he'd told *me*. I can take it. I've helped take care of Mom, and I've helped take care of Jared since then. I have to ask, did any messages threaten Jared or I?"

She shook her head. "No, thank God."

Footsteps pattered down the stairs. I jolted. Jared approached, rubbing his eyes. "Why are the p'lice outside?"

I looked to Corinne. She nodded, silently saying, "You got this."

To Jared, I said, "Oh, there were spooky creatures running through the neighborhood, and the police came to make sure everyone's all right."

Jared widened his eyes at Corinne. "Are you gonna catch ghosts?"

Corinne got down to Jared's level. "Oh, yeh! We ain't afraid of no ghosts."

Jared made spooky gestures with his hands. "Wooooo!"

Strickland returned. Corinne caught his eye and tilted her head toward Jared. "You see any ghosts back there?"

"Nope, didn't see any," Strickland replied. He beckoned me aside. I followed him down to the lawn, while Corinne stayed with Jared.

He took a pad and a pen from inside his coat. "No sign of your dad back there. You remember what he was wearing?"

"Khaki pants, black sneakers, a black Court of Thorns tee-shirt, and a maroon canvas button-front shirt."

He jotted that down. "Court of Thorns, eh? That band's so old, my dad patrolled outside the venue they played at."

I shrugged. "He played one of their tapes for me. Much better than I expected."

"That his car in the garage?"

"Yeah, we sold Mom's car."

"Right. You got anywhere you and Jared could stay while we find your dad?"

"We could stay with Mom's sister, Ariadne."

"Okay. I suggest you call her and tell her what happened, though if you feel better stayin' here, we'll drive by to keep an eye on things."

I nodded. "Okay. May I go to my brother?"

"Of course. We got plenty to go with here." I went back to the steps.

"So, where's Daddy?" Jared asked. My heart skipped a beat.

I glanced to Corinne. "He went out for something, and I guess it's taking longer for him to get back than we expected."

"Okay," Jared said.

I scooped him up. "We'd better get you back to bed, little man." To Corinne and Strickland, I added, "Thanks for keeping us safe."

Corinne dipped her head. Strickland gave us a two-finger salute. "It's what we do. Now, you kids be well."

November 1ˢᵗ – Morning and Early Afternoon – Nikki

The next morning when I got up, dad still had not turned up. The house phone rang; I answered it.

"Nikki? It's Chief Matthews."

The very sound of his gruff voice made me breathe a little easier, but I still felt my stomach flip inside me. "Oh, thank heavens. Have you found Dad?'

Chief Matthews paused. "I'm sorry to tell you this, but we haven't found him yet. We've called his work partners; no one's seen or heard from him. We've checked the Manuxet River and some of the creeks flowing into it."

Awful images came into my head of Dad's body floating face-down in Ice Pond over on Whipple Street or caught in a bend of Meadows Brook. "Oh God, that's something I won't get out of my head."

"Sorry about that. We had to be thorough. I called the school for you, to let your teachers know what's going on."

"Thanks. That's one call I won't have to make."

"We've also picked up the kids who tossed a pumpkin at your door."

"Don't tell me; it was Ryan McIlhenny and his dumb friends?"

"Yes, it was those guys. They had nothing to do with your Dad. We spotted them on the traffic cam at the corner of Manuxet Street and Main well before you called. We caught them throwing pumpkins at another selectman's house when she spotted them on her home security."

I nearly thwapped myself upside the head. That doorbell camera Dad had installed a few weeks ago. I made a mental note to check it as I replied, "Well, that rules them out. If it's who I think it was, they wouldn't kidnap anyone. They didn't see anyone at our door, did they?"

"Nobody other than your father talking to a kid in a costume, a bed sheet ghost from the look of it. No one says they saw anything weird after that, and a few people chose to carry on with trick-or-treating as usual."

"Anyone see any kids near the bed sheet ghost kid?"

"No, no parents either, but sometimes kids like to go up to doors by themselves and have the parent stay back on the sidewalk."

"It's still kind of weird."

"Best to get used to weird. We're widening the search. We've contacted the FBI. They should be sending an agent out to speak to you today."

"The FBI? Yikes, this is serious."

We exchanged polite goodbyes. Chief Matthews promised to call me as soon as anything turned up. I called Aunt Ariadne to come pick up Jared and take him to preschool, then went upstairs to get him up and dressed and make some breakfast for the both of us.

"I thought Daddy would get me up," Jared said as I poured out the last of the Boo-Berry for him.

"I think he went away for a few days to think things over. Remember how sad he was right after Mom died?"

He nodded. "I hope he feels better."

"I hope so too," I said.

Once Aunt Ariadne had come for Jared, I checked my email and the Facebook posts I had made about Dad's disappearance. I found a packet of homework waiting for me. Something to keep me busy while I watched for the Feds.

I worked on my algebra and nearly finished the assigned equations. The doorbell rang, and the video feed from the camera popped up on the screen of Dad's laptop. Three men in suits – one big with dark hair, one average-sized with brown hair, and one short with blond hair – stood just outside the door. I ran out to answer.

"Nikki Ross?" asked the big guy. He looked like he should be leaning on people who owed money to the Mob instead of holding out the billfold with his FBI badge and ID to me. "I'm Special Agent Dante Stamos. Behind me is Special Agent in Training Bradley Johnson." He tilted his head toward the average guy, who fumbled his credentials out of the breast pocket of his black topcoat. "And the gentleman in your bushes is Special Agent Blake Matherton."

The blond agent, a slight man, not much taller than me, with metal-rimmed glasses, had gotten down on one knee among the yew bushes beside the stoop, snapping phone camera shots of the shattered pumpkin laying there.

"One moment. I might have something here," Agent Matherton said.

"They ruled out the pumpkin tossers," Agent Stamos said with the patience of Dr. Watson dealing with Sherlock Holmes.

"You think that thing might be haunted?" Agent Johnson asked.

"Hardly. It's unwise to break a jack-o-lantern," Agent Matherton said, pocketing his phone and adjusting the cuffs of his black vinyl driving gloves before rising to join his teammates. "But this one doesn't appear to have been carved, which lowers the possibilities."

I let them enter, to get in out of the autumn chill. I offered them coffee, but they gently refused. I told them what I'd seen and what I knew.

"All this talk with the cops, and I never thought to check the video doorbell," I said.

"You had a lot on your mind, and you did say you hadn't had it long," Agent Stamos said gently, clearly understanding.

"May we view the footage from last night?" Agent Matherton asked.

"Yeah, sure," I said. I pulled up the link to the cloud server. I scrolled back to the night before, past when I had checked outside.

The car buzzed the house, the headlights flashing past our door. Something flew into sight, bouncing off the door and flying past the camera into the bushes.

Something walked into view from the front walk, dressed like a ghost with a pumpkin head. It walked up the steps and knocked at the door. Dad stepped into view, talking to the kid – or what looked like a kid – who held up their pumpkin pail to him. Dad shook his head, clearly telling them, "no." The kid tilted their head at an odd angle, not the way most disappointed kids would. Dad stepped back, going back inside. The kid looks around, lights showing in their eyes.

"The eyes," Stamos murmured.

"Pause that, please?" Matherton said. I tapped the monitor, pausing it.

"Maybe it's a mask?" Agent Johnson asked.

"How could they see? The lights are right in the center of the eyeholes," Stamos said.

"They look more like tapetum lucidum, those little… mirrors on the retinas of many nocturnal creatures," Matherton said. "Keep playing, please?"

I hit play. Dad stepped back into view, holding a bar of baking chocolate and putting it into the kid's bucket.

"That's gonna inspire the kid to TP the trees," Agent Johnson said.

The kid picked the bar out of the bucket, tilted its face down at the bar, then up at Dad. I swore the eye holes narrowed.

Things like vines shot out of the bucket and from under the kid's costume, grabbing Dad around his torso. They pulled him headfirst into the bucket. Somehow, the opening fit him. He vanished, flailing his legs, into the maw of the thing's pail.

I jumped back from the screen. "What is it doing?"

"What the hell?" Johnson shouted.

Stamos looked to Matherton. "A cryptid."

"Shit," Matherton muttered. He glanced at me. "Sorry."

"Don't be. I've heard worse."

"It's one of those," he muttered, passing a hand over his face.

I paused the video. "One of what?"

"I thought at first it was a manifestation of Sam Hain," Matherton started.

"Don't you mean Sow-wen?" Johnson asked.

Matherton sighed. "Yes, if you're referring to the Celtic holiday or the Gaelic name for November. But the misinterpretation made by an 18th century English writer has, quite obviously, taken on an existence of its own. That author identified Samhain with a 'Lord of the Dead.'" He raised his index fingers in very sarcastic finger quotes. "When the ancient Gaelic people had a '*Lady* of the Dead,'" so many people believed in the mistake that they created a kind of thought-form to which the name Sam Hain applied. When it does manifest, the entity appears as a costumed humanoid, usually taking on the shape of a classic costume: a witch, a ghost, a skeleton, a bat, things of that nature. But it would seem this thought-form has been hijacked by something else." He looked at me. "Have you ever read the writings of H.P. Lovecraft?"

"That really racist horror writer from the 1930s?"

"Philosophies rooted into junk science aside, he drew much of his inspiration from accounts of creatures we still barely understand, existing on the edge of reality as we know it."

"Tentacled monsters who didn't give a crap about us at best, and at worst have it out for us," Stamos added.

"Oversimplification," Matherton said. "It would seem that some of these creatures, possibly the offspring of Shrub-Nickelrath, have taken advantage of this legend as a scrim to hide behind and further confuse us."

"So, how do we get him back?" I asked.

"That bucket it carried. That likely serves as a portal to its home dimension," Matherton said.

"Like that weird 'the veil grows thin' stuff about Halloween?"

"On a symbolic level, it is," Matherton said. "If we can lure it back to this world, we may be able to use that portal against it."

My heart dropped into my shoes. "So, now what? He's in another world, and we can't get him back?" I wanted to scream and cry. I wanted to pummel a wall or a pillow, but none of that would bring him home.

Agent Stamos tilted his head to look me in the face. "Whatever it takes, we'll turn over hell to find him."

"How? You got a door into the Upside Down?" I asked.

Agent Johnson raised an eyebrow. "Cool! You watch Stranger Things?"

"Watched it with my dad." I couldn't hold the tears back. I braced my hands on the edge of the table, trying to be strong.

Agent Stamos leaned down beside me, putting his arm behind my back. "Cry all you need to. I got a daughter about your age, and I know life in general ain't easy. Add all this, and it knocks you sideways."

"You know?" I choked.

"Officer Denehy gave us the basics."

"Good. Thought you'd found it out by hacking my Facebook or something." I pulled away. Matherton gave me a look halfway between annoyance and boredom, like he'd heard that too many times, but he took several paper napkins from the holder on the table and held them out to me. I blotted my eyes with them. "Just find my dad and bring him home. Do what you have to do."

"We'll have to attempt summoning it tonight, and in the meantime, I have some... research to do and things to acquire," Matherton said, glancing up at Stamos. "I have to ask: are you religious or spiritual on any level?"

"We used to go to the Methodist church in town til Mom died. We haven't gone as often since then," I said. "Why?"

He drew in a breath. "You might want to call in a prayer circle or have your minister come to perform a deliverance after all this."

"I'll keep that in mind," I said. "Just get my dad home safely first."

Matherton looked me in the face for a change. "I can't make any promises, but we'll do everything possible."

"Fair enough," I said.

November 1st, evening – Nikki

I'd stayed off my phone as much as I could, aside from fielding calls from extended family and Dad's friends. Once Jared came home from preschool, Aunt Ariadne took over to give me a break so I could spend some time with Jared.

"When's Daddy coming back?" Jared asked as we colored some Halloween pages.

"Soon, I hope."

"I hope the ghosts didn't get him."

I tried not to think about the thing in the footage. "Nah, Dad's too tough and smart for them to get him."

My phone rang yet again. Aunt Ariadne took it. "Ariadne Baltrussis—" She raised an eyebrow. "All right." She handed the phone to me.

I put it on speaker. "Hello?"

"Nikki? This is Agent Stamos. We figured out what that thing in the security footage is and, more importantly, how to get its attention. I'm putting Agent Matherton on to explain."

The line rustled, and Matherton's cooler, high-pitched voice spoke. "Miss Ross, do you have any real jack-o-lanterns that you carved this year?"

"I have one on my windowsill, why?"

"We're going to need to smash it."

"What?"

"You know why people carved jack-o-lanterns in the old days, right?"

"To help light up the night so the spooks wouldn't come out of the woodwork."

"Precisely. The thing is, if you willfully damage a jack-o-lantern, that action diminishes your protection."

"So, in order to get that thing to come back and give him up, we have to smash a jack-o-lantern and get its attention?"

"Wise girl." His voice warmed a degree or two with approval.

"Okay, Jared won't like it, but I think I can make him understand."

"May we come to your family's house in about an hour?"

"Of course. What if we carved some more jack-o-lanterns?"

A slight pause was followed by a soft "Hrmm…" from him. He continued, "That's a good addition. If you do that, be sure to recall every Halloween memory you can think of while you're carving it in order to imbue it with… dare I call it, the right kind of spirit."

"That sounds a little woo-woo, but I guess the whole situation calls for something woo-woo."

We made our goodbyes, and I hung up. Aunt Ariadne had a look in her eye as she asked, "Are you sure these guys are really FBI? The whole thing sounds out there."

"And there aren't FBI agents keeping an eye on Area 51 and whatever aliens they have locked away there?"

"That's different."

"Tell that to the goat-staring guys the military hired in the 1970s."

I went to the kitchen, taking the big pumpkin from the kitchen table centerpiece. I laid out newspapers on the table and found Mom's pumpkin carving set – several blades and scoops and other tools with orange and black striped, wooden handles – in the back of the kitchen drawer.

"Jared, can you help me?" I asked.

Jared hopped into a chair to watch. "But I'm still too little to carve."

I thrust the largest knife into the top of the pumpkin, cutting a circle around the stem, making a lid. "You can still think of all the fun we've had at Halloween while you're watching me carve."

"All the jack-o-lanterns in the nice people's yard up the street, and the nice pumpkin man who lets us look at them."

I eased the lid off, scraping off the strings and goo and seeds. "And the Goosebumps books that his daughter hands out with the little bags of candy."

Aunt Ariadne joined us. "The time you got so scared at the haunted house in the recreation center on Livingstone Street, your dad had to carry you out at the end."

I chuckled, feeling better. "Yeah, and it's the kind of place I'd love now."

"Were you really that scared?" Jared asked.

I scooped out more of the slick stuff inside, dumping it onto the newspaper. "Yeah, I was a scaredy kid when I was little. I got another one: trick-or-treating, and Winona had that cat costume with the long, black tail and the long, black plastic claws."

"Oh, I remember that!" Aunt Ariadne said. "You went as a bat, with those wings under your arms."

I took the small detailing knife to score the outlines of the eyes, nose, and mouth. "The year April Bouchard dared me to knock on the door of a house with no lights on."

"Did you?" Jared asked, his eyes big.

"Sort of. I threw some gravel at the door. I wish I hadn't. The lights went on in the front windows, and a weird-looking old man ran out onto the front walk, yelling at us."

"That's scary," Jared said. "Mom made candied apples one year."

I breathed easier at that friendlier memory and cut into the eye outline. "You remember that?"

Jared nodded. "I was too little to bite into an apple, but Mom let me taste some of the candy part."

I gritted my teeth a little, continuing to carve the pumpkin, remembering the costumes Mom had made for herself and Dad, for me and Jared, when he came along. I remembered the Halloween parties we went to as a family, going trick-or-treating on Halloween night.

Aunt Ariadne found half an orange taper in a drawer. I lit it with the long-nosed lighter Dad used on the grill in the summer and turned it upside down inside the pumpkin to put down a pad of wax to stick the candle into before I replaced the lid. Once we brought down the jack-o-lantern from my room, we lit a second candle for it. I put out the kitchen light and let the jack-o-lanterns glow for a time, their insides warming and filling the room with the nutty scent that had filled so many Halloween nights.

The doorbell rang. I looked at the monitor on the counter. The three agents who'd come earlier stood there. Agent Matherton was setting something on the ground at the foot of the steps. Agent Johnson held what looked like a pair of baseball bats over his shoulder, and Agent Stamos peered into the camera.

"Let me get that," Aunt Ariadne said, going for the door. Picking up one of my jack-o-lanterns, I followed her, hearing her exchange greetings with them. "I hope you know what you're doing," she added.

"Trust me, I've dealt with things going bump in the night for twenty years," Matherton said, strapping something that looked like a telephone lineman's harness about his chest, under his coat. "There's some skills and knowledge you can only pick up in the field. Quantico's a bit slow on the uptake, but they're starting to realize that not every case can be quantified by the usual means.

"So, what we're going to do here is this: Agent Johnson and I will smash the jack-o-lanterns on the steps. As soon as the creature manifests, we're going to confront it, hopefully angering it enough that it will try and capture me. This harness I'm wearing will be connected by a cable to a reel."

He glanced to the object at the foot of the stoop, which Agent Stamos anchored into our lawn with what looked like metal tent pegs. "That will keep me anchored to this world. Once I find your father and free him, I'll bring him back."

I set the jack-o-lantern on the top step. Aunt Ariadne went back in, returning with the other. "We'll bring him back," I said.

Matherton raised an eyebrow as Stamos hooked the end of the cable to his teammate's harness, tugging on it to test it. "Excuse me?"

"It's my dad. I got mad at him before all this went down. I want to make this right. Besides, he'll need a familiar face with you when you find him."

He raised the other eyebrow but nodded, acknowledging this. "I must warn you, though: the place we're going is dangerous."

"I like this girl; she's got guts," Stamos said.

"I was about to ask why you're going in?" Agent Johnson asked.

Matherton didn't look at Johnson. "For the simple reason that I've been there before, or at least... a place like it." The hollow look creeping into his eyes told us more than words could have.

"And here I figured I was the expendable one," Johnson said, relieved.

A small ring of jack-o-lanterns carved from smaller, lumpy things surrounded the front of the stoop, leaving the path clear. I pointed to them. "What are those?"

"Turnip jack-o-lanterns. My wife carved 'em and volunteered a few," Stamos said. "Her Irish Grandad taught her how; said they make 'em like that back on the auld sod."

"That's kind of her," I said, inwardly questioning my sanity a bit.

"Stand back; this will get messy," Matherton warned. I stepped down the steps. Matherton glanced to Johnson, nodding to him. Johnson nodded back.

They raised the bats and, as one, smashed them down onto the pumpkins. I jumped back, pieces of pumpkin flying at my face and shoulders.

"I HATE HALLOWEEN!" Matherton roared at the smashed pulp on the steps. From the quiver in his shoulders, I knew he meant it. I looked at Stamos.

"He's got his reasons," Stamos said by way of explanation, and the look in his eye suggested things straight out of *Criminal Minds*, only real.

"I hate how it inspires idiots to call up things they can't put down," Matherton continued, not as loud as before but still as furious. "I hate how criminals put truth into some of those legends about trick-or-treating. And I hate those sexist, slutty whatever costumes!"

I had to agree with him, but I fought back a giggle at the last one anyway.

"Yeah! What he said!" Johnson yelled, a bemused smirk on his face.

A breeze rustled the yew bushes. Crisp leaves skittered across the lawn. Footsteps padded up the walkway when I hadn't seen anyone approach.

What looked like a kid dressed as a bedsheet ghost with a witch hat on their head approached, clutching a brown paper sack, like they'd wandered away from Charlie Brown's gang of friends out for tricks or treats.

"Trick or treat?" the thing asked in a weird, not-kidlike voice.

"Yes, you tricked this young lady's father and not in a very nice way," Matherton said, looking at the thing and talking like Dad scolding as he stepped closer toward it, the cable reeling out. I followed close behind him.

The thing hung its head sideways, trying to look like a kid on the business end of a scolding. The eyeholes in its sheet glowed with a weird colored light, like a stranger, darker shade of violet.

"Spit him out, Sam Hain," Stamos ordered.

"Surrender him, child of Shrub-Nickelrath," Johnson said, trying to sound like a wizard or cult leader in some weird movie. Stamos gave him an '*are you serious?*' look. Matherton kept his eyes on the thing, but he shifted as if he wanted to turn and yell at their agent in training.

The bag rustled as if it had something alive in there. Those tendril-things lunged out, grabbing Matherton and me around the waist. The bag didn't wide, but somehow, it fit us down the gullet of the bag.

We dropped into a forest, onto ground wetter and more squelching than any forest floor I'd hiked. Trees leaned over us with bark more like leathery skin and branches like limbs with eyes – or at least something like eyes – instead of leaves. Mist hung in the air, and it was far warmer than the New England autumn chill we'd left behind.

Matherton stood above me, offering one gloved hand to me. I took it, rising. "What is this place? The Upside Down?"

"Something like it, but something very different," he said. "As far as we know, this is a pocket dimension, inhabited by entities older than we are, perhaps even older than our universe – creatures which we still don't understand and that are hungry for anything: food, flesh, the essence of our minds…"

I looked up at him. "And it will take advantage of trick-or-treating to get a handout?"

"It would be a perfect place to hide in plain sight, with humans walking about in strange costumes."

"Dad?" I called out. I walked through the clearing we'd entered, along a rough path with Matherton at my heels. The ground squelched and sloshed under our feet. The trees turned their branches toward us.

We squashed into another clearing, the ground rising to a small hill set with boulders, some in a ring, some scattered about. On top of one in the center, Dad lay covered from neck to feet in a thick layer of what looked like sticky, green cobwebs or snot spun into cable. I ran up to him, punching at the crusty stuff. Dad trembled, opening his eyes to look up at me.

"Nikki?" he croaked.

Matherton took a bottle of water from somewhere inside his topcoat, cracking it open and holding it to Dad's mouth. "Don't try to talk; we're getting you out of here."

Dad took a long drink from the bottle, then sighed. I broke his legs loose. Matherton recapped the bottle and punched the crust close to Dad's arms, picking the stuff loose. Dad wriggled under the stuff, breaking more of it before he sat up.

We cleared the last of it from Dad's chest, then helped him down, letting him lean on us as we hobbled back to the exit. Once we reached the pool of light where we'd entered, Matherton tugged three times, then a fourth and fifth time, on the tether. I felt someone reel us in, back through the opening.

We dropped onto the path. Aunt Ariadne, with Jared on her arm, ran up, dropping to her knees beside Dad and me, hugging us both.

"Tom! Tom, are you all right?" she asked.

"Daddy! Daddy! The monster didn't eat you!" Jared yelled.

Dad put his arms as far around the three of us as they could go, murmuring over and over again, "I'm okay, I'm okay. I'm here now. I'm okay." He hung on like he'd hold us forever, and I pulled him close like I'd never let him out of my sight again. There was no sign of the thing, except for the bag it carried, which lay on the front walk.

After a long while, with the agents clearing up the area, Dad looked up. "Are you guys... with the police?"

"FBI, actually," Agent Stamos said.

"Unusual Cases, to be precise," Agent Johnson said.

"What was that place? What was that thing?" Dad asked.

"Something you probably wish you hadn't unwittingly awakened, from a place you never imagined existing beyond this world," Matherton said, unbuckling the harness from under his coat.

"Just because I voted to move the date of trick-or-treating?" Dad asked.

Agent Stamos took a large evidence bag from his breast pocket and opened it to slide it over the creature's bag. "A lot of things have rules you need to follow, or else there are consequences you may not expect."

"Sounds like you know a lot about this," Dad said.

"It's our specialty," Matherton replied.

"And you thought me ragging you was bad," I said.

Matherton eyed the creature's bag as Stamos handed it to him. "There's always something bigger and nastier out there."

"And when we can't cut the monsters down to size, we get people away from 'em," Stamos added.

November 1st, evening – Thomas

I hobbled out of a warm shower into Ariadne's master bedroom, where she'd laid out some of my scruffy clothes on the bed. I'd lost track of how long I'd let the warm water sluice over me, washing away the reek of that creature's domain.

"Those kids were smarter than you," she said, looking away. "You okay now?"

"The shower did me good," I said, slipping off the bathrobe and pulling on a pair of grey sweatpants. "Is this where you go 'told you so?'"

She shook her head. "I think you've had enough punishment."

I pulled on the Red Sox sweatshirt she'd laid out. She put a hand on my shoulder, steering me downstairs to the living room, where she'd lit the gas log in the fireplace and piled some real logs around it. She sat me down on a floor pillow set on the hearth before it. Nikki put a mug of something warm into my hands.

"Promise us the next time the town puts trick-or-treating to a vote, you'll leave it alone," Nikki said.

I sipped from the mug: hot cider with cinnamon, just what I needed. "How about a town Halloween party on the Sunday closest to Halloween and trick-or-treating on its usual night?"

"Fair enough. I have a feeling those FBI agents won't want to come back to pull you or someone else out of Monster World."

Something small with a sheet draped over its head shuffled up to us, a paper Market Basket in hand. "Trick or treat?" it hissed.

I nearly jumped back into the fire. Nikki grabbed the sheet, pulling it off Jared's tousled head.

"Jared, don't dress like that thing!" I cried.

"Yeah. It's too scary right now," Nikki said.

"Sorry," Jared said, dejected.

"Hey, it's okay, buddy. I'm a little jumpy after everything that's happened." I looked from them into the flames. The flames danced over and around the logs, licking through the wood.

Shapes like tendrils formed from the flames. Two spots of greenish blue appeared among the white flames. Maybe she's added apple wood, creating the colors. "Next year, I'm handing out full-sized candy bars."

"Really?" Jared asked, perking right up.

"That'll make it up to the kids in town," Nikki added.

"It'll make up for this year," I said.

The blue specks turned away, vanishing into the fire.

Born in Lowell, Massachusetts, R.C. Mulhare grew up in a nearby town in a hundred-year-old house near a centuries-old cemetery. Her interest in the dark and mysterious started when her mother read the faery tales of the Brothers Grimm and quoted the poetry of Edgar Allen Poe to her, while her Irish storyteller father gave her a fondness for strange characters and quirky situations.

When she isn't writing, she moonlights in grocery retail. A two-time Amazon best-selling author, contributor to the Hugo Award Winning Archive of Our Own, and member of the New England Horror Writers, her work previously appeared with Atlantean Publishing, Macabre Maine, FunDead Publications, NEHW Press, Deadman's Tome, and Weirdbook Magazine.

She shares her home with her family, two small parrots, seventeen hundred books, and an unknown number of eldritch things rattling in the walls when she's writing late at night. She's delighted to have visitors at:

https://www.facebook.com/rcmulhare

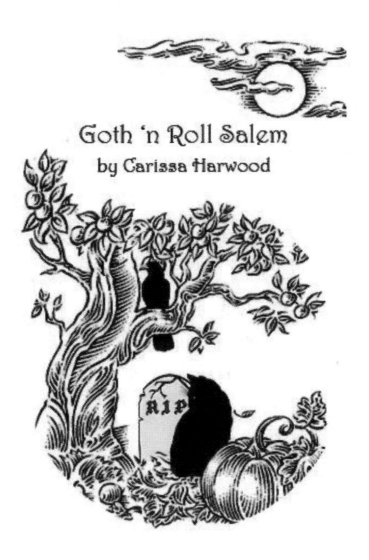

Goth 'n Roll Salem
by Carissa Harwood

SAMHAIN SECRETS

SALEM, 1987

Let me tell you about Salem, Massachusetts in 1987. I was a senior in high school at the time, and I don't think I would have been able to tell you this story without some of the old journals I found cleaning out the attic after mom died. What I found there helped me – no, made me – remember everything that I tried so hard, and succeeded, to forget.

In 1987, I'm sorry to admit, I was utterly Goth. It was my big stand against the quaintness and charming tourism of Salem. As a matter of fact, my house was frequently on the tourism line that would cruise languorously through our neighborhood, especially around Halloween, where my neighborhood would go all out starting September 1st with cobwebs and lights and pumpkins and ghosts.

I was so bored with it all, and sometimes I would sit on our ornate front porch and sneer at all the normal people in their mom-jeans and khakis and pastel sun visors. They would take pictures and point at all the ornate details of the house. It had started life as a farmhouse, I think, and then a boarding house during the Great Depression.

The best thing about it was that I had my own teeny, tiny bathroom that had a toilet that you used to have to flush with a chain. You couldn't actually use the toilet, but it was still kind of a novelty. My friends thought having your own bathroom was cool, especially the metal laundry chute that opened up in a dark part of the basement where my mom would leave a plastic laundry basket to collect everyone's dirty clothes and damp towels. You just chuck your clothes in, and whoosh! Down it goes to the basement.

One time, my friend, Winnie, tried to launch herself down when we were super drunk and staying up late to watch The Evil Dead on cable. She had smuggled in some horrible wine that tasted like stomach acid and got us wicked lit, and so we thought sending her down to land in a soft but smelly, mildewed pile of clothes was a really great idea. It wasn't.

Since it was so late, mom let Winnie stay the night instead of calling her parents but made her go home a seven in the morning, and I could hear her clunking her way down the sidewalk to the bus station in her ridiculous platforms. I don't know what happened to Winnie. We were best friends in that way that girls are really tight for forever, and all of a sudden, she was gone. Something happened to the family.

I remember driving by her house one night years later with a different and understanding best friend riding shotgun this time, and there were different people in the windows, like someone had changed the TV on me. But it was the 80's, and channel changing happened a lot. She probably wouldn't have recognized me anyway.

But back to my diaries. If you remember 1987 at all, this was the era of the Satanic Panic. My mom was a classic 80's housewife, and she loved her some Donahue. She would watch him religiously, and it made me wonder just how many lonely housewives he must have kept company while people like my Dad, who commuted to Boston every weekday, went off and did business in one of the high, glittering towers of the city. I couldn't even tell you which one.

Come to think of it, I'm not even really sure what his job was. While sipping drinks like Bloody Mary and screwdrivers, my mom would light a cigarette and settle in on the couch. She always got dressed up for the day, even if she wasn't planning on going anywhere. Usually, the corkscrew of the phone cord was stretched from the end table to her ear, and she'd spend the day chatting to one of my aunts or one of her friends from about the time she woke up until she'd make dinner for when Dad came home.

My mom was a Bloody Mary connoisseur and would even make me one once in a while. I wasn't one of those kids who had to really sneak around with alcohol. I mean, I didn't flaunt it, but my mom could definitely tell when I was hungover, and poof! There'd be a tomato-vodka concoction on my nightstand in the morning with two chalky tablets of Anacin. She just didn't like it when I had friends over who got loud. She was a quiet drunk.

So, Donahue. For anyone who doesn't know who he is, he was the talk show tabloid host in the 1980's, before there was Oprah. It wasn't until years later that I really thought about the way TV shows like this had such an influence on my mom. All of this leads to my Goth period in my teenage years and the Satanic Panic and its influence on Salem.

We have daytime TV plus my alcoholic and easily manipulated mother plus my mostly absent (and probably cheating) dad plus a weirdo, music-obsessed almost 18-year-old me with a love of Siouxsie and the Banshees and the Cure, Bauhaus and Metallica, who played Dungeons and Dragons. Stir in a magic wand, and you get… this.

For about four months before this all started, I had taken a bottle of black hair dye and smothered my hair in it in my tiny bathroom, getting black smears all over the place that I couldn't scrub out.

The thing to do at the time was to drench your hair in hair spray and kill it with a crimping iron, trying to get it as high and as big and tangled and scary-looking as possible, although, to be fair, the big hair thing was popular with normal girls, too. It's frightening in and of itself that big hair was ever a thing. Hair isn't meant to withstand that type of torture; it's amazing I had any healthy hair left after the early 90's.

Anyway, my wardrobe slowly evolved from the neon and pastels that I mostly had to scrounging through the thrift stores and Salvation Army, the only way a poor high school student could effectively change her wardrobe. I had babysitting money, but the weirder my look became, oddly, the babysitting offers started to dry up, and I soon had to go in search of a job if I wanted to maintain my goth 'n roll lifestyle.

I knew about the witches. How could you not? But it was historical and therefore boring, until I went Goth and acquired an interest in such things. Winnie thought the whole thing was contrived and basically to us, anything that wasn't Goth or rock in some way wasn't authentic, so we somehow convinced ourselves that we were going to find the real witches of Salem, not the stuff they sold to tourists.

And honestly, I went along with it because it seemed fun at the time, and I didn't believe in it. I didn't really believe in anything, but I thought, "What the hell?" Winnie told me it was the ultimate high. After all the heavy, black eyeliner and the fried, towering hairdos and thrift store black outfits that smelled like mothballs, which we ripped up and pinned with safety pins we bought at the drug store, freaking out the normies… after the look, the music, and the drinking, what else could we do to set ourselves apart from everyone else?

Oh, yeah… only the most cliché thing we could think of. We'd become witches. During the Satanic Panic. At Halloween. As I said, we weren't very bright back then but thought we were smarter than everybody. But some good came out of it too, I think, in the end. I don't know. I'm struggling to find all the right words. Things get a little fuzzy here.

I remember that morning, though, waking up in the before-noon haze of my darkened bedroom, coming downstairs to the TV on very low, feeling like something was wrong, or at least different. Neither Winnie nor I had enough money, but I felt weird, like I had been drinking. A little fuzzy, a little dizzy.

When I woke up, I saw that my mom had been in my room, leaving me a glass of water and some pills I assumed was the same Anacin she usually left. I didn't question it in the dark. I just gulped it down to prevent a headache and went back to sleep.

I was very rarely awake this early on a Friday morning, and it was Halloween night, or Devil's Night. I had already finished most of my classes and started to take creative writing classes at

Salem State College. I also found some crappy job working at a mail service for about five minutes, tagging people's doorknobs and windshields and mailboxes with Chinese menus one week, and car wash services or something the next. It paid shit, but it was money, and it was pointed out by a smirking teacher that I probably wouldn't get much better work for a teenager looking the way I did.

Yeah, I looked kind of silly, but didn't almost everyone in their teens? Maybe the parents of teenagers in the 50's thought poodle skirts were ridiculous. It only strengthened my resolve to look even weirder. I hated that everyone was so hung up on looks. I just wanted to drink and get spinny on music.

But that changed the morning I came down the stairs, wearing a band t-shirt I'd slept in, something with feathers and skulls, and just underwear because my dad would have left hours ago, and normally, mom was encased in her TV-and-nicotine coma. It didn't occur to me that maybe we'd have a guest.

I found myself wearing a t-shirt, underwear, and scrunchy socks in front of a very prim-looking woman I'd never seen before, who sat perched on the edge of an armchair that probably hadn't been sat in since Nixon was president. She was looking around our living room in a judgey way, and as soon as I saw her, I felt embarrassed and then angry at myself for feeling embarrassed.

My crunchy hair was tangled and smooshed flat against one side of my head, and I hadn't bothered to rub my makeup off before bed, having passed out. So, this is how I met Angela Richard, chapter president of Concerned Moms Against Witchcraft. Yes, that was the name.

Mom looked me up and down, as did Angela. Mom smiled tightly in an embarrassed mom way, like she was apologizing for me, and Angela didn't smile at me at all. She looked at me like something you'd pull out of the drain with tweezers, holding it as far away from you as possible before throwing it away. And it wasn't until that moment that the glow of Donahue's TV light shone dully on my copy of Scott Cunningham's Wicca for Beginners.

It took my sleepy brain a moment to realize that was *my* book. From *my* room. My mom *never* went in my room. Okay, well, she never went *through* my room. My mom was the type of mom to bring me hair of the dog when I was too hung over. It was her way of being nice to me and sort of acknowledging me as an adult. Or almost-adult. This – this was a huge violation of my privacy. And who was this woman, sitting there judging me like I was a total piece of trash?

"What's going on?" I asked, hating that my voice warbled a little.

"Cassandra." My mom never used my full name, signaling at once a peculiar type of formality, along with the use of the name she saved for when I was in really big trouble. "Can you explain what this is?"

My mom's chipped fingernails tapped the book with its relatively innocuous and plain cover. I remember thinking how nice Angela's nails were done, perfectly clipped and painted a delicate pink. This woman would never wear red, would consider it too lurid. I think it was at that moment that I decided that I would start wearing colors again. It's weird the things you notice in times like this.

I crossed my arms over my chest, feeling heat crawl up my neck and flushing my cheeks, trying probably failing to conceal the fact that I wasn't wearing a bra. I felt exposed under the woman's critical gaze and embarrassed, and why should I feel embarrassed? This was my house, and that was my book.

Before anyone could react, I dove for the book in the middle of the table and clutched it to my chest. It was now more precious to me than it had been before. My mind raced back to the day I bought it with Winnie at The Official Witch Shoppe of Salem. I mean, I bought it part out of fun but part because it seemed interesting.

I wasn't blind or oblivious to what the news said about rock music, particularly metal. While some of my friends played Rocky Horror over the weekends, I'd play Dungeons and Dragons with Winnie and a few of our other friends, but this woman's presence in my home made me assume that she had been snooping through my things. The second panicked thought I had was, *"Oh, shit, my diary!"*

My third thought was that this would be all cleared up in a few minutes, and I began to relax. All I had to do was explain that Wicca was in no way, shape, or form associated with devil worship and Satanism, whatever that was. I'd explain that Robert Smith was a little depressed and the looks were just aesthetic, but there was nothing there that could be connected to Satanism. Like at all. This was a misunderstanding. This would be cleared up, and I would be fine.

"You see," the woman, Angela of the perfect pink nails, said as she lifted her hand and waved it at me like I was a bad smell in the room. "She can't even speak. It's already got a hold of her."

I found my voice. "If I have trouble speaking, it's because there's a woman in my house implying I'm a devil worshipper or something." I ignored my mother's glare. I wasn't exactly feeling strong, standing there in my underwear, but I had to try.

"The practice of Satanism is very real, Mrs. Danvers, and they often target the young and impressionable. Exposing Satan's underground is what Concerned Moms do. We are certain it exists, the practice of evil in the Devil's name. It exists. It is real, and it is present in your very home."

My mother gasped, holding her throat. Angela sounded like a salesman, one of those women hawking wrinkle cream or cubic zirconia on TV late at night. I rolled my eyes so hard, I'm surprised they didn't fall out onto the floor. Wouldn't that have made Angela's point for her? Couldn't my mom see what was going on here? Where did she even *find* this woman?'

"When I first became aware of this war against God's souls, I was living in Florida, and God called me to Salem, Massachusetts. I know this is where wickedness thrives. It happened here centuries ago, when the good and the pure people of this village were also called by God to rid the world of the Devil and his followers. And now I am here to do the same." She leaned over and patted my mother's hand. "I feel certain God has called me to you, Mrs. Danvers." She was ignoring me, working on my mom with that salesman-like efficiency. She had found her mark.

"This is not a Halloween fable; this is the stuff of real nightmares. When my husband and I started this ministry, it was to help people like your family, your daughter. We have travelled all over this beautiful U. S. of A., and you know what we found?" She still didn't look at me. She was leaning in to speak to my mom, who had tears trembling at the corner of her eyes. "Satan is alive and well and resides right here in Salem. He's been here for quite some time."

My God! It was a talk show come to life in my living room. I couldn't help but burst out laughing, almost dropping my book. "Mom, you have got to be kidding me. You let this lady into our house? We don't even go to church!" I mean, sometimes we went to church on Christmas or Easter, when we remembered, but it wasn't that big of a deal in our house.

Mostly, dad was too tired and slept, and there was a Christmas special on or The Greatest Story Ever Told that we'd watch every Easter, but that was really it. I don't even think I owned any special church clothes since I was about five.

"Cassandra." My mother turned to me, looking awkward without a drink in her hand. She must have felt weird too because she took up a cigarette and a matchbook from the table. "I've been very concerned about you lately. All this black, the makeup, the… whatever you've done with your hair. And the kids you hang around with." She shook her head, then took a long drag on her cigarette. "This isn't normal, and aren't you supposed to be in school right now?"

"This is how it all starts," Angela interjected. The woman sitting in our living room, whom I now hated. "This is how they entice the youngsters in. The change in appearance, the music they listen to, the people they hang out with, the lack of inhibitions." This was clearly directed at me and my state of undress.

The youngsters? Was this woman from the 1950's or what?

I turned to go. I was going to go back upstairs, get dressed, and then... I don't know. Winnie would still be asleep. My mind started racing about the different places I could go. Maybe the cemetery, where we had kind of a little clubhouse, but would they know to look for me there?

"Honey, your father's on his way home. I called him this morning."

I froze where I stood, still clutching the book to my chest. Why would he need to come home? What for? She was acting like someone died.

"Why?" I felt like I had swallowed a live snake, and there it sat, writhing in the pit of my stomach. I was suddenly cold – really cold. The snake shivered inside me, coiling itself tighter and tighter. When I get scared, I feel it in my fingers, this tingling sensation. Calling my dad home was serious. It meant something was going to happen.

"Honey." My mom stood up, cigarette smoke surrounding her like a scarf. There were tears in her eyes. "You're going to go with this nice lady. She's going to help you get better. You're sick. The Devil has a hold of your soul." My mom was full-on crying now. Her voice sounded strangled. "We only want what's best for you, sweetheart..."

I didn't think. I just ran, clutching the book, up to my room. I slammed the door, but it didn't have a lock. I dragged the chair from my desk and propped it up against the doorknob. I didn't know if it would keep them out, though. I could hear my mother calling my name at the bottom of the stairs, followed by the low but firm sound of that woman – that hideous woman to whom my mom was perfectly content to just hand me over.

What did she even mean that I was supposed to go with her? That woman looked at me like I was a freak, like I was someone dirty and gross, but there was a hunger there, too – a kind of look that I didn't know how to identify. Later, I'd know it as zealotry. Angela was a true believer and couldn't wait to wash me in the Blood of the Lamb.

I hastily pulled on some faded charcoal jeans and a soft, grey t-shirt with U2 on it – all my t-shirts were band t-shirts – and I paced my small room, not sure what I should do next. I thought of my mom going through all my stuff and started going through my drawers, throwing their contents on the bed, looking for what was gone.

I whirled around, suddenly thinking of the music. Was it the music that made them think I worshipped the devil? Was it Dungeons and Dragons? A book about Wicca? All my records and tapes were gone, even the one I left on the record player. Everything was gone, even the pop stuff: Heart and Prince and Madonna.

I searched through my bookcases. Anything that was fantasy-related was gone, too. When had she done this? It had to have been last night, and coming in early this morning, I wouldn't have noticed everything missing in the dark.

My first thought was escape. Just pack what I had, what was light and not ransacked, and get out. I'd figure out where. Just get out; just go. I had some money in my backpack. I'd just gotten paid the day before. It wasn't much, but it was enough for bus fare. Bus fare to where, I had no idea. I'd figure it out. Winnie and I would come up with something.

I tried the window, and it didn't budge. What? There were two windows that faced the street, and I tried both. My sense of being trapped like an animal started to grow, and I felt more and more frantic, my armpits sweating and the back of my neck slick. *What the hell? Did they do this when I was sleeping? Could I have not heard this? What was going on?*

I sat on my bed, defeated. They had me trapped in there. That's why she hadn't stopped me from pounding up the steps. She knew I had nowhere to go. I started to cry big, bubbling sobs that I tried to stuff into my pillow. I didn't understand what was happening. I wasn't crazy. I wasn't a devil worshipper. Did my parents think I was? Did they think I was dangerous, like the kids we saw on Donahue, who slit their parent's throats in their sleep and had pentacles everywhere?

I lifted my head from the pillow and looked around, seeing they had left the posters on the walls, my Goth 'n Roll idols staring down at me, scowling. *"We told you this would happen,"* Siouxsie said, her sad eyes filling my wounded brain. *"Didn't I try to warn you they were all the same?"* I guess she had been right. They had all been right.

I heard a door slam outside and chanced a peek around the white eyelet curtain my mom kept on my window. I hated that curtain. It was so childish. And that's what this was really about, it dawned on me then. I was an only child, and I turned out to be a giant disappointment.

I listened to dark rock instead of classical music like the girls played at my school. Did my mom not know about these girls and how they pretended to be good but ran around with boys, smoked a lot, and drank as much as I did? Only I did it out in the open. I wasn't a hypocrite like they were, and now I was being punished for it.

My dad was home. I saw him get out of his car slowly, wearily... like every step hurt him. He stood with his tweed fedora and long, brown New England coat, looking up at my window, his expression unreadable. It was like I didn't know him, this stranger that shared a house with us. Maybe he was trying to communicate something with me, I don't know.

I jumped away from the window, like I had been burned, and really, hadn't I? The people I trusted and loved betrayed me, and I don't know if there's a worse feeling in the world. That feeling of having your heart broken by your parents. It hurts worse than any breakup because you know they were the ones who *made* you. They *formed* you. They did everything for you, until they didn't.

Until they started calling you a freak, a liar, a weirdo. Hadn't there been little digs? Was I just totally blind in that way that teenagers are, that they can't see around the next corner? I guess I was. Not anymore. If I got out of this, somehow, I knew things were changed between us all, forever.

I could hear the front door open, my dad's heavy footsteps, and low-murmured voices discussing my future without me. I heard him setting his briefcase down in the front hall. I listened to my mom's high, hysterical crying, the lower voice of the bitchy and more-than-capable Angela. Well, I wasn't going down without a fight.

Picking up my backpack, I walked to the bathroom and turned to look at my ransacked room. It looked like a hurricane hit it. Stuff was everywhere. Just more evidence they could use that I was crazy. Among the debris of life, I spotted my old patchwork teddy bear on the bed. As I heard three sets of footsteps ascend the stairs, for a reason I can't quite identify, I grabbed it, stuffed it in my bag, and shut the bathroom door.

There were no windows, and the door wouldn't lock. I heard the door to my room rattle. My eyes searched the room. Was there something I could use to fight with? I grabbed the giant can of hairspray. I could spray it in their eyes and try to fight my way out. But that would only work on maybe one person, temporarily. Despite what Angela probably told them, I wasn't hoarding knives or whatever, ready to plunge them into my unsuspecting parents as they slept. I'd leave that to the people on Donahue.

My dad called my name. "Cassandra? We only want to talk!"

Then my eyes saw it, finally. Maybe my panic made me blind before. The laundry chute. But Winnie had gotten stuck, and she was lighter and skinner than I. I hadn't done this since I was a kid. Well, it was worth a shot. It's not like I had a lot of options. I pulled open the laundry chute, and my heart sunk. The narrow tunnel unfolded from the wall, big enough for my backpack but probably not enough for me.

I tried putting my foot inside the metal hole in the wall, and it groaned under my weight, but it held. I got my other foot in and tried sliding inside. It was like being in a metal coffin. It was cramped; my arms were pinned to my sides, and there was no way I could get all the way down without making a lot of noise.

This was stupid. I'd never make it, but if I couldn't escape, then they'd have to work at getting me to go anywhere with that woman. If I had to go, I was going to make them work for it.

They were in my room, and I held my breath, closing the chute door, wondering how long it would be until they found me. I could see the faint outline of light around the cracks, and I did something desperate. I prayed to be invisible. I stared into the darkness around me, my eyes darting around, trying to hold onto something familiar.

I started shaking, biting down on my lip so I wouldn't make any noise. I was shaking like I did when I was sick with the flu during freshman year. Suddenly, I felt myself being pulled back there, looking up at my mother's face, her long hair falling over me, the tingles of the bubbles from the ginger ale she brought me. The fizz sounded so loud. She was gentle and smiling, telling me I'd feel better.

I scrunched my eyes shut. I wanted to cry again – my stupid, baby emotions. What happened to that mom? When did she stop being a mom and start being a stranger who thought I worshipped the devil? I opened my eyes, and when I did, I was looking up at my mom from the couch. Only, it wasn't my mom. It was a different woman, dressed in white. She was wiping my face with a wet washrag.

She whispered, "Do you want to be free of this?"

I nodded. I didn't know who she was, but I felt so safe. I felt like whoever she was, she cared... that she had the power to help me. I didn't ask who she was because I had a feeling I knew. "Will you devote yourself to me?"

I nodded. I felt eight years old, wanting my mommy to make everything go away... make everything better – totally willing and trusting that the adults would take care of things. I felt my patchwork teddy tucked next to me, and I longed for childhood again. A dim part of me registered that this wasn't real, and the teddy proved it. It was stuck in a backpack, which was currently lodged in a laundry chute with me as I hid from my parents. Something about this was wrong.

"Close your eyes," the woman said. I did as she asked and felt a sweet, soft darkness descend upon me, like I was floating on one of those amber-colored bubbles in the clear glass. I felt it, and I could taste it, sweet and ginger and sharp.

I woke up, disoriented until I figured out that I was in the soft but slightly smelly pile of laundry at the bottom of the chute, in the basement. The basement. I stood up quickly, almost slipping on a towel on the hard linoleum floor. I had a sense of time passing. I had somehow made it out of the laundry chute and, looking out of the basement windows, it was night now. I could hear voices above me, the creak of the floorboards as people walked back and forth. There were more people there; I could sense it.

Heavy-booted footsteps. Police? My mom softly crying. The lower baritone of my dad, that stranger. And, somewhere cool in the dark, I could sense her – the Professional Concerned Mom. I could see her clearly in my mind, which begged the question: if I could tell she was here, could she also tell that I was here? I waited for a few long moments, holding my breath. Nothing happened.

No one thundered to the basemen like I half-expected. Somehow, I knew that no one would come looking for me down there.

How did I know this? I wasn't sure. I remember a woman in white, a gentle smile. I heard a chair scrape against the peeling linoleum in the kitchen above me, a relic from the 60's renovation. More footsteps. Sooner or later, someone was bound to look for me here. Weren't they?

Not knowing how much time had passed or having any other plan except getting out, I looked at the cobwebbed window, filtering brownish light from the tall grass in the side yard. In the summer, it was my mother's flower bed. Now, it was a tangle of dead, dry husks. I climbed on top of the washer. Once out of the communal pile of dirty laundry, I felt cold, unbelievably cold. It took me a couple of tries to flip the lock and slide open the window. At least this space was big enough for me to go through.

I pushed the screen, and when it didn't give, I grew frustrated and tore at it with my fingers, leaving scratches that stung like papercuts. I stood on tip toe, threw my bag through the window, and managed to lift myself up onto the cinderblock windowsill, covered in dead flies and dirt, and managed to wiggle out into the dead garden.

Blinking in the dusk, I determined that it was about an hour before sunset, and the first thing I saw was a police cruiser in front of my house, lights off. They looked like they'd been there a while. A cackle from the inside startled me, and I saw a figure in the front seat speak into a mouthpiece connected to something on the dashboard. It was a man with a blue uniform and a mustache, and I froze when, as he was speaking, he turned his head and looked at me.

Stupid. This was a really stupid idea. I was busted. I must have fallen asleep in the laundry shaft and managed to fall out and land silently on the laundry pile. Covered by clothes, no one knew to look for me there. Or if they had, they just missed me.

To my amazement, he turned his head and kept talking into his speaker. It was like he didn't see me. I stood up, brushed myself off as best I could, and turned to look behind me at the wreck and the noise and the broken screen I had left behind. The window was closed and the screen intact.

I looked back at the police cruiser. I was standing up in the side yard. He had to see me. I looked down at my hands. They were a little cut from when I tore open the screen in frustration, little balls of blood beading on the cuts. I didn't register the pain.

I walked slowly around the house and saw my dad's car parked in the driveway. I saw trick-or-treaters who walked slowly by our house but on the other side of the street. Parents were pulling their kids, curious about the presence of a police car in front of someone's house. Behind the police cruiser was an ambulance.

A strange feeling came over me. Kids were trick-or-treating. That meant it was Saturday, Halloween. Almost a full day had gone by. What was going on? What was the ambulance for? Had my mom cried herself into hysterics? By now, I was in front of the house, in full view, not even caring that at any moment, I still could be seen, that I could be busted. The officer had put his speaker back and stepped out of the car, walking back to the house without even looking at me.

I saw my parents through the Cape Cod window that was perched above the garage. My mom was at the table, my dad standing pensively behind her, a hand on her shoulder, and that horrible woman, Angela, was still there. What was she still doing there?

She was standing by the window, looking right at me, eyes narrowed and practically blazing. They were reflecting back at me, like how cat's eyes reflect light. She mouthed something that could have been a prayer, but she wasn't raising the alarm, pointing at me, and screaming, "There she is!" I wondered why, but at that moment, I didn't care.

I did the only thing I could. I grinned, and I flipped her off and then took off down the street, toward town. Toward Winnie. I wasn't the same person I woke up as that morning. I was either dead or invisible, and that was fine with me. Either way, it was going to be the best night of my life.

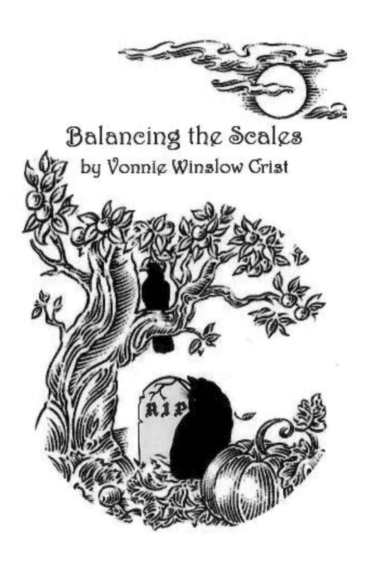

Balancing the Scales

by Vonnie Winslow Crist

With a morning breeze stirring the curtains, Lizzie sat in the main room of the house she and Billy Harper shared, listening to the Good Will Redemption Holiness Church's bell ring twenty-two times. Someone who was twenty-two years old had died.

"Billy," she whispered as she set aside the paring knife with which she was chopping vegetables for tonight's dinner. She stood and looked across the valley toward the church.

Don't be silly, she told herself as she gazed out the window. Today is too beautiful for tragedy. She studied the ghostly puffs of clouds drifting across an October sky bluer than her husband's eyes. She smiled at the orange, ocher, vermillion, and brown leaves still clinging to the trees, twirling in the air like whirligigs, and the woods alive with birdsong.

It is a coincidence that Billy is twenty-two, she decided. Attempting to downplay her premonition, Lizzie picked the knife and potato back up, but her hands continued to shake. Afraid she'd cut herself, she placed the blade and root vegetable back on the tabletop.

With every tick of the mantel clock, Lizzie became more certain her husband was dead. In her heart, she believed it was only a matter of time before the men brought his body home from the sawmill. *I'm probably overreacting*, she told herself as she reached for Billy's family Bible to look for a comforting verse to read while she waited. As she opened the well-worn Holy Book, a note fell out. She unfolded the paper and began to read:

Dear Lizzie,

If you're reading this, then I'm dead. I put this letter in the front page of my Bible on the twenty-fifth of October, knowing you'd pick up the Good Book for comfort – not the new Sunday School Bible but the old one with some of its pages taped into place. Now, I hate to add to your suffering, but no matter how they tell you I died, I was murdered.

Stop shaking your head, Lizzie. It's true.

You'll find a journal with entries starting this morning beneath the mattress on my side of the bed. I don't know how many entries I'll be able to make before he kills me. I'm hoping hundreds, but I think it will only be a few.

Lizzie, just let my family take the lead. Do what my people have done for generations when family passes. For sure, don't let on you know the truth about me being murdered. The murderer or murderers (he might have had help) will kill you, too. I don't want that. I want you to live a long life.

After mourning a reasonable time, you need to find somebody else. Someone to watch over you like I did. You can go back to the coast if you want. Just move on. It won't bother me. I want you safe and happy.

Forever yours,
Billy

Tears wetting her cheeks, Lizzie slid Billy's note into her pocket, then went to their bed. Slipping her hand between the mattress and box spring, she felt a thin book. After glancing over her shoulder to make sure she was still alone, Lizzie pulled out Billy's journal. Sitting on their bed with the sunlight streaming through the window like a slice of angel shine, she opened it up and began reading:

25 October

While working at the sawmill today, I saw Alvin Cubbins hit his wife, LeeAnn. It wasn't like it was that first time he did it. I'd seen him hit her before, but this time, he knocked her out. She just crumpled like a dress falling off the clothesline.

After Alvin went back inside the mill, I went over to LeeAnn and splashed some water on her face. Her cheek was red. Her face was already swelling up. That poor girl's eyes were rolled back in her head – it took a couple of minutes before they went back to normal. When she finally started to come to, I told her to go tell the sheriff about it.

LeeAnn said, "You're so sweet to worry about me, Billy. Why, I wish I'd married you instead of Alvin."

I never had a crush on her when we were young, so it was quite a surprise when she said that. I'd always had my eye on Lizzie Womack – never paid much mind to anyone else.

But Alvin heard it. I guess he'd come back down to check on his wife. That's when LeeAnn reached up, grabbed me around my neck, and kissed me hard on the lips.

I stood up, stared after her as she ran away laughing, then turned around to face Alvin.

"You too?" he shouted. "You after my wife like half of the boys in this county?"

I told him I'd never cheat on my Lizzie. Told him it was all a misunderstanding. Told him LeeAnn just said that and kissed me to upset him.

He replied, "I'm no idiot. I know what I saw. And you're gonna pay for messing around with LeeAnn." Then, Alvin stalked back toward the sawmill.

I think he means to murder me. I'm keeping this journal so people will know how it began

Lizzie shook her head as she flipped to the next page of Billy's journal. Only a fool would think Billy loved anyone but his wife, but the word fool described Alvin Cubbins. Known around town as a bad-tempered bully, he thought ill of everyone. She began to read again:

26 October

Last night, I had a hard time falling asleep. I suppose I should tell Lizzie about this business with Alvin Cubbins and his wife, but I don't want to upset her. Maybe I'm worrying about nothing – chasing "what-ifs" – but I don't think so. When I walked into the mill this morning, Alvin pulled an ax from the wall, pretended to be chopping something, then pointed at me. Two of the mill workers he's friendly with watched the whole thing. They laughed when he was swinging the ax.

Lizzie, this next bit is for you. I don't know what condition I'll be in when they bring me home. Hopefully, it won't be too gruesome. I hate to think of you having to deal with a mangled body.

Get my cousin Tate to move the recliner from in front of the funeral door. Remember last fall when you asked me about having two front doors? I explained one was for everyday and the other was for funerals. I didn't think we'd be using the second door so soon.

Back to preparations. Lizzie, the deadbolt on the funeral door might need to be greased and then hammered to get it to slide open. Tate will know how to get it unstuck. He and his brother, Bo, can grab the two sawhorses from the shed, then take off our bedroom door by the hinges to make a laying out board for me. Set it up in the deathwatch room. Of course, we've always called that room our parlor, but it was put there for funerals too.

After you cover the door with a spare sheet and lay m out, I'll need to be tied down. Tate and Bo can help you with that, too. There's twine and sisal in the shed. Nothing worse than a corpse twitching while folks are sitting up with the dead.

Your parents being in Newport News, I expect my Ma and her sister, Aunt Suellen, will be over to help you clean me up and dress me in my suit. If Alvin messed me up too bad, don't fret about my face. Just drape a scarf over it.

Honestly, Lizzie, I can't write anymore today. You are the best thing that ever happened to me. – Billy

"Why didn't you tell me about Alvin when he threatened you?" Lizzie asked. No one answered her as she glanced at the second front door, then back at Billy's journal. She turned the page.

27 October

I'm still not sleeping very well. I heard an owl hooting last night for hours. They say before you die, you can hear the owls calling your name. I just heard a bunch of who-whooing and no "Billy" being called, so I guess I'll make it until tomorrow.

This afternoon at the mill, I overheard Alvin telling the crew chief that some of the saw blades needed maintenance. He said he feared there was going to be an accident and that somebody was going to get killed. Maybe that's the way he's going to murder me. I hate to think of a whirling blade biting into my flesh.

Lizzie, I know you're going to be upset – probably not thinking clearly – so here's some things you need to be considering when they bring my body home:

1 – Buck Littrell or one of his boys will be in to measure me for my pine box. They're good carpenters and will do a fine job.

Make sure and pay them, even if they don't want to take the money. If necessary, you can slip the cash under their carpentry shop's door after I'm buried.

2 – Ma will talk to the preacher about putting me in the Harper section of the graveyard up on Dove Hill behind the church.

3 – The mill workers will likely want to help the men of my family dig my grave. Just don't let Alvin Cubbins help, though I expect it'd take more guts than he has to volunteer to dig a hole for somebody he murdered.

4 – They'll be bringing Great-Aunt Sookie up to do the saining. I know she's a granny witch, but she's the eldest woman in my family. She never scared you before, so don't be afraid of her now. She's got the gift – her being born with a caul – so it wouldn't surprise me if she gets to our house before my body. Trust her. She'll give you good advice.

Your parents were new to the area when you started at the middle school, so I don't believe you ever saw a saining before. Aunt Sookie will light a candle, then wave it over me three times. Next, she'll put three handfuls of salt in a bowl and place it on my chest, so make sure there's salt and a bowl out and ready for her.

I'm done writing for today. Though the mountains are golden with autumn and the last of the wildflowers are blooming, I feel a winter chill like I've been sitting in the spring house for too long. Sorry I'll be leaving you earlier than I thought when we said our vows last March. – Billy

Lizzie shivered. She felt a chill, too. With icy fingers, she turned the journal's page.

28 October
This morning, when I punched my timecard, I felt the hairs on the back of my neck stick up. I looked over my shoulder. With a scowl worse than our Halloween Jack-o-lantern's, Alvin Cubbins

was glaring at me. When he saw I was studying him, he drew his forefinger across his throat like a buck knife.

All day, I worked as careful as I could. Still, I know there are lots of chances for something to go wrong. Perhaps, I should see if they're hiring over at the big box store. Doesn't pay as much and it's farther to drive, but it'd make it harder for Alvin to kill me.

Lizzie, I've been remembering other things you'll need to do after I'm murdered. Aunt Sookie will help – or maybe Ma or Aunt Suellen – but you need to soak a dishtowel in soda water and put it over my face until the viewing. It helps keep the skin fresh-looking. My arms need to be folded over my chest, my feet tied together at the ankles, and a handkerchief should be tied under my chin and over the top of my head to keep my mouth in place.

I know this is distressing for you to read, much less do, but it needs to be done. Then, two coins need to be placed on my eyes. Some folks say it's to pay the ferryman – they might be right. What's more important is that the coins help keep the eyelids closed. Don't use pennies. Copper can cause the nearby skin to change colors. Don't use silver dollars. It's a waste of money, and someone might dig me up to get to the dollars. Any smaller denomination of silver will do. While dimes are a good size for young children, quarters are ideal for a grown man.

Now, I know you're going to want to put our wedding quilt over me – don't. Use an old quilt and keep the wedding quilt as a remembrance of our time together. Besides, after you, Ma, Aunt Suellen, Aunt Sookie, and dozens of others put flowers, herbs, and whatnot on top of the quilt, no one will recall which quilt I was buried under.

I'm thinking of the day we were married – the leaves just starting to come out. That March day was the happiest day of my life. I wish I had many more springs to spend with you, but I don't. Love you forever. – Billy

Lizzie thought of the carved pumpkins lining their porch steps. Billy and she'd joked they wanted to make their carvings scary enough to frighten trick-or-treaters. She pressed her lips together as she imagined Alvin's face scrunched up in an ugly frown. Then, she flipped to the next entry.

29 October

Today, I heard dogs howling in the woods at lunchtime. Sweets Carter said they weren't dogs; they were coyotes. I hope he's correct because to hear dogs howling like that can be a sign that death is near. It seemed every childhood superstition popped into my mind this afternoon.

A cat crossed my porch when I got out of the truck to pump gas. My heart was pounding like a woodpecker on a deadwood tree until I noticed that the cat was dark gray. When I walked into the store to pay for the fuel, I carefully avoided walking under the ladder a repairman was standing on, trying to fix the neon sign on the front of the store's roof.

Sweets says I'm jittery as a pig smelling a smokehouse. He probably thinks I've got a problem with alcohol. Meanwhile, Alvin and his buddies just stare, laugh, then stare some more. I don't know how much more of this I can take.

Lizzie, you asked me this morning if anything was wrong – if I was mad at you. No, my love. How could I be angry with you? A man couldn't find a better wife than you, my dearest.

Again, I must write of the day of my death. You need to cover the mirror in the bathroom with cloth – something dark like the navy tablecloth your parents gave us last Christmas. Draw the curtains closed, too. I don't want to be tempted to use the mirror or windows as portals to come back to this world and linger with my Lizzie. Though you do need to leave one window open behind its curtains, so my spirit can sail away.

Stop the mantel clock, for time will have stopped for me. After I'm buried, you can restart it.

The women will bring food to serve at the viewing. Put it in the dining room so people can grab a bit after the viewing before they leave. They'll also bring food for the luncheon after I'm buried. Thanking everyone in person is enough – don't worry about writing notes.

Ma, Aunt Suellen, Tate, Bo, Aunt Sookie, and the rest of my people will sit up with you through the death watch night. You don't need to be awake the whole time – let the others take a turn while you rest.

In the morning, Buck Littrell will bring over my coffin. He and the boys will load me in and drive me over to the church in the back of their pickup. Don't drive over to the church by yourself. Ride with a family member. I've enclosed several Bible verses and hymns I'd like used for my funeral. You can give them to Ma to pass on to the preacher.

You're going to do fine, Lizzie. I know sadness will be your companion for a while, but as each new season arrives, you'll begin to move forward. Before long, you'll find joy again. Love, Billy

Barely able to breathe, Lizzie unfolded four sheets of paper which Billy had placed inside his journal. On the first, she read:

Matthew 5, Verse 4: "Blessed are those who mourn, for they shall be comforted."
Psalm 23
Isaiah 57, Verse 2: "Those who walk uprightly enter into peace; they find rest as they lie in death."

She folded the sheet of paper and brushed away tears with her fingertips. The second sheet of paper was a copy of the music and lyrics for *The Old Rugged Cross*, the third a copy of *How Great Thou Art*, and the fourth a copy of *The Ash Grove*. Tissue in hand, she scanned the lyrics of *Ash Grove*. Her eyes lingered on the beginning of the last stanza:

> *"My lips smile no more, my heart loses its lightness;*
> *No dream of the future my spirit can cheer.*
> *I only can brood on the past and its brightness…"*

"Billy, I don't think I can do this," she said to the dust motes sailing on sunlight like unrealized dreams. After blowing her nose, she read the final entry in the journal:

30 October

This morning, I woke before dawn and studied your face, Lizzie. I got a terrible feeling it would be the last time I saw you on this side of the veil. I hope I'm mistaken.

I've decided to apply for a job tomorrow at the big box store. They ought to be hiring with the holidays coming soon. No more sawmill for me. I will tell you after work today about Alvin, LeeAnn, and the whole mess.

Lizzie closed the journal. Today was the thirtieth, so Billy wouldn't be able to finish today's entry, and there would be no more entries if the twenty-two tolls of the church bell she'd heard earlier were for him.

"Lizzie," called a voice from the front room.

She went to the bedroom door and saw Aunt Sookie standing in the everyday entrance to the house with her arms open. She ran to her.

"It's all right, child," said the granny witch as she stroked her hair. "They'll be bringing Billy home to you soon."

"What happened?" Lizzie asked as she raised her tear-stained face to look in Aunt Sookie's eyes. She wanted to ask, "How did Alvin Cubbins murder Billy?"

"A chain came loose on a flatbed full of timber. Some of the tree trunks rolled off all helter-skelter. Billy was caught beneath them. He didn't suffer – the end was quick. I came as soon as I could so I can help sew him together for you."

Lizzie gasped. *Sew him together.* The words sent a terrible image careening through her mind.

She realized Aunt Sookie was studying her. "He was murdered," she managed to say before she blew her nose on a tissue.

"I know," answered the granny witch. She patted Lizzie's back. "And I brought you something to read and something to use, if you have a mind to do so." The woman pulled an envelope from a crocheted bag she was carrying. She handed it to Lizzie. "You must read the note inside before the others arrive."

Lizzie nodded, sat on the sofa she and Billy had gotten for a wedding present from her parents, and opened the envelope. Inside were a handwritten letter plus a small bundle of hair and a black feather tied with a white thread. She looked at the granny witch.

Sookie pointed at the letter.

Lizzie swallowed hard, then began reading:

Dear Sookie,

If you've found this note, I am worm food. Do not flinch at my blunt words, for you better than most know the ways of beginnings and endings. I've taught you most everything I know about healing, birthing, foreseeing, and even a little magic. There is one more lesson, which I hesitated to teach you – but now that I'm gone, I will share: Calling a Demon.

Calling a Demon is to be done only in the most extreme cases – for once called, a demon will not depart until it has taken its prize. I have never done this magic, although the granny witch who taught me did call a demon once to deal with an evil person of extreme cruelty. On her deathbed, she told me the creature's scaly face and the screams of its victim still haunted her.

People say they hear a Panther crying out in the densest parts of the mountains, but it's not a Panther – it's a demon. I cannot say nor write any demon's true name. To do so would attract it to me. But you don't need to name this creature to call it forth. For safety's sake, I will call it a Panther.

Here is the procedure to call a Panther: First, gather a few hairs from the demon's prey. Second, pluck a feather from a living raven's breast. Third, tie the two together with a threat from a stillborn baby's grave cloth. Fourth, dip the bundle in spring-fed pond on the night of a full moon. Fifth, dry the bundle on the branch of a Judas Tree. Sixth, stand by a newly dug grave with the bundle in your left hand and say the first words of the Lord's Prayer backwards while turning anticlockwise three times. Lastly, you must stand still as a tombstone when a Panther manifests itself before you.

Hold out your left hand with the bundle balanced on your palm – much like you'd feed a horse a sugar cube. The Panther will take the bundle, then go fetch its prey. You must stand by the grave and wait. When the Panther returns with his prey, you must witness the victim's death. The Panther will come to you again. Say, "Thank you, Righter of Wrongs." Then, the Panther should vanish.

Again, I warn you not to use this magic without just case. Even then, hesitate before proceeding, for the Panther you call will watch you for the rest of your life. It is a monster of retribution. Should you turn to dark ways, it will return and claim you, too.

Until we meet again on the other side,
Tilly

Lizzie folded the letter and placed it back in the envelope before holding up the hair and feather bundle. "Is it ready to be used?" she asked.

Aunt Sookie linked her fingers, placed her hands in a prayer-like position in front of her waist, and nodded. "Yes. I foresaw Billy's death, visited the barber right after Alvin got a haircut, and prepared he bundle weeks ago. But I am too old for a trek to the graveyard in the dark. Therefore, if you seek justice – tonight as we sit with the dead, you must say you're tired. Go to your bedroom, but instead of taking a nap, change into dark clothing, sneak to Billy's newly-dug grave, and follow the procedure in the letter."

Lizzie pressed her fingertips to her lips. She knew Billy's murder would be ruled an accident, even with the journal. A judge would say Billy's journal was paranoia and speculation. A jury would believe Billy's demise was nothing more than bad luck. The only way to mete out justice was to call a Panther.

"I will call a demon tonight," she said as the vehicle bringing Billy's mutilated body pulled up beside the front porch.

Aunt Sookie smiled, gently squeezed her hands, and said, "That's my girl," before taking over the body and funeral preparations.

The sight of Billy's smashed and lacerated body being stitched together by Aunt Sookie was still fresh in Lizzie's mind when she hiked by candlelight to the graveyard on Dove Hill behind the Good Will Redemption Holiness Church. At midnight, as October thirty-first was born, she followed the instructions for summoning a demon from the dead granny witch's letter. She'd no sooner finished her third counterclockwise turn when a hulking black form manifested before her.

The demon's eyes glinted red like coals after a bonfire has burned down. Its long, scaly snout sniffed the bundle she held in her left hand before it grasped it between two of its shiny claws. Lizzie thought her heart would stop beating when it smiled at her before rushing away.

All she could think about was the demon's jagged teeth glistening a yellowish white in the candlelight as the minutes seemed to move slower than a dirge. Finally, the towering creature loped up the hill, dragging Alvin Cubbins. Lizzie had prepared herself for Alvin's screams, but instead, the demon squeezed Alvin's neck so tightly that the man couldn't utter more than a few gasps and gurgles.

Placing itself directly in front of Lizzie, the demon – or should she say dragon – hunched over its pretty and proceeded to devour Alvin. As Lizzie would later tell Aunt Sookie, the consumption of the town bully was neither quick nor tidy. After the Panther had finished crunching Alvin's bones and swallowing the larger parts of Billy's murderer, the creature got down on all fours and licked up the blood and body bits. The demon-dragon's tongue flicked out so rapidly and with such precision that Lizzie imagined no one would notice a thing awry when her husband's coffin was carried to the grave on Halloween afternoon.

Meal finished, the Panther stood before her, leaned close, and gazed into her eyes with his burning orbs.

"Thank you, Righter of Wrongs," she managed to whisper to the dragon.

The Panther rumbled a purr-like sound. Then, sniffing the palm of her hand one last time, he said, "I will remember your scent, Lizzie Harper," before bounding into the woods.

A week later, while waiting for her husband's cousins, Tate and Bo, to arrive to help load her things into the pickup truck's bed, Lizzie read the obituary section of the local newspaper:

HARPER, William W.

On October 30, William "Billy" Woodrow Harper, (22) beloved husband of less than a year of Elizabeth Ann Harper (nee Womack); and devoted son of Darla Lynn Harper (nee Sully) and the late Woodrow Tatum Harper, passed away suddenly. Billy was born in...

Then she flipped back to the front page and scanned an article about a missing person.

CUBBINS WHERABOUTS UNKNOWN

On Saturday, October 30, local mill worker Alvin Tunney Cubbins, age 31, was last seen about midnight leaving Rock Creek Tavern. Cubbins, reported missing by his wife, is 6 foot 2 inches tall and weighs 300 pounds...

As she folded the paper, she thought to herself: *There is no real justice – only the balancing of the scales.*

Billy was still dead, and Lizzie didn't have any interest in pursuing another relationship. Instead, she'd accepted Aunt Sookie's invitation to move in with her. After learning about healing, birthing, foreseeing, and a little magic, she hoped to receive messages from her husband again. Maybe more.

For on the night of his wake, after she'd returned from her dealings with the dragon-demon, Lizzie had uncovered the mirror above her dresser. And despite the likelihood of allowing multitudes of undead monstrosities into this world, she'd opened a portal for Billy on the day when the veil between living and dead was at its thinnest: Halloween.

Vonnie Winslow Crist is author of The Enchanted Dagger, Owl Light, The Greener Forest, Murder on Marawa Prime, and other award-winning books. A member of HWA and SFWA, her stories appear in Amazing Stories, Cast of Wonders, Chilling Ghost Stories, Killing It Softly 2, Monsters, Best Indie Speculative Fiction: 2018, Potter's Field 4 & 5, Curse of the Gods, Sea of Secrets, Zombies for a Cure, Haunted Hallows, and elsewhere. For more information, visit:

www.vonniewinslowcrist.com

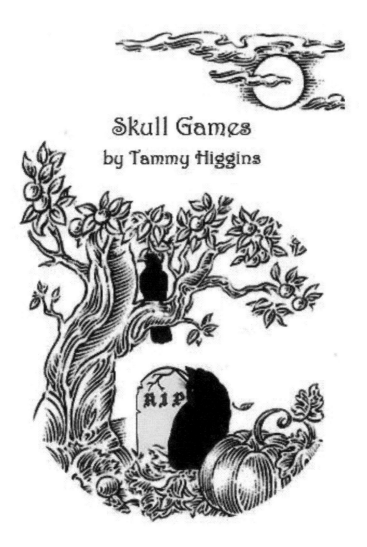

Skull Games
by Tammy Higgins

Jack crunched through the orange and burgundy leaves down the broken sidewalk being painted by the beginning of twilight. He could hear the joyous laughter of boys in a yard. He slowed down, searching for the game that seemed to be highly energetic and in full swing, and then kept walking. He came huffing finally to the top of a hill and stood gawking at the children, trying to catch his breath and wiping sweat off his brow. It was a soccer or kickball game before the night closed in.

He watched a triad of boys between ten up to fourteen kick a ball lightly back and forth. He took a swig from his flask of bourbon as a cool breeze brushed the top of his hair. He stumbled a little closer to watch before he went home, hearing porch chimes tingle softly in the breeze. Pumpkin candle flames flickered on the porch as he neared the children and their house.

It was . . . he shook his head, maybe he'd had to many rum-and-Cokes at the bar he favored. It wasn't a soccer or kickball game. It was . . . Jack squinted . . . a skull! An aged skeleton head. He gasped and sputtered at such vulgar habits of kids today. He stumbled back, turning to leave and weave on home. A voice called out in his direction.

"Our mother lets us. It's okay," said one of the boys. Jack wanted to laugh, thinking they were being smart aleck kids, but something in their voice sent his mind reeling and his hackles rising. He took another step backward, wanting to run.

"Wanna play?" yelled a red-haired boy as the two other boys turned in his direction, taking a step closer. He flinched at their dead, bruised eyes and pale faces, and he freaked at the rows of sharp pointed teeth smiling at him.

"No," he said weakly, then more firmly. "No!" He turned away and began to shuffle through the crunchy, crispy, crinkled leaves, his breath coming in short, cold bursts of air. He could hear them laughing at his back.

"Your grandma's head is next when we wanna play," hollered a plump baby fat blonde in a cold tone.

A chill ran down his spine as he walked faster.

Apparently, mom had come out on the porch, and she took her turn yelling in a sexy, cold voice.

"I want you, handsome. I'll be the one playing with your skull soon, baby," she said. She began to laugh in a loud, ancient, frightening way that was like nails from the grave on a chalkboard. His testes withdrew.

"Jack!!! Jackie!!!" the ghouls called after him, laughing in an evil, horrible way.

He hurried through the fallen leaves and acorns, disappearing into the dark. Under the starlit sky, he exhaled plumes of white clouds, desperately wanting to be invisible and to hide and erase the mental image that remained in his head.

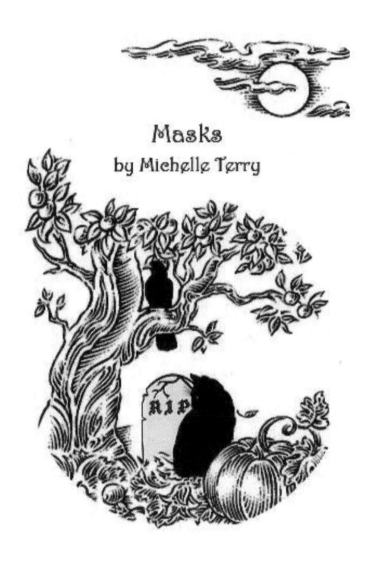

Masks
by Michelle Terry

Allyn crouched behind the car, watching the group of middle school kids. They were trick-or-treaters, dressed in stupid kids' costumes. There was no adult with them. Probably thought they were old enough to go on their own. They were a little old for trick-or-treat, really, but that was fine, because he wouldn't feel like a complete loser for scaring them.

He grinned and made sure his mask was situated just right. It was one of those serial killer masks from a recent scary movie. The character was popular this year. He'd seen at least a dozen guys wearing the same costume, and that was fine. He'd learned that wearing an original costume was a bad idea, because the cops in this crummy town would track it back to him, like they had last year.

He waited for the kids to pass by, then stepped out behind them, his feet making little more than a soft scuff on the pavement. He followed them for a few moments, listening to them babble about school, their parents, and other lame crap. He checked the street. Up ahead was a big, two-story Plantation house on the end of the street. Just past it was a vacant lot shrouded in darkness, then the intersection.

When they reached the dark space beyond the porch lights of the two-story, he sucked in a deep breath and moaned low in his throat. The younger kids turned as one, their eyes widened; they screamed and scattered. Three of them dropped their candy sacks on the way to safety. Allyn grinned and bent to pick them up.

It was then he heard the silver tinkle of female laughter. He stopped and straightened up to see who was laughing at him. There, across the street, was a feminine figure dressed in black leather. She wore shiny black motorcycle boots with silver buckles. Her black pleather leggings had been slashed at the knees and thighs to show just a hint of her long legs. He almost forgot to look at her face.

She raised her hand to her mouth, tittering softly again, and he dragged his eyes away from her pants, up across her shimmery silver tank top and her cropped moto jacket to her face. She was wearing a black and silver Volto mask, and a little silver halo on a headband.

Allyn stared. In the back of his mind he heard an electric guitar going through some intricate riffs, and his lips stretched into a goofy grin behind his mask. He couldn't resist the temptation, so he let his gaze slide back down her body in an elevator stare that reached her feet, then bounced back up to her breasts. She tittered a third time, and slowly crossed the street, driving him crazy with the sway of her hips and the slow, lazy motion of those long, slender legs.

She stopped in front of him. "See something you like?" she asked. Her voice was smoke and honey. He shuddered, a chill going down his back as he stared back at her. He could see her eyes behind that intricate mask. They were the palest blue he'd ever seen, and narrowed just a bit, as if she might be smiling behind the mask. "That was good." She pointed at the bags of candy in his hand.

He grinned. "Yeah. They really scrambled, didn't they?" He felt foolish holding three bags of kiddie candy, so he offered her one. "You want some?"

She gazed at him with those crystal blue eyes, then they narrowed with laughter again, and she held out her hand to him.

"Sure." He passed her the heaviest bag, just to be nice, then offered her his hand.

"Allyn."

She looked down at his hand, then grabbed it and pulled him close. She pressed it against her hip; his heart rate revved up like a jet liner when he felt the heat of her body under his palm.

"Lil," she said. He was so close to her now that he could smell something fruity. Her shampoo maybe, or body mist, or... he didn't care. It smelled great, and his heart was doing crazy things inside his chest. She pressed closer until he could feel the bulge of her breasts against his ribs and the taut muscles of her belly against his.

In that moment, he had a lot of thoughts, and most of them made his ears and cheeks go hot. He wanted to drop the bags of candy in his other hand, wrap it in her long dark hair, and... He shook his head. That wasn't cool.

"Lil."

The deep, resonant voice of an older guy drew their attention. Lil leaned around Allyn.

"Ash." Her tone was flat, and a little annoyed. "You coming?"

"Sure, yeah." She glanced back at Allyn. "You want to come? We're going to go raise a little hell." Her eyes were narrowed again with silent laughter. Allyn turned around. There was a group of teens standing beyond the light. He could barely tell they were there, except for vague shapes darker than the surrounding night. While he was staring at the cluster of dark shapes, a car turned the corner up the street; the headlights glanced off something shiny on one of the kids' costumes. For a second Allyn thought he saw detail in the quick flash of light, but then it was gone.

"Uh--" He hesitated. He wasn't keen on joining a crowd of guys he couldn't see.

"C'mon, Lil. He's chicken," said another female voice. "Give him a minute, Mara. He only just met us." Lil gave him another long, patient stare.

"Where you going?" he asked. She jerked her thumb over her shoulder.

"Down to Poplar. We're gonna egg some houses and maybe T.P. the churchyard."

Allyn thought about it, and grinned. "Yeah, sure. I'll come." He dumped all his candy into one bag and tucked it into his belt. Lil took his hand in hers. It was cool and dry against his palm; her fingers were light against his skin. He liked it. She led him forward and stopped a few feet from the group. Now that he was closer, he could see them better.

"That's Ash," she said, pointing at the tall, thick, black guy with the priest's cassock and a white half mask. There were three black teardrops on the left cheek of the mask. "Mara." She indicated the smaller girl with wide dark eyes, a thick mane of curly, black hair, and a skeleton costume. She wore a buccal mask that obscured her mouth, bearing the image of a skull's exposed teeth. "Sam." Sam was short and thick through the chest. He was wearing a butcher's apron stained with fake blood, and a burlap sack with eye holes cut into it. "And Steph." Steph was taller than Ash and dressed as Death. The hood of his costume was so deep that Allyn couldn't see his face. Allyn looked up at him and wondered if he should crack a tall joke, then thought better of it.

Allyn gazed at them, noting that they all wore masks, and decided that was probably best, considering what they planned to do next. Old Man Thompson, the minister at the Baptist church on Poplar, was strict and harsh with those who trespassed on church property. Especially on Halloween. And Lil had said they might go vandalize the church. It would be awesome, a real rush, but only if they didn't get caught.

"This way," Mara said. Her voice was husky. She took Allyn's other hand. Now there was no going back...not that he wanted to. He was sandwiched between the two girls in the group. What could be better? They walked down the street, then paused at the corner. Ash separated from the rest and moved to a car. He opened the door and drew out a big duffel bag, then carried it back to the group.

"Okay," he said.

They moved out onto Poplar street. Allyn felt like singing. He was going to have some real fun this Halloween. Last year had been lame. He'd done a few pranks, but he'd gotten picked up by the cops at the Gas-'N-Go at the edge of town because of his stupid costume. Then he'd been forced to do 'community service' by cleaning up the messes he'd made and visiting the old folks' home. So unfair. This year would be different. He wouldn't get caught. He was with a group of pros this time.

The rest of the night was a blur. None of the houses on the street escaped their mischief. There were spray painted 'Devil worship' slogans all over the sides of the church and up the path leading to the doors. They lit a bag of dog pooh and left it on Pastor Thompson's front porch. It was great. What a rush! But all good things come to an end, and so it was with the mischief.

They were just getting ready to smash a display of jack-o-lanterns outside a house that had gone overboard with decorations. Ash was poised, a baseball bat raised over his head. The blue lights of the Sheriff's car flashed across them, and the truncated blast of siren told them they'd been spotted. Ash dropped the bat and bolted faster than a guy that size should have been able to move. He was gone in a blink. Sam and Mara took off to the left, and Lil took off across the back lot of the house. Steph thrust his hands into Allyn's back, shoving him along.

"Hurry up," Steph grunted. He grabbed Allyn's upper arm and put on an extra burst of speed that Allyn almost couldn't match. He stumbled once, and almost went down, but Steph dragged him up by the arm and kept hauling him along. After what felt like an hour of running, they stopped on a street that was mostly dark. Trick-or-treat was long over, and the house lights were out. They collapsed on the sidewalk, gasping and laughing.

"Man, that was great!" Allyn gasped for breath and reached to raise his mask to wipe the sweat from his face. Steph grunted and grabbed Allyn's hand. Allyn pulled his hand away and glanced at Steph. Steph shook his head, once – just a slight motion of his hood that Allyn barely caught in the darkness. Allyn turned his face away and lifted the mask enough to wipe the sweat off his forehead and cheeks. He left the mask resting on the top of his head, enjoying the cool night air.

Steph leaned over and murmured urgently, "Put your mask down." Allyn turned toward him, surprised by the tone of his voice. "Hurry. Put it down." Hesitantly Allyn reached up and obeyed. Just as he nestled it in place, he heard a silvery laugh, and Lil stepped out of the darkness between two houses. She crossed the street and joined them. She flopped down on the curb beside Allyn.

"Wow. That was great." She let go another tinkling laugh and lay back on the pavement. Allyn looked around. The moment felt strange, and dangerous somehow, but he wasn't sure why. Was it Steph's strangeness about the mask? He wasn't sure, but he felt like something had been averted.

"There you are." Mara trotted toward them from across the street. Ash came from the left, and Sam followed in his wake. "What a rush, right?" She stopped in front of them and gazed down. Ash and Sam stopped a few steps behind her. Sam's stitched up burlap sack was fluttering with his breath. Mara's wide dark eyes were sparkling, and Ash was leaning forward, as though eager to find a new activity to expend his energy on. Allyn felt a little odd, but the moment soon passed. They were just a group of kids, having fun. So what if Steph was weird about seeing Allyn's face? It didn't matter.

"So," Lil said. "What's next?"

Steph stood up. He smoothed out his long robe, then looked left and right down the street. "It's almost Witching Hour. Let's go to the haunted house on Braun and do a séance."

"Is your board in the car?" Mara's voice sounded eager.

She glanced at Allyn. "Or are you too scared?"

"Séance? That's kid stuff." He wrinkled his nose. "You drive, right?" He pointed at Ash. "Let's go to the Gas-'N-Go and get some booze."

Sam chuckled behind his burlap mask. The fabric billowed out when he laughed; Allyn thought it was a bit creepy. "Yeah," Sam said. "Let's go." They stood and started moving back toward where Ash had left his car. Steph sidled up alongside Allyn and leaned down.

"Be careful about your choices," he murmured. Lil, on Allyn's other side, flashed a glance at Steph; the motion of her head was an annoyed little jerk.

They found their way back to Ash's car and piled in. Allyn found himself sandwiched between Mara and Lil again. Sam, Steph, and Ash were up front. Allyn wondered if the guys were jealous that Mara and Lil were paying so much attention to him, but he didn't think about it for long. Mara leaned her head on his shoulder, and Lil's slender hand rested on his knee. It was all he could do to keep from squirming in pleasure.

Ash drove the car to the Gas-'N-Go with the headlights off. Allyn was too preoccupied to wonder how he was doing that. Lil's hand was starting to explore his thigh, moving closer to his groin. He squirmed. He didn't want her to stop, but it felt weird with the guys up front. They stopped across the street from the station, and the guys turned around. "Who wants to be the gunman?"

"What?" Allyn felt something squirming in his stomach.

Sam chuckled, then pulled out a huge pistol.

"Paintball gun," he said, passing it back to Allyn. Allyn took it. It was plastic and had a CO_2 cartridge attached to the back end, but it looked real in the darkness of the car. "How 'bout you do it. This was your suggestion. Want the honors?"

Allyn swallowed hard and looked down at the pistol in his hands. Just a fake, he told himself. Fake pistol. Nobody's going to get hurt. Why not? It was fun, right? Just a little fun.

And they'd get the booze for free. Sure. Why not? He looked back up at the guys up front and registered that they still hadn't taken their masks off. That was weird, but at the moment, he didn't care. He nodded, stiffly, still nervous. "Right. Sure."

"Great. You keep the guy at the counter busy. We'll get the booze."

"And some snacks," Mara said. "Don't forget the snacks."

"Yeah," Sam said. "Snacks."

They piled out of the car and shuffled around near the trunk. Sam talked them through it, explaining how they'd go into the store in twos. Allyn would go in last and hold up the cashier with his gun while the others grabbed what they wanted. Then they'd bolt for the car. Easy as pie, right? Right. Allyn watched Sam stride toward the convenience store silently, wishing he'd said 'no'. The pimple faced kid behind the counter was going to piss himself when masked people started robbing the place. Ash and Lil went next, then Mara. That left Steph and Allyn standing on the curb across the road.

Steph turned to Allyn. "My turn." He started forward, then paused, and turned back. "There's still time to back out, Allyn."

"No way," Allyn said in a voice that was too high.

"There's still time, Allyn. Just remember that. There's time to turn back, until…" He paused. The clock in the tower of town hall chimed midnight.

"Witching hour." Steph shivered. "Remember. Until three o'clock, your choices are still your own. It's not too late."

He turned and jogged toward the store. Allyn stared after him. What kind of mumbo jumbo was that? He watched Steph step through the doors, then counted two minutes before moving toward the convenience store.

He pushed through the door and walked up to the counter. The kid at the counter looked annoyed when Allyn entered, still wearing his mask. The clerk's face was indeed pimpled and red. He scowled at Allyn a moment longer, but when Allyn didn't proceed to the back of the store the kid flashed him a dead, flat smile that showed the glint of braces between his lips.

"You can't wear the mask in here," he said. "Please take it off." His tone was perfectly flat and cool, but he was reaching for the phone.

Allyn yanked the pistol out of his pocket and thrust it toward the kid. "Give me the cash."

The kid stared at Allyn, his mouth dropping open in horror, revealing both upper and lower sets of braces in a silent scream. His eyes were huge, and his hands trembled as he fumbled for the register buttons.

"Sure. Sure. Fine."

He couldn't figure out how to open the drawer. Allyn slammed his palm down on the counter.

"I said 'give me the cash'." Allyn bellowed. The kid fumbled with the register's buttons some more, moaned and reached inside his shirt. He pulled out a key, slipped it into the slot on the front of the register, and turned it. The register made a ding, then the drawer slid open. The kid grabbed handfuls of cash and stuffed them into a plastic shopping bag, then thrust it at Allyn. Lil came up beside him and pressed her warm length against his side.

"Good job, babe." She grabbed his rear and squeezed. Allyn's heart was thundering like a race car doing a victory lap.

"Yeah," he shouted. Adrenaline surged through him. "Hell yeah." He thrust the gun toward the kid behind the counter. "And this thing isn't even--" He squeezed the trigger just as he said the word 'real', and a spray of red hit the display of cigarettes behind the counter. Allyn stared, frozen. The kid behind the counter raised his shaking hands to his chest, touched the red smear spreading on his apron, then his face twisted into rage. Ash blew a raspberry and started howling with laughter, and Sam shrieked in elation.

"You asshole!" the kid screamed. "I'm calling the cops. You asshole!" He bent down and grabbed the phone under the counter.

"Told you," Sam giggled, pounding Allyn on the back. "Paintballs. Just paintballs. Hurry up, c'mon."

They turned as a group and scrambled out to the car. They piled inside and Ash gunned the engine, then roared away from the convenience store. Halfway across town, Lil and Mara rolled the windows down. The car was speeding along the nearly deserted streets, still with the headlights out, and the wind whipped through the car, tearing at Mara's unbound hair. Lil leaned out the window and howled into the night, then flopped back against Allyn, laughing wildly. Up front, Sam uncapped a bottle of vodka, put it to his lips, and chugged.

Allyn leaned forward and tried to grab the bottle. "Hey, go easy." Sam turned around. The burlap sack that was his mask had been pulled up far enough to reveal his mouth. He grinned; Allyn pulled his hand back quickly. For just a moment, in the flash of the streetlights he thought Sam's teeth were jagged, like needles in his mouth.

"Don't worry, buddy. I got you one." Sam passed back a square bottle of whiskey with a black label. Allyn hesitated a moment, but Sam was grinning at him; his teeth looked normal. Allyn took the bottle, uncapped it, and took a long pull. He swallowed, leaned back, and sighed. The warmth of the liquor burned down his throat and settled in his belly. Lil's hand was on his thigh again, slowly massaging, moving closer to his groin. Mara's hand was on his chest, rubbing up and down, and her head was on his shoulder. He could feel her breath on his skin; it gave him a little thrill when she sighed against his neck.

Ash turned a corner and took them deep into the old section of town. The streets became rough and cracked, and the houses became older and more dilapidated. Eventually they pulled around the side of a house and into the back yard. Ash shut the engine down. Lil and Mara leaned away from Allyn, reaching for the doors of the car. Allyn shook himself out of his pleasant daydreams and looked around. One look told him where he was. The 'haunted' house on Braun.

Ash was around the back of the car. He opened the trunk and pulled the duffle bag from the back. The girls got out, as did Sam and Steph. Allyn stepped out on Lil's side and followed them into the abandoned house. As his foot crossed the threshold, the clock in the town hall's tower struck one o'clock.

Steph, ahead of Allyn, turned and tilted his head. The motion seemed to say, 'remember what I told you'. Allyn considered turning around at that moment and heading for home, but he wasn't done having fun yet. He shook his head to clear away his doubts, took another slug from the bottle of whiskey, and followed Steph through the door. The house was pitch black. Allyn hesitated at the door. Ash leaned past him to pull the door shut. "Hey," Allyn protested. "We won't be able to see."

"We will," Ash said. His tone was neutral. He locked the door, then grabbed Allyn by the collar of his shirt and pulled him further into the house.

"Ash," Allyn said, yanking on his shirt to pull it from the bigger man's hand. "What the hell?"

"Just relax. I know the way," Ash said. He led Allyn forward, then turned to the right and into a wide-open room. It smelled musty and cold. Ash let go of him and crossed the room. Allyn wondered how Ash could see where he was going. There was no light from outside. The windows were boarded up.

There was a soft click, then the cold, white light of a battery-powered lantern flooded the room. Allyn flinched from the light, then blinked away the spots dancing in his vision. When he could see again, he looked around.

The room was big, and still furnished. The walls were painted a faded gold color with dingy white molding everywhere. There was a crystal chandelier in the center of the ceiling, surrounded by a wide circle medallion. Allyn took a moment to study the molding, the ceiling, and the chandelier. The house was decorated in the style of a long-gone era. He didn't know what one, and didn't care, but he was stunned that the house was untouched by vandals or vagrants.

Lil let go another of her silvery laughs. "What's wrong? Never seen a haunted house before?"

Allyn tore his eyes from the ceiling to look at her. She was sitting on a dusty gold divan, her long legs crossed at the knee, and her arms spread across the divan's back. Mara was next to her in a delicate Victorian-style wingback, her legs slung over one of the arms. Ash was perched on the wide coffee table in front of the divan, and Steph had moved to the back of the room, where he stood tall and unmoving beside the fireplace. Sam was crouched near the boarded-up bay window, rummaging in Ash's big duffle bag.

"I've never been inside," Allyn confessed. "I always wondered what was in here."

Lil giggled again. "Well," she said. "Now you know."

"Why isn't it torn up? I kind of expected something else." "Don't know," Lil said, and shrugged her shoulders.

"Have you guys--" Allyn looked around at the placement of things in the room, taking note of the pile of garbage near the door, the lantern, the grocery bags of snack food on the window seat near Sam. "Are you living in here?"

"Only for a few days," Mara said.

"Why?" Allyn blurted. It sounded rude, but he couldn't understand why these kids would choose to live in a dusty, abandoned house. Mara tossed her head back and laughed.

"We wanted to get away from home for a while," she said.

"Oh." Allyn felt stupid. He knew what that felt like. He'd
be a senior in high school next year, and his parents were
always riding him about something. Dad wanted him to
wrestle, mom wanted good grades, they both wanted him to
go to college. It was too much for him sometimes. These
guys probably had the same crap going on at home. "Sorry."

"It's fine," Ash said. Sam walked over with the Ouija board
and planchet and put them on the table. Ash got down on his
knees on the hardwood floor and motioned everybody to gather
around. "Who do we want to call up?" he said.

"C'mon," Allyn said. "That's kid stuff. It's just a trick."
"Really?" Lil's voice had the suggestion of amusement to
it. She crossed to him and took his hand, leading him toward
the coffee table. "Then you won't mind playing along while we
scare ourselves silly."

Steph hung back a moment while the others settled
themselves around the coffee table. Allyn looked up at the tall
man, wondering why he hesitated, but eventually Steph joined
them on the floor. They each put a hand on the planchet, and
Ash asked again who they wanted to call up. Lil giggled. "Let's
call for ZoZo and see if he comes."

"Really?" Allyn gave her a long look.

"No, silly." She shoved him playfully. "Everybody knows
ZoZo isn't real."

"Lizzy Borden?" Mara said.

"Can't. This ain't her house," Sam said. "Let's just ask who's
available?" Steph said.

"Sure," Ash said. He spoke to the board. "Are there any
spirits that would like to make themselves known?"

Allyn didn't expect anything to happen, and so, when the
planchet rocketed across the board, it surprised him enough
his fingers almost slipped off. It moved to 'Yes'.

"Ah," Sam said. "Who's speaking?"

The board spelled out the name 'Jeremy'.

"No way," Allyn said. He almost took his hands off the planchet. Seven years ago, a kid named Jeremy Bartlett had disappeared on Halloween night. Goose flesh broke out on his skin. Did these guys know about Jeremy?

"Don't break the circle," Steph said. His tone was mild, but there was urgency in the way he said it.

"What's wrong?" Mara said.

"Jeremy is the name of a guy who disappeared seven years ago. No body. Cops think he ran away from home or fell in the river or something."

Allyn's mouth felt like cotton. He wanted to grab the whiskey bottle, but Steph's warning stopped him from taking his hands off the planchet. Ash and Lil shared a long look, then Lil glanced toward Steph. Ash's head turned toward Steph slowly. The motion held a repressed emotion that looked a lot like anger from where Allyn was sitting.

The planchet came to life again, and moved under his fingers, gliding across the board at a speed that almost jerked his hands off the planchet. It spelled out 'They killed me.' Allyn narrowed his eyes and shook his head. "Did you guys know about Jeremy?"

"No." Sam shook his head. The edge of the burlap sack scratched against his shirt and apron; Allyn registered the fact that they were all still wearing their masks. "We're not from around here."

"Where are you from?" Allyn said. "South," Ash said.

The planchet started jerking around the board again, moving so fast it almost felt like Allyn would get whiplash from holding on. It spelled out three words, then paused. Allyn stared at the board. The three words it had spelled were 'Don't', 'Mask', and 'Off '. What the hell was that supposed to mean?

The planchet moved again, zooming across the board, spelling out the same word three times, then zipped across the board hard and fast to the word 'Goodbye'. It zipped right over 'Goodbye' and flew off the edge of the table onto the floor. Allyn tried to wet his lips with a tongue made of sandpaper. The board had spelled out 'Run, run, run.'

Nobody moved for a long moment. They were all staring at the planchet where it had fallen to the floor beside Allyn's knee. Allyn picked it up with shaking hands and examined it. There weren't any magnets or motors to make it move. Just a plain, brown, plastic triangle with a magnifying lens in the middle. He dropped it back on the board with numb fingers.

Ash blew a raspberry into the silence that followed and started to chuckle. "Guess it is just a crock," he said. Mara clapped her hands and Lil giggled.

"I'm starved," Sam said. "What did we get at the gas station?"

Mara moved to the window seat and rummaged for a moment. "Gummy worms, jerky, candy bars, chips, beer--"

"Gimme the gummies." Sam held out his hand. Mara passed him a brightly colored bag. Sam pulled up his mask far enough to expose his mouth and used his teeth to rip open the bag. He tilted his head back and lowered a red and blue gummy worm into his mouth. He chewed for a long moment, swallowed, and groaned in pleasure. "Love gummies."

He offered Allyn the bag, but Allyn held up his hand and shook his head. After the thing with the spirit board he wasn't in the mood for snacks. He watched Sam stuff more gummies into his mouth, then follow them up with a huge gulp of vodka. Booze sounded good right now. After the board had spit out the name of a dead kid, Allyn needed a drink. He grabbed up the whiskey bottle, lifted his mask enough to let the bottle reach his mouth, and chugged from it. When he lowered his head and wiped his lips, he realized they were all staring at him.

"What?"

"Way to go, there, champ." Ash chuckled and slapped him

on the shoulder. The warmth in his belly had nothing to do with the whiskey this time. He took another long gulp from the bottle, then passed it to Mara.

They spent a while munching on the snacks and drinking their stolen booze. Allyn started to relax. His belly was warm and his mind fuzzy. The feeling of well-being filled him, and he listened to the others trading stories about Halloweens past and the fun they'd had. He liked this feeling. He was part of something.

Mara and Sam were leaning close to each other, laughing about a story Ash had just brought up. Sam put his arm around Mara, and she leaned over and kissed the side of his neck. Allyn looked away, but that put him eye to eye with Lil. She ran her hand across his chest, pulled him closer, and kissed him. The fruity smell of her filled his nostrils, and he realized what that scent was. Apples. She smelled like apples.

She kissed him again, long and slow; her tongue flickered against his lips. His mind started to buzz with the effect of the liquor, and the pleasure of kissing Lil. Her hands were all over him, doing interesting things. He let her lead, just enjoying what she was doing. Her fingers knotted into the collar of his shirt. She climbed into his lap and kissed him harder. Her fingers knotted in his hair; he reached up and wrapped his arms around her. Nothing mattered right now. Not the grubby house around them. Not Ash or Steph sitting nearby.

His mask started sliding down the back of his head and hit the floor. He didn't care. Lil's lips were softly kissing their way down his throat. He heard Ash give a soft exhale that sounded like satisfaction, but he didn't bother to wonder about it.

Sam stood up. Mara had her legs wrapped around his waist and her arms around his neck. He carried her up the stairs like that. Allyn paused to watch them go. Lil stood up, then, and offered him a hand. He took it, and she led him up the stairs after Sam and Mara. He followed her up the darkened staircase and down a pitch-black corridor, but it never entered his mind to wonder how she could see. All he cared about was getting to someplace private. He heard her open a door, then close it again.

She led him across the room, then pushed him down onto a bed. There was a quilt. He could feel the stitch work beneath his fingers as he pulled himself further onto the bed. It never occurred to him why the bed still had a mattress or covers. Lil's hands were undressing him. He gave up thinking at all when she straddled him and pressed her lips against his mouth.

The clock struck two. Allyn woke alone. He lay still for a long moment, listening to the night sounds outside, then pulled his jeans on and stepped out into the black hallway. He fumbled his way down the hall, using his hand to guide himself along the wall until he found the stairs and went down. From there he could see the light from the main room. He peeked in, found it empty, and took the hallway to the back door, where they'd entered. Where was everybody?

He stepped outside, realized the car was gone, and started to get nervous, but then he realized that all the gear was still where they'd left it. The spirit board was still on the coffee table too. The crew hadn't left him for good. They'd just gone out somewhere. Maybe for more snacks. He walked to the back of the overgrown yard and relieved himself. Something swished through the long grass behind him. He turned, startled, and the being behind him jumped back.

"Careful," Steph said, his tone a mild reproach. Allyn must have peed on Steph's shoes.

"Sorry, man. Don't come up behind a guy while he's taking a leak." He gazed up at the taller man while he adjusted his pants. Steph had taken off the Reaper costume; Allyn could now see more of him. His face was still nothing more than a pale shape in the darkness, but it was narrow and long, like the rest of him. His hair was dark, and slicked back.

"Forget it." Steph turned and looked up at the moon overhead. "Enjoy yourself?"

"Wha-?" Allyn scowled.

"Lil. She show you a good time?" Allyn didn't want to answer that.

"The stars are lovely tonight," Steph said. Allyn relaxed. Steph was a little weird, but maybe the guy had problems. Maybe he wasn't good with people or something. They stood a moment longer, silently staring at the night sky together, then Steph said, "Allyn, you should go. Quickly."

"What? Why?"

"There's still time. It isn't yet three."

"What the hell are you talking about?" Allyn shook his head. "You think I have a curfew or something?"

"No." Steph turned toward the house again. "You lost your mask, Allyn."

"So?" Allyn jogged to catch up to Steph. "What about it?"
"Do you know why people wear disguises on All Hallows' Eve?"

"What?" Allyn wrinkled his nose. "This isn't a history lesson, is it? You're like a geek or something, aren't you?"

"No." Steph shook his head, then passed into the darkness of the house. "But understanding the history behind traditions can be very important."

"What do you mean?"

"Remember, Allyn. Thrice I warned you. Three times. Whatever choices you make are yours alone."

"What? Is this some kind of role-playing group? Did I get mixed up with some weirdos playing a live action game?" They went through the door and into the darkened corridor leading to the main room. Steph paused before passing into the room and turned toward Allyn. His face was gaunt, and his eyes deep set. In the bright white light of the lantern it looked like a skull with skin stretched tight across it. Allyn took a step back, startled. Steph entered the room. Allyn hurried after him.

Steph was standing near the fireplace again. He had his back to Allyn, gazing at the boarded-up space where the fireplace grate would have been. Allyn started to cross the room. Something moved in the periphery of his vision. He slowed and turned toward the motion. Sam came at him faster than his eye could follow, a thick fist cocked back. Sam's fist pistoned out and slammed into Allyn's face. Stars burst behind his eyelids, his cheek hit the wooden floor, then he blacked out.

His head hurt. He opened his eyes and raised his head. He didn't know where he was. He turned his head, trying to see.

The walls were stone. In the corner of the room, Sam sat on a pile of crates, scraping a big carving knife across a whet stone. Sam's mask was gone. He had a square chin, heavy brows, and a button nose that looked like it had been broken many times. His hair was blond and cropped short.

Allyn looked for Steph. He found the tall man in a shadowy corner, standing stony and silent. Allyn tried to raise his hand, but he couldn't. He tried to roll onto his side but couldn't do that either.

The sound of a door opening above them drew his attention. Allyn looked up and watched Ash descend a set of wooden stairs from the floor above. Two girls came after him, whimpering softly, followed by Lil and Mara. When Ash reached the floor, he glanced around until he found Steph in the corner. "There's another up there. Go bring it." Steph climbed the stairs silently. Ash crossed to Allyn and looked down at him. "He's awake."

"Oh, good. It's no fun unless they struggle." Lil clapped her hands, giggling. The girls, standing at the bottom of the stairs, hugged each other and started to cry. Steph appeared in the square of light at the top of the stairs. He paused to close and lock the door, then descended, carrying a guy over his shoulder. He dropped the man on the floor near the crying girls, and joined Ash standing over Allyn.

Sam stood up and checked his watch. "About time for the main course," he said, grinning. He crossed to the girls and looked them over, then crouched to examine the man. After a long moment he pointed his knife at one of the girls. "You," he said. "I like your looks." The girl he'd indicated dropped to her knees and sobbed. The other one tried to hit him. He grabbed her wrist and spun her around, laughing. "But you," he laughed. "I like that spirit." He pulled her in and slow danced her in a circle. "But that won't help you," he said. His eyes were cold and hungry. He scrubbed his lips with the back of his hand, then licked them, eying her. She backed up until her heel hit the steps. She sat down hard and stared up at him with frightened eyes.

Allyn stared at Steph. "What's going on? What kind of sick joke is this?"

"No joke, cutie." Lil giggled. Her eyes were still ice blue, but the pupils were elongated, like a cat's eyes. She grinned at him with the teeth of a leopard.

"Do you know why people wear disguises on All Hallows' Eve?" Steph said. "It's so the spirits can't tell who's mortal, and who's not."

"Steph, cut it out. Untie me. This isn't funny."

"I'm sorry, Allyn. Thrice I warned you, but you didn't listen. Your choices brought you to this moment. There's nothing more I can do for you."

"What? Who the hell are you guys?"

"That's right," Mara said. "We never introduced ourselves.

Not really. My name is Mara. That's Lilith." She pointed to Lil. She swung her finger toward Ash. "Ashtaroth, Samael, and Mephistopheles."

"You almost spoiled everything," Lilith said, casting an accusing look at Steph. Steph shrugged.

"It's in my nature. You know that."

Allyn's gaze darted from one to the other. His five new friends didn't look like people. Sam's eyes were gleaming gold that glowed in the darkness like fire light. Lilith had cat's eyes of blue ice, and claws on her fingers. Mara had tusks and skin the color of a corpse that had been submerged in water for a long time. Steph had the face of a skull, with sunken, dark eyes and hollow cheeks, and Ash--

Allyn inhaled a sharp breath when he saw Ash's eyes. They were pure black. When Allyn looked into those eyes, he felt a dizzying sensation that sucked the breath from his lungs and replaced it with ice. It was like looking into nothing. It was the absence of--everything.

"How long did you know?" Ash said, giving Steph a hard stare.

"Since the police chased us off Poplar. He raised his mask," Steph said.

"And you tried to keep it from us?"

"I offered him a choice. You know that's the nature of who I am."

"Is that why you kept finding excuses to be alone with him?"

"Perhaps." Steph shrugged. "But he didn't heed my warnings, so it doesn't matter, now, does it?"

"No," Sam said, grinning. "It doesn't" He ran his finger along the edge of his newly sharpened knife. "Should I do him now?"

"No. Wait until three."

"What's going on?" Allyn said. "What are you guys doing?"

"All right. I guess you can't go anywhere," Ash said.

"We're demons, Allyn. Hunting mortals on Halloween is a special treat for us. It's one of the few nights of the year when we can be--more than spirit. We try not to take prey from the same town every year. It keeps mortals from seeing a pattern."

"What?" Allyn looked from one to the other. "You guys are crazy. Let me up. Joke over."

"Lilith already told you. This isn't a joke. You revealed yourself. We caught you fair and square. Now we're going to kill you."

"And eat you," Mara added, leering at him. The girls on the stairs wailed, hugging each other. Allyn tried to process what Ash had told him. They tried not to hunt the same town every year. Seven years ago, a boy had disappeared. Allyn had taken his mask off, even though Steph had warned him not to, and during the Ouija session Jeremy's spirit had said three words. Don't. Mask. Off. It should have been obvious. Jeremy had been warning him not to take his mask off. Ash and his crew must have been here seven years ago.

"Jeremy. Is that what happened to him?"

"Finally figured that one out? The spirit board almost gave us away. Good thing you're so stupid."

The clock in the tower at town hall struck three. Ashtaroth chuckled low in his throat. The impossible blackness of his eyes seemed to bleed out and cover his entire body without losing its depth. Allyn stared, watching his five captors transform. Then he screamed.

Second Times
by Irene Ferraro-Sives

"So, look," said Miranda to Darlie, "Here's what I'm wearing." The dress was simply elaborate in a pile-your-hair-up-on-top-of-your-head kind of way.

"Wow, or is something else to be said," said Darlie.

"It is a vintage piece," said Miranda, "I bought it in that second-hand place on Blame Avenue."

"It sure has a lot to it," said Darlie.

The dress fell in flowing lines that brushed the foot. It was swathed in layers of black silk and lace trimmed with black pearls. The sleeves flowed open in wide cuffs.

"The bride of Dracula," Darlie giggled.

"I thought she wore white," Miranda said, "I hate to be a copycat." She fretted with the fabric, bringing the wide skirt out for display. She curtsied.

"Who's that bow for, the Prince of Darkness?" said Darlie.

"Oh, come on, Darlie, it is for a Halloween party," said Miranda.

"You've got me there. It is very suitable for Halloween. I can't believe anyone wore that for real," said Darlie.

"So, what's your costume?" asked Miranda.

"I think I'll get a black suit and cape, some plastic fangs, and go as your husband, The Count," said Darlie.

"Cool! I love it! Let's do it!" said Miranda.

The night of the party was chilled like a tumbler on ice and filled with scattering autumn leaves. The room was full of people and the smoke of burning candles. A man in wolf ears lit a cigarette from a wick atop a skull. The flame accommodated his quest admirably. He blew a long stream of smoke from his mouth. A woman in a long, white, trailing dress walked across the floor through the smog of the smoke machine. The man with the cigarette stopped her with a wave.

"You're smokin' tonight, Angel," he said.

"I can see you are, too. When are you going to stop, Wen?" said Angel.

"When you stop, but Wen won't stop you, not your kind of smokin'," said Wen.

"Mama loves sweet talk," said Angel. "Wen knows," said Wen.

"Here's our husband and wife team," said Angel.

Miranda entered the room in billowing streams of night. Darlie stood beside her, neat in her man's suit, necktie, and plastic fangs, all in the appropriate places. Angel extended her hands in a hostess greeting.

"Welcome Count and Countess, Prince and Lover of Darkness," said Angel.

"We have the deed, so we are more than lovers," Miranda smiled.

"Congratulations, you two," said Angel, and she kissed them both on each cheek.

"What is that divine smell?" Darlie asked, sniffing the air. "Smells like rum to me," Miranda answered.

Angel smiled. "Help yourselves to the hot punch."

A van outside unloaded its burden of horror and fantasy with touches of history and myth here and there. Marie Antoinette in a powdered wig, strawberry blond curls protruding in odd places, entered the room like a queen.

"Where's the cake? Tell me before I lose my head," said the doomed queen.

"Later on, in the evening, I could lend you one of my chains," said a man who had entered at her side. A sheet of white cloth was draped over his head. Chains hung from his arms.

"I know what you're thinking. Not a chance. You look as if you've just left the Bastille," said Marie Antoinette.

"I never left," said the ghost.

"I know. That's what I meant," said Marie the queen.

Miranda and Darlie found their way to the table. There was the warming punch bowl and an assortment of goodies in witch and pumpkin shapes, along with trays of food in less festive contours. Miranda and Darlie sipped their hot punch and nibbled on treats.

The lateral light of the glowing moon penetrated the windows and danced with the candlelight. Miranda felt herself flush as Wen came toward her.

"Smoke?" said Wen, offering her a cigarette.

"No, thank you. There's enough of that in here. All I need to do is take a deep breath," said Miranda.

"Not as satisfying as what I've got ," said Wen, but he put the open package away in his furry pocket.

Miranda observed Wen from under her half-closed eyelids. She decided he was handsome. His calm and easy confidence attracted her. She hoped she was not showing her feelings. She felt that Wen, once in a relationship, would not be faithful. She wistfully took in his carefully carved good looks.

"I'm a wolfman tonight," said Wen to Miranda.

"But I'll bet you're always a wolf," said Miranda, slyly. Darlie came over and stood between them.

"I'm sorry, Miranda, excuse me. Are you married?" said Wen, with a knowing smile.

"I never let him stand in my way," said Miranda, "Think of him as a green light." The hot punch had made her a little reckless. She did not care at the moment if Wen turned out to be the biggest gigolo of all time.

"I'm not the jealous type," said Darlie.

Marie Antoinette joined the trio, brushing strands of powdered wig out of her mouth. She took a deep bite into a soft breadstick that looked like a severed finger. She turned to Darlie with her mouth full.

"Aren't you a stud," Marie Antoinette said to Darlie, without losing any of her breadstick.

Miranda smiled at Wen, extending him an invitation to get to know her better. Then, she turned to Marie Antoinette.

Miranda lost her smile and narrowed her eyes. Wen noticed a change in Miranda's demeanor.

"Miranda?" said Wen.

"I know you. You had them set fire to me. I was burned to death," said Miranda.

Darlie giggled. Marie Antoinette turned to Miranda with an appreciative grin. She stopped smiling when she saw Miranda's face. Miranda did not appear to be playing the role. Her expression was serious.

"Will you look at her marvelous deadpan," said Wen. The queen and Darlie resumed their mirth.

"Come along, little chicken, let's get some more rum," said Wen. He led Miranda away from the other two women.

Wen gave Miranda a comforting hug. "What's wrong?" Wen asked her.

"I don't know. All of a sudden, I felt like it was really Halloween," said Miranda.

"It is really Halloween. We're at a Halloween party. We're all good friends." He gave her another hug.

"I know, but I suddenly felt like I was really a monster, like I am an evil witch."

"Maybe that was me bringing out the bad girl in you," Wen murmured in her ear.

"Or maybe it's too much rum and not enough food. Let's get something to eat."

Miranda and Wen skimmed the holiday buffet table. They emptied a basket of black bread rolls onto their plates and stuffed them with cold cuts. Wen finished his first sandwich with carnivorous bites. He rolled his eyes at Miranda and she laughed at his antics.

"I made you laugh. Glad I could help," said Wen.

"I want to have a good time, stay out as late as I can, and, when I am too tired to think anymore, go home and sleep, sleep, sleep," said Miranda.

Wen winked. "I'm with you. You're my kind of woman."

After the punch bowl and plates were emptied and the last streamers had been trampled underfoot, Miranda and Wen left the Halloween gathering. They were among the last of the party guests to depart.

They walked hand-in -and to Miranda's place. The light in the window told her Darlie was home.

"I'll call you," said Wen. "Sure, you will," said Miranda.

She looked at the window, the light from inside melting into the glass, and tried to figure out if Darlie were asleep. Wen waved good-bye. Miranda waved back and closed the door.

She wondered what Wen was all about. At the last minute by the door, he had been only a friend.

Darlie had fallen asleep in front of the television. Miranda turned off the picture box and gave her roommate a shake. Darlie woke up right away. She recognized Miranda through sleep's haze and breathed a sigh of relief. "Are you alone?" she asked Miranda.

Miranda waved her arms in the spaces of air around her. "Yes," she said. "I'm going to my bed and I may sleep for two days."

"Do you need help taking off that big, black horror story?" said Darlie.

Miranda carefully untacked the fluttering, black dress. She hung it up on a sturdy hanger and left it on a coat rack to air.

"A big, black horror story. Sounds more like your last boyfriend," said Miranda.

"Walter was nice. He wasn't really standing me up. He was working. I'd see him again, if he ever had the night off," sighed Darlie.

"Ha. I don't believe him," said Miranda.

Miranda stepped into the shower to wash off the day's events. She soaped up, rinsed off, and stepped out again. She dried herself and slipped her nightgown over her head. She turned to the autumn night, lifting the window shade to look out over the rooftops and falling leaves. The full moon was a silver button waiting to be unfastened so the sun could show itself and the moon could sleep. Miranda yawned and closed her eyes. She opened them slowly to say goodnight to the moon.

When she opened her eyes, Miranda saw a shrewd man's face peering at her through the windowpane. Two hands gripped the side of the house like the building had been spread with glue.

The man smiled slyly. "My love," he said through the window glass.

Miranda screamed and jumped back, colliding with Darlie as she rushed into the room.

"What's wrong?" said Darlie, recovering from her momentary stumble.

Miranda pointed frantically to the window. "Someone is trying to break in," said Miranda.

Darlie studied the window carefully. She opened it and stuck out her head to look around.

"There is no one out there."

"But, Darlie, a man was hanging outside this window, trying to climb in," Miranda insisted.

"What were you and Wen smoking?"

"Nothing like that happened tonight. I am totally sober and sane."

"Miranda, there is nothing outside this building on this side for anyone to use to climb up to this window. How could someone be at this window, trying to get in?" said Darlie, knocking calmly on the windowpane.

"He climbed up that tree and jumped and held on. He climbed up the fire escape around the other side and crawled to this side. He used hooks and ropes. I know I saw him. He was there!"

"Why didn't he use another window? Why this one?" asked Darlie.

"Because he knows I sleep in this room."

"In your dreams, Miranda." She checked the window to make sure it was locked and pulled down the shade. "Go back to your dreams. I'm going back to mine." She left the room.

Miranda stood in uncertainty and her nightclothes. Darlie's mattress creaked as she settled in. The house became silent. Only the ticking of a vintage clock and the dripping of the bathroom faucet interrupted the quiet.

"Got to get that fixed," Miranda thought to herself as she lay down in her own bed. She pulled the covers up to her chin. Her mind rested on Wen. Would she ever figure him out?

Miranda fell asleep with Wen on her mind. That night, she dreamed beyond reason. She dreamed that the man at the window had climbed into her room. The window glass had disappeared, and he stepped easily onto her wood floors. He smiled at her with that sly, knowing smile. She was amazed at her own calm. "I guess being asleep makes the difference," she thought to herself. She watched his actions without alarm.

"You know I can't refuse an invitation," said the intruder. "It's nice to be pursued," replied Miranda.

When she woke up, her gentleman caller was gone. Miranda sat up and looked around the empty room. The window was still closed and locked. To Miranda's surprise, it was late morning.

"It's Saturday, Sleepyhead," called Darlie. "Thanks for nothing," Miranda called back.

She raised herself from her rumpled bed. She paused to consider her restless night before she straightened the sheets and blankets.

She joined Darlie in the kitchen. Scrambled eggs and bacon were already sizzling on the griddle. Miranda pushed bread down into the toaster.

"I had a weird dream last night. The man I thought I saw at the window came into my room. We spoke. Then I woke up. I thought I had been asleep only a short time, but it was late. That's when you called me," said Miranda.

Darlie looked at her with serious interest.

"You say time lapsed and you don't remember?" she asked. "I was sleeping," Miranda defended.

"But he was in the room and you don't remember what happened?"

"And?" She took a sip of coffee.

"Vampires do that," said Darlie, "You got strange last night in that dress. Maybe a vampire wore that dress once upon a time and now she wants it back."

"A man came into my room last night. Shades of our time. Maybe he was a drag queen?" said Miranda.

"Be serious, Miranda. Maybe he was her lover and he thought you were her because nobody ever wore that dress but her," said Darlie.

Darlie looked at Miranda's neck.

"Maybe he didn't bite you, or maybe we don't see the bite," said Darlie. She put her hand on Miranda's shoulder in a comforting way. "We'll have to watch you, for your own good."

"Darlie, stop," said Miranda.

"If you become a total vampire, you know what we have to do. But I don't think you are. We'll keep our eyes open for signs, to be safe," said Darlie. She patted Miranda's shoulder.

Miranda took a forkful of bacon and eggs. She snorted a short laugh, then felt a cold chill of dread. She had lost her battle with Darlie's words. They rooted in her mind and grew there, quickly, becoming a dense tangle of meanings. She fought back tears between mouthfuls and tried to put those thoughts from her mind.

The day passed without further mention of vampires. It was a lazy kind of a Saturday. The two girls sat around all day watching movies. Miranda was relieved that there was no further mention of vampires. Darlie's warning seemed like part of her nightmare.

The ordered pizza for dinner, and Wen came with the delivery person. The delivery person left, but Wen stayed on, helping himself to a slice. Miranda was glad he was there, but she was not sure how much.

"It's a good thing you're here. You can help us wash the dishes," Miranda said to Wen.

"There are other good reasons for me to be here," said Wen. He reached into a satchel of no particular distinction and pulled out garlic and a crucifix. Through mouthfuls of pizza, he said, "Not to worry, Miranda, we're on it."

"He didn't bite you, yet. We're going to prevent that," said Darlie.

"I'm going to stay here. I'm sleeping with Darlie, in her room," said Wen.

"Wen found out about this house. There used to be rituals of evil here. The man that presided over them lured young women like us to this house. He would sacrifice them to devils in rituals. He would kill them and drink their blood. And, get this: he would drain their bodies and keep their blood in jars and bottles. He would drink their blood at his leisure, like a favorite wine. We think he's the man that's after you. He must have been a vampire, or something like that," said Darlie.

Miranda's mind banged around on several mental objects before it settled into blankness.

"Someone is trying to kill me?" she asked.

"Not quite. Someone wants your soul," said Darlie.

Wen stared at Miranda, grimly. Miranda nodded with resignation.

"Do what you can," she said in a low voice that was filled with despair.

"It's just a precaution. We don't think you're there, yet,"

said Wen.

Darlie gazed at Miranda, her eyes filled with profound sympathy.

"We've been friends for too long," Darlie said. She stroked Miranda's hair.

"Go to sleep, now, Miranda. We'll watch over you," said Darlie.

Miranda found her bed, resolving to free herself of fear. She lay her head on her pillow and saw the shadows under her door as Darlie and Wen left a crucifix and garlic. The same was already hung through her bedroom. Miranda felt she would have trouble sleeping, but the next thing she knew, it was morning. She had slept a deep and dreamless sleep that did not leave her rested.

Miranda opened the door to her bedroom. The garlic and cross were gone. She stepped across her threshold and entered the kitchen. Darlie and Wen were seated at the kitchen table. They were not smiling.

"Did you sleep well?" asked Darlie.

"Yes. I fell asleep so fast and hard, when I woke and saw daylight, I felt like I had just closed my eyes," said Miranda.

"Do you remember anything?" asked Wen.

"No, I didn't wake up once. How long have you two been awake?"

"Since before dawn. You don't remember that noise?" Darlie asked.

"Yikes! No, I don't remember any noise," said Miranda. "There was a noise, like something tapping on your

bedroom window. It was so persistent, it woke us up. You had gotten out of bed," said Wen.

"We found a bat. We think it was banging on your window, trying to get in," said Darlie.

"Knock, knock," said Wen.

"Where's the bat, now? Is it dead?" asked Miranda.

"No, it is not dead. It turned into a man and flew away," Darlie answered.

Wen gave Darlie a sharp, warning look. "Be careful," he said.

"Miranda, we must watch your every movement. You are not remembering your nights capades," said Darlie.

"Are you still my friends?" said Miranda.

"Of course, we are, no matter what happens. Would we protect you this way if we were not your friends?" said Darlie. "Miranda, we think you ought to take a leave of absence from your job. And, we think you ought to take a temporary

hiatus from your personal relationships," said Wen.

"The only personal relationships I have are you guys," said Miranda.

Wen looked at Miranda long and hard. "I am so glad to hear that." He took Miranda's hand in his own.

Miranda awoke early to her first day of suspended life. The garlic and crosses had been removed with the dawn. Darlie and Wen were both gone until evening. They were continuing to go to their jobs.

Rather than leave Miranda alone, they had hired a caregiver for her. The young woman came upon the departure of Darlie and Wen in the morning. Miranda had agreed to lock herself in her room when the sun began to go down. It was autumn, so sunset came early. Wen and Darlie did not want Miranda near the caregiver when the sun disappeared from the heavens. Darlie and Wen would both be returning, because Wen had moved into the house.

Tanya, the caregiver, had been told that Miranda had a type of heart condition. They showed her an array of medicine bottles. Tanya did not have much interest in the pills. She was not responsible for administering the meds, so she did not care about them. She never bothered to read the labels to find out what was in them. It never occurred to her that the pills were expired prescriptions for coughs and sneezes, or tooth infections, or pulled muscles that had been cleaned out of the medicine chest and closets and purses. She only seemed to be care about her paycheck.

Tanya's scheduled duties for the day were simply watching Miranda. Tanya had been convinced with warning that Miranda's condition could cause sudden death. She was to stay with Miranda at all times. However, if Miranda retired to her bedroom, she was not to be disturbed. Once again, Tanya questioned nothing.

Miranda found Tanya in the kitchen making noncaffeinated herbal tea. The toaster was on. She could smell the no sodium, no fat, whole wheat bread burning. Miranda pushed the blackened bread out of the slots. Just as she wished her life had taken a different turn, dread clutched her heart. She threw the toast in the trash, and, out of character, said nothing about ineptitude. Miranda felt the future throw shadows in her mind.

"I'll make my own toast. I can do something," said Miranda.

With faux buttered toast in hand, Miranda sat down in front of the television. She pondered on the remainder of the day, wondering how she would pass the time and grateful that it would pass no matter what she did. She longed for sundown when she would be left alone. She was frightened by her longing.

Tanya sat down with Miranda in front of the television. "What do you want for lunch?" said Tanya.

Miranda sighed at the coming hours.

But the time did pass. The light of day began to recede.

Miranda's anxiety rose as the sun sank into the horizon.

Miranda lifted herself from her comfortable seat. "I've been sitting all day and I am so tired. Can you believe that? I am going into my bedroom to lie down," said Miranda.

"Okay. Let me know if you need anything," said Tanya. She

cracked open another pistachio nut. The television and the snacks held the better part of her attention.

"The ad must have said 'get paid for being lazy and stupid'," Miranda muttered. She exited and actually did lay down on her bed. To her surprise, she was exhausted. She looked once to make sure her door was locked. Sleep overcame her before she fully closed her eyes.

Miranda woke up in her recent, usual manner, without realizing she had been asleep and that more than a few minutes had passed. When she opened her eyes, her room was dark. Noises outside her door told her that Darlie and Wen were home.

Their speech was hushed, but furious. Miranda longed for the day that their intense discussion would have indicated a disagreement about what to have for dinner. Knowing something was not right, Miranda roused herself with effort and opened her bedroom door.

The hallway was still and dark. All the light and noise were beyond, in the room where the television was. Miranda approached her friends with dread. She turned into the room, slowly.

When Darlie saw Miranda, she stepped back with caution. Wen faced her entrance with determination. Miranda took them in, then looked for Tanya.

Tanya was still in her seat before the television. She was sprawled out, her legs before her, her arm hanging over the side. It appeared that her throat had been sliced, and from the look of her remains, all her blood had been drained. Her sucked in skin was the color of pale moss. Miranda had not seen many dead people, but she had never known a corpse to look like that. Tanya's skin was shedding some kind of dust. Miranda shrieked with horror.

"You did this, Miranda," said Wen. His voice was dark with unknown meaning.

"You're not a vampire, after all," said Darlie, "You are a rebirth of the killer."

"We did the wrong thing. We did not prevent you," Wen told her.

"The killer shows himself over and over, through past centuries. You bought the dress you must have once worn, to kill. When you put the dress on, your past was reawakened," said Darlie.

"The killer was a man," Miranda objected.

"Many of his co-conspirators were women. They were devil-worshippers and witches. They can't ever really be killed. You were burned for your crimes, but you didn't die."

"Who else could have done the killing, Miranda?" challenged Wen.

"I may have opened the door in my sleep and let the killer in," said Miranda.

"We didn't tell you, but we changed the locks. The doors lock from the inside, too. Only we have the keys," said Wen.

"The killer is supernatural. Maybe he walked through the door."

"Enough of this," said Wen. He seized Miranda and held her, reaching around her and pinning her arms. He lifted her off her feet and proceeded to carry her to the upper floor.

"I've loved you for too long, Miranda. I don't want them to know what you did. We're going to hide you and keep you from harming others," said Wen. His voice quavered as he spoke, but his arms were strong. He brought Miranda to a room upstairs that had been prepared for her. He kissed her, passionately, before he locked her in.

The room was a master bedroom that they had never used. Miranda looked around. It was now the cleanest room in the large, old house. A bed had been placed against the wall. There was a dresser, a table, chairs, a television, radio, books, but no phone or computer. *What will we they tell our friends when they don't hear from me?*

The adjoining bathroom was stocked with soaps, towels, tissue papers. *They want me to be clean and comfortable,* Miranda thought.

A refrigerator and microwave were set up in a corner. There was a free-standing pantry filled with food. Plates and cutlery on a table told her she would receive regular meals. *So, I never need to leave.*

She sat down on a plush recliner and cried. *I didn't know Wen would ever say he loved me.*

Miranda lay down on the bed that had been made for her. The locked and shuttered windows admitted the darkness of night just as they had let in the light of day, in slow trickles. The clock on the dresser told her it was close to midnight.

Wen had brought her a cooked dinner. "Darlie doesn't want to see me, does she?" Miranda had asked. She received no answer. Wen had looked grim as he left.

The lamp shed golden lights across the room. Miranda reached over and turned the lamp up a notch. She studied the windows. She had already tried the locks, and they would not budge. One day, when they were gone, if she smashed through the windows and shutters….? She could not remember if there was anything to climb down on. The third floor was pretty far to jump.

Murmuring from downstairs filtered through the floor. The voices of a man and a woman seesawed back and forth. Miranda could not make out what they were saying. She fell asleep in despair.

A timid knock roused Miranda. The dim sunlight spilling over the edges of the locked shutters told her it was early. The day had just begun.

Miranda got herself up and walked to the door. She opened the door to find her breakfast at her feet. An iron gate had been set up, extending beyond the threshold by one foot. *How long have they been planning this?* thought Miranda. She picked up the plate and closed the door.

She ate in spite of herself. She fixed herself some coffee and sipped it while watching the morning news. There was no mention of a missing person or homicide in the area. *What have they done with Tanya's body?* thought Miranda. *Doesn't anyone notice her missing? How did they hide what I did?* For the first time, Miranda found herself admitting guilt. The moment was fleeting, for with the next thought, she rebelled against herself. *I did not do that. I am not a murderer. I am their friend. How could they think I would hurt anyone?* Miranda started to cry. *Why don't I remember being awake when I was sleeping?* Miranda let her tears overtake her. She sat and cried and cried until she couldn't cry anymore.

The afternoon burned down. Since there was no knock on the door at lunchtime, she fixed herself a can of soup in the microwave. "Darlie must have gone to work," thought Miranda. She thought about what her own day would have been like if she were not a supernatural suspect. She had never known Darlie or Wen to let their minds run away with the wind. What had she done to make them both believe she could be capable of sipping blood like some kind of dreadful cocktail? Miranda had felt strange since she wore that dress, but she did not feel she had changed so much she could kill.

Miranda had heard that people have feelings inside them that they don't know about. Could she have a homicidal fiend buried deep inside her? She loved and trusted her friends. Why would they believe she was a murderer if it were not true? Did she have more confidence in her friends than she had in herself? She felt that she did.

Miranda waited for sounds of Darlie's return. The first sign that her housemate was home was the knock on the door at dinnertime.

"Darlie, don't go. I won't open the door. I want to talk to you," Miranda said.

"Thanks for leaving the dishes outside so I could take them," Darlie said in a strained voice.

"Darlie, I wouldn't love you the way I do if I were capable of killing. I would not be worthy of such love. I think this house is haunted by the spirit of the killer. I think the killer's ghost killed Tanya. He tried to make me do things for him, but I didn't do what he wanted. I didn't kill her, Darlie!"

"Yes, you did, Miranda. You were never what you seemed to be. I don't know why Wen trusts you, even in a locked room. Maybe it's because you throw yourself at him. I would burn you to ashes myself if I could," said Darlie.

Miranda heard the gate crash closed and the lock fall into place. Miranda opened the door. Her dinner plate was there, but Darlie was gone.

Miranda was more fretful on this second day of her imprisonment. She did not eat as much and cried a little more. Sometime toward evening, she thought she smelled smoke. She brushed it aside, thinking she had imagined it. When the smoke alarms went off, she screamed with fear, knowing she would be trapped in this locked and shuttered room.

Miranda banged on the cage until her hands were bruised. "Darlie, what are you doing?" Miranda shrieked.

The smoke alarms cut off as suddenly as they had started. "How does it feel to know you are going to die?" Darlie snarled.

"Darlie, did you burn my dinner?" Miranda said.

"I'm not feeding you anymore. Take care of yourself," said Darlie.

"Where's Wen? Wen will bring me dinner," said Miranda. Darlie did not answer. There was no sound in the house.

Miranda was chilled with dread. She noticed her banging had loosened screws on the gate. Miranda was not a genius of home repair, but she knew loose screws meant loose gate. She quietly closed and locked the door. She would wait until she knew Darlie was out of the house to work on her escape.

Once again, Miranda awoke to find out she had been sleeping. She could not remember laying down on her bed. The last thing she remembered was standing by the door. She lay in bed for a while, listening for sounds of Darlie's presence. The house was still as could be. Miranda could hear her stomach rumble. She was munching on crackers and jelly when she quietly opened the door.

Not only had the screws been tightened, but the gate and hallway were crawling with rats. The rodents observed Miranda with eager, red eyes. Miranda slammed the door shut and locked it. She could not hear the creatures moving outside her door. She peeked out to see if they were gone. They were still there. One of them scurried toward the opening, trying to enter her room. She pushed the creatures into a furry ball with her foot. It sprawled against the opposite wall.

Miranda stared at her bolted door. Was she still asleep and dreaming or was there a menace in the hall?

A long, gray tail hung over the table where the jelly crackers were. The rat was chewing on the sweet snack. The animal glared at Miranda, its red eyes shining with unseen light. Miranda grabbed the rat. Without thinking, she threw it into the hall. She stood still in her room, trying to understand her situation.

"Miranda," someone said. She thought she heard Wen's voice call her name. She did not move and listened very hard. "Miranda," the voice said once more. Her name floated out of the walls and hung in the air, a disenchanted balloon of joy.

"Where are you, Wen?"

"Darlie lied. Creature of evil," said Wen. "Wen, tell me," Miranda begged.

"Find me."

"Where are you?" said Miranda. There was no answer.

"Wen, if I had ever known how you felt about me, I would have told you how I feel. I love you. If you knew I loved you, none of this would have happened. You would have trusted me. I would never have bought that silly dress. I would have been with you. No one really has any power over me but you. And I have self-control, but not as far as you are concerned. I know I did not kill anyone. I could never do such a thing.

"I wish I were with you, now. Why won't you tell me where you are? I will find you if you tell me where you are," said Miranda. She began to weep tears of anger and despair.

"Don't cry, Miranda. I will find you," said Wen, "I love you."

"Wen, will you let me out?" There was no answer.

"I will be patient. I will trust in you. I will wait for you," said Miranda.

Miranda washed and dressed with more eagerness to greet the day than she had felt lately. Her anticipation level was raised by joy. She and Wen had found one another under the strangest of circumstances. Would they laugh over this, someday? She would not be dissuaded by circumstance.

Miranda ate more than she had since the night of the Halloween party. "Love makes you fat," she said, aloud. She laughed at her own remark. She laughed until tears ran from her eyes. "That is so funny," she said.

Miranda looked around to see if there were anyone who heard her. Wen was not there, yet, so who could hear her? "Silly Miranda," she scolded herself.

The bright, autumn day settled into dusk. Slivers of twilight blue pushed through chinks in the shutters. Late afternoon let go of daylight and darkness came to take its place.

Outdoor evening sounds seeped through the silence. Miranda became aware of her breathing. The muffled clinking of metal outside her door caught her attention. She held her breath, waiting a moment. She walked quietly to the door.

When she peeked outside, she found the gate had been opened. The rats were gone. Nothing stood in the way of her escape.

"Wen!" said Miranda, ardently.

She looked up and down the hallway. The corridor was empty and still.

"Wen," she called again, softly.

She crept outside, trying hard not to make too much noise. *Where is Darlie?* she thought. She no longer cared if Darlie were convinced of her innocence, as long as Wen believed in her.

The house looked pretty much the same, except that there was the odor of death. *What have they done with Tanya?* thought Miranda, her skin prickling. She found her way downstairs, though the house was mostly in darkness. Her bedroom was as she had left it. The bed was still unmade.

Further down another flight, the house seemed devoid of presence. No lights were on except for the television. The volume was down. A game show host was soundlessly awarding money to a contestant. The only audience in Miranda's house was Miranda.

Miranda looked all around. She could see the outline of someone sitting at the kitchen table in the dark. She approached the unknown quietly, entering the room on tiptoe, with caution. The person seated at the table seemed to be Wen. Miranda smiled as she turned on the light.

The person unseen in the dark was Wen, but not as she had known him. Wen's eyes were mere hollows. His lifeless body had been tied to the chair, propping him up in a sitting position.

Miranda felt as though her own life had been drained from her. The sense of loss was unbearable. She grabbed the back of the chair to hold herself up. Her hand brushed Wen. He was cold and had been for some time. Miranda wailed with grief and fear.

"Wen! Wen! Wen!" she screamed several times. Her voice

reverberated throughout the house.

It was not the rats that Miranda called to herself. "Hello, dear girl Miranda," said Darlie, from behind. Miranda turned sharply.

Darlie was dressed in black, the black dress of unspeakable frills that Miranda had worn to the Halloween party.

"We laughed together over that dress," Miranda said with bitterness.

"You stole my dress and then you tried to steal my man. Wen is mine forever, now. You will never have any part of him," said Darlie.

"His spirit doesn't belong to you. Wen is free of you, forever," said Miranda.

Darlie placed her hand on Wen's forehead and pulled his head back. She lifted the lid of his sunken eye. Wen's exposed iris turned, slightly, searching for Miranda, and resting on her.

"He's not dead!" Miranda exclaimed.

"Not in any way that your dull, little mind could understand. Miranda, dear, I can't die. And now, neither can Wen. You stole my dress. I had to steal your mind. I tried to make you think you were me, but you did not have enough intellect to work with. You have an abysmal lack of imagination."

"I did not kill Tanya," said Miranda.

"Of course, you didn't. I killed Tanya," Darlie confessed. "You pretended you were my friend," said Miranda.

"Not quite true. I found you a very amusing companion. You are always cute and harmless. You were never a threat, until you found this dress, and Wen," said Darlie.

"I don't want what's yours. It's just a stupid dress. Wen belonged to me. He gave me his heart and soul. You stole Wen from me," said Miranda.

"It's not just a stupid dress. It's the dress I wore when they hounded me for what I am. I was burned to flame and ashes in this dress. But the dress and I have magic. We are both here, with you," said Darlie.

"You are an evil witch!"

"Evil is like my dress. Its power and purpose are relevant to the woman who uses it."

"I hate you, Darlie. You're not my friend anymore," said Miranda.

Darlie threw her hands over her head in supplication and worship.

"Great Evil One! Master of my desires! Come to this kitchen and admire my work," said Darlie. She reached for the hatchet-type utensil that Miranda had once used to cut up chickens. Darlie aimed the sharp edge at Miranda and came toward her.

"With all my love and friendship," said Darlie, as she swung the weapon at Miranda.

Miranda backed away. Frantic moments rushed past her, lifting clouds from her vision. She opened the flame on the stove and threw an old newspaper on top of it. Darlie fended off the smoke and fire. Miranda grabbed a bottle of cooking oil from the counter and opened it. She threw the oil on the stove. The golden fluid immediately ignited. A ridge of flames covered the stove and counters. The fire spread rapidly.

The walls of the kitchen collapsed inward, pushing the escaping flames wherever they would go. The fire spread further into the house, finding its way to other floors. Darlie shrieked, her sharp, piercing voice splitting time. Her unearthly scream made Miranda's ears bleed.

"Not aga-a-a-a-in!" Darlie screamed.

Shadowy, transparent figures flew out of the crumbling walls. They brushed passed Miranda and seemed to crush her within the oppressive smoke. She screamed, again, as a young woman with a tooth-baring grin flew past her, arms flapping like a bird. Flames were visible through the see-through girl.

Wen smiled slightly, though his eyes were grim. He stood up and walked, slowly and steadily, to Miranda. He put his hands on her shoulders and stared into her eyes. Though he was wasted, his skin glowed with passion.

"I knew you couldn't finish her off without me," said Wen. He lifted Miranda in his arms and carried her through the parting flames. Once outside and past danger, he set her on her feet.

"I'll be back!" Darlie howled from inside the house.

With groping fingers, Wen brushed the singed hair and soot from Miranda's face. "I can't stay, now, Miranda. I have to go," he said.

"But we'll be together, always, anyway, won't we?" "You know I'll be back," said Wen.

Flashing lights and sirens came closer.

"I will never let anyone hurt you, again," said Miranda.

Wen kissed her lips, softly, before he disappeared into the night.

A crowd of people had gathered at a distance. They stood well beyond the reach of the flames. Emergency vehicles arrived on the scene. Water was poured on the burning house, but every thirsty, flaming tongue just licked it up. The house was reduced to ashes.

Miranda stared at the charred, smoking skeleton of her former residence. Her house was gone.

"I have nothing," Miranda said in amazement.

"Can you tell me what happened?" someone asked her.

The man's voice was lost in a blue haze.

Miranda stopped time with her dazed expression. "I'm not sure," she said, "I was upstairs, in my own room when I smelled smoke. I saw fire. I called my friend, but she didn't answer. I wasn't sure that she was home. I ran out of the house," said Miranda. She was not sure that she was believed. She cried as convincingly as she could.

Miranda received a blanket to protect her from the autumn chill. Total strangers offered her solace and hot tea. One woman offered her a place to stay. All Miranda could think of was Wen. She had the rest of the night to be with him. She wanted to get away from the crowd, the flashing lights. If she were with Wen, everything would be fine.

Wi! they find Tanya's bones in the ruins? thought Miranda, *And Darlie? What do mortal remains look like when someone can't die?*

Miranda couldn't fathom her future. Tomorrow's coming crushed her. She decided she did not have another day, at least not one worth living. With an unheard sob, Miranda ran through the night. She wished the darkness would never end.

"Wen, Wen," she called between her tears.

Miranda ran as far and as fast as she could, searching for Wen. She avoided light, trying to hide from the moon and stars. She had not run very far when, exhausted from tears, she fell into a pile of autumn leaves that were dank with decay. The fallen leaves were pungent with farewell. She cried with her whole mind and body. She wished she were anywhere else but where she was.

"Miranda." Someone called her name amid the piles of rustling leaves.

Wen was standing over her. With the moon behind him, his face was in darkness. Miranda stood up and clasped him around the neck. His face was wet with tears.

"If I had ever told you how much I love you instead of playing all kinds of games, none of this would have happened," said Wen.

"Don't blame yourself, Wen. Darlie would still have been jealous. She was evil," said Miranda.

"She is evil. You don't think she's gone very far? She is not so easily departed," said Wen.

Miranda thought, *I am alone, and helpless, and in the dark.*

Wen stroked Miranda's burned hair. "I could never hurt you," he said. He had read her mind.

"What about Darlie?" asked Miranda.

"She and I are equals, now," said Wen. He took Miranda's face in his hands. "When daylight comes, I'll be gone. Go back to your own life. They are waiting for you and there are many questions they will ask you. I will come to you, from time to time."

"I don't want my life back. I will live in the dark, with you," said Miranda.

"Miranda, my needs are different, now. How can you live in the dark, with me?"

"I will find a way. Love overcomes obstacles. That's what people say. Let me try," she begged.

"They will look for you. Through you, they will find me," said Wen.

"They will look for me for a while, but then they will stop looking. We will hide from the light," said Miranda.

"In some ways, we always hid from the light," said Wen.

His voice held the memory of a smile.

Miranda touched the cold skin of Wen's face.

"There's that abandoned house in the open field. There is a forest on the outskirts of that property. It is not too far from the river, and well off the highway. I always wanted to renovate the house and live in it. This is as close as I will ever come," said Miranda.

"There will be no lights or running water. How will you eat? Or keep warm? It's no good, Miranda. I can stay there, but not you," said Wen.

"I won't have it any other way. I am coming with you," she insisted. "Tomorrow, I will be rested. I will think of some way to live there."

"Tonight, you will rest. Tomorrow, you will find a way to live. What will I do?" said Wen. Miranda saw the slight gleam of humor in the hollows of Wen's eyes. It was the old Wen who looked at her with amusement.

"Let's go to the house, now."

They moved silent and unseen through the night until they arrived at the old house. The house was predictably cold and dark and dusty. Miranda felt the airborne particles swirl all around her. They settled on her skin and in her eyes and throat. Life had never felt more unworthy of living. Yet, Wen was the light of her life and he walked beside her. He would be her guide to that place of peace.

"Here we are in that deserted old place," said Miranda.

She giggled.

Wen put his arm around her shoulder. "I wish I had some warmth to give you," he sighed.

"Being here with you is hot enough." "Where will you sleep, Miranda?"

"I will sleep wherever you sleep," she said. "I don't feel like sleeping," said Wen. "Then I will remain awake, with you."

"Miranda, you can't do this for very long. You will die." "Then, I will never have to leave you. We can be together,

forever," Miranda smiled.

"There is no guarantee. You may go your own way... unless I take your life," said Wen.

Miranda took in Wen's words and meanings. Wen spoke to Miranda's silence.

"I have power now. Otherwise Darlie would be here to torment us both. If you pass to the other side due to your own actions and will, you have chosen a path all your own. If I put you in the other world, I will have captured your soul with the pain of parting, and you will be mine, forever. You will be like me, and you can stay with me," said Wen.

Miranda's eyes brightened. "I would do anything if it meant I could stay with you."

Wen walked away from her. He stared at the moon

through the cracked and dirt-crusted pane. "I want this to be as quick and as painless as possible," said Wen. He played with and pulled a large piece of broken glass from the window. It came loose with an easy squeak. It brought down other loose pieces. Some of them fell on Wen's hand. The skin was opened, but Wen did not bleed.

Wen tested his piece of glass for sharpness. He rubbed his fingertips along the edge and nodded. "This is good," he said. He looked at Miranda with sad and empty eyes. "Come here to me, Miranda."

Miranda walked to Wen as though she were a bride. Her hands were folded in front of her. Her eyes gleamed with mystery.

Wen opened his arms to Miranda. Miranda smiled as she stood before him. When she saw the piece of glass close to her, she began to shiver.

"Are you cold, Miranda? Soon, you will not feel the cold, anymore."

Wen turned Miranda around. He kissed the side of her face as he pulled back her head, exposing her throat. Swiftly and accurately, he drew the sharp edge of the glass weapon across her neck.

Miranda sighed as her blood flowed. Wen stuck his tongue in her wound. He licked and sucked and tore with his teeth,

Miranda saw the room glow larger. The dusty windows towered over her, giants in a new dream. All her energies were building to release. She reached her finish line panting, trying hard to catch her breath. When she arrived at the end of her final race, the trophy disappeared. There was no release. There was no transition.

Miranda understood that she had changed. She no longer felt cold in the nearly uninhabited home. The chill was merely there. Temperature had no importance to her. Heat and cold were simply experiences. Fact would always be a kind of intellectual digestion.

Miranda wiped the blood off her neck. She licked her red-smeared palm. There was no taste on her tongue. A thrill pursued her senses, starting in her mouth, but it wasn't enough. Miranda found herself craving the satisfaction that only the blood and flesh of others could provide.

Miranda turned to Wen.

"We shall be like this forever. Together forever," said Miranda.

"We will find our victims. They will be people that don't matter to us," nodded Wen.

"Yes, Wen, I do not want you to suffer for hunger. I don't want you to watch me suffer, either."

Wen embraced Miranda in a kiss. There was no search for fulfillment.

"Come, let's go find someone we don't care about," said Wen.

Outside, the flower of night was blooming. Each of its dark petals uncurled in beauty and mystery. The moon and stars were its frost and dewdrops.

The driveway that connected the house to points beyond was silent and empty. The overgrown gardens and woods, depleted by autumn, were populated by seekers. Alongside the ghosts who kept the secrets of the house were the normal police, parked in unlit cars and crawling silent and unseen through the trees and bushes.

"She kept me locked up in a room upstairs. She was not right anymore. She killed that woman she hired to clean the house. She changed. I don't know why," they heard Darlie saying. "Like I told you, I wasn't home tonight. I was out. I had a date with my boyfriend, Wen. He never showed up. He was probably with her. She was after him. She was jealous of me in every way. She stole my clothes and pretended she was me. I should have read the signs a long time ago. I should have seen this coming."

"Where are they, now?"

Darlie pointed to the dark house that blanked out part of the sky and its stars. "They're in there. Look, the house is totally dark. They can see in the dark, like bats. I don't know how they do it." She talked in an excited whisper.

Duty and honor surrounded the old house. Darlie crouched beneath the dropping leaves of an oak tree. She was breathing rapidly. Her eyes were wide with hunger.

"Hurry, they may get away," she urged.

The armed man beside her in the night did not answer.

He waited in the dark. Darlie was intimidated by his silence that was like absence. She could hear herself panting. She knew he was there. His quiet aroused her. She reached for him in the dark, but, to her amazement, she could not find him. She turned around, searching for her intended victim. Stealthy shadows were approaching the looming building in the dark. Her escort was on the move.

Darlie ran toward the moving figures with her brand of lust. She licked her teeth in lascivious anticipation.

The group came toward the house on all sides. Darlie was at the back of the building in the once gracious garden. Now, the flower beds were overgrown with the remains of weeds. The fountains and ponds were dry. The stone figures stood, forlorn and lonely.

Darlie was eager to enter the house and had stopped to revel in the moment. She put her hand on the statue of a boy feeding pigeons. She pulled back with rage and surprise when the child wept beneath her hand. The marble boy was shedding tears.

"You are not going to get attention. This is my moment. Nobody rains on me," Darlie snarled. She tried to push the stone child over, but the figure began to scream. The cry could be heard at a distance.

The night was still with listening. The group moving toward the house stopped. The statue screamed again.

"You are just stone. You can't make noise," said Darlie. The marble boy wailed with sorrow.

A voice whispered in Darlie's ear. "The boy is a carved rock and he screams and weeps. You are flesh and you feel no pain."

Darlie scoffed, "I should never feel pain. I am above common misery."

The night was filled with stealthy movement once again. All of it was coming to Darlie. She waited with ravenous patience. Every second brought her satisfaction closer to her. She growled in anticipation, pushing her tongue out of her mouth until it was as long as a snake. There was the silence of stillness, again.

Then, the quiet night was filled with sadness. There were murmurs of grief and sobbing that covered the autumn decay with a living blanket of broken hearts. Darlie stamped the ground under her feet and giggled. She wanted to smash the broken spirits into the ground.

"You are all glass dolls, stomped to pieces under my shoes," Darlie snickered, "Cry as much as you like."

The thudding of Darlie's feet and the ensuing cracking of twigs and dried leaves brought the stalking group to her. When she saw the first men and women approach her, she waved her long tongue around like a whip. She caught one of them, wrapping her tongue around the man. Her captive gasped with horror.

A woman of his kind sliced the air and Darlie's tongue with a machete she had used to cut through the brush. Darlie gagged and spun around, her teeth gleaming in the woman's flashlight. The woman reached for her revolver. She shot Darlie in the chest several times with her bullets, sending one of the tiny missiles clean through Darlie's heart. The ancient witch crumbled to the waiting earth, which embraced her with cold arms and would not let her go.

Messengers from hell slithered through the mat of leaves and twigs. Darlie answered their call. She let them take her in.

The freed man and his female liberator observed the empty spot where Darlie had been. The woman kicked the leaves and twigs aside. She felt only the ground.

"There's no hole. Where did the beast go?" asked the woman.

"I did not see anyone," said the man.

"Yes, you did. She had her foul tongue wrapped around you like a snake."

"It just looked that way in the dark," said the man. "So, you did see someone."

"She must have gotten away," said the man. "Must have?" said the woman.

"We've seen a lot of weird stuff. What's one more?" said the man.

The woman nodded. "Yes, let her go. What's one more stranger."

Miranda and Wen circumvented the searchers who never found Darlie, or Miranda, or Wen. They never looked in the right places.

From the outside, the house seemed to have only a past. The clouded windows and cracked façade seemed to indicate all the life it would ever have had already happened. One could look upon the dwelling and dream of the memories that must walk its halls in solitude. One would never guess, unless one had been touched by a cold breath, that the house had a present and a future.

Evening broke open, spilling out the moon and stars. The diamonds overhead sparkled with organized brilliance. Beneath the twinkling masses of light, Miranda and Wen walked. The autumn breezes had laid bare the outstretched arms of the trees. Only the evergreens bore the green of eternal summer. Miranda avoided these tokens of perpetual life. She had forgotten how much she used to love them.

A raccoon bared its teeth and snarled at the two wanderers. The animal's eyes gleamed like lanterns in the moonlight. Miranda charged the raccoon, snarling in her turn and reaching with a claw-like grasp. The animal held its ground, but the raccoon was no match for her strong grip and her ruthless teeth. Wen chuckled with delight as the two of them ripped the animal open. After they had finished, Miranda and Wen chased one another through the trees. They jumped from one shadow to the other, hiding their existence. They screeched and laughed.

It was the laughter that sparked the flame of memory in Miranda. Laughter used to set her spirit free. *My soul will never be free, again*, thought Miranda to herself. She hid from Wen behind a tree. Her heart pounded, an empty bell that could not make music.

Wen came out of the darkness and leaped at her. "Boo!" he said, "I got you." He did not touch her. He stood and gazed at her, not speaking. His face was devoid of joy.

Miranda was suddenly overcome by a frightening hunger. "One way or the other, I can't walk two paths," Miranda found herself saying. "I'm hungry, Wen."

Wen nodded. "So am I. The raccoon was not enough." "What will we do?" said Miranda.

"We'll do what comes naturally. We'll look for something to eat," said Wen.

"Remember, no one good, only bad people," said Miranda. Miranda and Wen walked through the woods. Lights were visible through the thickness of trees and undergrowth. The heavy thumping of bass could be heard through the walls of the club. The house of entertainment sat just outside the trees and thicket. It was on a dirt road that eventually connected to a highway. It had been raided by the police from time to time, but this night the parking lot was not filled with milling uniforms. There were assorted vehicles in the dark, the transportation of anyone who had come to drink at this well.

A man and woman stood beside one parked vehicle. They made broad gestures. Their voices were indiscernible and shrill. They seemed to be arguing. Their words were permanently intertwined. Streams of steam followed each vehement denial. The woman shot one, last invective at her mate before she ran into the noisy building, past the line of silent engines whose windshields were idly collecting frost. The man was left outside, alone in fuming contemplation.

At this opportunity, Wen leaped upon him. Miranda followed and joined in. Sinking their sharp teeth into his neck, they chortled with glee as they ripped and sucked him dry. The man was too startled to cry out. He succumbed to shock before he could offer resistance. Miranda and Wen had their way with him.

When they were done, they ran joyfully back into the woods. Miranda leaped through the trees with gladness. For the first time in her life, she felt like a healthy, young animal and nothing more. She glanced at Wen, who ran beside her. He looked back at her, reveling in his moment. Miranda was disappointed that his expression did not share his satisfaction with her. She perceived a kind of mistrust of her in the way he held back.

"How did you like that?' called Miranda to Wen. He ran on ahead of her. He did not answer.

Miranda looked back at the remains of the dead man. She couldn't see him anymore through the thick darkness of trees and the kindness of night. She knew no one had discovered him, yet. The silence stretched from the parking lot to where she stood. She looked toward Wen, who was well ahead of her. Oddly, Miranda could still see him as though the trees and lack of light could never stand between them.

"Wen," she said, quietly, and he stopped. He turned to face her. His face was a somber map of personal interest and thought. He walked toward Miranda. Miranda felt a twinge of self-pity and regret.

"How do you feel, now that we've done it for the first time?" Miranda said to Wen.

"How do you feel?" countered Wen.

"We have to kill. It is our nature, now. We have no choice."

Wen looked through her at some point she could not see. "Part of me felt his life leaving him," said Wen.

"His life entered you for safekeeping. He was bad. He is kept from evil by you," said Miranda.

"That is not true, Miranda. That is not how it felt," said Wen.

"This is what you said you wanted."

"No, Miranda, we bargained. This was the settlement." "This was a choice you and I made after we had no choice.

That's what you mean. And I am a part of the trap," said Miranda.

"No, Miranda, you are not a part of the trap. You are the whole trap," said Wen. "If it were not for you, I would not be where I am now."

"None of this is my fault," said Miranda.

"Yes, Miranda, all of it is your fault. All of this is because of you," said Wen, "You didn't need to chew on that man with so much gusto. You didn't seem to mind at all that he was still moving. Maybe for all her worthlessness, Darlie was right about you. There has always been something of the murderer about you."

Miranda sucked the bitter seed Wen had planted within her. She could still feel pain and repulsion, after all.

"You always had Darlie in your heart, no matter what you said. Wen, don't go," Miranda said as Wen turned and ran away.

Miranda stared at the face of the dark woods that had swallowed Wen. The tree branches had not even rustled with his departure. Miranda followed his tracks to the house. The cold, dark halls barely echoed with her footsteps. She was fading away into some other dimension of being. The part of her that could lick a man's heart till it stopped beating was becoming all of her.

She found Wen by an ash-strewn hearth. The fire had gone out long ago.

"What will we do, now, Wen?"

"Why do you ask me? I am looking for an exit," said Wen, "I don't know if I will find one."

"There is no way out of eternity, Wen."

"There has to be a way to make right what is wrong. We are wrong. I see that when I look at you. You are someone else, now," said Wen.

"No, I am who I have always been."

"Maybe that's the crux of the matter, Miranda. You are no different from what you have always, really been. Your true soul is showing itself," said Wen. He turned to face Miranda. He kept his sad and cold eyes upon her as he walked toward her. In the darkness, he lifted in the air what he had concealed in his hand. The long stake was fashioned from a tree and he plunged it through Miranda's heart.

Miranda's eyes squinted shut in outrage. An awful scream spun out of her mouth, rising from her insides and spiraling out into the world beyond the forsaken house. She was heard by those persons who had come seeking killers in the woods.

The body in the parking lot had already been found. Terror had sparked the ensuing hunt that now rushed to find the screamer and be at her side.

"Now, it's my turn," said Wen to his still and supine Miranda.

Shouters knocked down the door and crashed through the

windows. Stampeding feet rushed into the room where Miranda lay. Wen pulled the sharp stake out of Miranda and rushed the first group that entered. A volley of shots from several guns brought him to his knees, and then onto his face, not far from where Miranda lay. He reached out and clutched her with his hand as he took his journey onward to another life.

Their bodies were covered with grief and soil. Time quieted mourning. The noise of tears was laid to rest with those that had passed on.

The dusty house remained standing. Recent events became memories and the abandoned building retreated into anonymity. Only the curious paid any attention to the empty halls and the creaking beams.

Darlie looked down as the floor groaned under her feet. "It's all different, now," said Darlie to Miranda and Wen, "Though we are together, the three of us."

"We are the same, but there are still differences," said Miranda. "No grave can hold us. This completes us but gives me no satisfaction."

"Stop complaining," said Darlie, "Things could be worse. You could be like you were, before."

Outside, under the cloud-banked winter sky, a car pointed bright headlights through the skeleton trees and the heavy evergreens. The car headed right for the old, abandoned house and parked outside.

Darlie, Miranda, and Wen waited in gleeful silence. "They don't know we can't die," whispered Darlie. "Shhh," said Wen, silencing her.

"We're all three of us still friends in spite of everything," said Miranda, in a very low tone.

Wen waved her to silence. And silence was all that remained as the house and the grounds were still.

"Curiosity seekers," said Darlie. "No, they are dinner," said Miranda. "Shhhhh," said Wen.

Darlie made the floorboards creak, again. There was no noise in response. Yet, the house seemed more still than it had before. Someone was listening.

The floorboards creaked, again. This time, they were not sure if it were one of the three of them, or the persons who had entered the house. The trio was stilled with anticipation when the doors crashed open and a crowd bearing crosses spilled into the room. Wen roared. Miranda and Darlie hissed. The three friends drooled from their bared teeth. Before the dawn came, Miranda, Wen, and Darlie had been impaled with stakes in their hearts. They were laid in boxes in a mildewed corner in the cellar of the abandoned domain.

And there they lay while the house around and above them was renovated until it was like new. The land around the house was pruned and refined. The statues were cleaned. The water flowed again in the fountains and the fishponds.

A brick wall was built around the three coffins. A heavy door was fitted into the wall. The door was locked and bolted. Only one man had the key. From time to time he entered the room where the three lay to make sure they were still sleeping. He wanted no escape from his captive monsters. He did not know from whence the two women and the man had come, nor did he care.

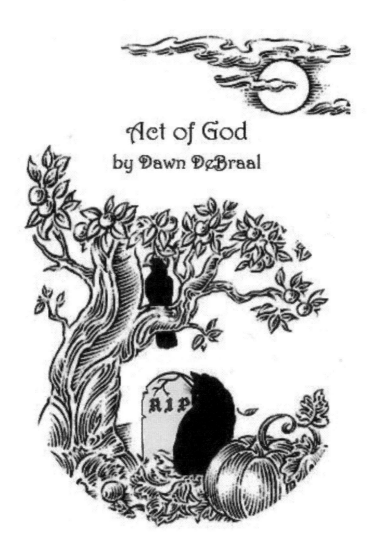

Act of God
by Dawn DeBraal

She was fifteen and being forced to take her little brother out Trick or Treating. How humiliating.

"Put the princess costume on," her mother said. Angela rolled her eyes.

"Please, Angie," her little brother Bradley pleaded in his cute four-year-old beg. She sighed and rummaged through her closet for the stupid princess dress. She was amazed at how much better it looked on her this year. A year's worth of maturity had her looking pretty good. She even found the fake rhinestone tiara at the bottom of the closet. She would show Bradley a good time, she decided. Who wouldn't want to show off this costume?

Angie piled her hair up, attaching the tiara. She put the dangle earrings on and donned on the white gloves. The pale blue dress looked perfect on her. She secretly loved the way she looked, but she wouldn't tell her mother and father this. She had to act as if she was doing them a huge favor by taking her brother out. They wanted to watch over the house to make sure the pranksters didn't do anything, and to hand out candy to the neighbors.

Angie came down from her room. The look on her parents' face said it all. Maybe they shouldn't have forced her to wear the costume. It was precious. She laughed.

"Come on, Bradley, are you ready?"

He screamed in excitement. He was dressed as some intergalactic soldier of some sort with a light beam and a cape. They all looked the same this year. Everyone wanted to be Mace Adams, the warrior who saved Galactica Major. The movie had played over and over this summer. When Angie started at the front door, there was another Mace Adams walking across their yard. She called Bradley to follow her. It was just getting dark outside.

"Don't hold my hand. I'm almost five," Bradley told her.

She let go of his hand.

"Okay, but stay close," Angie said.

While she waited for him, Bradley ran up each walkway, shouting "Trick or Treat" with the other kids. The doors opened and candy was put in each bag. Angie thought she would be able to convince her brother to share some of the good stuff - not the taffy stuff, but the chocolates – if she played her cards right. As the night crept in, she turned on the flashlights and gave one to Bradley.

The streetlights gave off enough light, but Bradley was starting to run with a bigger crowd, and now there were three of Mace Adams in his group. He was the middle-sized one. The flashlight helped her see him right away. Bradley allowed her to drop the flashlight into the pumpkin bag. The light shone through, making the bag look cool, so Bradley didn't argue with her, and she could see him instantly in the crowd.

Angie stood down by the road, watching the kids collect the candy. A car, some hot-rod looking thing, pulled up on the curb. The guy behind the wheel beeped.

"Hey, Princess. I Wanna Lay Ya. Get it? Princess Leia! Ha ha!"

Angela ignored the guy. She felt creepy and resented the guy for making fun of her. She pretended not to notice him. Bradley joined her again, and they walked to the next house. The car sped off. She was relieved the guy was gone.

Mr. Danbury, her neighbor, came up to them. "Did that guy say anything to you?"

Angela looked embarrassed she said he was just being a jerk. Mr. Danbury told her to stick close, and he would watch over her and Bradley. Angela felt a little better. If you couldn't trust the neighbor, who could you trust?

They reached the end of the block. Bradley wanted to go around the corner. Mr. Danbury said it was time to go home, but Bradley could only see the endless lights down the street.

Mr. Danbury turned to Angela. "I think it's best you both

come with me. The way you fill out that dress could spell trouble for you and Bradley." Angie flushed with embarrassment.

"I think we will be fine. Thank you, Mr. Danbury," Angela responded tersely. She grabbed Bradley's hand and went around the corner. *What a jerk.* How could he think it was all right to say something like that to her? She had a good mind to tell her parents. Angela allowed Bradley to hit a few more houses. She didn't want to be anywhere near Mr. Danbury. He was as bad as the punk in the muscle car, just sneakier about it.

"I'm tired," Bradley suddenly said. "Okay. Let's go and sit at the bus stop."

Angela walked Bradley to the bus stop, and they sat on the bench. He picked through his bag.

"Wow, I have a lot of candy!"

Angela peeked in his bag. It looked like there was plenty of chocolate. She would have to bribe her brother when they got home.

"You do! Wait until we get home to check it over. You know what Mom and Dad said." Bradley pouted, but knew that was one of the rules their parents set so that he could go trick or treating. It was already 8:45. Trick or treating would be over at nine. "Do you still want to hit the other side of the street on the way home? We have fifteen minutes!"

Bradley jumped up and pulled her across the street. They were back on their block. She watched Bradley get a second wind as he ran back and forth from the sidewalk to the doors and back to the sidewalk. Angela could tell his little legs were getting tired out. One by one, the porch lights turned off, the sign that trick or treating was over. Bradley's face fell, but she could tell he was bushed and didn't have it in him anymore to continue to run. They walked with plenty of other people toward their house.

The orange car showed up again. Angela looked straight

ahead and continued to walk. Looking around, she realized it was just older kids walking home. Most of the parents had given up after eight. She wished they had done the same.

"Princess! Yoo-hoo, Princess," Shouted the creep.

Bradley asked her, "Why is that guy calling you? Do you know him?"

Angela told Bradley to keep his eyes forward, ignore the guy and keep walking. They were still pretty far from home. She regretted not going back with her creepy neighbor. He would never do anything to her, at least not while Bradley was there. She could feel her eyes tear up. Why did someone think it was okay to treat anyone like this? Make them fear, make them feel bad about themselves. Stupid princess dress, why had she worn it? She'd thought she looked so beautiful, and now she had drawn attention to herself.

The car stopped. Angela could feel her heart pounding. "Bradley, run home as fast as you can. Tell Mom and Dad about this car, an orange Camaro with a black roof."

She stopped and pushed her brother, turning to meet the punk who suddenly hesitated. He did not expect that. A little girl taking a stand. She had guts. It stopped him dead in his tracks. Angie snapped a picture and sent it.

"I have sent your picture to the Sheriff 's Department," she bluffed. She ran down and took another picture of his license plate and sent that. He looked panicked. His plan, whatever it was, had been destroyed. The scare angle had been turned on him. He was angry with himself for not anticipating her cleverness. He walked up to her.

"So? There's no law in talking to someone."

She took another picture of him, sending it. "Stop harassing me. I have asked you to leave me alone. Your picture and license plate have been forwarded. Please go away and leave me alone."

Angela started walking. She thought she had successfully

ditched the punk. She continued at a pace that was fast, but not panic running. She heard the car start up. Relieved, she thought he was moving on, but he hadn't stopped. He followed her at a close distance. She heard a cough. He was behind her, and someone else was driving the car! She hadn't seen the passenger. Now she was doubly worried. She pushed 9-1-1.

"9-1-1, what is your emergency?"

"I'm being followed. My name is Angela. I live at 225 Saunders Road. There is a man driving an orange Camaro, license plate number…"

He knocked the phone out of her hand, then turned it off. "Get in the car."

Angela knew if she got into the car, she would be dead. She started to run, shouting. She went up to the nearest house and pounded on the door. The curtain cracked.

"Please help me, this guy is trying to force me into the car."

The man came up behind her. "Ma'am this is my wayward daughter. She is fifteen, and she is dressed like a tart, walking the streets at night. Look at her! What would you do if you were her father?" He turned to her. "You will go home now, young lady!" Angela watched as the woman closed the curtain quickly. The man grabbed her arm and squeezed it tightly and painfully maneuvered her down the sidewalk. The driver turned his head away quickly, but not before she saw him.

The driver, who moved back to the passenger side of the car, was her neighbor, Mr. Danbury.

"Shut up, Angela, and get in the car. We'll drive you home."

She screamed, and the woman shouted out of the house door. "Let her go, or I'm calling the cops!" The woman stood in the door punching the phone.

"My name is Angela Slater, at 225 Saunders Road, please! Help me."

The guy forced her into the car, and they took off down the street. Angela knew she had to be smart. Suddenly they stopped in front of her house.

"Get out," said Mr. Danbury. "What?" she was stunned.

"Get out. What did you think we were doing? Dressed like that, you were asking for trouble. Consider this your warning to watch what you wear in public."

Angela got out of the car. Mr. Danbury did, too. He walked her up to the house. Her parents opened the door, looking at Angela strangely.

"Is everything all right?" Her father pulled Angela into the house.

Mr. Danbury stepped forward. "We wanted to make sure Angela got home safely." He turned to her and looked her up and down.

"Trick or treat, Angela." He laughed.

Angela couldn't believe what had happened. How could they do that to her?

"Bradley! Where's Bradley?" she asked.

"Here I am! Look at all this candy!" he shouted.

"Bradley, didn't you tell mom and dad what I told you to say?"

He shook his head. "I told them you were outside talking to some people."

Angela started to shake. This couldn't be real, what they did to her. The phone rang, and her mother answered.

"Yes, she just got home, safe and sound. Thank you!" Her mother looked at Angela, confused. "That was the police department. They wanted to make sure you got home safe and sound. What is going on?"

Angela told her it was all a mistake, that a lady had call the police on a bunch of teens. She told her parents she was going to bed.

Her phone buzzed.

"It was real nice to see you tonight." The voice belonged to Donald Danbury.

Angela dropped the phone. What was the man doing? She

was freaked. She couldn't go to sleep now. She needed to find a way to get rid of this guy. It was bad enough to know he watched her tonight, but somehow, he had her phone number. He was going to make her life a living hell.

Angela waited until everyone was in bed.

"Good night, Bradley!" she called out to him. She was still wearing the princess dress, and it wasn't a Princess I Want to Lay Ya dress. She still had the crown on. She was going to make Donald's life a living hell instead.

Angela climbed down the arbor outside her room. It was dark save for the streetlights. She walked down the sidewalk dressed as the princess until she came up to Donald Danbury's house. She peeked in the window. The other creep was with them. They were watching a horror movie, drinking beer with their feet up on the coffee table. They would say something and laugh. She knew they were talking about her. What they had done to her, the scare they had given her, was just the beginning of what the two were capable of. They were dangerous, and would only get more so, and Angela could not let that happen.

Donald got up and walked to the refrigerator, getting out another couple of beers. He handed one to the guy who owned the orange Camaro. They toasted by clicking the necks of their bottles. She hated that they were enjoying their lives while she was forced to live in fear after tonight's experience. She decided she would get even. She texted Donald back. She heard the ting.

"Holy Shit!" Donald Danbury jumped off the couch, whooping.

"What?" asked his partner in crime.

"She answered back! Look at this." He showed the phone to his friend.

She had texted, *I don't think what you did was funny tonight.*
He quickly texted back.

"It wasn't meant to be funny, it was meant to be a warning.

You are too beautiful for your own good." He was excited to see if she responded. Angela quickly turned off the pings and warnings on her phone. It wouldn't do to have them knowing she was standing outside their window.

She needed a weapon. Why hadn't she brought one with her? She looked around and found a heavy branch. It had the heft of a shillelagh, stout and solid. The wind picked up, and it looked like they were going to have a storm. Angela moved from under the old tree which swayed in the breezes back and forth.

"I'm gonna have a smoke," said the other guy. Angela had no idea who he was, but the door slammed at the back of the house. She watched him step up to the tree, where he looked down to light his cigarette. He took a deep drag and was sighing with relief when she punched him in the stomach with the end of the branch. He didn't know what hit him, and the wind was knocked out of him. He leaned forward in pain. Angela brought the stout stick down on his head, caving in his skull. The man fell down into the grass and didn't move.

Did I kill him? She watched his lifeless body. She had no idea she could do all this damage with a stick. Her martial arts training over the past eight years had paid off. It was funny how it didn't even upset her to see the scum on the ground, blood coming from his head.

By this time, Donald wondered what had happened to his friend. Angela hid behind the tree. The wind had picked up and was thrashing the branches. She was a little scared of the tree toppling over.

"Eddie!" Donald called out the back door. Through the streetlights, he could see his friend's form on the ground. The door caught in the wind and blew it shut with a loud slam. Donald Danbury staggered drunkenly out to see what had happened to his friend. He bent over.

"Eddie, what the hell. Are you all right?" Danbury knew

there was something drastically wrong with his friend. Suddenly the chunk of wood struck his skull and cracked him open, and he fell next to his friend, moaning and groaning. He grabbed Angela's ankle. She screamed as she pulled herself forward to get away from his grip. She hit him a few more times. He let go of her ankle to protect his head.

A lightning bolt strike the tree. Angela ran toward the house. The tree cracked loudly, and a huge branch fell on Eddie and Donald, crushing them both. Angela took the club with her. She hoped that when the two men were found, they would call it an accidental death.

She sneaked back to her house, climbing the arbor. She took a shower and washed the remains of the brain matter off the club. The two deserved what they got. She scrubbed and scrubbed until the wood came clean, and then she hid the club in her closet. Trying to go to sleep was lost on her now with the storm raging outside and what she had done to the two men who had tried to scare her. She knew they would never have left her alone. She looked at the message she had left. She texted another message, thanking Mr. Danbury for the ride home.

She paced back and forth. The wind was blowing sideways, and her mother shouted for them all to get into the basement. There was a tornado coming. They went down the stairs and waited out the storm. All the lights went off for a time. When the wind died down, there was nothing but pounding rain. They came back upstairs to the sound of a fire engine that had stopped near their house. Her father ran outside to find out what had happened.

"Danbury's house is on fire!" her father shouted. He ran over to see if he could help the firemen. An electrical fire engulfed the entire house, which was a total loss.

They found Danbury and his friend crushed under the tree

in the backyard.

Angela applied the last of her costume while looking in the mirror. She had been roped into taking Bradley trick or treating again this year. He was almost six, and he wanted to go as a pirate. Angela would not go as a princess again. She was smarter this year with her choice of costume. She picked up the pipe and put it between her bearded lips. She wore an elfin hat cocked to the side, along with pointy shoes with small bells on them. She clattered down the stairs. Her parents laughed at her costume. Angela was dressed at a leprechaun, complete with a shillelagh.

"I'm so glad you got into the spirit this year!" her mother smiled. "Thank you for taking Bradley!"

"No problem. Bye, Mom and Dad."

Angela allowed Bradley to run ahead of her. He carried his bag with the flashlight in it. They would stay to the designated route tonight. Bradley had his pirate costume on with a feathered stuffed parrot on his shoulder. Inspired by his swashbuckling outfit, he ran alongside her, swinging his saber back and forth.

They passed the empty lot where Danbury's house used to stand. The whole neighborhood talked about how the fire was started by the same lightning strike that brought down the tree on top of both Mr. Danbury and his creepy friend Eddie. It had been ruled an Act of God.

"Come on, Angela!" Bradley said. He ran up the yard to holler and trick or treat at the next neighbor's house. She watched him closely and followed behind him. This year, she wasn't worried about their safety.

She walked softly and carried a big stick.

Dawn DeBraal lives in rural Wisconsin with her husband Red, two rat terriers, and a cat. She has discovered that her love of telling a good story can be written. Published stories with Palm-sized press, Spillwords, Mercurial Stories, Potato Soup Journal, Edify Fiction, Zimbell House Publishing, Clarendon House Publishing, Blood Song Books, Black Hare Press, Fantasia Divinity, Cafelit, Reanimated Writers, Guilty Pleasures, Unholy Trinity, The World of Myth, Dastaan World, Vamp Cat, Runcible Spoon, Siren's Call, Falling Star Magazines, 2019 Pushcart Nominee and others.

https://www.amazon.com/Dawn-DeBraal/e/B07STL8DLX?

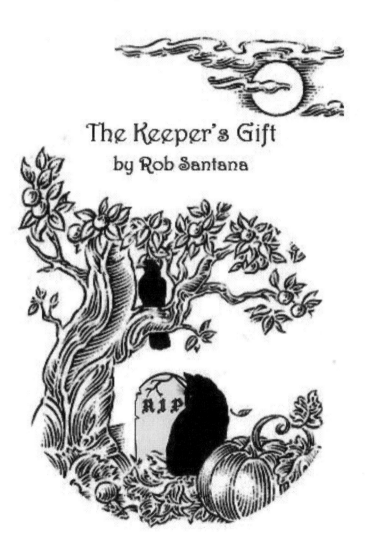

The Keeper's Gift
by Rob Santana

Dave and Troy had been warned by Miss Fritz, who lived across the street from the Keeper's aging one-family house.

"I wouldn't trick or treat there," she said to the pre-teens. "Not this year."

Dave's costume for this blustery Halloween night came straight out of a popular comic book detective from before his time, complete with yellow fedora, matching wool overcoat and a fake hook nose. Troy paraded the narrow small-town street as the gray-suited Sherlock Holmes, carrying with him the signature un-lit pipe. They regarded the red-brick home where the mysterious Keeper lived alone, with its shuttered windows and billowing tar-black chimney. The lawn was scraggly, unkempt. Weeds grew instead of grass during the summer.

"Does he ever go out?" asked Troy. He had to continually adjust the hat, which seemed too large for his head. Miss Fritz shook her head.

"Not since he got back from jail," she said, her withered sixty-five-year-old frame shuddering. She stared at the chimney, shifted, and gasped. A swarm of costumed kids had approached the Keeper's doorbell.

"No! Uh-uh! Do *not!* Do *not!*" She waved them off the sidewalk facing the gravel path. They frowned and moved on to the next house. The Keeper's sanctuary was situated fifty yards between other, more refined dwellings.

"When'd he get back?" Dave asked.

The retired schoolteacher kept gazing at the chimney. "Last month. He hasn't stepped out since," she said in a hushed voice. "For all we know he could be looking out his window at us. At *me.*"

She pulled the boys inside and shut the door. Her living room smelled of old cat, dull and musty. Dave hoped she would hand out her plastic trophy of assorted candies and coins. She hovered over them instead, her eyes wide, her lips quivering.

"You boys must promise not to repeat what I'm about to tell you."

Troy gulped. "About the Keeper?"

"Oh, yessss," she hissed. "Have you ever noticed, on your way to and back from school, the moans coming from somewhere inside his cellar's window?"

Dave imagined a low, guttural whine, a pleading din, like a dog on a leash waiting outside for its owner. "Is it his dog?"

She leaned forward, her wrinkled face inches from his fake nose. "He doesn't own one."

Dave and Troy, friends since kindergarten, exchanged wary glances.

"Promise me," she insisted.

"I promise," the boys said in unison.

She pushed aside the drab yellow curtain, peered out, and closed it tightly. "There's a demon trapped inside… What's so funny, David?"

Dave had to stifle a grin. "Ain't no such thing. Is there?"
"Like, what kinda demon?" Troy asked, his mouth open.

"A *female* demon," she said. "Dark, scaly skin and eyes the color of hate. There's no whites in its eyes but red. Its mouth a nasty gash of rotted fangs. Its wings like that of a bat's."

"How do you know the demon is female?"

She straightened and scowled. "That's enough for now. You stand warned. Keep away from the Keeper." She opened the door to let them out. No candy or coins tonight. Bummer.

Every small-town neighborhood has its own psychological bully. Evansville, population eight-hundred fifty, had Willie, who was dressed as the tired, clichéd Dracula. How original, thought Dave, as he crossed paths with his hulking crew-cut classmate and neighbor. Willie shifted to block Dave and Troy's path.

"Where you headed, hook beak?"

"Gimme a break, Willie," said Dave, immune by now to Willie's Gestapo tactics. It occurred to him that Willie would look cooler revved up as a Nazi stormtrooper. He'd counted ten kids sporting either the Drac or wicked witch costumes. How lame.

"Who a' you supposed to be?" Willie asked. "Hook Beak."

Willie turned to Troy, smirking. "And you?"

Troy looked embarrassed, palming his thin flashlight. "Umm-Sherlock?"

Willie chuckled. "Sooo un-Halloween, your outfits, no lie."

"Yeah, nothing original like *yours*." Dave shot back.

Willie let that one pass. "What were you guys doing in Miss Fritz's joint anyway? I heard she's givin' out nada this year."

"I'm hip," Dave said, holding to his promise not to divulge the old woman's story. He was about to pass Willie, who held up a hand.

"Me, I'm ringing Mr. Lynch's doorbell. Care to join me?"

"I'd skip the Keeper's house," Troy blurted.

"The who?"

"That's what Miss Fritz calls him." Dave said.

"Skip Mr. Lynch?" Willie asked. "After what he gave out last Halloween? Are you serious?"

The Keeper's treats to the brigade of kids that resided within his province had been overly expensive: the latest in PSP3's *Super Streetfighter* series or video game consoles. To Dave's amazement, no parent questioned the generosity and there were no reports to the police. A rumor spread that Mr. Lynch worked at a warehouse that had relocated sometime in August.

"And who knows what he might be giving out this time?" Willie said. "Worth a shot, dontcha think?"

"Pass," said Dave.

"Me, too," Troy murmured to his leather lace-up shoes.

Willie nodded, hands on hips.

"Wimps. I'm guessing Miss Fritz didn't tell you about the time she practically invited herself into Mr. Lynch's house."

Dave cocked an eyebrow. "When was this?"

"She went straight to my dad after and told him about the *stank*.'"

Willie's father, a police officer, had been off duty the night Miss Fritz pounded on his door. She had decided that Mr. Lynch, a bachelor pushing sixty, was attractive after spotting him leaving for work one early morning. His thick forest of white hair and smooth, clean-shaven face surprised her. She chanced an offer of baked cookies that night, hoping he would invite her in. It was a bold move, but she was lonely 'and drunk,' according to Willie's dad.

"My dad could smell the booze on her breath," Willie said, sniggering.

Dave was in no hurry to get past Willie now. "What happened?" he asked, picturing the spinster alone with the Keeper.

"The old prune claimed that once inside, she heard someone hammering on Lynch's cellar door, crying out like a walrus in pain. And that this – *'stank'*, she called it – dropkicked her nostrils. And that's when Lynch panicked and screamed at her to haul ass. She did and ran to our house."

"Then what?" Troy asked, glancing over his shoulder at the Keeper's home. Willie grinned. There was a camp-fire tone to his delivery.

"Then this," he whispered. "My dad? Got mad curious cuz this guy Lynch is real secretive about his whereabouts, never speaks to anyone, yet the last three Halloweens he's been handing out these awesome treats like they was candy, only it ain't candy, is it?"

Dave still played with the pricey game console the Keeper had given him the year before, and the retro Game Boy the year before that. "So, what'd your father do?" he asked.

Willie smiled. "It's when the old prune claimed some kind of demon was kept hidden in the cellar and was causing the smell that my father formed this notion."

"Notion?"

"Yeah, dummy, notion. That maybe, just maybe, the old man had kidnapped someone and was holdin' him in the cellar against his will. So, he knocked on Lynch's door, right? Began questioning him. Then he asked what that board was with the numbers on it. A kind of flat board. That's when Lynch went batshit. Dad had to call in reinforcements."

"How come?"

"Dumb-ass! The old guy punched Dad and had to be dragged into a patrol car. The assault charge sent him to jail. Except the precinct never bothered to get a warrant 'cuz they thought Miss Fritz was a nutcase."

Willie beamed, fingering the bow tie that colored his dark blue tuxedo. He nodded towards the Keeper's house. "He served his time, got off early. And now he's back."

Dave noticed that the other trick or treaters avoided the chain of houses that led to the Keeper's area.

"So, who's coming with me?" Willie said. "I bet he's got the latest Omega Collection behind that door, just waitin' to be handed out."

Dave backed away. "I'm happy with what I've got." "Me too," said Troy.

Willie sneered. "You guys are pathetic."

"Didn't your dad warn you not to disturb him?"

Four blocks down, other masked kids entered a deli with their black and orange bags.

"My dad's on duty tonight," Willie said. "What he don't know won't hurt me."

Dave craned his neck. The deli clerk had filled the kids' bags with goodies. "Not tonight, Willie."

Troy nodded. "Yeah, maybe next year, Willie."

Dave and Troy opted to watch Willie from a safe distance. The Faux Dracula rang the Keeper's doorbell and waited.

No response.

Willie buzzed again.

A shadow spilled under the door. Dave edged closer. Troy stayed put.

"Is he crazy?" Troy said. Dave shushed him.

The shadow seemed painted on, like an illusion that teased the senses with its unforeseen stillness. Willie swiveled his head towards the boy detectives, then dipped his head at the shadow. Was the Keeper aware of Willie's presence? The shadow persisted with its lull. From where Dave stood, Willie looked comical in his Dracula rig, his cape billowing, alone, with no one to sink his fangs into.

The shadow shifted and disappeared. Dracula turned to Dave with a quizzical expression.

Dave, with Troy behind him, scurried over to Willie and yanked him to the side of the house. Willie did not object to this show of spunk from Dave. His eyes were rattling like pin balls. Dave now knew he'd been allowed to take charge.

He pointed to the ground-level window that held a partial view of the cellar. Troy, inspired by Dave's boldness, took out his flashlight and trained it on the darkness below.

"Now you're talking, Sherlock," Willie said. "Willie, be quiet," Dave warned.

"Sorry."

They hunched closer, the detectives and the vampire, to the square porthole. The flashlight's weak beam nonetheless illuminated a shape writhing on the wet, chalky cement floor alongside a decaying pillar. It undulated, squirming, until its round distended belly swerved and faced the ceiling. Dave tensed.

Demon. Female.

"It's – it's pregnant," David said, staring down at the beast's ballooning paunch. It looked ready to burst. Willie had seen enough. He raced towards Miss Fritz's porch and watched from there, bug-eyed, perhaps waiting for Dave and Troy to follow suit. It was only when the beast let go a hideous bellow of pain that the boys joined Willie.

Dave regretted not bringing his iPhone. Troy and Willie's presence leveled his breathing. The section was now devoid of revelers. The empty stillness chilled Dave. The wind had picked up. Leaves scattered along the pavement as if on cue. Sparrows began chirping and a black, muscular cloud strangled the moon.

Troy shivered. His Sherlock costume was too light for the sudden change in climate. It had gotten colder. The wind swept debris along his line of vision. The Keeper's lights shut off as one.

Then the chimney's cavity began to glow. "What the f-" said Dave.

Willie lost his nerve and banged on Miss Fritz's door. Like a good Samaritan, she let them scamper into her home, then shut the door. They rushed to the floor-length window and looked out, their knees indenting the green sofa as Miss Fritz stood behind them.

"I knew it!" she shouted.

The bowels of the chimney shimmered to life. From within, a batch of what appeared to be large birds streamed out and flew east and west, circling the roof before diving towards the street. A woman wearing a housecoat further down opened her door and stepped out, looking up.

A bird, or whatever it was, swooped down and attached itself to her face, its black, oily wings flapping maniacally as it pecked at her cheeks. Her screams echoed but no one surfaced.

She collapsed on the lawn as the thing clawed at her clothes, then shot to the sky. Miss Fritz drew back and made a noise in her throat. The creatures now cross-hatched the area, singing their dark songs, a swarm of destruction.

Garbage cans were toppled. A car's window was shattered. The witnesses in Miss Fritz's shelter froze, watching. Dave wondered if anyone had called the cops. There should have been police sirens heard by now.

From out of nowhere, one of the creatures slammed against the window and Dave could see its face as it pressed against the pane, its spindly hairy legs leaving a trail of slime as it slithered across the glass, its vast red eyes darting across the room until they fixed on Miss Fritz. The face looked vaguely human, pink in contrast to its sooty torso. Its teeth were not fangs but normal, a perfect row of ivories that would thrill a dentist. The tongue lashed out, imprinting its glop with a smooth slide along the surface.

Then the creature soared away, its residue a smear no one would dare wipe off. In the peripheral distance, a kid could be heard shouting. Doors opened and slammed shut. A lone police car braked. Its passengers sat frigid as the creatures swirled above them before vanishing *en masse* into the horizon.

No one moved or spoke for a full minute.

"Holy Jeez," Willie said, breaking the silence. Dave turned to Miss Fritz, whose bony hands clutched the buttons of her thick granny pajamas. She had backed up against the wall, tremoring, murmuring nonsense. He went to her.

"They're gone, Miss Fritz."

No one within the perimeters of that block could make sense of the pithy blitzkrieg of those winged animals. The local news at eleven focused on the Halloween festivities that took place along the commercial strip. The cops who had witnessed the horde filed it under 'bird frenzy.' Dave had to plead with them to check in on Mrs. Felton, the lone attack victim. Although amused by Dave's costume, they rejected his imploration to visit the Keeper's home.

It was Willie's father who took action later that night. The Keeper was eventually hand-cuffed and booked for harboring a… what?

"Dad saw it." Willie told Dave. It was pre-dawn Saturday morning. No school today. Time enough for neighbors to wander the street, some looking up, others in hushed conference.

"What was it?" Dave asked, ignoring his mother who stood waiting impatiently by the door one block over. Troy had been ordered to bed without protest.

"It's just like the old prune said, only Dad still won't call it a demon. I think he used the word 'mutation' in his report. Told me it looked like some kind of…oversized bat. I just wish he'd have let me see it for myself." He smiled. "Weird kind of fun, wasn't it? Best Halloween I ever had."

A throat cleared. They whipped their heads to face Miss Fritz. She crooked her finger at Dave. Willie slapped his palm on Dave's shoulder and walked away. Dave could hear his mother.

"In a minute!" he said, waving her off. Miss Fritz stood poised, the fear in her eyes gone. "You okay, Miss Fritz?"

"Come in for a moment, David." Her voice was slow and breathy. Dave looked back. Mother stomped her foot, frozen under Dave's front door. He raised a hand. Mother, in her night coat, exhaled, looked at the sky a moment, and waited. Dave entered Miss Fritz's house. She held up an object.

"Do you know what this is?"

Dave recognized it as a Ouija board and nodded.

"The Keeper showed it to me, David. The Keeper insisted I join him. Right there in his living room."

"Was that the time you… invaded his privacy and smelled the *stank*?"

"Oh, yessss." Her eyes bulged from the memory. Dave caught a glimpse of Mother approaching, her arms folded.

"I held back the truth, David. Who'd believe the truth?"

She took a step towards him. He stepped back. Mother rapped on the door. It was ignored. Miss Fritz would have to hurry her punchline.

"Miss Fritz, I have to go."

"He took the opportunity to involve me, David, into conjuring the father of the off-spring coming from that abomination in his cellar. Do you understand what I mean by that? If the Keeper hadn't allowed the planchette to slide off the surface of the board…"

Mother began hammering the door. "Ma! In a minute!"

Miss Fritz quickened her cadence. "If he hadn't left the board, David, he wouldn't have had to wet-nurse that thing! It materialized from below, David. From Hell itself! All the Keeper wanted was to be Santa Claus to the kids. It's all he cared about…"

Thump-Thump!

"Maaaa!"

"…giving out gifts, like it was Christmas. But that monster! It upset his plan, took up his time. When I refused to take part in the conjuring, he-he screamed at me to get out."

From outside: "David? Out! Now!"

Miss Fritz shoved the board under the sofa, opened the door, and smiled.

"Hello, Mrs. Wilder. Happy Halloween."

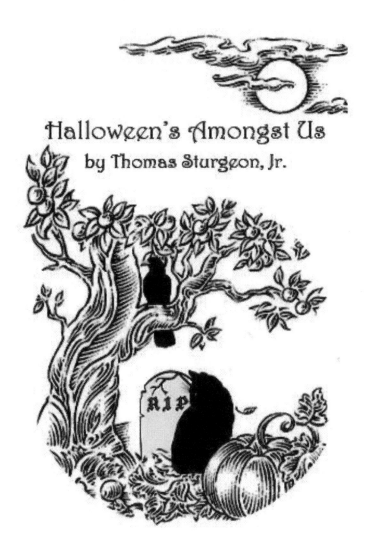

Halloween's Amongst Us

by Thomas Sturgeon, Jr.

Tonight was Halloween. I'd been looking forward to this night for months, now. I was looking forward to trick or treating with my sister, Macie. As we put on our costumes with Mom and Dad looking out for our safety, we were anxious to go out into the night in our own neighborhood, which was connected to the suburban area.

I dressed up like a clown and my mother applied the make-up to my face along with an orange wig. My sister, Macie, was dressed up like a vampire. My sister was older than I was. She was ten and I was eight.

Our uncle, Boris, had been staying with us as he was trying to get a job. He was older than my father and he was my father's brother. He was forty, and he had circles underneath his eyes. He had a very hollow voice, which boomed every time he spoke. He didn't like Halloween and didn't enjoy the parties and the candy and such as much as we did.

"Don't let the real monsters get you tonight. That would be bad. Just be careful out there with them kids you got, Jim," Boris told my father.

My father nodded at Boris as we got into the car with our parents.

There were tricksters nearby, and we had already gotten our candy from the first few houses on the left. We heard real screaming from further down in the neighborhood.

"Get in your houses immediately. There's monsters coming! There's monsters coming!"

We just ignored the panicked screams as we had finally caught sight of the real monsters that were heading our way. We shrieked as we ran across to our parents' car. Suddenly there was laughter all through the night, and we realized without a doubt, Halloween was amongst us. Our own nightmares were blending in with reality.

HALLOWEEN'S AMONGST US BY THOMAS STURGEON

SAMHAIN SECRETS

Thomas Sturgeon Jr is a 33-year-old author and poet living in Chatsworth, Georgia. He's been published in Black Hare Press's World's, Monsters anthologies as well as Organic Ink volume one by Dragon Soul Press. He loves his family and has

a cat named Tigger. He also has a story included in the upcoming Black Hare Press's Apocalypse.

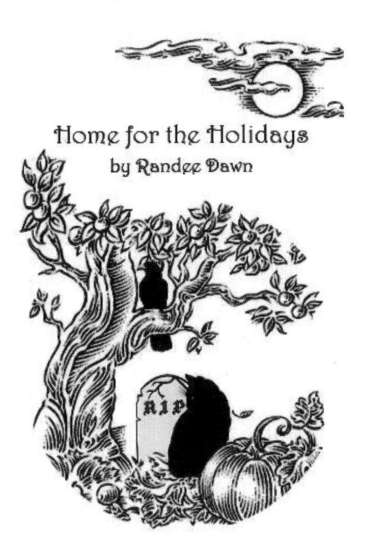

Home for the Holidays
by Randee Dawn

Giles Sanderson was a very bad man. Bu Jesus, he was a hell of a decorator.

But maybe I'm getting ahead of myself a little here. Nathan Jacobs is the name, and this is my territory. Some call it a neighborhood, but when the houses are this damn huge and each comes with three-quarters an acre of property, I start thinking of it as a territory.

I'm not alone. Folks 'round here mark their space better than dogs — why, just take a turn onto our main drag off I-35 and you'll see 'em, ten-foot high wood-slat fences with no space between for even a casual peep. 'Cause Christ knows you shouldn't be eyeballin' who's got Oprah on the tube or who's throwin' the ball with his kid, or even who's buryin' something under the old oak tree in the far back corner.

Or, in the case of Giles Sanderson, when you hauled off and backhanded your half-Mexican wife 'cross the chops for not scurrying fast enough to get the mud clots off the Italian tiled floors. Mud that you, Giles, had clomped in in the first place.

You wouldn't want nobody to be seeing that.

Yes, the backs of our territories are duly cut off from the rest of the world by the butt-ugliest of fences. But the front of those homes … well, that's a different story.

We're Dellians, y'see. That's the computer giant that employs us, and sets us up in these fine McMansions, one cardboard cut-out like the others, with just enough shades of difference in the rock façade or the hidden two-car garage or the overhanging porch to make it seem as though they were all thought up by original brains. But the truth is they all look the same, and when you're driving past, they're just a blur of beige-and-gray like the dusty ground that used to surround Austin, before the builders came and resettled the place.

Dell employees don't stay too long in one place. They come,

they unpack, they get settled, wave a little at the locals, and then they're off again, relocated like Army brats, only ruled by the whims of the computer industry. Houses in this area get to be two, three years old and they've gone through just about as many families. There are no long-timers.

Except us. The Jacobses. Or "Jacob's," if you're partial to the misprinted nameplate Jill bought me when we moved in. I've been here with her and the little ones – that's David and Astrid – goin' on five years now. I'm a Dellian like the others, but I've got a snug little executive spot with a window overlooking … well, overlooking I-35, but still *overlooking*. I know about half the folks who load in and load out of our little cul-de-sac – that's Tempest Cove to you. We wave and send over Jill's cranberry muffins when they arrive and sometimes, they wave back until they're waving goodbye a few months later. It happens.

Giles Sanderson never was a Dellian. He worked for one of those big box stores, somewhere up in management, with some kind of title that includes the word "vice," and that's about all I know about that. And, it turned out, his wife is allergic to cranberry.

I still remember when they moved in, 'bout four years ago, right directly south-west to our homestead. Jill did her muffin thing, comin' back to tell me that evening how the wife – never did get her name – stuck her head out of that front door like a mouse from its hidey-hole, took the basket, and darted right back in.

"It was dark in here," Jill told me later. "And they had the A/C on full blast, so I felt like I was peeking into a goddamned cave."

She also said that the wife had on sunglasses.

I put it out of my mind until our doorbell went that night: A big "ho ho ho" 'cause I'd bought that ringer with 17 different rings and since it was past December first, we were gearing up for the big holiday season. But on the other side of my front door was like a big "no no no." Without preliminary or nothing, Giles Sanderson – face all aflame like he was gonna stroke out – pushed my wife's basket into my arms.

A chewed-on muffin rolled on to the floor. Sharky, our golden retriever, shot forward and had it before dust could even think about gathering. That retriever is a garbage disposal, and no mistake.

"Just what the fuck do you think you're doing with my wife?" Sanderson steamed at me.

Behind me, I knew Jill was sticking her neck out of the kitchen. Such a loaded statement had to be seen to be believed.

"More importantly, what are you doing with my wife's basket?" I tried to get things light. Folks in Texas, even near the civilized oasis of Austin, do love their firearms.

Weirdly, it worked. The red went to pink and then to a sort of mottled orange-gray. Sanderson wasn't a very big man, with a flattop crew-cut an aircraft coulda landed on, and his clothes were just a cat's whisker from being too tight. I got the picture: Former jock. Holding off middle age with both hands. Probably pumped iron three hours a day.

Finally, when he realized I was kidding, he stuck out a meaty paw. Manicured fingernails glinted under our outside porch light. "Sorry. Overreacted. Just – just the wife's – she can't have berries. None. Blows her up like a balloon."

"No problem," I said, and took his hand. He squeezed so I could feel the bones folding in. I'm not a small man myself, even if I was never a football player. But I know overcompensation when I see it. Or feel it. This wasn't a handshake. This was a test. So, I didn't wince, I just gave it back. And the handshake went on a few breaths longer than it should.

A tap came on my shoulder and I let go. Jill came around

and gave me a look warning about testosterone contests. "Howdy," she said. "Jill Jacobs. So sorry I caused a fuss."

That Jill, she's a lady with the outside folks. Butter wouldn't melt and all. With me, though, she's a real person and swears like a sailor. Just one reason I love her.

He turned red again, but this was a blush. "Aw, sorry, ma'am. Giles Sanderson." He pronounced it with a soft "g," and it all rhymed with "piles." I just bet he was the kind of guy who'd blast off if you pronounced it wrong.

"Nathan," I nodded his way.

"We just got in and – well, it's a little funny to have a Welcome Wagon," he admitted, running his paw around the back of his neck. "Just never know who could come by and start offering food, so I got a little … concerned."

Jill passed me a look. We knew folks who got … concerned like that. It never ended well. And in the neighborhood where I grew up in North Austin, it could end up in blood, sweat and tears, let's say. Suddenly the wife's sunglasses inside made sense.

Disarmed, Sanderson stood there and babbled a little longer, told us what they were doing here, and how they didn't have kids but were hoping, and then the phone rang and we both begged off. When I shut the front door finally, I think everybody was relieved.

"At least he won't be here long," I told her. "How do you make that?" she asked. "Because nobody stays here long."

"Except us," she winked. "Muffin?"

So, that's how it started. We met the Sandersons, one at a time, and that was it. They never waved back, so we didn't strike up a friendship. And I didn't have time, not in that December month. Because I was getting geared up for one of my favorite things of all.

Dressing up the house.

Yeah, it might seem a little candy-assed, but when you got kids, you get into the whole cornball of everything. You sing with "The Lion King," and you act like Dora's a fuckin' genius and in a way, you actually believe it all because they do. So, starting when the kids were about two and three, I got into the holidays all over again.

Started with Halloween. Spook day meant I could wire the house for sound and movement and make lights flash and witches fly, send up plumes of dry-ice smoke and put the doorbell on to make it go "whooooo." Every year there was more shit at the store to test out – the skeleton I put in the front hallway which lurched out at you when the door opened scared off so many trick-or-treaters I had to retire it – but turning the garage into a haunted house brought them back. I reigned unquestioned supreme as Halloween House on Tempest Cove.

Partly that was 'cause all of the Jesus freaks around here got Halloween seen as anti-Christian. These evangelical nuts got all worked up over the fact that their favorite holidays might actually have — saints preserve us, where are my smelling salts — pagan histories. So, the competition I might have isn't participating. Oh, sure, their kids go candy-grubbing. Some of 'em even have the little ones show up with pamphlets. But they don't dress up and they don't decorate the house and they give you the hairy eyeball in the H&B when you start checking out the bowl with the mechanical hand that grabs back.

So, it didn't surprise me 'tall that Giles Sanderson's house was dark that first Halloween. I thought about egging it, but between the haunted house and taking Dave and Asty around the territory I didn't have time. And then we all crashed out after too many Reese's Peanut Butter Cups, so I shrugged my shoulders and let it go.

Then came Christmas.

Christmas, now, that's a different animal. The neighborhood goes certifiable. I shit you not. Every year, we go for a post-meal Thanksgiving constitutional – I need a walk before all that pie – and catch parents with their kids climbing trees and scaling ladders, already putting up the gaudy red and green lights, or staking out those blow-up Santas and snowmen to flap in the breeze for the next whole month. Every house – and I do mean every house, except the ones not occupied – has some kind of decoration up, from Santa in his sleigh on the roof to multiple trees in the window.

Just who needs more than one tree?

Still, I was guilty, too. I didn't start out to make it a competition. But my taste for fame got whetted with the Halloween success, and it felt like the area was looking to me to take the lead in decking the halls. So, who was I to let them down?

I wouldn't go gaudy. I did all white lights and maxed out with three things in the yard. We only had one tree. But it was tasteful. Pleasant, and clean, and easy on the eye. Cars would slow-drive on Tempest Cove and pause before our home. They took pictures. And then they'd ease on out, going a bit faster past all the rest. We had it down. We were kings of the Cove.

Not bad for an atheist and his lapsed-Catholic wife. Then came Giles. He upped the ante.

That first Christmas he came, he waited until we had our whole display out. I knew he was eyeballing us – you could see him staring from his second-floor media room window, cradling a cup of coffee in one hand, sipping it in slippered comfort while I banged hell out of my fingers trying to get all the pieces in place.

The day after I finished, Jill went out to snag the morning paper. She took so long coming back in, I went to see what was what. Sharky trotted alongside. That dog follows me everywhere.

"Bad news?" I asked, nodding at the still-folded paper under her arm.

She slid her eyes over at the Sandersons'. "Son of a bitch," I muttered.

Sanderson had mirrored our hard-designed, long-admired house beautiful on his side of the cul-de-sac, down to the flickering candles in the windows. His house was a different model than ours, but there was no mistake. All white. Icicles from the eaves. Candles in the window. And lighted deer frames on the lawn. But then I saw it. The deer heads were bobbing up and down, grazing. They were ghostly, ethereal, heartbreaking. My lawn looked like shit next to that. One small difference, and it changed everything.

Just then, Sanderson came out to get his paper. I started forward. Jill grabbed my robe, but I yanked free. My slippers slapped against the tarmac as I pounded in his direction.

"You like?" He winked at me.

"Has the ring of the familiar," I barked back.

Behind Sanderson, a mouse stuck her head out of the door, watching.

Maddeningly, he shrugged. "It's the most wonderful time of the year!" he said.

"You stole my design!" I shouted, knowing the whole neighborhood could hear, knowing I sounded like a four-year-old. I didn't give a rat's ass.

He grinned. "Imitation is the sincerest form of flattery." "Quit flattering me."

And just like that, the grin still on his face, he gave me the finger.

I took one step – and this time, it wasn't Jill tapping on my shoulder. It was Asty and David, each grabbing an arm. "Daddy!" they cried together. "Daddy! Come see!"

I glanced down, wanting to shrug them off. I was livid, infuriated on some deep, instinctual level by this creep. But when I looked back up again, he was already inside.

So, I dropped it.

The second year, I vowed to be bigger. And I was. We added on. Jill looked at me askew but didn't say anything. And when Sanderson still did us one better — he had music synched to his lights, for good mother's sake — the cars slowed down to look at his place. Third year, he got so complex he was hiring illegals to come out and help him get all the decorations up. That year the local paper did a story on his designs and then the local news picked it up and it got put on the Internet and landed about 100,000 hits or something ridiculous. We were left in the dust.

Only, we shouldn't've been. We still had a kick-ass set of decorations. But every time I brought in a new innovation — words on the roof! Light panels in the driveway! — Sanderson had one more trick up his too-tight sleeve. And it always was the one thing that made his place perfect, and my place like an amateur's.

Taste went out the window that third year, and Jill even complained. "I can't find our front door any more with all of this shit," she told me. "I'm blind just carrying in the groceries."

"Use the garage," I snapped.

And when she tried to take one or two items down when I wasn't home, it was my turn to blow my top. We retired into our bathroom and had it out. She made perfect sense, and I was completely unreasonable in return. But it was the only thing I became immobile with her on. *Do not fuck with my decorations,* I told her. *It's the principle of the matter.*

And she threw up her hands and said she was learning to hate this holiday.

Strangely, so was I.

Meanwhile, Sanderson took in the accolades and the

applause. Always him doing the talking, his wife standing in the back behind, blinking with wide, dark eyes. Then the news trucks would disappear, and his house continued to blare out at the rest of the street with its permanent snowfall and eternal pine scent. If you stood outside to admire it in the late, late hours you might even catch some sound from the house – noises that had nothing to do with December celebrations.

No, the screaming and the shifting and the breaking reminded me much more of Halloween than Christmas.

This year, Jill said she had enough; they were going to spend Christmas with her parents in Colorado, and I could come, or I could sit at home and stare at Sanderson's like Pink does at the TV in *The Wall*, she didn't give a shit.

Of course, she did give a shit, but that's how she puts on a brave face. Y'see, this year, what broke her was the contest. I don't know for positive, but I'm pretty goddamned sure that Sanderson was behind the institution of the Holiday Decoration Contest with the local news station. You know, the one that got him on the Internet a few years back. It was co-sponsored by our local rag, which had printed that his decorations were "elegantly reflective of the joy the holiday brings," or some other high-falutin' crap. Basically, everyone in this zip code could enter, alls you gotta do is decorate, send in a 3-minute video about your place, and the finalists got a visit from the station's judging committee. The winner? A blue ribbon and a picture in the paper and a hundred bucks.

So obviously, it wasn't about the ribbon or the paper or the hundred bucks. It's the fuckin' principle of the matter. The last four years this joker had stolen every good idea I got and colored outside the lines and gotten outside help and then took it to the media, which made everybody start upping their game until our whole neighborhood turned into like one of those side streets at Disneyland. It was the least happiest place on earth, though.

I kissed Jill and the kidlets goodbye at Austin-Bergstrom and told them I'd be along directly but had to stick at work for some last-minute development meetings. Jill gave me another hairy eyeball, like she didn't think I was really gonna show. I kissed her again and promised to make it.

"When was the last time I let you down?" I asked her.

And she had to look away. She knows I don't go back on my word.

The plane took off and I left the car at the airport, taking a cab that cost me more than the prize money would have, sneaking in the back door of my place just as full dark came on. I don't think anybody saw me, they shouldn't've, since I left all our decorations turned off. We were out of town. Nobody home.

I took a quick look at his handiwork, which glowed even more bright now that it didn't have to compete with mine. I caught the live-action Santa in the front yard, grinnin' away, wavin' his hand, leanin' back in his big old ugly sleigh. And I gave him the finger.

It wasn't but a quick walk across the street to Sanderson's, but I had to be circumspect. I went out the back again, all dressed in black with my hunting knife hid good and tight in its sheath against my leg. I got low to the ground and hugged that blockade wood fence that keeps all of us safe and tight from prying eyes, swooping around the back of the Browns', The Changs' and the Cohens', until there I was, in the one place Sanderson didn't want to be observed — his own backyard.

I hunkered next to his backyard deck, behind the grill, and waited.

It was quiet. And that was odd, because except on Halloween night I knew the Sandersons never went out, never had people in, never went on vacation. Sanderson came home from work every night at 7:30 and was gone again by 6 in the morning. When he was home, mostly all you heard was the TV blaring, except for the nights when you couldn't sleep and you got a breath of fresh air outside and could hear the whimpering or the moaning in the late night, so late it was really morning. But now – I heard nothing.

Something wet came out of the branches and fastened on my hand and I jumped a mile.

"Jesus Christ, dog," I growled at him. Sharky, who followed me everywhere, thought we were playing a game. "Git. Go home."

He didn't move.

"Aw, fuck, animal," I said, and gave him the one command he did obey: "Lie down."

Immediately, his blond bulk dropped flat and his nose went between his paws. He would stay like that until the earth opened up under him or until I gave the signal. "Good dog."

I glanced off to my right. There it was – the one thing I was looking for. Same spot as on my McMansion. I pried open the fuse box with a lock pick, preparing to mess up the innards with my knife. Nobody was gonna give out a prize to a house that couldn't even get itself lit. That was all I was gonna have to do, and then I could receive the judges with open arms the next morning, just a few hours before my flight was taking off.

I had just pulled out the knife when I heard the thud.

It was a dull, crashing thing but it all came as one big noise, as if someone had dropped a sack of laundry from a height. I froze and glanced at Sharky, who had an eyebrow cocked, but had not moved. Inching over to the deck, I crouched down low just as the backyard light popped on and the glass backyard door slid open. A figure emerged, pulling something behind it. A mouse, lacing her fingers under the armpits of a former jock, taking minute backwards steps on to the deck. Her breaths came hard and fast, audible even above the shushing of his clothes against the wooden deck slats. She stopped and righted herself, and then I heard soft sobs.

"Hey," I said, standing tall, the knife re-sheathed. "You okay?"

The mouse whipped around, eyes wide and staring. One seemed sunken in, almost blending with her boy-cropped brown hair. It was a shiner like none I'd seen, and it got my blood boiling. The light cut across her mouth and I caught a crust of blood on one of the corners, a rough texture against the swelling there.

"It's okay," I said, staring down at Giles Sanderson. Let's just say, he looked much, much worse than the mouse, thanks to having his skull stove in. From the size of it, I'd say she clocked him with a vase, or maybe pot. Maybe even a claw hammer. It didn't matter. He wasn't breathing.

Is it wrong to say I felt a small thrill run up my backside?

I caught my flight with plenty of time to spare the next morning. For once, Delta was on time, and I knew I'd be with Jill and the kids in time to see them opening the gifts. But I was also glad I'd have a few hours more to rest. Every muscle in me was aching by the time I got on board.

Y'see, I didn't have much time to sleep that evening. The mouse and I – you know, I never did get her name – had to expend a lot of energy making sure Giles wouldn't be found, at least not right away. At first, she wanted to bury him under the tree and pretend he vanished, but I told her that was going to look suspicious in about five minutes. And then they'd bring out the dogs and sniff him out and it wouldn't work.

What she needed to do is just be out of town for the

holidays. Leave the house look broken into. I'd take care of the rest. So, at two in the morning she was packing, and at three she was heading to the train station, and at four I was doing a little more decoration on Giles Sanderson's house.

It still looks like mine, of course. Yes, there's always that one extra bit that completely fucks with my design and elevates his. But this year, I'm the one who made the adjustment. It's a very personal addition – a lifelike, human-sized Santa figure in full costume, propped up in a sleigh on the front lawn. The reins are in his paw-like mittened hands, and the mask over his face makes him eternally jolly and delightful. Can't do much about the lack of a twinkle in his eye, though.

It's too bad it isn't Vermont, but Texas has been cold these last few seasons, so I don't think anyone will say anything about Santa's body odor until at least Dick Clark is counting the ball falling. By which time the mouse will have returned, and noted her husband missing, and the search will commence. Nobody will ever think her capable of causing him harm, and nobody will certainly think she could have moved him that far, and by then all of her injuries should be well-healed.

I know it may seem counter-productive to add to Sandersons' landscape. The Santa figure lends a touch of fantastical reality that no other house – including mine – can approach. There's no doubt that Giles Sanderson will win the contest this year.

But he hasn't got a chance in hell next Christmas.

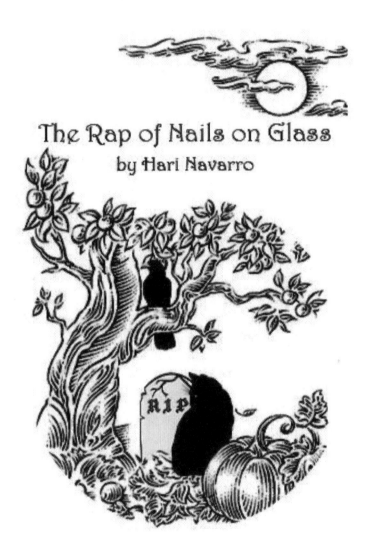

The Rap of Nails on Glass
by Hari Navarro

I sit naked and dripping at a table in a tiny room with no windows and only a door.

I have been dead for five years. I know this due to the novelty flip clock that has Christ the Redeemer taunt me as he slaps down both time and date in exacting repetitive succession with a comical flick of his wrist.

I know because I have heard the rap of nails upon the window that is set into the door four times now to date. And I also know that in a few impossibly long moments I will hear their cold thrum yet again.

So, yes, I guess there is a window, a panel of glass in the door that lets me see just what it is that I am to become. I sit here and I stare at it. Actually, I don't, I stare at the curtain that dresses it from top to bottom in a fall of yellowing lace.

I know every last looping floral swirl of its design and I am obsessed with and haunted by the gentle parting decay of its threads. I hate it but through the stretch of my long, long days I find myself singing to it. And I talk to it and I cry to it and, sometimes, its designs move and form into eyes and lips, and then... and then, I love it.

It makes me laugh. That horrible hollow flavor of laugh that has nothing to do with humor and everything to do with fear. It's a fucking curtain and yet I plead, and I beg for it to love me. To love me right on back.

I am frozen. My arms and my legs have been drained of use and they lock me into my chair. This horrible place, this cold dark box allows me but the most scant sensation of feeling. It lets me feel the sticky contraction of my muscle as it lifts and parts from my bones. It allows me to sense the minute shifts in my weight as I drip and fill the smooth patina grooves of the wood where I sit with the waxy sag of my bare, bloated skin.

Death is not supposed to be like this. Death is finality and this hell is anything but. This hell that plays by its own sickly rules. Rules that offer me a choice.

Once a year on this night and this night alone, it offers me the chance of escape.

Halloween, or Samhain, or the night of my senseless murder, call it what you will, but tonight I will be propositioned yet again.

I can feel it happening as we speak. The blood once again sluicing down and into my veins. I feel the prickle at my fingertips and my hands roll and ball on the tabletop and I can feel the stirring dull thud at my chest. I inhale the first breath in all of a year and, at once, I can taste the stale wet taint of my rot.

The minute approaches. This anniversary of my violent end. Or was it more a violent beginning? This night on which I was dragged by my hair. My screams fusing with those of the witches and the demons and the ghosts and then...

The night I was pushed to that filthy brick wall and fat fingers snatched the life from my throat, I remember in those first moments of my death wondering just how this could be happening to me. These kind of horrors only happen to other people. Faceless people on the television news.

Poor. Lost. Souls.

And then he cast me down into the water, and the water swallowed me whole.

On this night, death repairs me and allows me to stand. It allows me to make my way across to the door and it lets me gaze through the curtains. It lets me see they who knock at my door.

I can open it and escape but each and every time that I

see through that lace my hand trembles and stops at the handle.

I see the demons and I see the witches and the rotting dead, and I know that they are real. I can feel the seething of their evil.

Open the door, step out into their fold. Become something. Feel something. Tear something. Kill something.

I sit at the table and I marvel at the bones that crackle and join beneath the failing flesh of my hands and I hear the gentle rap of fingernails – tap tap tap – at the glass. And, then, comes the insistent knocking and soon there will be a frenzied pounding of fists.

I sit and I smile. For tonight I will not stand, and I will not relish this thing that passes for life that blooms and spreads in my veins. I know that no part of this is truth.

I am dead and I will sit here for year after year, and I will wait until my mind crumbles and flakes to the floor. I smirk at their anger. It pisses them off, and I know I am beating them. I know I can win.

One day when there is nothing of me left, perhaps that will be some kind of peace. I won't beg them, and I will not plead, but I hope that then they will allow me to rest.

THE RAP OF NAILS ON GLASS BY HARI NAVARRO

Hari Navarro has for many years now been locked in his neighbor's cellar. He survives due to an intravenous feed of pureed extreme horror and Absinthe-infused sticky-spiced unicorn wings. His anguished cries for help can be found via 365 Tomorrows, Breachzine, AntipodeanSF, Horror Without Borders, Black Hare Press, and HellBound Books. Hari was the Winner of the Australasian Horror Writers' Association (AHWA) Flash Fiction Award 2018 and has also succeeded in being a New Zealander who now lives in Northern Italy with no cats.

https://www.amazon.com/Hari-Navarro

It Came from the Film Can!
by Mark Osborne

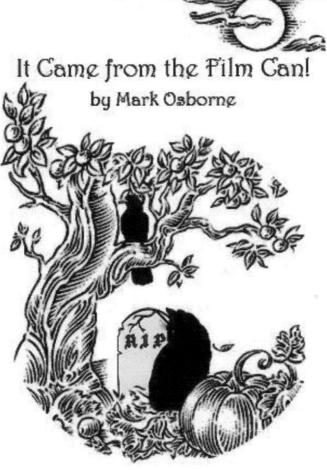

IT CAME FROM THE FILM CAN! BY MARK OSBORNE

OCTOBER 31ST, 1983, NEW YORK, NY – THE EAST VILLAGE

After Sam Angulio twisted open a can of Pringles, he said to Judy Clowery, "Now that you got your VCR fixed, instead of us super-self-absorbed film students going to 42nd Street theaters to watch hokey, Grade Z horror movies, we can study their nuances from the safety of your crime-ridden neighborhood."

Judy brushed her dyed-black bangs away from her eyes, paused the videotape and said with a smirk, "At least at those theaters, I'd just have to hear a bunch of dopey guys talk to the screen instead of one guy blah and blahing to me—and making me miss some dialogue."

"Give me a break! You can barely hear what these actors are saying here! Just…proceed with the not-so chilling conclusion of *The Blood of Satan's Beast*, maestro."

Judy pressed the remote's PLAY and watched the 1932 horror movie unfold, straining to hear cliché-filled dialogue that blended in with the soundtrack's hisses caused by the film's advanced age. Both laughed at chunky character actor Billy Gilbert staggering through a forest; gasping and glancing back in wide-eyed terror as raindrops and tears poured down his face.

"Back, you beast. Back!" he cried.

"What the hell is *that?*" Judy asked after seeing the film's first appearance of Satan's Beast. "Now that is one bad Halloween costume. If he tried trick or treating tonight, he should give the people giving out candy his *own* candy—to apologize for wearing such a piece of--"

"Stop blah and blahing! I'm trying to watch. But, yeah. Just what the hell is *that?*"

The beast looked as if its poor-excuse-for-a-costume would have been deemed unworthy to film by Ed Wood. It resembled a diminutive albino gorilla with lopsided hands that on closer, paused, still-frame inspection appeared to be oversized white gloves with black paint haphazardly splashed on its fingertips. Two ill-fitting unicorn-like horns sprouted from each side of its furry head and four jagged fangs obscured most of its black lips. A close-up of its face revealed it to be Rondo Hatton, who Sam noted was "an actor afflicted with Acromegaly and his worst movie role ever."

"This hackneyed plot is too complicated," Judy said. "Let me get this straight. So, what that actress, Joan Blondell, thought was a glass of tomato juice, was really Satan's blood and—"

"And once Joan drank the blood, she turned into an extension of Satan slash Rondo Hatton—Satan's beast. Got it?"

"For now, I do. Wait a second. Do you recognize the set?" "Don't tell me—it was used on a Universal Film—um

—*The Ghost of Frankenstein*, 1932?" Sam guessed.

"Close. *The House of Frankenstein*, 1931," she corrected him. "You're so right. God, am I slipping—and so is Billy boy."

They watched a sobbing Billy Gilbert continuously slip and fall on wet leaves in between thunder crashing and lightning flashing on his face. He stopped running to snap a crooked branch from a dead tree and hold it high over his right shoulder as if it was an axe. The beast half-growled and half-chuckled, then showed Billy that its once non-existent fingernails now resembled ten-foot-long rusty tent spikes.

"Hey! We should tell Freddy Krueger slash Robert Englund that someone stole his fingers slash fingernails," suggested Sam.

"Shhhhh!"

The beast wiggled its fingers as if they were playing a piano keyboard, then ripped the branch out of Billy's hands.

"I said back, beast! Go back to where you came from!" cried an exhausted Billy as he fell to his knees.

A close-up of the beast's bushy eyebrows bobbing up and

down was abruptly replaced by a grey placard that read:

"Last reel (#13) of 'The Blood of Satan's Beast' lost The Blood of Satan's Beast
Directed by
F.W. Murnau, Alan Penrod and
Franklin Pingborn"

"That's it? We don't know if the beast did in Billy?"

And why did it take three directors to direct one crappy movie?" Sam asked.

"Because two of them died of heart attacks while filming most of the film. And the third one died after he filmed the last reel," Judy said as she ejected the videotape. She placed it on one of the many stacks of punk records positioned under posters of Ramones album covers and Stanley Kubrick movies that filled her studio apartment's walls.

"What the hell ever happened to that reel?"

"I read that 53% of movies made in the U.S. prior to 1950 no longer exist. And I read that one of *The Blood of Satan's Beast*'s directors, F.W. Murnau—after he finished filming the last reel, he said that filming the Satan movie would kill him."

"A lot of directors say that after a tough shoot."

"Yeah, but do a lot of directors die in a car crash a week later—like F.W. did?"

"Not that I know of. Jeez, *now* I'd like to see how that crappy movie ended."

"For the last 51 years, no one has seen that reel. But for the next billions of years, everyone will because—hold on."

She went into her bedroom and returned, holding a round and dust-covered metal film canister. Handwritten in faded black magic marker on frayed yellow masking tape covering the canister's sides was *The Blood of Satan's Beast, Reel 13, 1932.*

"I hold in my super-self-absorbed hands *the* last reel!" Judy announced.

"Where did you get that?"

"Remember how I told you my grandfather owned an old film lab and was selling it in a month?"

"What about it?"

"When they were cleaning that lab out, they found a storage room full of super old canisters. And one of those film cans buried under other film cans—is that!"

"And what are you gonna do with *that*? God, I bet the film's just as filthy as its container."

"I know. That's why I'm gonna clean the film then give it to the American Film Institute for eternal safekeeping."

"Please. You know about as much as cleaning film as your Johnny Ramone knows about playing a guitar."

"I'll show you. Step into my laboratory, Igor."

She grabbed his right hand and led him to her bathroom. Nine empty, pint-sized brown medicine bottles and an aluminum paint roller tray filled with a liquid that looked like watered down ginger ale sat in her bathtub.

"The tray's filled with Isopropyl alcohol. It cleans film," Judy said.

"Who doesn't know that?" Sam laughed. "Okay. Ready for the unveiling?"

Judy removed a pair of white cotton gloves from her back pocket, slipped them on, then twisted open the film canister, unleashing an eye-watering odor.

"Whew. That smells kinda like—"

"Bad vinegar, right?" Judy finished. "I read that's because when old film decays, its acetate releases a chemical that smells kind of like vinegar."

"And I bet you read how to get rid of that smell *and* clean it all up, huh?"

"How did you know I'm so well-read, Samuel?"

"And I know you're venturing into unknown territory here. I mean, what does a 19-year-old video store clerk slash film geek know about cleaning a 51-year-old film?"

"Who better to take care of film than someone who loves it…and now knows how to treat it right? Starting now."

She carefully removed the film from the canister and unspooled two feet of it to show that it was red.

"Uh, when is a black and white movie red?" Judy asked. "Guess this reel was tinted red or something. They did
stuff like that way back in the day."

"Looks that way. Pew! Someone hasn't taken a bath in 51 years. In your tub ya go."

She submerged two feet of film in the tray and gasped when it instantly dissolved; leaving behind a liquid that was the color and viscosity of blood.

"Did you read why that film just did that?" Sam warily asked.

Judy removed her gloves, dipped her right index finger in the tray, placed it under her nose and noted, "It even smells like blood. How could that be? It's just film."

"Wrong. It's not *just* film. It's *cursed* film!" "And who cursed it?"

"Since it's called, *The Blood of Satan's Beast*, I'd say Mr. Satan did a curse on it. And-And-And since you just restored the film, the beast lives once again in that restored blood—which is Satan's Beast blood!" Sam nervously said. "And you found the canister 'buried,' like Dracula's always found buried, and th-then Dracula gets 'unburied' and lives, and, and, and, and, and now that film's curse is 'unburied' and lives too! In a rent subsidized apartment!"

"So, I have the power to restore a film and a curse?" Judy laughed.

"Who am I or you to say?"

"I say as long as I don't drink it like it's tomato juice like Joan Blondell did in the movie, I should be okay."

"Did those three directors who died drink that blood? No way! I say an angry Satan cursed those directors for making a crappy movie about him and then they all died."

"You're beginning to kind of make scary sense. And it's s-s-s-scaring me."

"Is it?"

"Absolutely not, film geek boy! I'll just have to read more and find an explanation why that piece of film just did what it did. As for you, isn't it time for you to get to work at our favorite video store tonight?"

"It sure is," Sam said, looking at his wristwatch. "Just to play it safe, maybe you should just mail that reel to the American Film Institute. Let them clean the rest of it and get cursed. Not you."

"I think you're right."

He grabbed his knapsack filled with textbooks and walked with Judy toward the apartment's door. After Sam stepped into the building's hallway, he reopened the door to warn in his best Boris Karloff voice, "But remember. She or he who even touches the Beast's blood, dies...or even worse! Happy Hell-o-ween!"

Judy faked a hearty laugh and retreated to her bedroom, which she called her Cocoon Room. Her bedroom was a place where, with the help of the Ramones, she shielded herself from the outside world and her place in it. Judy much preferred having Joey Ramone's voice and Johnny Ramone's guitar fill her head than her own questions.

Why won't Sam ever ask me for a real date? Or just try to kiss me—then kiss me like he's Humphrey Bogart and I'm Lauren Bacall in To Have and Have Not? Is the reason we'll never kiss is because we work at that same video store and if we break up, we'd still have to see other? No, that shouldn't be the reason. We have way more in common than just our workplace. We're both majoring in film, both gangly and both find it uncomfortable to look into a pair of eyes unless they're on a movie screen and, and him kissing me, might be too weird for him. It'd be like him kissing himself I guess."

Should I change my major %om 'Film Studies' to another non-money-making career like being a social worker? Oh, enough of me!

Judy put an end to mulling her future by opening her Walkman, plopping in the Ramones' new *Subterranean Jungle* cassette and slipping on headphones. She pressed PLAY and let the sheer volume of guitars, drums and words blow all self-doubt out of her head as Joey Ramone reassured her that:

"When you're feelin' low and he fish won't bite
You need a little bit o' soul to put you right."

God bless Joey! She thought. Judy believed that the hurt permeating Joey's voice derived from all the years he spent silently and repeatedly taking the same taunts she had once heard in her suburban school rooms:

"You look like a stork wearing a bad black wig. You're soooooo tall. How's the weather up there? God, you look like Shelley Duvall's and Jerry Lewis' love child! Stop hiding your eyes behind your bangs! Are you a boy or girl? Do you ever wear a color that's not black? Do us a favor. When you go to a movie theater and watch your weird movies, don't come out. How could you listen to *that* music? You're sooooooo weird. Oddball. Will you ever fit in? *Just what is wrong with you?"*

Judy's "formative years" consisted of her ignoring most words spoken without musical accompaniment and focusing on words that were either sung behind jarring guitar chords or spoken by movie actors and actresses. When side one of the tape ended, she placed her index finger on the EJECT button and noticed them. Hairs. A patch of quarter-inch high, bristly white hairs was at the end of her right index finger.

"How did these get here?" she thought as she chewed the hairs off. "Wait. Did that happen because it touched the blood of that 'cursed' film? And, and, I'm turning into that albino beast thing? No, it must be a dermatology thing...I hope."

The hairs unnerved her so much that Judy went into her small kitchen to make a Bloody Mary to calm her nerves. She played the Ramones tape at such an eardrum shattering volume that she did not hear a stolen credit card slip in and jiggle by her front door's lock. The door creaked open and two burglars wearing worn Wolfman masks crept into her foyer. Gary Lipmein and his slim, dim-witted partner in crime, John Benza, looked like a mutant version of Laurel and Hardy... that is, if the old comedy team were unkempt, perpetually sweaty, had pockmarked skin, wore torn white Converse sneakers and stained t-shirts, rarely bathed and were junkies in their mid-30's, constantly looking for their next fix and an apartment to raid.

Gary, the chunky Oliver Hardy of the pair, accurately surmised, "Damn. This place looks like a college student lives here. They have less coins to rub together than we do." He ordered John to look in the kitchen while he went into the bedroom to see if there were any signs of jewelry.

John walked into the kitchen to see Judy pouring vodka into a glass of tomato juice on a rickety table. As Judy sang along to the Ramones, she did not hear John creep behind her. He wrapped his right arm around her shoulders to secure her arms and placed his left palm over her mouth. She shook the bulky headphones off her head but wished she never removed them after hearing approaching footsteps and Gary's voice snarl before her face:

"Try to escape or scream and I'll kill you. Do you understand?" She nodded. As John released her and gulped down her drink, Gary demanded, "Take us to your money."

"Look, guys. I'm worth nothing. I work at Louie's. It's a lame mom and pop video slash bookstore that'll most likely close soon. How much money do you think I have from working there?"

"Yeah. By the looks of this place, we're even doing better than you, man," John said, then laughed to show that he was in desperate need of caps on most of his yellowed teeth. "If that's possible."

"Shut up you!" Gary ordered. "As for you—" Gary grabbed Judy by her black t-shirt and slammed her against a wall. "Tell us where you have cash, or we'll tear this place apart looking for any—starting by breaking every album you have. Beginning with 'A' which is the soundtrack to *A Clockwork Orange* and ending with—"

"Don't do that! Okay," Judy surrendered. "I got a couple of hundred hidden under my bed."

"Now you're talking. Take us there," Gary snapped.

She led them to her bedroom, got down on her hands and knees and looked under her bed. Balancing on top of two ten-pound dumbbells was her cardboard safe, the soundtrack album to *West Side Story*. She handed it to Gary, who ripped it apart. Ten twenty-dollar bills floated to the floor. As John picked them up and Gary admired the album cover, Judy grabbed a dumbbell and stood.

"Does your mother know what music you listen to, sister? What old school crap!"

He looked up from the album to see her hurl a dumbbell that barely missed his head. Judy then went for Gary's face with her black fingernails, three of them leaving bloody scratch marks on his right cheek. John tackled her to the floor.

"Girl, you got some nerve," Gary roared as Judy's right heel thudded into John's groin. She made a break for the door only for Gary to grab her by her right wrist.

"No! Don't kill her!" John pleaded.

Gary backhanded Judy across her face then landed an uppercut to her chin, knocking her unconscious.

"Is she d-d-d-dead?" John asked.

"N-n-n-no. But she won't be waking up soon, which'll give us time to temporarily live here. Rent free."

"What do you mean?"

Gary pointed to the $200 in John's hand and roared, "Go get the junk from Leroy around the corner on Avenue D and bring it back here. We'll shoot up safe and sound here, man. *Capisce?*"

John rapidly nodded and replied, "*Si. Muy capisce!*"

He ran out of the apartment, leaving Gary to wipe a smattering of blood off his face. Out of his Strand Bookstore tote bag, he took a spoon with black burn marks on its bottom, a batch of cotton balls, two hypodermic needles and a wrinkled red, white and blue tie. He went to the bathroom to half-fill his spoon with water, and he noticed *The Blood of Satan's Beast*'s canister in the sink and the paint tray filled with what looked like a small pool of blood.

What's with her and this blood? he thought. *Is she some Bela Lugosi vampire? Hell, she's pale and dresses all in black like one. Maybe she is.*

Gary saw the 1932 date on the masking tape. *That makes this an antique. Which could be worth something to the right film nerd.* He picked up the canister, reentered the bedroom, stepped over Judy's prone body and sat on the bed.

"You messed with the wrong junkie, sister," he chuckled.

Judy awoke to a splitting headache. She wondered why she was lying on a floor and who had badly bruised her bottom lip and jaw. Her memory was jarred when she heard Gary cackle.

"Well, gabba-gabba-hey-oh-let's go! Josephine Ramone awakens!"

Judy looked up to see Gary, wobbly, standing in her bedroom's doorway and sipping from her pint of vodka. She instantly recognized the junkie chic look he had no doubt been cultivating for years: the heavy-lidded eyes, the head half-bowing then suddenly standing at attention, and limp hands wiping away droplets of forehead sweat.

"Where are you, man? I said bring it in here now!" Gary barked as he poured a half glass of vodka.

An uneasy John entered the bedroom, his shaky hands holding the paint tray filled with blood. Gary filled his glass of vodka with the tray's blood then brought the glass to Judy's lips.

"Have a *real* Bloody Mary on me, gorgeous," he said. "You know where you can stick that, scum," Judy said.

Gary then punched her in the jaw, knocking her unconscious.

"Why did you do that for again, man? Leave her alone and let's just leave," John pleaded.

"Yeah, let's," Gary agreed. "But before we do—"

Gary dipped his hypodermic needle in the tray and pulled up its plunger until it was filled with blood. He brought the needle closer and closer to Judy's throat, then lowered it until it hovered over a purple vein running along her left forearm.

"This is where I'll stick it, gorgeous. In you. Trick or treat, sweets!"

He shot the film's red fluid into her and sang the first stanza of *I Wanna Be Sedated*. Judy's eyelids slowly creaked opened to see John holding a stack of her albums and the thirteenth reel of *The Blood of Satan's Beast*.

"No...Don't take that reel...it's cursed," Judy mumbled before she passed out; the needle half-protruding from her forearm.

"Curses to you too! Foiled again, eh?" Gary laughed.

After Gary had packed as many of Judy's belongings of

value as he could fit into his tote bag and left the bedroom, he returned to mock her labored breathing. "Tsk, tsk. Look at you. Just another soon-to-be-dead junkie who never knew when enough was enough."

As the burglars left the apartment, white bristly hairs slowly began to sprout and spread along Judy's left forearm, then envelop her entire body.

"Judy? Are you there? If you are, pick up!" Sam's voice pleaded through her phone's answering machine.

But Judy was no longer in her apartment. Her form was now the one of a beast that had once haunted and hunted down three film directors who thought they could freely mock Satan without receiving any harsh repercussions. In 1932, two of these fabulists were stopped from completing the film when they were literally scared to death by encountering the real-life version of the fictional beast. The third director, who had finished the film for them, had swerved his Packard one night to avoid a shadowy, monstrous form standing in his car's path and crashed into a telephone pole. Now, Satan decided that two drug addicts who dared to treat a deadly curse lightly would be duly punished for contemptuously injecting hallowed blood, Satan's resurrected blood, that was now inside and changing Judy's body into a beast like it once did to Joan Blondell's character in 1932.

The beast could only see in black and white and hear mostly hisses, as if it was still living in a scratch-filled print of a long-forgotten 1932 movie. It could barely make out Sam saying through an answering machine, "Hey Jude. Right before I started my shift here, these two lowlifes came in and tried to sell Louie your *Blood of Satan's Beast* reel. Louie told them we just deal in videotapes. Fortunately, one of those morons registered for membership here and put down his home address in Brooklyn—433 Atlantic Avenue, Apt. 403. I'm going there now to see if I can reason with him and get your film back. See you."

The beast's instinctive thirst for revenge sent it out of the apartment's front window, down its fire escape and dashing down Greenwich Village sidewalks, causing passers-by to either step aside and laugh, or sarcastically remark, "Cool white gorilla costume, man! Extra-happy Halloween!", until it stood softly growling outside a run-down apartment building in a part of Brooklyn called Prospect Heights. It could now hear the start of a thunderstorm, and John's voice as he wondered in his living room, "I still don't believe it. How could a fifty-year-old film not even be worth fifty cents?"

"I guess video stores don't buy films, idiot. We'll shop it around more tomorrow," Gary replied.

"I bet we'll have better luck selling her records, man."

"We will. Yeah, in honor of Josie Ramone, let's hear her big brother Joey sing," Gary scoffed.

John flipped through Judy's records in Gary's tote bag. He found a Ramones album, placed it on his record player's turntable and dropped the needle in the middle of its second side.

"C'mon, stooge. You can play it louder than that!" Gary said.

John twisted the volume knob until the walls vibrated because of Joey Ramone singing *Animal Boy*. As both badly sang along to the Ramones, neither heard a tent-spike-sized fingernail jiggle by their front door's lock, the door creak open and two white fur-covered feet creep into their foyer to enter the dark living room.

"What the...?" John gasped as a flash of lightning burst through their living room window and revealed the 5'2" beast, its hands looking like white gloves with black paint splashed on its fingertips.

Gary menacingly approached their intruder and said, "If you and your piss-poor Halloween costume don't get out of here on the count of three, I'm going to kick your little ass right out of your albino monkey suit. One—two—"

The beast, a foot shorter than Gary, wiggled its fingers as if it was playing a piano's keyboard. John and Gary looked at each other and laughed.

"I get it. You need a manicure. I think you need fingernails for that, chimp," mocked Gary. "Now, where was I? Oh yeah. One-two—*What the hell?*"

Gary stopped counting when he realized that what were once non-existent fingernails had been replaced by fingernails resembling ten rusty, sharpened tent spikes. Three slashed through John's throat, exposing torn arteries spurting blood and Gary as a simpering coward. As John took his last breath and toppled to the floor, Gary cried, "Who—what are you?"

The beast's pupils and unicorn-like horns turned from black to dark red, sending Gary screaming for help, running to the bedroom's window, opening it and stepping outside to the fire escape.

Sam approached the apartment's open door and walked inside, noticing the last reel of *The Blood of Satan's Beast* on the torn couch and John's blood-drenched body lying in front of it. Sam followed the sound of Gary's faint cries to the bedroom's window, where he watched Satan's Beast chase him into a rainstorm and the forests in nearby Prospect Park.

"Just what the hell is *that*? Is that—it really is! And it's alive! Alive!"

Sam grabbed the reel, ran out of the apartment and sprinted toward the park. He zig-zagged through dirt paths toward Gary's hoarse voice; which grew louder in volume with each step Sam took. He stopped running when he heard Gary repeatedly cry:

"Back, beast! Back!"

IT CAME FROM THE FILM CAN! BY MARK OSBORNE

Sam hid behind a faux nineteenth century gas lamppost on a path, where he watched a sobbing Gary continuously slip and fall on wet leaves in between thunder crashing and lightning flashing on his face, as if he was reenacting the last reel of *The Blood of Satan's Beast*. Seeing that the beast was gaining on him, Gary stopped to snap a crooked branch from a dead tree and held it high over his right shoulder as if it were an axe.

I'm watching <u>The Blood of Satan's Beast</u> *again—and now it's in color*, Sam realized. *And that guy's Billy Gilbert—and the beast was some woman who got filled with Satan's blood? Like Joan Blondell was…. wait. Can it be—?*

The beast half-growled and half-chuckled, then ripped the branch out of Gary's hands.

"I said back, beast! Go back to where you came from!" cried an exhausted Gary as he fell to his knees.

The beast's bushy eyebrows bobbed up and down as it backhanded Gary across the face, then landed an uppercut to his chin, knocking him unconscious. Sam watched the beast repeatedly slash Gary's neck and face with its nails, leaving a bloody corpse. The throat slashing stopped when the beast turned and noticed a stunned Sam staring at the gory scene. The beast took a step toward him then slowly spread its arms wide, as if it wanted a hug.

"Judy? Is that you?" Sam asked.

The beast looked up at the sky and pointed at a full moon emerging from the black clouds.

"Help…me," Judy's voice meekly begged as she collapsed to the ground. As Sam approached, the 5'2" beast physically transformed from a white, furry creature to a 6'3" Judy dressed in black. Blood oozed from the sides of Judy's mouth as her eyes slowly closed. Sam kneeled, placed his right ear to her chest and screamed:

"No! You're not going to die! I'll—I'll save you! But—how? I know!"

He ran to a streetlamp, removed the reel from its canister, unwound the film until its near ending and held it up to the fluorescent light.

"What a stupid cliché movie. It figures it'd do that. You're supposed to turn into some monster when you see a full moon, not turn into a human again like Judy did but--how do I get her to stop dying? Is the answer in here? I think…There it is? No, there *we* are?"

The last frames of the movie unnerved him so much that it caused his hands to shake and goosebumps to form on his arms. They showed an actor and actress who were the spitting images of himself and Judy, as if both had time traveled back to a 1932 soundstage's forest but were still wearing clothes from the 1980's, which included Judy's Ramones t-shirt.

"Who the hell directed this reel?" he whispered.

Sam shook the inexplicable image out of his head and searched for any film frames that would show how to save Judy.

"There it is! That's how I'll do it!"

Sam ran back to her and mimicked the film's conclusion. He gently lifted her left index finger, then her right one, positioned them to form a cross then kissed her; only to see that her eyes remained closed.

"C'mon, Judy. Be the ending of the movie! Be the movie! You can do it…Please?"

He kissed her again, longer and lovingly. This time, her eyelids fluttered, then shot up.

"At last!" she gasped upon realizing that Sam was finally kissing her. Judy threw her arms around his neck as if she was Lauren Bacall in *To Have and Have Not* and asked, "But—how did I, we get here? What happened?"

He laughed, helped her to her feet and replied: "We just had a happy ending."

Reminders
by Stephanie Scissom

I left work early, hoping to avoid the sight of the little ghosts and goblins racing down the sidewalk. I hadn't celebrated this night in over 40 years.

Yet, there they were already, clutching their jack-o-lantern pails, running from door to door. I walked faster, past the old cafe where my mom used to work, trying not to think about how my brother and I used to dance around the jukebox while she was cleaning up after her shift.

Usually, I hurried inside my house, turned off the lights and went to bed early, but for some reason, I couldn't bear the thought of sitting there alone tonight. I got my car out of the garage and drove.

I drove until the city lights disappeared, until there was nothing but dark country road ahead. I turned the satellite radio to the 80s station, the music I'd listened to as a teenager. The singer was crooning about never being free. I didn't like where that thought took me, so I turned the station.

Something crashed against my door and splattered on my window. I screamed and swerved, before I realized what it was. An egg. Just an egg.

Damn kids.

I drove a little farther, then pulled over to see if they'd dented my door.

I wiped the egg off with some fast food napkins, conscious of all the nighttime woods sounds around me, then climbed back into the car. I drove another mile before I realized I was no longer alone.

The face in the rearview nearly stalled my heart. Garish green Hulk mask with an obscenely red-lipped snarl. The ill-fitting plastic costumes we'd worn in the 70s.

I don't know how I didn't wreck, but I somehow wrenched the car to the shoulder of the road. The tiny Hulk just sat there, his hands folded in his lap.

"What are you doing here?" I sobbed. "What do you want?"

I knew, even in the dark, that the eyes that stared back at me were green, the same shade as my own. I knew his little plastic pants were purple.

He said nothing, but I heard his labored breathing beneath the mask. It had been so hard to breathe in those things, so hard to see. That's why he tripped that night. That's why I got away and he didn't. I squeezed my eyes shut, hot tears streaming down my cheeks.

My mom's boss had made her work late that night. Reluctantly, she'd let Carlton and me trick or treat alone, but just on our block. Just at the neighbors we knew.

When the man in the station wagon pulled alongside us, we knew not to get in when he promised to take us to his house for homemade candy apples. What we didn't know was what to do when he threw the car in park and ran after us.

For the rest of my life, I would remember Carlton screaming my name and turning to see him reaching for me, his mask askew, as the man dragged him on his belly through Mrs. Marshall's leaf pile. I didn't mean to leave him, but I did. When I opened my eyes, I was alone. This was my penance. Carlton would always be a part of me. I couldn't hide from my guilt. I couldn't run.

When I found the Reggie! bar wrapper in my backseat the next day, I wasn't even surprised. Carlton's favorite, named after his idol, ballplayer Reggie Jackson. The candy was introduced during his last summer alive in 1978, discontinued in 1982.

A reminder of him. There was always a reminder.

Stephanie hails from Tennessee, where she works nights in a tire factory and plots murder by day. She's published in romantic suspense and horror. You can stalk her at: www.facebook.com/stephaniescissom2019/

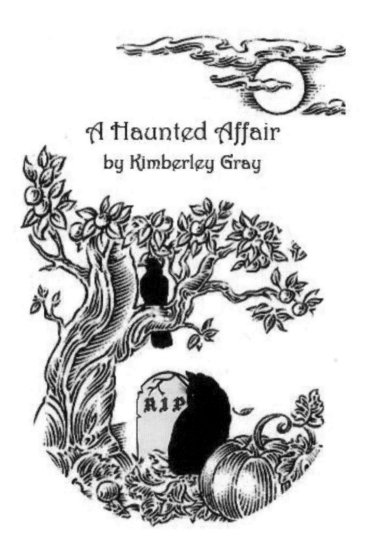

A Haunted Affair
by Kimberley Gray

Jaclyn Bowman stood out from the crowd because she was the only one not wearing a Halloween costume. Sure, she wore an awesome red dress covered in black lace, but it was more of a masquerade dress than costume. She must have misunderstood the memo. She came for a masquerade party, not a costume party, but if anyone asked, she'd tell them she was a vampire. Her eyes looked out behind a black lace mask with red beads above and below the eyes.

She searched for any members of the Paranormal Searchers, her favorite paranormal group, but figured they'd be in costume so she wouldn't know any of them. Winning a ghost hunt and a party with them on Halloween night was a dream come true and something to scratch off her bucket list. She danced with a few people, wondering who was behind the costume. She was happy to see that everyone wore masks with their costumes, so she didn't feel too out of place. Then, *he* walked up and asked her to dance.

Jaclyn tried to keep herself from shaking. She'd know those eyes anywhere. Shane Alexander, her crush out of the group. He had the warmest brown eyes she had ever seen. And there they were, looking into her blue ones. He was a divine dancer, and she wished the song would go on. He stayed on for another song, a waltz.

Too soon, the party was over. Jaclyn went to her hotel room to change. She had to meet the group at the same room as the party, and then they'd go to the house they were investigating. She all but floated back down the stairs to the hotel's grand ballroom. Opening the side door, she walked in. They all sat at a table that had been cleaned off from the party. They turned and looked at her.

"You must be Jaclyn Bowman, our contest winner," the leader of the group said.

"Yes. That's right."

"Come on over. We're just going through everything."

He introduced her to the group, and they got back to business. Jaclyn glanced over at Shane. He stared at her with a look that said he was thinking about something hard. Jaclyn felt the heat rise in her cheeks and looked away.

They gathered in a van and headed to the house.

"They say that a woman dressed all in black haunts this house. It is rumored she was in mourning for her husband that never returned from war. We've never been here, so this is a new place for us. Once we start, you and I will go first. Then, each one will go with you. Then, we'll go again. And so on and so forth. All right?"

"Okay," Jaclyn's voice cracked. "You alright?"

"Yes. Just a little nervous."

"There's no need to be. We do this all the time, so we know what we're doing. And, besides, we won't bite."

Jaclyn smiled a bit. She fought the urge to look over at Shane again.

They arrived at the plantation-style house and got their flashlights, cameras, voice recorders, and headlamps together. Shane equipped Jaclyn with a headlamp, voice recorder, and flashlight.

"Thank you," she said without looking at him.

He was silent, and Jaclyn didn't know how to take it. She walked away.

They began their investigation on the first story of the house. It was all uneventful. They asked questions and waited for a possible reply. Then, they decided to move up to the second floor, and things picked up.

Jaclyn and Shane walked into one room, and Jaclyn got chills. She looked around the room. Shane finally spoke.

"All night, I've been trying to place you. I knew I had seen your eyes before. You were the girl I danced with toward the end of the party. You were dressed in a black lace covered red dress."

"That's right. But, why did you wait all night to say something?"

"I wanted to be sure. Now that I am, there's something I'd like to do if it's all right."

"What's that?"

Shane closed the space between them. He turned his camera off. Jaclyn's eyes widened. *'Is he going to kiss me?'* she thought. He cupped her cheek and tilted her face up. She closed her eyes halfway. He bent down and very softly brushed his lips across hers. Her knees buckled. He wrapped his arms around her and kept her steady. He deepened the kiss, and Jaclyn kissed him back just as hard. They broke for air. Jaclyn smiled.

"How did you know I wanted you to kiss me?" "I took a chance."

"I'm glad you did."

Jaclyn leaned toward him again but stopped dead still. A beautiful woman appeared. She wore a vintage black dress with a big, black hat and a veil attached. Jaclyn's eyes widened again, and she stumbled back away from Shane.

"What? What's wrong?"

Jaclyn just pointed. He started his camera up again.

"I'm not seeing anything. Is this your way of rejecting me?"

"No. There's a woman. You can't see her at all?" "No."

"Quick. Get the voice recorder," Jaclyn said. The woman spoke directly to Jaclyn.

"You can see me?"

"And hear you, apparently. Who are you?" "I'm Katherine Garrison. I used to live here."

"So, you know you're dead?" Jaclyn couldn't believe she was having this conversation.

The woman looked around. "Yes. I know. But you're the first one who I can really communicate with. How is that?"

"Lady, if I knew myself, I'd tell you."

"You must have a gift. I want to tell you my story." "Okay.

What happened?"

"I was waiting for my husband to come back. I couldn't wait to tell him my news. He hadn't been gone too long, you see. I was with child and knew he'd be thrilled. Then, I got word that he didn't make it. I was devastated. I couldn't eat or sleep. Then, I lost the baby. I couldn't live with myself. I wore this dress and hat. I ended up dying from malnutrition and a broken heart. I had to tell someone about the baby. No one knew. I've waited all these years. Now, you can tell what really happened. I can go now. Thank you."

Tears fell from the woman's face as she vanished into thin air. Jaclyn felt at ease – a bit shaken, but at ease. She looked at Shane. He stood, wide-eyed, with his camera and voice recorder.

"She's gone now. She won't be back." "You can talk to ghosts?"

"I guess so. I guess you think I'm a weirdo now, huh?" "No. I think it's amazing."

Shane grabbed her and kissed her again.

"Let's go tell the others and listen to the recordings." "Jaclyn, I want to see more of you. Do you want to get something to eat later today?"

"Of course, I do. I like you, and I'm glad you like me."

Shane smiled and took her hand in his. They left the room and the house. The rest of the group raised their eyebrows at them. Shane kissed her hand.

"Nothing like that happened, but we are together.

Anyway, you guys will not believe what *did* happen."

Jaclyn told them everything that went on. They listened to the recordings and couldn't believe they got most of the conversation. Since Jaclyn could see and talk to ghosts, they invited her to join the group, much to Jaclyn and Shane's delight. Nothing else was ever mentioned about the woman haunting the old house, but Jaclyn knew there wouldn't be.

When not writing, Kim spends time with her two kids and husband in Northwest Alabama. She enjoys listening to music, reading, crocheting, watching television, and working word search puzzles. She has always had a love of reading, which grew into a love for writing. She's a big Alabama football fan and loves the Dallas Stars hockey team.

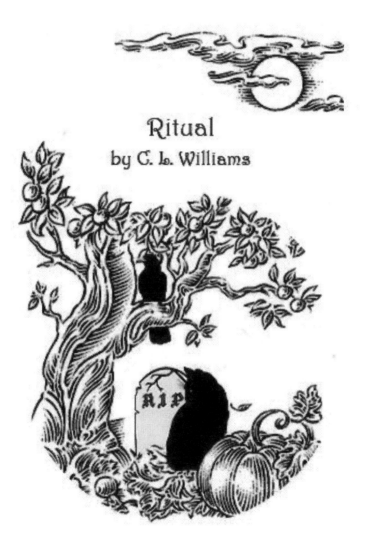

Ritual
by C. L. Williams

After going to a Halloween party, Ronnie and his friends, Scott and Ezra, make their grand exit. By grand exit, Ronnie got so drunk that he was kicked out and his friends left because they know he's too incoherent to walk or drive home. Scott and Ezra get on either side of Ronnie to help him stand straight without having any issues.

Given Ronnie only lives a block away, Scott and Ezra decide it's best to just walk him home. They know a shortcut that will potentially avoid any cops. It'll lead to the back yard, meaning Ronnie's parents won't see a belligerent Ronnie enter the house, and it also gives Ronnie a chance to possibly sober up before getting home.

While cutting through the woods, the three see a beautiful woman dressed in a witch costume. The three of them stare in awe as she just takes in the compliments from the three.

"Hi, I'm Abigail," the witch introduces herself.

"I'm Scott, that's Ezra, and this passed out mofo is Ronnie," Scott says, returning the courtesy.

"What's wrong with your friend?"

"We went to a party and he got drunk," Ezra tells Abigail. "We're cutting through the woods to avoid the cops. Ronnie is not only drunk, he's under 21."

"I was just sitting out here with some friends," Abigail then reveals a thermos. "I have coffee. Want to sit him down and I can share my coffee with him, sober him up some?"

Scott and Ezra look at one another and shrug. They decide to follow Abigail into the woods as a way to sit a near deadweight Ronnie down, but they also want to see if Abigail has friends as attractive as her.

Abigail leads the three guys to where she and her friends are sitting. As it turns out, her friends are still sitting around a campfire, drinking coffee and roasting marshmallows. Abigail asks two of her friends to move over so Ezra and Scott can put Ronnie down for a moment. Given a few of the girls have had their fair share of alcohol before, they move away in case Ronnie should start to vomit.

Scott and Ezra introduce themselves to Abigail's friends while Abigail introduces her friends: Stacey, Jess, Nora, and Hailey. Scott and Ezra trade small talk with the five women, all dressed as witches, and enjoy one another's company until Ronnie manages to mutter some gibberish.

"Uyhguy," comes from Ronnie's mouth. "What did he say?" Hailey asks.

"He's drunk, right now he's not going to say *anything* coherent," Scott tells Hailey.

"Abigail, thermos," Hailey yells out.

Abigail tosses the thermos over the fire, managing to avoid the campfire altogether as the thermos reaches Hailey's hands. Hailey opens the thermos and gives Ronnie some of the coffee. Ronnie, hating the taste of coffee, begins to gag.

"What's wrong?" Hailey asks.

"He hates coffee, give him more!" Scott says, acting immature.

Even though it was a crude suggestion from Scott, Hailey looks at the girls and they all agree that she should give Ronnie more coffee. She shrugs and begins to give Ronnie more coffee. Ronnie soon vomits out the coffee along with everything else he had during the day.

"What the Hell!?" Ronnie screams.

"Dude, we can't take you home drunk," Scott explains, "These beautiful ladies offered us the opportunity to lay low here while we try to sober you up!"

A few of the witches blush at Scott calling them beautiful, and Ronnie looks up and sees Hailey, the one giving him coffee while he's drunk.

"Why is this angel dressed like a witch?" a drunken Ronnie blurts out.

Hailey's face turns shades of red. "I've never been called

an angel before."

Ronnie then turns his attention back to his friends, "My parents are out of town this weekend. I could've puked and slept all I wanted to! I'm out of here!" Ronnie attempts to get up and make his way home, but he's still feeling the effects of the alcohol and almost stumbles into the fire. Hailey grabs him before he faceplants the fire.

"Now can you sit here, sober up, and enjoy the company of those around you?" Ezra asks Ronnie.

Ronnie looks at Hailey and agrees to Ezra's request. He sits back down next to Hailey, "Where have you been all my life?" Ronnie asks Hailey, trying his best to flirt with her.

"Casting spells?" Hailey hesitantly responds while showing off her witch's outfit to Ronnie.

"Seriously, though," Scott asks, "Why are the five of you here in the woods instead of partaking of the Halloween traditions?"

"You mean the Legend of Samhain?" Abigail asks. "Sawwin?" Ezra asks.

"Halloween began as Samhain," Abigail educates the three guys. "It's the time of year when the human world and the other side are closest to one another. It allows goblins, werewolves, vampires..." Abigail pauses and glances at her friends before saying, "Even witches are able to invade the human world for a little fun."

"So, let me get this straight," Scott asks, "You five dress as witches and call yourselves witches because it's Halloween?" Ezra then sneaks in a quick chuckle.

"What do you mean, dress up?" Nora asks.

"It's Halloween?" Ezra responds, "That's what people do," he adds, while in a state of confusion.

"Honey," Abigail responds, "who said anything about dressing up? We're not like these infants; we're not pretending to be witches. We *are* witches."

Scott and Ezra both laugh until Abigail holds out her hand, forcing the two of them to become quiet. She then speaks in a language unfamiliar to the three guys. While uncertain of what Abigail's saying, the three of them are now bound and unable to leave the woods. "You see, boys, we have been around for centuries. Sadly, our pets don't live as long as we do. That's where the three of you come in. You are going to be our new pets!"

Scott and Ezra try to scream; unfortunately, the spell Abigail placed upon their mouths makes it impossible to scream or even let a noise exit their mouths. Abigail places a weaker spell on Ronnie, in fears of possibly killing him. He lets out one cry for help. Abigail then places the same spell on Ronnie, but it's too late. Ronnie's cry for help happens to catch the attention of a police officer checking the perimeter. "Ladies, gentlemen," the officer says as he reveals himself,

"I believe I heard some screaming. Is everything okay?"

Hailey places the thermos of coffee next to Ronnie while the officer is looking around. "I'm terribly sorry, sir," Hailey says, trying her best to make it look an accident, "My friend here wanted some coffee and I guess it was still hot and he burned his tongue."

While Hailey's talking to the officer, Abigail places a spell on Ronnie forcing him to agree with everything Hailey says.

"Thorry offither," Ronnie says, attempting to come off as someone with a burnt tongue, "Pain thas extheme!"

"Okay, kids, be careful. Also try and get home. You know Halloween is almost over, right?"

"It's okay, officer," Nora says. "This land is my neighbor's land. We'll be going back sooner than you may think!"

The officer exits and Abigail once again makes sure the three guys are silent, "You boys are nothing but cubs to us.

We want to give you the meaning in your pathetic lives that you've never had before!"

"Meaningless lives!" Jess chimes in, echoing Abigail's

monologue.

"You see, boys," Abigail speaks once more. "We used to have pets." She plants an image of their history in the minds of Scott, Ronnie, and Ezra, showing the five witches holding leashes that contained werewolves almost the size of the witches themselves. "But our pets don't quite live as long as we do! That's where you three come in. YOU THREE will become our new pets!"

"I'm so sorry Ronnie," Hailey says to the drunken one sitting next to her, "I really did like your sweet talk, but I'm a little old for you, and I need a wolf pet more than a boytoy pet!" The five witches, looking like five beautiful models, then reveal their human forms are nothing more than a spell the five cast upon themselves. Once released from their own spell, instead of five beautiful girls, Ronnie, Scott, and Ezra are now looking at five creatures. The witches are now grey in color, visibly older than the three guys, and clearly inhuman. The three want to gasp at the sight of the witches but are unable to do so due to the silent spell Abigail placed them under.

Abigail grabs Ezra and places him in the campfire. The five witches breathe his essence into themselves as his flesh burns. All five witches let out a simultaneous exhalation as Ezra's charred body lies in the fire. Abigail then recites a spell in an unfamiliar language as a cloud of smoke covers the campfire. Once the smoke clears, Ronnie and Scott are now watching as Ezra's once lifeless corpse transforms into a werewolf and steps its way out of the campfire. The remaining two young men want to scream in terror, but the spell that Abigail cast upon them is still active and making a sound is impossible.

Nora and Jess grab Scott and throw him into the campfire next. Just as they did with Ezra, the five witches breathe in Scott's essence while his body burns. His life is being drained from him until nothing remains but a charred, lifeless body. This time around, Nora and Jess recite the ritual Abigail recited minutes earlier. Just like with Ezra, a cloud of smoke covers the campfire and Scott's lifeless, charred body. Once the smoke dissipates, a werewolf steps out of the campfire and walks over to the two witches that recited the incantation.

"Can you remove the spell?" Hailey asks Abigail. "You know I love the sound of a cub screaming." She then looks at Ronnie, "Your screams will almost be as delicious as me draining you of your life essence." She then gives Ronnie a kiss on the forehead.

Abigail removes the spell as Hailey kicks Ronnie into the fire. While he is screaming, Hailey is breathing in every ounce of his essence on her own until he is nothing more than a burned body. The other four look at Hailey in awe as she begins reciting the ritual incantation, turning Ronnie into her own personal werewolf. A once drunken Ronnie emerges from the fire, now a werewolf, loyal only to Hailey.

"Should we stay here and join in on this *Halloween* fun, or should we go home?" Stacey asks Abigail.

"That man that was here earlier said that Halloween is almost over. We should consider making our way back home before the borders of worlds begins to widen once more," Abigail decrees.

The other four mutually agree that it is time to go, because they now have new pets in the forms of Ronnie, Scott, and Ezra, human beings that were put under witchcraft and transformed into werewolves, pets loyal only to the five witches. While there was a desire to have five werewolves for the five witches, no one is complaining at having three new pets and three less humans.

"Ladies," Abigail says as she begins to open a portal, "I know it's the Legend of Samhain, but these pesky humans want to say *Happy Halloween* so I guess I'll say it," she then looks at her five sisters, "Happy Halloween, ladies!" Abigail then steps through the portal.

"Happy Halloween," the other four respond as they soon follow, bringing their three new pets with them.

C.L. Williams is an international bestselling author currently living in central Virginia. He has written eight poetry books,

four novellas, one novel, and a contributor to various anthologies. He is getting ready to release his first novelette, Lucifer's Lost Love. C.L. Williams is currently working on the book Bed Bugs, a tie in to the MMH Productions film of the same name.

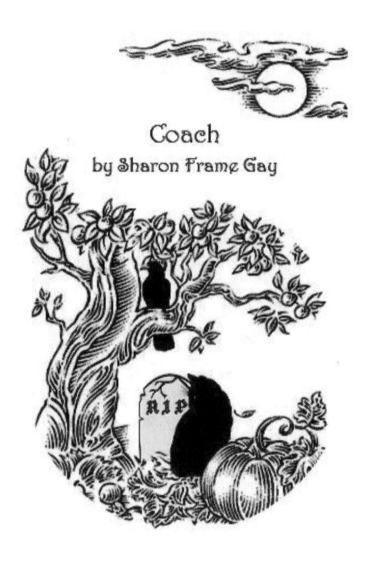

Coach

by Sharon Frame Gay

JOURNAL OF LINDSEY STONE, 1985

My name is Lindsey Stone. I'm writing in the darkness under a blanket with a fading flashlight.

Whoever finds this will know who killed me. I'm hiding this journal in the locker at school. I know I'm dying. It is just a matter of time. Of opportunity. My bones already ache from the frost of death, my heart silent as the deep woods.

When you read this journal, ask yourself, 'What would I do?'"

It all began this September when school started. The happiness of junior year was shadowed by the disappearance of four girls this summer. Three lived in townships close by. The fourth, Julie Taylor, was a freshman here at Lincoln High in Pine Falls, Missouri. Two were found. They were stabbed, mutilated, and tossed into Fletcher's Pond. Two are still missing. A cloud hovered over our school, our festivities, our studies. The whole town was jittery. Nobody goes out past dark until they find the killer. Girls walk in pairs or groups, never alone, and NEVER after the sun goes down.

Monday started off like any other day. We laughed and joked, huddled in corners with friends and chatted in the lunchroom. But behind our smiles, there was a deep foreboding.

My dad dropped me off at the front doors of the school as he always did. It was a crisp fall morning, the leaves a brilliant red and orange against the backdrop of a deep blue sky. My friends gathered in groups and talked about classes, the upcoming football game on Friday and music, until the bell rang. There were promises to meet at lunch or in study hall.

My best friend Katy and I stayed after school that afternoon to help with cheerleading try-outs. We planned on riding home with Jason, Katy's older brother. After the tryouts, Katy and I were heading for the showers when Jason jogged down the hall.

"Wait up," he said. "We have a problem here." "What's the matter?" asked Katy.

"The old crappy clunker broke down in the parking lot. The tow truck is coming to pick it up and take it to the mechanic. I have to ride along. Hurry if you want to come downtown in the tow truck with me. Dad will pick us up from there."

"No way," said Katy. She jutted her chin out. "I have stuff to do at home. I won't waste time sitting around in a stupid garage. Lindsey and I can walk. It'll still be light when we leave. Right, Linds?"

I glanced at my watch. It was getting late. I hesitated, then nodded. "Yeah, we'll hurry home."

"Ok, have it your way, but you better hustle," Jason said as he turned and walked away. "See you at dinner."

Downstairs, the girls' locker room was silent. Everyone had left for the day. I decided not to clean up until I got home, pulling on a grey hooded sweatshirt and jeans, stuffing my gym clothes in a backpack. Katy said she wanted to take a quick shower, so I waited in the dressing area for her. I paced the floor, hoping she'd hurry.

"Get a move on," I called out. I heard the shower start. A few minutes later, it stopped.

Katy called out in a worried voice. "Lindsey! Get in here!" "What?" I asked, poking my head around the tiled stall.

Wrapped in a towel, Katy pointed past the shower head to the ceiling.

"Does that look like a camera to you?"

I peered upwards. There was a small black disk perched on a stalk protruding from a rafter. Maybe it was a fire sprinkler. Maybe it was a security camera. A security camera? Here in the girls' shower? That would be an invasion. Far away, I thought I heard footsteps. Then silence. I put my finger to my lips. We listened, but all we heard was water dripping from the shower head.

"I don't know what it is. Let's get out of here. We can tell the office tomorrow and have them look at it. Come on." I looked at my watch. "Now!"

Katy dressed quickly, running her hands through tendrils of damp red hair. She tossed a bottle of soap and the wet towel into her backpack. We hurried down the corridor, past a series of darkened classrooms to the double doors, pushed them open and set off across the football field toward home.

The sun was dancing lower on the horizon. We broke into a trot along the well-worn shortcut kids took through a stand of trees. Although it was a dense wooded area, it was the quickest way home. Our feet pounded along the trail as we brushed past shrubs and low-hanging branches. The last of the remaining sunlight flickered in and out of shadow, forming lacy designs on the trail. A cold wind picked up, trees swaying overhead. In the distance, a dog barked.

Katy caught her foot on a root and stumbled. She stopped to adjust her backpack and bent down to tie a shoelace. She straightened, took a step. There was rustling in the trees to our left. Branches snapped. We looked at each other, frightened. My heart raced. Katy's green eyes widened as she stared into mine.

"Let's go," I mouthed. I took a step towards home, but Katy wheeled around and raced back down the trail towards the football field.

"Katy, come back," I whispered into the wind.

Instead, she ran faster through the woods, leaving me far behind. I stood there, confused. I didn't want to continue alone, yet I didn't think going back was the right thing either. But how could I leave Katy? I sprinted down the path toward the school, the forest darkening in the fading light.

Reaching the edge of the clearing, I stopped and looked around. Katy was nowhere in sight. Did she make it back to the building? Did she double back into the woods, thinking I hadn't followed? I stopped and listened, the only sound my labored breath. Fear clouded my brain. Deep shadows crept across the football field as I strained to see.

Then I heard a muffled noise coming from the woods. It must be Katy.

"Katy?" I whispered.

There was no answer, just the wind in the trees.

Holding my breath with every step, I approached the area.

I smelled it first. The coppery tang that hit my nostrils and set my head spinning. Blood, fresh and heavy over the lower notes of the forest. In the deepening dusk, I stopped, terror rising. There was Katy's backpack, lying under a broken shrub, and a flicker of yellow through the branches beyond the path. I stepped off the trail and into the bushes. Parting the leaves with my hand, I peered through the foliage.

Katy was lying on the forest floor, eyes half closed, her throat slit and still pumping blood, clothes sliced in shreds. Standing above her was the killer. He was drooling, eyes glazed, knife in hand. The man kneeled above Katy's body, ripping at her clothes, lost in a frenzy. I gasped, inhaled sharply. He froze, turned his head, and we locked eyes. Recognition came to both of us. I backed away in horror as he turned towards me with the knife.

"Wait!" he yelled.

Panicked, I turned and raced deeper through the trees. He followed me. I veered right, scrambled across a small brook into a horse pasture. Now he was right behind, as though he expected this was where I would go. Somewhere familiar.

Somewhere open. I burst forward, turned toward the barn, but changed course at the last second, darting past the building and onto the rural road that circles our town. I sprinted down the middle of the road into the setting sun, running for my life.

Headlights came up over the hill in the dusk. An old white pickup truck topped the rise, driving toward me. I waved frantically. The car slowed, then pulled over, motor idling.

An older man rolled down the window. "What's going on?"

I didn't recognize him. He could be dangerous, too. But anybody was safer than who I had just seen. I hesitated to tell this stranger what I saw. He might drive off, thinking it was a prank, or worse yet, hand me over to the killer lurking somewhere behind me. So, I lied.

"Help! I need a ride to Springfield. My brother's hurt and I have to get there right away."

"Springfield?" he asked. "What's the big emergency? Can't your parents drive you? A kid like you shouldn't be hitchhiking."

"No, they can't drive me. They're already there! He was in an accident and I'm heading for the hospital."

He gave me a suspicious look, then nodded. "Hop in, I'll take you as far as the edge of town, then you're on your own." "That's fine," I said, running to the passenger side. I looked behind me as we drove on. There was nobody in sight. But he was there. Hiding in the trees. Plotting, planning, waiting to get me. I needed to get as far away as possible. I knew him all too well. And he knew me, too.

The killer was our high school coach. He was well-respected in town. The police might not believe me at first, giving Coach time to get to me. He'd twist things so that nobody suspected he was capable of murder. Coach would make my death look like an accident. I didn't know what to do.

Where was I going to go? There was nothing in my backpack but books, some makeup, and a few dollars. I only knew, for now, I couldn't go home. Coach would kill me.

The truck driver said his name was Dan Olson. He had white hair under a farmer's cap and wore faded overalls. The truck smelled like smoke and sweat. Beneath my feet rolled used soda cans and crumpled papers. He asked my name. I told him it was Janet. He made small talk on our way to Springfield. I answered as best I could, my heart tripping.

All I could think of was Katy. She knew Coach too. Katy probably ran right up to him, thinking he'd walk us home in the dark. I shuddered at the thought. Now Coach was after me. Mr. Olson peered at me from time to time, asking questions. My voice sounded tinny and fake as I tried to speak normally, even though I was bordering on hysteria. I thought of Coach, of Katy, the camera in the locker room, the girls who had

disappeared and felt bile rise in my throat. My spirit shattered.

After an hour, the truck slowed as Mr. Olson turned off the highway, rattled and stopped in front of Springfield Regional Hospital.

"Here we are," he said. "I brought you all the way to the hospital instead of drop you off somewhere. It isn't safe, with all those girls gone missing." He looked over at me, eyes milky behind thick glasses. "You should never hitchhike, you know. Especially now. I hope your brother's okay."

I nodded, thanked him, and got out of the car. He sat there with the motor running, watching me, a deep frown on his face. To avoid suspicion, I walked through the hospital doors.

It was busy in the lobby. People were wandering in and out, talking in hushed tones. Babies were crying, small children running back and forth, patients in wheelchairs. Uncomfortable looking chairs lined dull green walls. Still shaky, I settled in the far corner next to a potted plant. I set the backpack down, clasped trembling hands together between my knees, and closed my eyes.

What should I do now? I longed to call home. Say I was okay. What if Coach found out I called somehow? Would he hurt my Mom? I couldn't take the chance. No, it's best to hide out until I can figure out what to do. At least for now, I was out of danger. I hunkered down in the chair and tried to stay calm, but everything came back again and again. *Katy. Oh my God. Katy.*

Katy and I had been best friends since first grade. She lived down the street in a white Colonial house with green shutters. Her mom was a doctor, her dad an accountant. Her brother Jason was a year older than we were, always teasing us, calling us the "Terrible Two." I remember walking to school together when we were six, holding hands, trailing behind Jason every morning.

Katy's fiery red hair glimmered in the sunshine, so different from my blonde pigtails. She was the risk taker, the one who loved a challenge, while I hung back and watched her do something first. Then, like a faithful puppy, I followed. You seldom saw one of us without the other.

By the time we entered high school, I was taller than her by several inches. Katy was tiny, always the girl at the top of our cheerleading pyramids. I held her up, her feet on my shoulders while we cheered at all the games. And now, she was gone.

I felt like I let her down somehow, unable to lift her up from death. Coach had known her all these years, too. How could he betray her, betray me, betray the whole town? My mind whirled. I couldn't get the image of Coach out of my head as he stood above Katy's body. Nothing will ever be the same.

Hours went by. Night had gathered outside the window. A constant parade of people shuffled by. Nobody seemed to notice me. I felt safe here among all these strangers. What irony, I thought. To feel more secure with people I don't know than those I do.

Closing my eyes again, I leaned my head against the wall and tried to rest. Maybe if I fell asleep, I'd wake up and discover I'd been dreaming. My mind kept returning again and again to Katy, to Coach, to the grisly murder.

Somebody grabbed my sleeve. I gasped, jumped backwards and bumped my head against the wall. Looking down, I saw a small boy in a blue sweater tugging on me.

"Is that you?" he asked, pointing to the television mounted in the waiting room.

There I was up on the screen, along with a snapshot of Katy. Beneath the photos a banner read "Two girls missing in Pine Falls. Police are asking for your help. Call 911 if you have any information."

Pulling the hood over my head, covering my blonde hair, I looked down at the boy, swallowed hard. Tried to smile. Sweat trickled down my ribs.

"Now, how can I be on TV and be here in the hospital at the same time?" I asked him. "How silly! That's not me."

He thought about it, nodded, then skipped back to his mother. I picked up my backpack and walked down the hall to the cafeteria, where I bought a banana and a sweet roll. I tried to stay as invisible as possible. I turned toward the window, shielding my face from the others, and sat there until the sky lightened. Then I stretched and headed back to the waiting room.

There were more people in the lobby now than last night. I couldn't stay here much longer. In the ladies' room, I washed my face and hands. I ran a brush through my hair and tucked it inside the hood. Looking in the mirror, a pale version of myself stared back.

Opening the door, I turned towards the lobby. A deep voice said, "Stop right there."

Startled, I tried to duck back into the ladies' room, but a strong hand grabbed my elbow. I looked up. The voice belonged to a sheriff. He towered above me, his badge right at eye level, beefy face lowered towards mine.

"Are you Lindsey Stone?"

I thought of lying. But my name was on the backpack. I had identification in my wallet. He'd know the truth soon, anyway. I couldn't run. He still gripped my arm. I nodded in defeat.

"Come along, Lindsey. We're glad you're safe. Everybody's been looking for you. We're taking you back to Pine Falls and your family."

He propelled me through the lobby and out the doors into the back seat of a waiting squad car. Another officer was in the passenger seat. He turned around and smiled. He looked like Coach, and my heart skipped. As we pulled away from the curb, I saw the little boy in the blue sweater with his mother, pointing at me. I was so lost, confused and afraid. Then I put my head in my hands and cried.

"Lindsey," said the sheriff, peering in the rearview mirror. "Do you need anything?" His voice was soft, sympathetic.

I shook my head.

"Listen, we're taking you to the station in Pine Falls. Your parents will be there. The police want to ask questions. Don't speak now about what you may have seen. Just sit back and relax. Wait until you talk to the local police."

I nodded, peering out the window at the start of a bright autumn day, remembering Katy with her blank eyes, her mouth open in surprise.

We pulled in front of the tiny building that housed our police station. The officers led me through the door and down a short hallway, into a room with bright overhead lights, metal chairs and a table. On one side of the table were Mom and Dad. They both stood up and moved toward me.

"Lindsey!" Mom cried. "Thank God you're okay!" She trembled as she put her arms around me. Her face was ashen and drawn. In the harsh light she looked like a ghost.

I turned to Dad. He put both hands on my shoulders, squeezed. "Honey, are you okay? Is everything all right?"

I swayed, feeling faint, knees buckling.

"I think I need to sit," I mumbled, and Dad led me over to a chair, sat me down, and kept his hands on my shoulders.

Two officers walked into the room, greeted us, then began the interrogation. They started by saying they found Katy's body. They were sorry to tell me she was dead. Katy's brother said we had been together after school.

The police asked if I had been with Katy. Maybe saw something that can help. One man turned on a tape recorder, pushed it towards me and invited me to speak. I took a deep breath and began to talk.

I told them we had gone separate ways on the trail, and I'd lost her. That's when I heard a faint noise coming from the woods and thought maybe Katy was hiding. I saw her backpack near a bush and parted the shrubs. Katy lay on her back, throat slashed. I told them she was lying there alone. I said I completely freaked out, running in terror through the woods to the highway. Afraid the killer was hiding nearby, I took off in a panic, asked for a ride out of town from a stranger.

Twisting my hands in my lap, I lied and said I never saw the killer, never heard his voice, had no idea who it could have been. They asked me the same questions over and over again, trying to trip me up, but I remained solid in my lies and told them I had seen nothing but Katy's body. There was too much at stake to tell the truth.

Mom prodded. "Are you sure you saw nothing else, Lindsey?"

I looked at her, then over at Dad. He raised his eyebrows in question.

"I'm sure," I said, crying. I looked into Dad's eyes. "Please believe me. I saw nothing."

He stared at me for several moments, nodded slightly in understanding, then turned to the police. "She's telling you the truth, officers. I know my daughter. I know when she's lying and she's giving you honest answers. Lindsey's exhausted. Please let us take her home for now."

Eventually, the police took up their recording devices and notebooks and told me we'd talk again. Maybe something would come back in my memory that might help. Call them anytime. They said we were free to go.

I barely ate dinner that night. The three of us sat at the kitchen table, each overcome with different emotions. Mom and Dad stole worried glances at me. I know they suspected I wasn't telling the whole truth. I kept my head down, stared at the plate. Weary, I rose from the table on unsteady feet.

"I need to go to bed" I mumbled. Climbing the stairs with shaky legs, my heart thumped with each step. Soon. I would die soon.

Closing the bedroom door, I shoved the dresser against it,

double locked the window and pulled the blinds. Rummaging through the closet I found an old baseball bat, set it down on the bed. Then allowed myself to cry, for me, for Mom and Dad, for Katy and her family. I felt the desperate pall of terror wash over me and vomited into the trash can next to the bed. Spent, alone, frightened, I wrote in this journal. Every creak on the stairs, every scratching limb on the window, every night noise, was no longer a source of comfort but an invitation to death. Fatigue overtook me and my eyes grew heavy.

I must have slept, waking with a jolt when Mom knocked on the door. She said it was time to get up, have breakfast and set out for school. I washed my face, got dressed, took great care to stow this journal in the backpack, and walked downstairs. My parents sat at the kitchen table. Mom buttered a slice of toast and put it on a plate. She told me I didn't have to go to school today. I told her I wanted to go. In my frantic mind, I thought it might be safer in a crowd. I could finish this journal at school.

I sipped at some orange juice and felt it burn as it slid down my throat. I wanted to say something to my mother, warn her. But I also wanted to protect her. Maybe it's for the best, I thought. Maybe it's as it should be. I felt my soul surrender to the horror of what I saw, to the horror of what will be coming.

Dad and I did not speak as he drove me to Lincoln High that morning. We rode in silence. I held my backpack clutched fiercely to my chest. This time, instead of dropping me off at the front doors, he parked the car and we walked into the building together, his hand on my elbow, guiding me. We had a meeting this morning with Mrs. Roberts, the principal, to discuss what happened. Friends smiled sadly as we passed through the big double doors, hugging me, murmuring words of sympathy about Katy, shaking Dad's hand as we made our way down the hall. They were relieved I was found. In the midst of all this sorrow, at least I was spared, they said. Or so it seemed to them.

We reached Mrs. Robert's office. She rose from the desk with tears in her eyes and closed the door behind us. She gave me a hug, tucked a strand of hair behind my ear with a gentle hand.

"Thank God you're home, Lindsey. This is a nightmare. Such a tragedy. I'm sorry for you. For poor Katy. It's horrible, but it's over now. You're safe." She gestured to a chair. "Here, honey, sit down so we can talk."

Then, smiling at my father, she gestured to the other chair by the window.

"Have a seat, Coach."

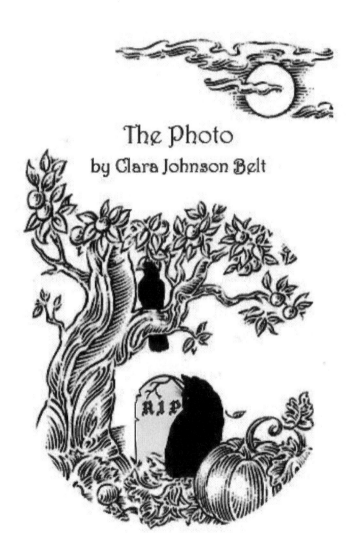

The Photo
by Clara Johnson Belt

It was that time of year again. Halloween, filled with horror movies, costumes, and silly pranks to scare your friends and family. It was also the time I'd spent with my father. He loved Halloween, so much so that he would take me to those haunted theme parks where I held his hand as we traversed through the haunted houses and carriage rides.

Five years later, I still can't accept invitations to go to those places with my friends.

Amanda had offered me a ride to a park in Lancaster, as she does every year, despite me telling her every year the exact same thing: "It's not the same without my Dad."

Maybe she didn't get it because she still had her dad. He liked Halloween, too, but he never had time to go with her due to work. So, she would invite her boyfriend and friends like me.

My alarm clock read two-thirty. I went downstairs to get a snack when I heard Mom cussing up a storm about something.

"What's wrong, now?" I asked not really wanting to know.

My mother's eyes were wide with panic. "We have no water. Go check in the basement to see if there's a leak."

Wonderful, I thought. This was a problem every year. When the temperatures dropped, the pipes would freeze in the basement and we would have no water until they finally melted. Sometimes, that lasted for days on end.

Grabbing my coat, I went outside to our basement. The entrance sat underneath our porch as it was an above-ground basement. The door was built to look like the rest of the house, with white sliding.

I pulled the door open and walked in, only to find two inches of water on the floor. A quick glance upward told me the cause: the water line for the hose outside. I shut off the valve that was closest to the pipe.

Luckily, the heater was not in the water. Good thing I had

put it on boxes to keep it off the floor. We've had issues before where the water pipes burst. This was the third time the one for the hose broke. It traveled down the door, so it had the most exposure to the outside temperature.

But if it's that pipe that burst, that meant something else was wrong. The water to the hose wouldn't take all the water from the house.

I checked the gauges at the water heater. One of them I assumed was the water pressure in the house. The needle was down to five, almost zero. We had no water pressure, which was most likely due to the freezing temperatures.

Going back outside, I noticed Mom was leaning over the railing on the porch. "What's going on with the pipes?" she asked.

"The water line for the hose broke, but we also have no water pressure. Either the frozen water is preventing flow, or the thing is broken," I explained.

She rolled her eyes and mumbled something I couldn't hear. The nights were already getting colder, and we didn't need to this to add to our problems.

My hot breath formed smoke in front of my face as I shivered against the cold. I had a feeling this was going to be a long week.

It was several days before he plumber came by and told us what was wrong with our water pressure. Turns out, the switch was going bad and suggested that we increase the heat downstairs to prevent the water from freezing.

I barely had anything in my bank account, but between Mom and I, we were able to purchase two more heaters. I made sure that they were placed above the floor in case another pipe burst. It made Mom unhappy because she began worrying about the electric bill. Running that many heaters in one house would cost more money for anybody.

I was outside the basement as Mom talked on the phone to my grandmother. From what I could hear of the conversation, it wasn't going well. Mom was practically yelling at the phone now.

"I gotta go now, Mom. I'll talk to you later," she said before she hung up the phone. My grandmother probably didn't appreciate it. She hated it when Mom did that.

Mom walked down the driveway and headed towards the open basement door. She put her hands in her pants pockets and stared at the water heater, mumbling something else I couldn't hear, nor did I really want to. The last thing I wanted was a fight.

"Your father gave up everything to keep this house going. He'd be heartbroken to see how bad it's gotten." Mom's face fell and she wiped her cheeks.

I didn't respond. It was true. Dad had spent money he didn't have between this house and the painful divorce from some woman he was with before he married Mom. He tore the entire house apart to replace everything from the floor to the electric and plumbing. He tried to make a good home with his own two hands, but the house was just too far gone for him to save.

Now the weight of a broken house weighed on Mom and me. We had to keep it going. We had no money to move out thanks to our crappy landlord.

She began to step out the door when she paused. Turning around, she stared at something on the floor and picked it up. "What is it, Mom?" She didn't answer me and continued

to look at the thing in her hand.

I walked toward her to see what it was she was holding. She handed it to me. It was an old ID tag with Dad's picture from a company he used to work for when I was a kid.

"This… this was on the shelf, wasn't it?" I knew it was there.

I'd seen it years ago and again just the other day. It was nowhere near the edge to just fall off due to wind.

Mom looked at me, spooked. "It just fell. Face upwards and everything."

I stared at my father's awkwardly smiling picture. Is it possible that his spirit is here with us? Is he trying to tell us that he's here? On Halloween of all times, too. What did this mean?

"Maybe Dad's spirit is here reminding you that he loves you and is here for you," I offered, hoping it would give her some comfort.

"I don't believe in ghosts and all that." She waved her hand dismissively.

Annoyed, I asked, "Do you have another explanation?" Instead of answering, she walked away from me.

Mom always joked that it was the Native American side of my Dad's family that made me believe in ghosts and otherworldly things. I wasn't much of a believer in God and the Devil, but I did believe there were things for which no reasonable explanation existed.

I felt my eyes water as I stared at my father's photo. It was as though I could feel him trying to say, "It's okay. Things will work out. I'm here." I could hear the voice in my head as clearly as if he was standing right in front of me.

For the first time in weeks, I smiled. Genuinely smiled. "Thanks, Dad."

I may not have been able to see him, but I felt he was there. Somehow, he knew what was going on and wanted to remind me and Mom that he was still here with us.

I drove to the nearby gas station to buy Mom and me some cigarettes and a snack for my brother. She'd given me money, as she'd ended up smoking all of mine. I also purchased some flowers for a stop I'd make before heading back home.

The church was barely a quarter mile from the gas station. Pulling in, I noticed one of the spots were recently filled. It must've been dug just this past week by the looks of the dirt.

I stopped and placed my car in park before getting out and walking over to my Dad's grave. The grass had barely grown after all these years. My uncle had told my mother he'd put some grass seed down, but it seems like it didn't take.

I placed the flowers down on my father's headstone. "Happy Halloween, Dad. Wish you were here."

I left, feeling a sense of calmness. It was like a hand reached out to touch my own. Dad appreciated my visit and was wishing me a Happy Halloween.

Clara C. Johnson is a poet and storyteller who has been writing since her time in high school. She has written short stories, novels, and poetry with a particular love for epic fantasy. She spends most of her days at her computer plotting her next project, spellbound in a book, and spending time with her husband and cats. She has a B.A. in English at the Pennsylvania State University. Besides writing, she also enjoys painting and gaming. She currently lives in PA with her family.

Sign up for Clara's newsletter for news on upcoming releases and special deals!

www.authorclaracjohnson.com

Candy Snatchers
by N. M. Brown

Halloween. Yeah, I don't celebrate that day anymore. That day ruined my life. Now I know what you're thinking: maybe somebody snatched my candy bag as a kid and soured me on the holiday, or maybe the cute girl at the Halloween party shut me down, forever altering my confidence. But it wasn't anything like that. This was something real, something far worse. Pure evil.

When I was fourteen or so, a couple buddies and my girlfriend Hannah showed up at my back window. They wanted me to go out with them. My parents were so busy screaming at each other that they didn't care that I was even there, much less have any objections to my absence. I could have gone out the front door if I wanted, to be honest, but it was more fun to sneak out, even if my jaw was throbbing.

The arrival of colder weather brought the worst out in my broken tooth. I'd been lying to my mother about it to avoid the dentist and having to miss school. My girlfriend was in an after-school club with me. It was our only chance to be together for more than just five minutes here and there between classes.

The night air was cool and damp, and it felt good on my skin, like liberation. Considering what my friends had in mind, that's honestly the most appropriate word for it. Plenty of children would be liberated from their candy bags tonight.

See, we were candy snatchers, punks, the ruiners of fun for little children. We told ourselves at the time that any kid out that late had it coming. Eddie would say, *"It wasn't our fault they were in the right place at the wrong time."*

Besides, everyone knew that Halloween candy got marked down 75% at all the stores the next day anyway.

It never fails. Sympathetic parents will buy candy by the droves to satisfy a broken-hearted child. Those kids made bank because of us. At least that's what we thought... that's what I told myself the year before. I'll tell ya what though, I saw those kids crying every time I closed my eyes until Thanksgiving.

I swore to myself I wouldn't ever do it again, but my parents had me feeling some kind of way. There was anger, anger I didn't I understand much less know how to express rationally. Destruction was instant gratification, and it fueled my needs.

Now, we weren't bad kids. Bag-grabbing was the most harmless crime kids our age could have been up to that night. The rest were out partying, drinking, driving or vandalizing. We weren't in the woods drunk with some girls' legs up in the air. We cruised around the streets, hanging out and listening to music. Sure, there may have been a joint or two, but that was commonplace back then.

We weren't in the car but fifteen minutes when we saw them: four little kids all dressed in the same costume. It was the weirdest thing I'd ever seen. They wore red robes with devil horns and red masks that covered only the area around their eyes.

Their heights told me they were various ages. It was probably some bored mother's idea. She likely made the matching outfits for her kids.

I almost felt sorry for them at first, to be honest. They just stood there without emotion. Those kids had to have heard us coming, though none looked in our direction. There was barely any reaction when we grabbed their bags; no sadness or outrage, just blank stares on their faces. It wasn't until started to drive away that any movement occurred. As I looked out the back window, all four of their heads snapped up in our direction.

I was no expert, but I was certain that I'd never seen any kids like these before. Their eyes glowed red all at once, like they were caught in an eternal camera flash.

That was the only movement their bodies made. It didn't even look like they were breathing. There were no puffs of warmth on the cold night air, no rising of shoulders as they inhaled breath, nothing.

Glowing eyes, like hot coals, stayed visible through the fog long after their forms fell away into the shadows of distance. Chills wrapped around my bones, one by one. They settled there, no matter how much I hugged myself to create a rise in temperature. My head felt heavy, so I closed my eyes. The children's eyes burned into my subconscious.

We got to my house not long after. Our hauls were poured into the middle of the floor, and each person took what they liked. In no time at all, we were smoking in a rotation and an eighth of the candy was gone. I tried my luck with a Kit Kat bar – bad move. Bursts of agony shot into my left ear and temple like a knitting needle. Clumps of chocolate peppered the sink as I spit out the candy. Warm saltwater soothed my tooth like a warm blanket.

A clatter from the living room cut my relief short. It sounded like someone broke something; that's all I needed at that moment. It felt like the side of my face was kicked by a donkey, and now people were breaking stuff. *Greatttt.*

Hannah was screaming my name repeatedly; someone else was yelling to call for an ambulance. The scene before me was pure chaos.

Those sounds I heard belonged Eddie's body as it fell to the floor. His bones twisted and creaked with convulsions. Crimson and brown foam bubbled forth from the depths of his throat, and his eyes were fixed on something within his skull that we could not see. His turbulent heartbeat turned erratic before stopping altogether.

Hannah was soon to follow. Her death came swifter and more gracefully than Eddie's She hadn't eaten nearly as much candy as he did. The last words she uttered on this Earth were about children.

"The children...why are they laughing?"

Burning pains consumed my torso, bringing me to my knees with pain. The wind was knocked out of me as my body slumped to the floor. It wasn't fair, I didn't even fully eat one single piece of candy. Tinkling squeaks reverberated off the walls of my living room. I understood what Hannah meant then. The last thing I heard before my consciousness was robbed from me completely was the ethereal sound of kids laughing.

I came to in a hospital bed. A charcoal treatment saved my life but also left me with mental disturbances that I'll never be rid of. Whenever I'm around a fire, I'm still convinced I can taste it. But perhaps that's just my burden to bear.

Maybe that's just what happens when you steal candy from children.

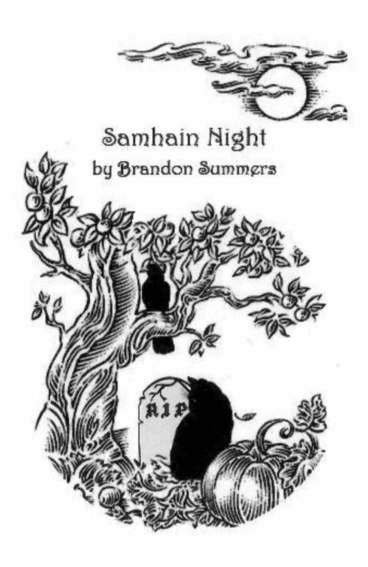

Samhain Night
by Brandon Summers

It had been a long day. School, then trick-or-treat with her little brother, then scary movies and popcorn with her friends.

For one year, though, she had been waiting for that day, and that whole day she waited for only one thing. The midnight hour. The dark that came between the last day of October and the first of November belonged to her.

Samhain!

Lorrie Mulhare slipped out of the house unseen and took her bicycle to the end of the block before zipping down the suburban lanes. She did not wear a costume, just the clothes she'd had on since morning: a blue hoodie, long sleeve black tee with a skull on the chest, jeans, and blue sneakers. Her long, straight brown hair was swept up by the wind of her speed.

It was quiet. Gray clouds traced across the pitch-black sky, and over the blazing orange foliage and moist brown and deep green of the earth.

The community's Halloween festivities had ended, but there were still plenty of pumpkins and paper ghosts and streamers in sight, lights on in a few of the quaint homes, and rowdy teens in skeleton costumes raising hell or an adorable facsimile of it.

Lorrie smirked. They had no idea of the night's importance, its true meanings.

The silence became absolute as she left the small neighborhood, going from city streets to country lanes and into the deep mountain woods, to one of many secret paths.

She stashed her bicycle and began her ascent. It would be a long march through the woods, and even as she enjoyed the crackle of leaves and snap of twigs, she took care, pushing away spindly branches and stomping over gnarled roots.

There was no need for courage, only resolve. She was well acquainted with the woods. It was her passion. She belonged there. The woods were the only place where she felt real. To her, it was a magical place. No danger could hope to diminish her excitement.

She continued upward, ever nearer to the goddess.

The history of their village and the surrounding mountains had always fascinated her, and she drew inspiration from it as she trekked. The pious town masters, with torches and pitchforks and whips, had driven the witches and heathens into those woods, some simply to be exiled, many more to be slaughtered.

Lorrie had found one of the burial sites, badly weathered over the centuries. The markings on the three remaining graves there had long since become illegible.

She could have told her friends about it and even thought about bringing them there. They thought her interests were awesome and supported her beliefs. Samhain was not a game to her, though. It was hers alone.

Lorrie reached the site, arriving in good time for traveling in the dark. She removed her hoodie, setting it upon the clearing's fine white sediment and using it as a blanket.

She convinced herself that she liked the cold. A chilling wind blew against her, and she imagined the howl of a wild animal being carried upon it.

She took out two objects from her sweater pocket. With the lighter, she ignited the wick and set before her the carved turnip. She had given it a face, and nothing more. Its light flickered warmly in the space as she rested on her knees.

"I am here, goddesses. Earth Mother and Mother Moon. I know you're with me. I feel the life energy of your loving womb. The rays of your wisdom shine upon me."

Alone, and at last free of the burdens of her life, the oppression of her family and peers, she was able to truly be herself, enjoying the night as she summoned the earth's energy into her waiting soul.

Lorrie looked to the sky and addressed the goddesses, pleaded with them, as she did so many nights in her prayers.

"Show me your world. I want to see magical things! I know they exist. This town's dumb. The people here are so lame. They don't get it. But I do! You empower me. Let me celebrate you! Oh, to play among nymphs and dance with the moth-man and swim with werewolves."

She shifted, pulling her legs from under her, and leaned back, relaxing as she dreamily watched the busy gray clouds veiling the deep blackness above.

There was no more wonderful time than Samhain. The town would never hold a festival, and there was no harvest, but she could feel it inside, the coming of winter, and with it the arrival of her fantasized "dark half."

A smile played at her pale lips. Tomorrow, she would awaken to a different world, the other realm given dominion. The fires would burn, if only in her mind, because they did not have a fireplace and arson was still illegal.

"Mew!"

Lorrie gasped, jolted as she sat up. She spun around, searching, and caught the shifting in the shadows behind the stone marker.

The lurking black cat emerged, yellow eyes blazing in the dark.

"Hey!" Lorrie cooed. She leaned forward, setting her hands on her knees. "You found me, huh? Cute little guy. Who are you?"

"Meow."

Her jawed dropped, and she stilled.

"Harold? But I can understand you? Your name is Harold!

I totally understand you!"

She giggled as she reached and collected him, cradling him. He was hefty and mature, despite his size, with wonderfully soft fur.

"Meow!"

"No. Not your name... Herald. You're a herald. You bring, but..."

A chill suddenly swept over her. The wind howled in the spindly branches of the ancient giants towering over her and swept away the leaves, their frantic rustling all but deafening. Under the howl there was a bellowing woof, like a dark laugh.

The cat sprang from Lorrie's arms, scurrying to safety behind a stone marker. The site glowed around her, though the moon was hidden. And there was a smell, like the stink of rot and wet mold, so potent it seized her senses. She shrank in place, trembling, searching for a reason for such strange phenomena.

Finally, the wind began to calm. Around her, though, the world had changed. The trees were much taller and far thinner. The earth was black, and the sky was a bright ruby red.

The brightness concentrated before her into a single formless mass. The newly arrived spectral being looked down upon Lorrie, and she had no doubts about its divine intelligence. She smiled just as brightly as she jumped to her feet, big-eyed with awe.

"Hi. I mean, hello! Oh, wow. It's so nice to meet you." The ghostly thing did not move. Lorrie reached out,

feeling its wispy, glowing vapors. As a child, she had fantasized about dancing with the dead under the moon's pale light.

"I have come far..."

The voice arrived from every direction, an echoing shout sounding off the far hills and a whisper directly into her ear.

"Help... We need your help..."

"I can help you. What can I do? I've dreamed of this moment! Do you need help with unfinished business? Or, laying your remains to rest? That's a thing. I can feed your cat!"

For a long moment, the ghost said nothing. Its manner,

like its tone, was filled with sorrow.

"We are under attack." "Oh, no!" Lorrie cried.

"He comes for us. He finds us. He sets his hounds upon us. They eat us. We are devoured, but do not die. The screams are unending."

A tear streaked down Lorrie's cheek. "Can't you fight back?"

"I'm only a child. It was cold, and the sickness took me."

Lorrie looked down, fussed back a step. She never would have known the grave she was resting on had such a small imprint.

"I'm so sorry."

"We need a warrior spirit. A fearless heart. We have waited for you, hoping every year, but you did not come."

"I'm here. I'm here now!" Lorrie cheered. "I'll be your warrior!"

Her heart ached. Lorrie knew suffering. Every day, people judged her. And she did not want the ghostly child, or anyone else, to have to suffer, too.

"It is not easy. To join us, you must cross over. And for a mortal with a living soul, it comes with great sacrifice."

Lorrie did not even have to think. It was why she existed. "I'm ready," she declared.

The ghost's light suddenly shined upon Lorrie, into her, through her...

She gasped, as though her breath had been stolen from her. She felt cold, like she had fallen into an icy lake, and hot, like she was boiling from the inside.

Her teen body shivered, quaked. She couldn't help jabbering, the noises erupting from her.

"Aw, gawd..."

She huffed. Her throat ballooned and she heaved violently, projecting yellowish slime onto the black earth, a long, unpleasant outpouring. Her eyes were open and watering.

"You must be vacant," the ghost said. "You must exist as will and energy, as a ghost exists."

The torrent finally ended, and Lorrie flung back, whining. "What..."

She held up her hands. Her skin was translucent white, veins thick and bright green.

Crack!

Lorrie cried out. Her index finger was instantly longer! The cracking came furiously as all her fingers lengthened between the knuckles.

She wailed, itching all over. Hairs, thick and dark, grew over her arms and legs and chest, and parts between.

"What's happening?!" she cried.

"You are becoming! You remain mortal, but to become as a ghost, transformation is required. You must change, your shape and your very essence."

Crack! Crunch! Crackle!

Lorrie twitched, jerked madly as her limbs lengthened. Hairy arms extended from her sleeves and jeans hiked over hairy legs as she elevated. She sobbed. The sensations weren't tortuous, but overwhelming to her young human mind.

She groaned as she was reshaped, like having a good stretch, only one that would not cease as her muscles and bones were pulled.

"Aw, no, my feet! My feet!"

She lifted off one foot, then the other as her sneakers flexed and warped. Bones crunched and shifted until her shoes came apart at the front. The material flapped as her hairy feet grew outward, warped and arching until she was resting on fatty toes. The remnants of her shoes clung to her heels and ankles.

"Gaw!"

Her forearms and calves fattened, parting the dark hairs and showing green pulsing veins, the same that bulged at her huge neck.

She was beginning to stink, too, no longer just sweating, but excreting, all the wastes that had been in her body made into a glistening slime. She reeked of putrescence, like a body wasting in a bog. Like a ghost.

"Naw, my back!"

She hunched forward as her spine lengthened and dense back muscles swelled. Her shirt tore, giving the fat hump space to grow. Long arms dangled, so her large knuckles nearly brushed the sodden ground.

"The transforming is nearly complete."

Lorrie roared, eyes bulging as her head reshaped. Her hairline receded and from the back of her head her hair grew long and mangy. Her skull widened. The crunching of bones in her head made her want to vomit, faint. Her eyes pushed apart, and the newly vacuous sockets grew large and dark as voids.

Teeth dropped from her face and lips thinned to non-existence, and from green gums thin pink tendrils slithered out. Her nose and ears remained.

The ghost, though it had no face or shape, beamed brightly with elation.

"It is done. In this new form, your mortal soul is no longer bound to the earthly plane. You may join me in the realm of the ghosts!"

Lorrie whimpered. It was too wonderful, too extraordinary. She could not believe her dreams had come true.

She staggered, feeling the weight of her new body on her new legs. She angled her head down, fearing its mass would propel her forward and make her fall. Her jeans had ripped apart up to her knees. Her shoes were tatters over her monstrous feet. Her stomach had shrunk to a pinch. She looked at her forearms, hairy and huge like a sailor's, and at her long fingers that curled like spider's legs.

Though her new form was awkward and different, she felt powerful, correct. It must be the way a knight felt, she thought, when he donned his armor to battle a great beast.

She felt purer, smarter, luminous. "The time has come."

A swell of light burst over the site as a portal opened to the other realm.

The ghostly being hovered into it, and stomping forward, with a weight that shifted from side to side, Lorrie followed.

She blinked from intense flashing of the supernatural light.

The first incredible sensation she had to accept as the new normal, among so many others, was her muscular eyelids sweeping over the vast scope of her now massive eyes.

But what those eyes could see!

Before her, melding with the black earth, there was a lake of liquid onyx. She peered over it, looking at a reflection of her new self as cast by an inky mirror. Hulking and hunched, gangly and powerful... she was truly beautiful.

"Follow me."

The ghostly being guided their descent down the mountain.

Above them, the night sky was emerald green. Stars blazed like white fire. Falling! Fire raining upon her! It impacted, soft and tickling and tangible. She unfurled her large hand and collected more in her palm. It was some sort of magic pollen.

The journey was slow and awkward.

Lorrie adjusted to her new feet, her mass balanced on the meaty paws. Her body tingled all over. She no longer had blood, but cosmic energy, the stuff that held together the layers of many realities as one.

She knew such things because she was special, and she cherished it.

They approached the village. It was her hometown, but reduced to ancient ruins, dilapidated and assaulted by wild vines and overgrowth, every window vacated and filled with moths and butterflies.

The dense vegetation swept over everything and grew freely. It was like her home had been consumed by God's garden.

The many bushes stirred, and pixies emerged. What else could they be? Bright and sparkling, spindly-limbed and big-eyed. They captured the gently raining fire pollen in their small hands and chewed on it like fruit.

There were many creatures in sight, and she knew all their names. Glitter snakes. Cooing slime pods. Grazing in a wooly patch of grass, there was a tri-horned goat. *Spark!* A burst of light! She looked over, and scampering freely was an electro bunny! They were all eating the vivid flowers and grass, which smelled of candy, and eating the many bugs.

There were so many bugs! Hardly one inch of space was not occupied by insects. The world was not only alive but slithering and squirming and chattering and buzzing.

Worms, caterpillars, centipedes, beetles and roaches feasted, too, upon the living earth. Not one of them was the boring brown or black of her world. Each sported a dazzling rainbow of neon colors.

She did not fear them. She found them interesting and unique, like ambassador aliens of their shared world. But that many bugs all at once and all over, most people would have considered it a waking nightmare.

Seeing so much life, so much living, inspired untold emotions in Lorrie. It was too much beauty to comprehend.

She swung her huge head about and stared, and though she no longer had a mouth, she gaped joyously.

It was all that she had dreamed, only greener and greater.

Bang!

A sudden harsh flash of lightning illuminated the green sky and wondrous land, a million micro shadows flickering into existence and disappearing just as quickly.

"It is the demon electricity," her ghost guide mused. Lorrie wondered. Electricity is the work of the devil? There were no paved streets in that version of her home, only sodden earth veiled by swirling mist. Each heavy footfall was met with a splash. She had assumed it was just the moisture of a recent downpour, but as she watched a busy centipede travel in front of her, the mists parted, and looking down at her odd feet, she realized she was walking in a streaming rivulet.

A ruby rivulet. Blood! It was the blood, the spectral conduit, that was enhancing her vision and sustaining her with tickling energies.

She was part of that world, and it was a part of her.

The hovering ghost brought her to the town square, only it had been obliterated, the ground torn up by large columns of white stone that did not exist on Earth or in their galaxy. It came from the farthest edge of the universe, found only at its crest. It was the very material of the creation event itself.

Collected amid the communal amphitheater's columns were several figures, all cloaked in darkness, though their silhouettes were distinct enough.

The woman in center, Lorrie could see, did not possess a head.

As she entered the magical theater of stone and earth, light swelled around the seven figures, but not beyond them.

The slender, headless woman wore an elegant, lacy white gown. At her muddy bare feet was a small black pig.

With the woman were a black man in a top hat, a man with a flaming pumpkin head, a maiden with a ribbony hennin, a hologram man of the 31st century, a living scarecrow, and a shrouded woman in black leather with many piercings.

"Welcome," the woman greeted. "To the girl who once was Lorrie Mulhare, now reborn as the demonite warrior-goddess Sharddal."

Fluttering pixies brought Lorrie a crown of twigs and buds and writhing bugs and set it upon her bulbous head.

Lorrie released a series of squeaks and whistles that made

her tendrils flap. She could no longer speak, but she did not fail to express her gratitude and sincerity.

At her side, her ghostly escort had taken its true form, that of a small boy, gaunt and sickly, wearing 19th century clothes like she had seen in movies. The sight broke her heart. She gave a whistling coo, expressing sympathy, though the sound was not intended. Her emotions were no longer hers to keep.

"You must help us, Sharddal," the woman pleaded. "We are scared. Each night, we are besieged by a monster born of your world. He is Danaan, the Mad Monk!"

Lightning erupted, scorching the sky in four directions at the mention of his name.

"He eats us. He eats the young among us. He does it to make the Goddess cry. And he terrorizes us with his hounds of the hunt. We are the hunted."

The woman's words sang from the prismatic light, and in the shining fractals Lorrie could see images, memories, realized like the oil paintings of old.

A man. A miserable, elderly man. Lorrie wasn't surprised. He wore holy crimson robes. Its hood cast deep shadows over his skeletal visage, and its drawn cord dripped with the thick residue of the corrupted energy surrounding him.

The hounds – there were six – were muscular and powerful, their eyes glowing white and exhaling clouds of bluish fire with their barking breaths.

"See what he does," the woman said. "See what he does, and weep."

The images began moving, and with them Lorrie could feel the terror of a small ghost, just an infant, floating along in the deep woods and aware of the danger at hand, as it was seized by the hounds, chewed upon, not dying but in eternal torment.

The dogs consumed its spectral essence, and the monk devoured its pain.

"My kindred here, and even I, have failed to subdue his

influence. Only a girl who is brave and awakened, and no other, can defeat the evil that eats our babies. Sharddal, you must be our demigoddess knight."

Lorrie let out a long, chirping coo, drooling out, but it was no mere noise. It was a declaration, and it was precisely received.

She was ready. She would help them.

"You will know what to do, and at the correct moment you will act. That moment is soon. You must be strong, or our doom will pass on to your world, and for generations you and yours will know only nightmares, sleeping or not."

The gathering was interrupted by a maniacal cackling that dwarfed the world itself.

The glow of the amphitheater was vanquished, leaving the figures suddenly standing in only the green rays of the moon.

The headless woman shivered.

"He comes?" the man in the top hat asked. "He is arrived," she intoned. "Danaan!"

Lightning struck again, thunder booming with it, and he appeared at the end of the red-sodden boulevard. The Mad Monk!

The many millions of insects swarmed away from his presence, like a chattering rainbow wave, and his blue flames erupted in their wake.

Danaan was just as Lorrie had seen in her visions, frightening in his crimson robes and preceded by his six hounds.

The ghostly child ran into the dark beyond the columns, knowing what fate awaited him should he catch their vicious gaze.

The monk's deep voice roared down on them.

"If you come out, you will burn. If you stay, my hounds of the hunt will devour you."

He laughed, and the earth trembled.

The black pig skittered anxiously behind his mistress. "You, who darkens our days, who poisons the dreams of

children, who brings fire even as he spits at our names. You show yourself, at last. Why? What is it you want?"

The monk's dark laughter ceased.

"It is no longer enough to make you cry. I must cause you pain. This world must burn so I may profit. And finally, you must be destroyed, so all that is good will splutter and die, and I can be truly happy. My dogs are hungry. It is time we feast!"

His hands shot out from his robes and at the silent command his muscular hounds raced ahead as one, snorting and barking blue flame.

The kindred charged to meet them. They knew the strength and awful deeds of the hounds, but their concern for the safety of their goddess was far greater, and they did not hesitate to act in her defense.

"We must protect our headless mother!" the pierced woman called.

The scarecrow cried, "We must save the Queen of the Zygents!"

The hounds lunged and the kindred grabbed them, wrestling the biting animals. Some were knocked to the ground by the force, and all were burned by their atomic breath or sliced by their black razor fur.

Lorrie released a whimpering coo, teary-eyed and uncertain. She glanced back. The headless woman remained in place, no less powerful or confident.

"I have faith in you, Sharddal. Know our magic. Become the realm. This is your time."

The words electrified the teen, and she stood as a titan.

Lorrie looked across the boulevard, at its black mud and rivulets of living blood. Compelled forward, guided by instinct, her hulking mass ambled onto the slop. Her warped feet once again touched upon the wet earth, and instantly she could feel it. Magic! It was there. Its power could be borrowed, made her own.

Not having to reach far, she scooped the slimy mud with her long hand. Her pink tendrils flared out and her drooling mouth hole opened. She brought it to her face and ate heartily.

She did not question why she was doing it, sucking up and squelching the mud, juicy and rich with minerals and nutrients, but she could not stop and did not want to. It was delicious! The noises she made as she feasted were obscene.

Her stomach gurgled loudly, obscuring the growls of the attacking dogs, the peals of thunder, and maniacal laughter of their foe.

As the kindred wrestled, the mad monk strode forward.

With each menacing step, he impacted the air an inch above the ground, not even touching the swirling mists, his sandals flat and level with the earth.

Lorrie glanced up. The mad monk, ever nearing, regarded her with disdain.

"This is your newest pet? Disgusting," the mad monk spat.

"You revered us once, Danaan." The headless woman's hands swept out in pleading. "You came to this place in worship."

"I believed in you. Yes, I believed in goodness. You were the symbol of beauty, prosperity. And then you declared me evil, and my worship a sin."

"We need not be at war. We both suffer."

"You believe it is just, though, for some to suffer. Even I would never proclaim such a thing. My existing is not a crime against you!"

"Yours was not a selfless worship. You brought darkness with you. You demanded reward. You expected a taste of the power that was always out of your reach because only the truly good can know it. When you were warned of these things you took it as a personal affront, and when invited to leave our realm, you took it as a declaration."

"My suffering..."

"We would never turn away from the suffering of another. We turn away, though, from any being, of any identity, who would inspire suffering in others."

For the moment, Danaan was quieted, unable to reconcile the truth of her words and greater truth of his rage, his pain.

Lorrie did not stop eating the black mud covered in ruby slime. Electricity coursed through the otherworldly matter that comprised her new body.

Under her hunched form, her stomach ballooned outward, larger and larger, making the worst noises as it expanded over the top of her soiled jeans.

Fistful after fistful of mud, teeming with nematodes and fungi and crystallized star matter, was shoved into her sloppy mouth hole, her throat undulating to accommodate its dense mass. She did not mind. To her, the sensation was satisfying, and the mud as tasty as brownies and syrup and cake and frosting!

"I have nothing left. You have stolen happiness from me, denied me hope. Now, I only know the pleasures of inspiring horror and eating the soul energy of my victims. My gut will fill with the meat and tears of your subjects, mother goddess."

The mad monk started forward, only a few paces away from Lorrie and the amphitheater just behind her.

"You will never set foot upon this holy place," the headless woman warned. "Turn back."

"Will your pet stop me? This reeking, misshapen..."

With Danaan only two steps away, a small wet trench between them, Lorrie completed her mission, at last satiated. She flung her dirty hands back and released a buzz saw shriek, its waves powerful enough to make the bloody muck ripple and mists disperse.

The mad monk, to the surprise of them both, recoiled some, raising his hands in defense.

Lorrie heaved violently. "Gwark! Gwark!" And with each wretched belched she whistled around her drippy mouth tendrils.

The sensations were abnormal but came to her naturally. She understood. She was different. She was changed. She allowed it, encouraged it, knowing it would somehow help to save the magical realm.

Her bulging, translucent stomach, the size of a giant watermelon and just as pink and green, pulsed with life. With each horrible heave the dense mass inside of her began to lift, elevated by her otherworldly gasses.

"Gwark! Gwark!"

It propelled upward, making her ribcage crack loudly as it parted, and her throat ballooned. The wet ring of her mouth hole stretched wider and wider. Pinkish slurry oozed out. Her long arms lifted, and she raised her large hands to her mouth. The juices splashed over them as she kept heaving, knowing she could not stop. It was not an uncomfortable act, but urgent. It had to be done, or so many worlds would be doomed.

"BRAAAK!"

The large object, crowning at her mouth, popped out amid a torrent of goop onto her hands, and Lorrie released an exhausted whistle.

It shined in the greenish moonlight, a bright red orb, its slick surface mottled and pitted.

"What magic is this?" Danaan asked fearfully.

Lorrie did not know, just as curious and entranced by the object she had birthed.

"That is the magic of the earth realm," the headless woman said. "The true magic, of growth and renewal, and born of light and faith."

"I do not understand these things," the mad monk sneered.

"How could you?" the woman replied. "You only know pain."

Lorrie clutched the egg in both hands and broke it, pulling it in half and releasing a bomb burst of whitest energy.

Danaan cried, wailing as he was burned alive, every atom of his being eradicated by the light, and his influence was destroyed with it.

The light waned and darkness was restored. The monk was gone, and his hounds of the hunt had become blue vapor.

Lorrie only stared, astonished by her achievement.

One by one, the kindred stood, each battered and weary, and approached. As they returned to the amphitheater, they each gave Lorrie a warm hug, embracing her great mass, and she returned their hugs in kind.

With the kindred restored at the sides of the headless woman, Lorrie stood before them and let out a quizzical whistle and woofing.

"That? It was the light of good, the light of truth. It is the warmth from within that inspires all beings to do good and believe there is value in doing good. Hate, like darkness, is destroyed by the light. That light came from within you, Sharddal. It was your goodness that saved us and saved the world."

The kindred applauded. From behind the columns, the ghostly child returned, beaming with gratitude. She had saved him, too.

"The choice is yours. Stay with us. Join the kindred as a demonite demigod. Or, return to your realm without shame and the earthly rewards of your mortal life."

Lorrie had forgotten. She had another life, belonged to another world beyond theirs. And like a dream, those memories returned to her.

She missed it horribly, and the idea of losing it forever wounded her.

Watching horror movies with her friends and laughing at the gore effects. She had so much schoolwork to do and enjoyed doing it. She was excited about college. Her whole life lay ahead of her. Her family would miss her, too, and she would miss them, even her brother. He was a brat, but he could be a sweetheart sometimes.

Her large head lifted, and huge black eyes swept around, gazing at the green sky, radiant moon, the wet landscape and bugs, and the powerful beings who inspired such hope.

She could be one of them. She just wasn't ready. No matter how emboldening their offer or beautiful their world, it was a truth she could not escape.

Her gaze returned to the headless woman. The woman bowed some, the moon's rays gleaming off the meaty red remains of where a neck had once been.

"We understand. You are always welcome here, and we hope you will return one day. Maybe, in one year's time?"

Lorrie let out a series of giddy squeaks and whistles, her mouth tendrils flapping. She was glad to have such understanding friends.

The kindred all nodded reverently and cheered as the ghostly child escorted Lorrie down the boulevard. The insects had already returned, and they neared her in veneration. They would continue their good existence, a part of the living earth and the earth a part of them, just like she had become.

They returned to the mountain hills. The ghostly child hugged Lorrie's leg tightly before soaring back to the village. She sniffled, touched.

Lorrie began her ascent when, before she was ready, a flash of intense light enveloped her. She shrieked, falling down a tunnel of swirling energies. Her gangly arms swept up in fear as unholy scents and cosmic sensations assaulted her.

She staggered and stumbled and fell onto her front, striking the ground hard. She convulsed, shrieking and whistling as the reversion came. Black fluid rushed from her, vomiting from her mouth, spewing from her eyes and ears and nostrils, and gushing out lower.

The teen flopped about. The light had changed her back, made her human again, making the changes a grueling, unpleasant experience that she wanted to end.

Her body steadily shrank. Bones crunched and crackled. Giant feet drew into the flaps of her torn sneakers. Her hump reduced, and her shoulder blades and spine compressed. Arms and legs shortened, and fatty forearms and calves dwindled. Her skull reduced, eyes shrinking and tendrils slithering into her mouth. Her lips puffed. As she breathed out, her teeth chattered, restored along with the rest of her.

The black fluid soaked into the earth, and around her grew grasses and vibrant flowers, pillowy soft under her resting form.

Lorrie blinked and gasped as she sat up. She clutched her head. It was dark and quiet around her, the wind gentle and brisk.

"What... Did I fall asleep? Was it a dream?"

It couldn't have been a dream, she realized. The beautiful patch of flowers and grass under her, bright even in the night of the dreary woods, had not been there before. She would have found it and delighted.

Lorrie stood and moaned as the cold licked at her exposed back. She caught her torn shirt as it started to slip away from her front.

"It did happen! I changed. I became a, a..."

Not *monster*. That was the word her tongue wanted to release, but it wasn't true, so she did not allow it.

The correct word, her heart knew, was *goddess*.

Lorrie stood, feeling uneven and weak. Of course, she did.

She'd been on an incredible journey, and there was nothing left inside her. A sandwich was needed.

She wiggled her toes at the ripped fronts of her sneakers. Her jeans were shredded up to her knees. It was no surprise she had a chill. She collected her sweater from the ground and put it on, smoothing her long hair after.

The sky started brightening as she descended the mountain, heading home. Wrapped tightly in her hoodie, she smiled. She had loved her trip to the other realm, but her future waited ahead, and she was excited to discover it.

Besides, she thought, there was always next Halloween. "Just one year until the midnight hour," she mused.

"Until...Samhain!"

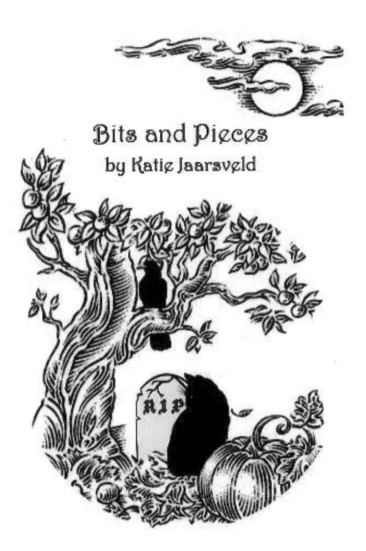

Bits and Pieces
by Katie Jaarsveld

Emanuel

"A cult, by its own definition, could be a system of devotion toward a holiday, religion, person, or an object. On the flip side, it could be viewed as a sect in society, having to do with beliefs and living souls in a colony.

"Throughout history, there have been many religious cults who performed mass suicides or mass murders. Has no one considered the idea that maybe no one has changed in any way? Maybe they saw a part of themselves that they were comfortable with, so they acted on it?

"Given the opportunity, would you not take the chance to expand the knowledge in every part of your mind and body? To act on every emotion that you have ever felt without having to worry about the consequences of your actions?

"Imagine this. A car cuts you off, almost running you off the road. Do you let it go? No. You're livid, your pulse is racing, your temperature is rising, *and* you have an adrenaline rush. You're trying not to change into your alter ego, the *real* you, so to speak. Your hands are clenching the steering wheel so hard that your knuckles are white, and it would take a crowbar to pry your fingers from around it.

"Under your breath you curse, steadily accelerating until you hit them, forcing *them* off the road. You both get out of your cars and you feel like beating the living crap out of them. "Instead, you pull your hunting knife out of the sheath on your belt and stab them repeatedly until your anger is sated, the white spots in your vision have diminished, and you no longer hear the voices screaming in your head. You cut his heart out and place it in your cooler to feed to your cat later.

You toss the body aside to feed the wild animals.

"You take a deep breath, close your eyes, exhale and feel the peace of forgiveness wash over you. Welcome to free will. You just purged yourself clean. You justified taking a life to save your cat's and wild animals' lives. You get back in your car, go home, take a shower, have sex with your neighbor then start your day all over again.

"It's that simple. Everyone, have a good day, and I'll see you at dinner."

Everyone stood. Some came over to thank me for my enlightening point of view. They all looked to me for guidance. I could tell this herd of cattle anything and they would still follow me. The lost souls who believed in nothing before me and felt even less. No matter what they were.

I had the ultimate plan to be rid of those who had wronged me, ridiculed, and tried to make *my* life a living hell. The plan was already set in motion. My flock could try to exorcise their own demons, while I was feeding mine.

To do everything in someone else's name for the honor of glory *and* be self-righteous at the same time was such a joke. I called my flock sheep, because of the way the poor, lost souls were. In reality, they were made up of broken-down Halloween creatures. Fewer people believed in Halloween, and I tried to build these sheep up, just to satisfy my inner demon. They were just souls trapped in a purgatory known as the human body.

I was so caught up in my musing, I didn't notice a stranger standing at the back of the big dinner hall that we used for eating, meetings, and such. There were no children. Their cries irritated my demon no end, so they were not allowed.

The stranger walked up to me. "Isaiah is the name, friend. May I ask yours?"

He held his hand out for me to shake, and I bypassed it by turning halfway around.

"Emanuel. May I be of assistance? This is a closed commune for me and my flock."

As I turned back toward him, his eyes flashed with an emotion that I hadn't seen in a long time and almost failed to recognize. It was gone as fast as it had appeared.

"I've lost my way, and something led me here."

His eyes flashed again. I offered him a chair to sit in. One of the women came over with a tray of sandwiches and a pitcher of iced tea with two glasses.

"Please help yourself. Margaret, leave us."

She smiled and left through the side door, not looking back. She knew better. She was the most obedient of all my flock, after the disciplining.

"Isaiah. You haven't changed much over the years."

Isaiah was blond, with thin hair hanging without style to the top of his shoulders, and a thin mustache in need of a trim, and it had always been the same, whereas my raven black hair was thick, styled short, and I sported a thick anchor-style goatee.

"Names are of no consequence. How did you get in, and more to the point, what are you doing here?"

"You know why I'm here. To help these lost souls who you have convinced that you are watching over and guiding them. If you are watching anyone, you have a plan. Does it come to their end or yours, is the question?"

I had to give it to Isaiah. He was direct, if not foolhardy in thinking that I would give up my flock.

"I think you should leave, Isaiah. This flock of souls belongs to me. I'm not going to hand anyone over. There are no innocents here. All of these are mine. They are consecrated for evil, branded, smell of Sulphur, and have earned their right to live with me instead of simply going to hell. They are in purgatory on earth without even realizing it. They were lost before, and now I have given them a purpose."

"A purpose? I could lead what's left of these people and give them light again. Give them to me to redeem. Let me lead them to a more righteous path."

"Isaiah, they can leave at any time. But, make no mistake, when they decide to leave my flock, they will cease to exist, one way or the other. And, by the way, I don't remember you blessing your weapons for the good of these kind of souls."

Isaiah started to protest, but realizing he needed to rethink his plan, he stood to leave.

"I will be back. I'm not turning away from these people."

"Why not? You turned away from me." Sarcasm dripping with hatred was my favorite language.

I picked up the tray to carry it back to the kitchen. When I turned back around, Isaiah was no longer there. Once again, it was just me. I should be used to it by now.

"Margaret." I called out, and she returned. "Yes, Emanuel? Our visitor has left us?"

I wanted to torture her for addressing me so informally and questioning, but it wasn't her I was mad at. However, the opportunity had presented itself. I asked that she go to the basement and bring up something. I didn't even know what I had requested. As she started down the stairs, I walked up behind her, and withdrew her soul from her, and into me. Her human remains fell down the stairs. I didn't care for witches much anyway. They seemed to like being disciplined and that threw my punishment to pleasure, not what I had in mind at all.

I closed the door. I would let someone else find her body. I was in no mood to deal with more drama today. I left and went to my study.

Preparing a sermon of sorts for the flock was simple. A little inspiring and pushy without being hypnotizing, for the most part. We were not political or included in a terrorist movement, not specific to religion or faith healing, not into snake practices though I wouldn't be against it. It came to me so easily.

We are a flock of people who regard each other as equals. While some desire acceptance, belonging, or a place to be led from and not be judged, others need a small place to gather away from the cruelty of society, to practice their beliefs and share them, to create for ourselves our ideal family.

We don't need religious ceremonies or rituals. We are who we are, and we accept each other for that very reason. We don't need a statue or someone else saying we can't speak openly to who or what we believe in, that we have to go through someone of higher status.

I don't believe that. I never did.

Man, was I good or what? Writing this drivel was as easy as having pie and coffee.

There was a noise coming from outside. Someone in a loud, booming voice saying what I was writing. It could only be one such person. Isaiah.

I rushed from my office to see him standing on the steps of the well and preaching down on my flock with my words. They were mesmerized. Their souls were dancing, hovering just above their bodies, ready to go with him.

I ran toward him and shoved him backward into the well, striking his head on the crank mechanism, tearing flesh and skin and leaving it there on the stone. He had almost been scalped.

I expected screams of terror or excitement. I turned to look and was met with eyes filled with wonder and confusion. Questions came from several at almost the same time.

"Why?"

"Was he an enemy or did he wrong you in some way?" "He was only saying what you were writing."

It was my turn to almost fall backward. How did they know this?

"You are a part of each of us. You both are, he still is. You thought we were mindless sheep, doing your bidding. We were lost, about that, you're right. But we're not anymore. Thanks to you."

Thanks to me? I felt a blow to the back of my head.

I tried to focus and heard talking, but I could only pick

up pieces of the conversation.

"They have almost the same head injuries. What do we do with them, Jude? Keep them tied up and gagged?"

Jude

"Leave them as they are, and we will all come up with ideas. I'm not a leader like they were. I'm the voice of everyone here. There will be no more struggles between souls. There are many of us. We can decide together."

"Everyone will share in duties. Men and women alike will hunt. We will see who is the best at what positions and assign them from there."

"What if someone is good at nothing? Isn't that a reason for being here? To belong and find what we are good at? To heal and take back our souls?"

"Yes, Marie. For the moment, continue your day as it is every day. I will make a list with Margaret of what we all do, then who does what. After that, we will switch places or have a game to see who can do what. How does that sound?"

They were all nodding their heads in agreement.

"Has anyone seen Margaret?" Looks of confusion ran throughout.

"Please search for her." I addressed everyone.

I went to Emanuel's office and looked through papers and books. I found names with numbers on them, as well as notes on us and our misgivings. No birth certificates, diplomas or any important documents, except one. The contracts where they signed over their souls. I looked at his book of teachings and saw where we were called cattle or sheep repeatedly. He had lied to us all. It was never about us, just him and feeding his demon souls.

I decided then that we would no longer be cattle. We would be wolves. The weak would be cut into bits and pieces for their souls to be eaten. My shoulders ached, and I was guessing it was from the new burden placed on them. The good and evil were making my head hurt.

My good, naïve side was always out. It was time to let my

demon come out and play. Maybe if they had equal time, I could be a good leader. My headache was almost totally gone on one side. That was a sign good enough for me.

"Jude! It's Margaret! Come on, please, hurry!"

This couldn't be good. I'd figure it out. Margaret was sprawled out on the landing at the bottom of a flight of stairs. By her body and head position, I would guess her neck was broken by her fall. But then, a niggle of doubt entered its head and made me think Emanuel did it after Isaiah's visit. A sense of calm washed over me as I realized that Emanuel had killed one of us and claimed her soul for all eternity.

"We were her only family. We will bury her remains at nightfall. Marc and Jane, please get the excavator with tooth bar on the bucket. She loved the big oak out back, so we'll start a cemetery nearby. Be careful not to dig at the tree roots." I made eye contact with Jane and Marc. "Make it deep."

The twinkle in her eyes told me she knew exactly what I wanted to do. We were going to end this. Marc nodded yes.

They both agreed and went outside. I asked Marie for an old blanket to wrap Margaret in. Some volunteered to help carry her up. We went down together and brought her up, placing her on a blanket.

The rest of the commune that came to help carry her and place her in the ground were Eugene and Ras. Isaiah and Emanuel were brought out by Marie, Betty, Kym, and Izabel.

While they were busy with Margaret, I pulled the sword from beneath my robe and with one clean slice, I removed the heads of both Emanuel and Isaiah. Ras pushed their bodies into the grave while Eugene kicked the heads in after their bodies.

Marc and Jane leapt down from the excavator, intent on decapitating Ras and Eugene with their swords. I stopped them with mine. I swung with both arms, cutting Marc and Jane into two pieces at the waist.

Gabriel

Jude tossed their swords toward the bodies in the grave. He knew there could be no witnesses to this, and as much as it pained him, they all had to go. All their souls would be released to Hell.

I knew this cult would never last. There were too many who wanted to rule, and not enough to be ruled. In essence, it ended itself. Sometimes you just had to remove a head from the conversation in order to think clearly.

The sheep tried to become wolves and were sheared for the thought of it. Jude could have been a good leader, if not for being more demanding than all the others.

The idea of creating your own family wasn't a bad idea. People did it every day. You just had to be careful not to cut off your nose to spite your face, as the proverb went.

Jude lit a cigarette, then reached inside his robe and pulled out the contracts. They ran to him just as the contracts caught fire. I watched the well overflow and empty its water, making the land into a nasty swamp that smelled of rotten eggs. The souls were being ripped from bodies, and as the remains fell into the water, the souls were sucked up into a fiery Hell.

As for me, I was only the bystander to make sure everything played out correctly. I was known as Gabriel.

Katie lives in the Netherlands with her husband, dwarf pinscher Jubjub and 2 cats, Scout and Jack.

When not spending time with her husband, pets, family and friends, she can be found engrossed in a favorite book, reviewing an author's latest release, or most importantly, writing her next bestseller.

Katie started by writing horror, and though that is still her favorite genre, she has also released stories in contemporary, paranormal, supernatural, fantasy, mythopoeia, young adult, and even romance.

Changelings
by S.B. Rhodes

Arietta

They say that the veil between realms is thinnest this time of year, and I agree. It is the one time of year when others can see what I see. Spirits and fairies have been part of my life for as long as I can remember, coming and going. Sometimes, they are kind and helpful, offering a friendly ear and departing once I've helped them to move on.

Others, however, are less than welcoming… territorial spirits who refuse to share their homes with the living, demons who keep escaping through the gates of hell and terrorizing people, and the less-than-benevolent fairies who feel that humanity is beneath them. "Evil is in their blood," the fae queen liked to say. "It's who they are and who they'll always be. Let's not concern ourselves with their kind."

Thankfully for me, Tilani was not a very good listener. She is my best and only friend. I had a sister at one point, but I never met her. Her name was Aubrey. The plague took her before I was born, and my parents never liked to talk about her. I wish I could have met her. I always wanted a sister. Then I met Tilani, and she became that sister for me.

She was the one who helped me cope when my father left, then when my mother passed away and left me all alone. Having no other family, I would have been completely lost without her. The rest of the village turned their backs on me, always treating me as though I was an outcast.

"She reads too much," they often say. "She is a strange child with a strange imagination… always talking of fairies and spreading nonsense. It is time for her to grow up and live in the real world." Ah, yes, the real world… and yet, for one magical night each year, even they choose to believe.

They can't truly see the fairies and spirits the way that I see them… at least, not all of them can. However, they can feel the magic in the air and the joy that it brings to those who do believe. So, they come together for Samhain, offering up their sacrifices and making pleas for protection over themselves and their families. How silly it is to ask for help from someone in whom you do not truly believe. What good can they do if they do not exist?

For all their begging and pleading for protection from others, they are not so quick to offer it themselves. They turned a blind eye when I was in need, pretending not to see the lonely little girl with no home and no food. They ignored me, but Tilani didn't. She welcomed me with open arms, helping me to build a special "fairy" house in the woods. She was a frequent visitor, stopping by for tea and to help with the gardening. Nobody had a greener thumb than she.

Unfortunately, she eventually stopped coming around, and I never found out why. I will not give up, though. She is my best friend. The last time I saw her, she swore that she would return, this time indefinitely. She would not lie. Something must be preventing her from returning. I know that she would not abandon me, nor will I abandon her.

As Samhain approaches, I am preparing for a journey that I know will be tough. When the full moon shines high above the earth and the barrier between our worlds is at its weakest, I will cross over into the world of the fae. I *will* find my friend.

Laughter fills the air as I make my way through the village, watching passersby live their lives and celebrate with one another. Samhain is a magical time of year. Spotlessly clean hearths are filled with fresh firewood that is set ablaze. The fires are left to burn as the villagers tend to their harvest, whistling and perhaps even singing while they work. Soon, they will return to their homes and prepare for the festivities. They will carve their pumpkins and choose crops for the market, while the biggest and best are reserved for the Pukah.

The market is where I am headed, for I will need supplies. I do not know how long it will take me to find my friend, so I am preparing for the very real possibility that I will not be returning anytime soon. The portal between worlds will close at dawn; if I am not back by then, I will be trapped in the fae realm until next year.

The air smells of spice, and even the stodgiest neighbors are able to find joy in the festivities. Children run through the fields, playing their games. Women are making their way through the market, practically glowing with each new purchase. Men stand off to the side, laughing and drinking. Tonight will be a good night... and perhaps the last I will spend in my home world for quite some time.

Knowing how the fae queen feels about us humans, part of me worries about what the future brings. It is no secret that we are seen as inferior, and my presence in their world will not be quite the cause for celebration that theirs is in ours. Nevertheless, this is something that I must do. Tilani is my friend, and I know that she would come for me if I had vanished without so much as a word.

Besides, part of me is excited to finally see the world of the fae in person. Tilani has told me so many stories. She has a way with words and is able to describe her home and customs in great detail, making it easy for me to visualize it. After all these years, I will finally experience it for myself.

Having been lost in thought, I am startled by the sounds of screaming in the distance. With a jolt, I look up to see a crowd gathering around one of the homes as a woman emerges, screeching. She has just given birth and now holds her baby in her arms, crying hysterically.

My heart sinks as I imagine the worst. I know this woman. She has never had a kind word to say to me, but in this moment, I am filled with concern. I rush over to lend an ear and possibly a helping hand. As I get closer, I hear the happy coos of a newborn babe. I see the little bundle of joy holding his momma's finger, oblivious to the world around them. Such a sweet child.

What could be wrong? I wonder. The child seems perfectly healthy and happy. It is then that the mother pulls back the blanket, and I see that the child is missing a limb. The poor babe will undoubtedly struggle when learning to walk, but all children do. I am sure that he will be just fine, and there is no need to panic. Of course, all good parents want what is best for their children. So, I can understand her being upset, but I try to reassure her that the baby will be fine.

However, the rest of the village does not agree. They cry out, blaming the fairies. "They did this! It's another one of... those things!"

"Those things?" I ask, confused. "What do you mean?"

"Changelings," says the father, joining his wife on the porch. "The fairies have taken our child and replaced it with this thing."

This only confuses me further, and I ask them to elaborate.

"Stupid girl," says old Mrs. Wilder, the village gossip. Always one to pass judgment and spread nonsense, it is no surprise that she has something to say on the matter. "Those rotten fairies are always playing tricks on us humans! They take our precious children and replace them with their deformed spawn."

"Some of them don't even do that much," chimes in Peter O'Connor. "Look at what happened last year. That poor couple was so distraught that they moved away, and nobody's seen them since."

"What happened?" asks one of the newer neighbors.

"Their little one was replaced by a log. Fairies have been doing this since the beginning of time. Sometimes, they replace them with their deformed offspring, and other times they'll leave behind a rock or a log... and sometimes, they leave nothing at all. The child just vanishes without a trace."

"That's absurd!" I shout. "Look at this child. He's perfectly happy. He's fine. Look at the way he's already bonding with his momma. How can you think such an awful thing about him? He is not a changeling."

"Really?" says Mrs. Wilder. "I thought you of all people would be a little more accepting. After all, aren't you the one who is always spreading nonsense about fairies and spirits?"

"It is not nonsense, and if you are so sure that these fairies and spirits are not real, then how can you blame them for this child's condition? Either they exist, or they don't. You can't have it both ways. Besides, just because there are fairies, it doesn't mean they would do such a thing. What would be the point? Most of them don't even like us, so why would they take our children?"

Gasps emerge from the crowd, and I realize what I've just said. I rub my forehead, knowing this is not going to go well.

"You heard her! The fairy lover herself says that they don't like us. We were right. It is them. They're taking our children to punish us. They will pay for their treachery!"

With that, the child's parents turn toward me, and the mother shoves him into my arms. "You love those beasts so much? Here! You can have this thing they've left behind. Tell them I will find them and make them pay for this." She turns on her heel and heads back into her home, sobbing into her husband's shoulder.

What on earth is wrong with these people? I look at this sweet child's face as I cradle him in my arms. "Hi there, little one.

Aren't you so precious?" This will be difficult, especially knowing what I am up against as I go to find my friend, but I am not afraid. I will succeed in my mission, and I will protect this child as if he were my own son... because that is who he is. His parents may have turned their backs on him, but now he has me. "Don't worry, love. Momma has you, and I'm never letting you go."

The harvest work is complete, and the last of the villagers are leaving the market. None of them have even acknowledged our existence since the ordeal outside that couple's house, but that is okay. Alistair and I rather enjoy our little corner of solitude.

This is when villagers typically gather their families and join the Druid priests in the lighting of the community fire, but tonight will be different. Their suspicions have them on guard, and they are not in the celebratory mood.

Much debate took place as they decided whether or not to participate in this, the third and final night of this year's celebration... and whether they ever would again. Some of the villagers expressed concern about abandoning tradition. After all, it is widely believed that the gods will punish anyone who fails to participate. Was this something that they were willing to risk?

The general consensus was that they would. "If the gods can turn their backs on us while these creatures invade our homes and take our children away, then we shall turn our backs on them."

The only people who are joining us now are the witches and the Druids. We will continue our traditions, even if nobody else does. The priests gather together with their wheel, lighting the fire and beginning the celebrations.

Night has fallen, and it has been a lovely celebration. As we depart, we take a flame from the communal fire. The others retreat to their homes, lighting their hearths with the flames. Though I typically do so as well, tonight I will be taking the flame with me into the fae realm. It will guide us along our path. The priest knows of my plans, and he has offered his blessing. May the gods be with us as we travel an unknown land. May they see fit to aide me in the search for my dear friend.

I make my way to the portal, a doorway to the fae world shown to me long ago by Tilani. Cradling Alistair in my arms, I stand before the portal in complete awe. Although I've seen the portal before, I've never been this close – never felt the magic radiating from it. Holding my new son close to me and shielding his face, I step through the portal and into the world of the fae. I pause for a moment, bracing myself.

I take a deep breath, then open my eyes. As I look up, I see hundreds of fairies and other fae creatures roaming about. I walk through the crowd and am greeted with smiles by those I pass. Some nod, and others offer a simple greeting: "Hello" or "Good day" or "Blessed Samhain." Despite my intrusion into their world, I am not met with the hostility that I anticipated.

On the contrary, everyone is quite friendly. I continue walking, not sure yet what my next move should be. I ask a few fairies if anyone knows Tilani, but so far, nobody has been able to help.

I come across a pond and kneel down to grab a drink of water. As I lean in to scoop up some of the water, I am caught off-guard by my reflection. I no longer recognize myself. No longer do I see the shaggy brown mane and haggard appearance for which I am known. Instead, I see long, curly red locks. I see elongated ears, eyes the color of emeralds, a slender body... and large, glowing wings!

How can this be? Surely, I must be mistaken. I look around, but there is no one else around. It is truly my reflection in the water. *What is happening? I don't understand. Is this because I'm in the fairy world? Do humans who cross over the threshold look like fairies while they are here? No, that can't be it... though it would make sense that we would be protected, given the queen's hatred of us.*

My thoughts are interrupted as Alistair begins to cry. I set his basinet on a nearby boulder and attempt to comfort him. I pull back the blanket and notice that his appearance is unchanged. I look around and see several mothers with their young, all of whom have wings and features befitting the fae. *Why would my appearance be changed and not his?* Suddenly, it dawns on me. I remember the conversation in the village that led to his being placed into my care.

Noooo... it can't be. What is it that the villagers called him? Changeling? If he were a changeling – the offspring of the fae – then surely, he'd have wings as well. If a human crossing over takes on the appearance of the fae when crossing the threshold, then certainly one of their own would...

I nearly collapse as the realization hits me. Alistair is not the changeling. *I am.* I stare blankly at our reflections in the water, having great difficulty processing this information.

"Are you all right?" asks a wood nymph. "You seem as though you are deep in thought."

Deciding that now is not the time to panic, I turn my attention – and the conversation – to my mission. "Hi, sorry. My name is Arietta."

"Hello, Arietta. That is a lovely name. I'm Blarington, and that lovely lass over there is me wife, Milah."

"It is nice to meet you. I'm looking for my friend, Tilani. Have you seen her? She's tall and--"

"Oh, no need to describe her. I know exactly who you're talking about. Tilani is a kind lass, always making friends with everybody. It is a shame what happened."

"What? What happened?"

"Oh, you don't know? I apologize, little lady. I thought that was why you were looking for her. The queen has her. She is being held for sentencing."

"Sentencing?! For what?"

"That, I don't know. I can't for the life of me figure out why the queen would mean her harm. Tilani wouldn't harm a hair on a wee goblin's head."

"Where can I find them?"

"Why, at the palace, of course." I start to ask where that is, but I do not want to draw attention to myself as an outsider. Though I am apparently from this land, I was not raised here, and the fae may not take kindly to strangers invading their sacred land.

They. Their land. Will I ever feel at home here? Should I feel at home here? Do I stay and discover my roots, or do I return home after I find Tilani? I never felt truly at home in my world, but that was because I was treated like an outcast. Then again, I suppose I was one all along, and not for the reasons they suspected.

Focus, Arietta. Now is not the time for an existential crisis. I must save Tilani before it is too late. But first, I need to find someplace safe for Alistair.

Tilani

I am Tilani of Aranathica, and this is my story…

I was the youngest of a rather large family of aquatic fae. We live near rivers and streams, contributing as best we can to the fae community. The various species each have their own benefit in society. The wood nymphs and gnomes, for example, tend to the forest creatures and heal the trees that provide us with the air that we breathe. Aquatic fairies make use of the water and its curative properties. We are the healers, along with the nature spirits who tend to their crops and lend us the herbs we need to create potions and cures.

I've always been fascinated by the human world. I loved crossing over into their realm during Samhain, and sometimes I'd stay even longer. Only a few of us fae folk knew how to open the portal, coming and going at will. However, we are always so careful to conceal our identities… either through disguise or by hiding in the shadows where the humans cannot see us.

The first and only time I allowed myself to be seen by a human was when I met Arietta. She was beautiful and complex – unlike any human I'd ever observed. She had fierce intelligence and a fire in her eyes. She loved to read and did not waste her time pursuing meaningless relationships.

She was standoffish and found it difficult to make friends – so unlike me. I found this strange at first, wondering why she had a hard time trusting the others. Then I saw the pain in her eyes. I watched her from a distance as the other humans taunted her and excluded her from their activities, treating her like nothing more than a nuisance. She could make friends if she tried. It would be easy. Simply take an interest in the things they enjoyed and mimic their behaviors. That seemed to be the human way.

However, that was not her. She would not pretend. She

would not allow them to change her. She could never taunt and tease another person to make herself look and feel better.

She had a kindness and purity that made me instantly fall for her. I had to get to know her better, so I threw all caution to the wind and approached her.

"Hello," I said to this mysterious creature who captivated me so. "My name is Tilani." I extended my hand and waited while she looked at me – perplexed, perhaps wondering if she should trust my kindness.

After a brief moment of awkwardness, she shrugged and took my hand, shaking it slightly. "Hi. It's nice to meet you. I'm Arietta."

We hit it off instantly, though it would still be quite some time before I revealed my true self to her. I had to get to know her better and be completely certain that I could trust her. Revealing your true self to a human is a very intimate moment for a fairy. It is not something to be taken lightly. However, she proved herself worthy.

I will forever remember that day and how it started with one of my frequent trips to the human world. I had just stepped through the portal when I heard some commotion coming from the eastern section of the woods, near Arietta's home. Worried, I began running as fast as my feet could carry me.

When I arrived, I was relieved to find that Arietta was standing near a tree. She seemed to be okay, but then I heard her yelling. I inched forward a bit and saw that she was holding a stick and threatening another human. My heart sank as I started to reevaluate our friendship and my trust in her.

So many thoughts ran through my mind at that moment. *What is she doing? Is she going to hurt them? This is so unlike her. Have I been wrong about her all along?*

Then I saw the tiny, helpless puppy caught in a juniper

bush. As I listened intently, I discovered the cause of my friend's distress. Some villagers had found the puppy and, instead of helping the poor creature, began to pelt him with sticks and stones. Arietta discovered them attempting to hurt the animal, and she stood between them, protecting him. She threatened to return the favor if one more object was thrown in the animal's direction. The others backed away, hurling insults at her as they left.

As soon as they were out of sight, she dropped the stick and kneeled down to untangle the puppy, setting him free. The poor, frightened creature backed up quickly and stared at her as if he were studying her and trying to decide if she was friend or foe. She kneeled on the ground at his level so as to not seem threatening, and she waited for him to warm up to her.

I watched as he approached her and started sniffing. When he wagged his tail, she reached up slowly to pet him. She was so kind and patient, not wanting to frighten him. He had been through enough, and she just wanted to help. I knew at that moment that she was more than worthy of my trust.

I walked around the tree, and the puppy ducked behind her. She comforted him and greeted me warmly, smiling. "That was incredible," I said.

"Oh, you saw that?"

"Yeah, I did. There is something that you need to know." She furrowed her brow and asked if everything was okay. "Yes," I replied. "It's nothing like that. It's just that I've been hiding something from you. You have to understand that I was hesitant. I've never revealed myself to anyone before, so I needed to know that I could trust you."

"I understand. I have a hard time trusting others as well. Don't worry, though. You can trust me. I would never betray you. I promise."

I took a deep breath and removed my robe, revealing my wings. I pulled back my hair so that she could see my pointed ears. I allowed her to fully see me for who I was, and there were no longer any secrets between us. My fear gave way to happiness when she showed enthusiasm and excitement about being friends with a fairy. She wanted to know everything about my world and my culture. She seemed genuinely interested, and I was happy.

From that moment on, we have been the best of friends. She even gave little Puddles to me to keep me company and ensure his protection, knowing that the other humans could not hurt him if he remained in the fairy world with me.

I continued to visit her as often as I could. She was there with an open ear and a pot of tea whenever I needed to rant, and I was there for her when she was lonely and hurting. I was there for her when her father left her and her mother for another woman. I was there for her when her mother passed away and she was all alone in the world.

I'd never seen someone so broken as she was the day of her mother's funeral. The only human to ever truly love her was gone. It hurt my heart to see her like that, and I wished that I could take away her pain and bring her mother back. There was nothing I could do about the loss she suffered, but I vowed that I would never leave her. I would be the family she needed.

Arietta and I were inseparable during my trips to the human world, but I could never stay there for very long. I had to get back to my own realm before anyone discovered the portal was open. Samhain was a different story. During this time of year, the veil between worlds was at its weakest, allowing for safer travel back and forth. Nobody cared if we went to the human world because we would have no trouble getting back, as long as we did so before dawn.

The only stipulation was that we be careful and not allow humans to travel to our world. The portal was only meant for use by the fae, and it would be all of our heads if our borders were ever breached by the humans.

It was only a matter of time before the queen discovered what I was doing. She caught me attempting to travel to the human world and confronted me. Not one to lie, especially to the queen, I told her everything. I thought that she of all fae would be understanding. How could anyone not see how special Arietta was?

Unfortunately, the queen was not so easily swayed. She forbade me to see my friend any longer, even on Samhain. When I refused, she hurled all manner of insults, saying that evil was in their blood and that they were not to be trusted. I knew better, though, and I was not going to turn my back on Arietta as the other humans had done. I was all she had left, and she was not going to lose me.

So, I continued to sneak through the portal. My visits became even more frequent, partially out of rebellion and partially because I was finding it harder and harder to be away from her. I had grown attached in a way that I never knew possible. I could not bear to part.

The last time I was in the human world, I gave her a hug and told her that I would see her soon and perhaps even stay indefinitely. Her face lit up with those words, and we were both so thrilled about the future and all the things we could do and see together if I didn't have to worry about rushing back each day.

Unfortunately, those plans fell through just as quickly as they were made, for the queen and her guards were waiting nearby when I walked through the portal. I was captured and brought before the court for sentencing. Having refused the queen's order, I was guilty of an "unforgivable" crime. No amount of pleading would sway her.

I was permitted visitation by my family at various times while awaiting punishment. I asked that my grandmother, an oracle, use her ability to check in on my friend. She did and revealed to me a truth that I never expected. Arietta was no human as I'd thought all this time. She was half fairy.

When she was born, her mother was in grave danger, being pursued by a powerful warlord who sought the destruction of all magical creatures, especially her because she refused his advances. Not one to be turned away, he pursued her relentlessly and threatened her life.

When she became pregnant, she sought refuge for her daughter. Then she gave birth and named her daughter Arietta after her mother, Arielle, and her grandmother, Henrietta. Not wanting her daughter to live her life in fear, she gave her away to a human woman who showed her kindness and had just lost her own daughter to illness. She hoped that this would keep her daughter safe, while also healing the poor woman's broken heart.

I had a hard time wrapping my head around all of this, and I wondered if Arietta had any idea. I suppose she didn't. Surely, she would have told me. I tried talking to the queen and revealing the discoveries I'd made, but she was unrelenting. In fact, she claimed to already know all about Arietta and having a rather strong grudge against her mother for giving her to a human rather than entrusting her to the fae.

I cannot blame her, though. If a warlord was after me and waged war against magical creatures, I would not want him anywhere near my home. I am not sure I could leave my child in the same world as he, but it would do no good to bring her here if he followed them and brought the rest of the humans here to capture us and conquer our realm.

I will not give up, though. There must be a way out of this. Arietta deserves to know the truth, as do the rest of the fae. They deserve to know that all humans aren't as wicked as they are portrayed to be. Sure, there are those with dark hearts, but they do not speak for the species as a whole. Arietta certainly is nothing like them. I only wish that I could see her now and talk to her about all of this. If only I wasn't stuck in this wretched prison.

"Tilani?"

Surprised at hearing my name in that familiar voice, I turn slowly until I find myself face-to-face with my Arietta. Though she looks so different now, I still recognize her immediately. I can see it in her eyes. It is unmistakable. I lunge toward the bars, shaking them wildly. I am more determined than ever to break free and embrace her once again.

"You found me!"

"Of course, I did. When you didn't return, I knew something had to be wrong. I knew you wouldn't abandon me."

"Guards!" cries out the familiar voice of the queen. "Seize the intruder!" The guards approach. I yell for Arietta to run, but she refuses. They grab her and open my cell. I expect them to throw her into the cell with me, but they do not. Instead, they grab me and lead us both to the stocks, where we are to be executed.

"Tilani of Aranathica, for your crimes against fae kind and against the queen, for your treachery in choosing the humans over your own people and leading them here, putting all our lives in jeopardy, I sentence thee…

And you, Arietta of Earth, for breaching our borders and for your and your mother's crimes against the fae, choosing the humans over our people, for risking our lives to save your own, I sentence thee…"

"Wait, what do you mean?" I ask, confused. "Arietta never put us in jeopardy. She came here to save me… to save one of us. She would never harm us. And her mother didn't put us at risk either. She gave up her own child rather than risk leading an enemy into our realm. She gave up her child for us as well as for the human who was suffering a tremendous loss."

I turn to see that Arietta is looking at me with a confused expression. "You... you knew that I was a changeling?"

"A changeling? No, changelings are nothing more than myths that people use to explain the unexplainable... a way to make sense of things, while placing all the blame on us fae as they do with so many other magical beings. You're not a changeling. You are half-fairy, half-human. Your mother was running from someone who hurt her and wanted to harm all of us. To save you – and us – she gave you up. She gave you to a kind woman she trusted... a mother in need of a child to care for a child in need of a mother."

Tears streamed down her face, and I wondered if I'd hurt her by telling her the truth. She turned to me and said, "Thank you. I'm glad to finally know the truth."

"Of course. You deserve to know the truth. But I don't understand. You know how the queen feels about you and humans in general. You knew that you would be in danger if she discovered you. So, why did you come here? Why would you risk your life in this way?"

"Don't you know?" she asks, her eyebrows raised and a slight smile revealing her dimples. "I love you. How could I not come for you?"

Before I can respond, the queen walks over and kneels before Arietta, staring into her eyes. I recognize this move. She is looking into Arietta's eyes for any sign of weakness or deceit. Finding none, her expression softens, and she looks at her as if to study her. "Can this truly be? Can someone raised in the human world learn to love one of us and even risk their life in the name of that love? Can a human truly be that selfless?"

Standing once again, she turns toward the crowd that has

gathered. The fae world, usually filled with the laughter and noise of everyday life, is now completely silent as we await the queen's next move.

With a deep breath, she addresses her kingdom. "My people – my beloved kingdom – it appears that I have made a grave error in judgment. This human… nay, this fairy before you means us no harm. She has risked her life to cross over into our realm in an effort to save one of us. This makes her a friend to us all, and we must welcome her with open arms." She turns to her guards and gives them one more command. "Release them."

Once we are free, she turns to us and apologizes. Arietta surprises the queen by leaning forward and embracing her. "Thank you, your majesty. I will never forget the kindness you have shown me."

"But, child, I almost had you executed."

"That is true, but you didn't. You were doing what you thought was best, and when you learned the truth, you let me go. All I want now is to be able to spend my life here with my best friend – my soul mate – and to raise my son here as well."

"Wait a minute," I say, confused. "Your son? When did this happen?"

"Oh, yeah, about that… there's something we should discuss…"

S.B. Rhodes writes science fiction, fantasy, young adult fiction, and horror. She loves all things fantasy and supernatural, and she has a passion for steampunk and history. She has had stories published by Zombie Pirate Publishing, Wild Dreams Publishing, Irish Horse Productions, and more. Look for her novels, set to release in 2020.

Search for an Identity

Lilith

Don't miss Zeta Phi Massacre, a co-written novel by S.B. Rhodes, Katie Jaarsveld, and J.A. Cummings. Releasing February 1st, 2020!

She enjoys spending time with her loving husband, two children, two fur babies, and scaly baby. She also loves to travel and hopes to see the world someday. She enjoys meeting new people and would love to have new Rhodies join her Facebook group here:

www.facebook.com/groups/SBsRhodies

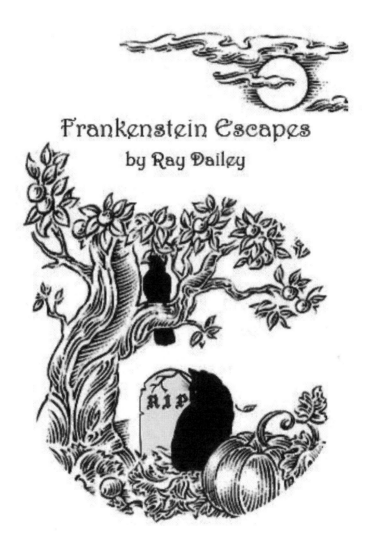

Frankenstein Escapes
by Ray Dailey

CHAPTER I

"Elizabeth! Stop it! You're killing them" Henry Clerval grabs the whip from her.

Elizabeth Lavenza glares at him.

The horses bolt at the sound of a large explosion up ahead, throwing Elizabeth and Henry from the carriage. They both feel the heat of the blast on their faces.

Henry, panic in his voice, says, "It came from the castle."

Elizabeth struggles to her feet. "I never should've left him. The horses have bolted. Let's hurry on as best we can on foot."

They arrive in short order to find, as they fear, the castle destroyed with the epicenter Victor Frankenstein's laboratory. Smoke, overturned laboratory equipment, and smoldering debris is everywhere. The sound of wood and metal creaking and groaning can be heard, suggesting the remainder of the badly damaged structure will come crashing down at any moment. Heedless of the danger, Elizabeth rushes in.

"Victor! Victor. Please answer!"

Henry, surveying the ruined castle, calls out. "Victor! Can you hear me? Elizabeth, please be careful. It looks as if these walls may crumble at any moment."

"I don't see how anyone or any...thing could've survived this."

Elizabeth stops herself. She has said too much... "What was that, Elizabeth? Any... *thing* did you say?" "Nothing Henry, I must've just misspoken, that's all." "If anyone could've survived this, it would be Victor." "Dear Henry, I only wish I shared your confidence."

Elizabeth inwardly breathes a sigh of relief. Attempting to explain the being she and Victor had created would be both unexplainable and unbelievable. Henry is simply out of his depth.

"I'm sorry but I fear we are too late. Victor's folly...*our* folly, may have cost him...everything."

"Why... What do you mean?"

"Henry, there are certain things you don't know."

"Whatever it is, if it will help Victor, you must tell me."

"Henry, you're loyal to a fault and we love you for it...

Wait. I hear someone coming."

An officious-looking man approaches them, picking his way through the smoldering rubble.

"What's all this? Who are you people? What is your business here?"

Elizabeth is indignant. "And just who might you be, Sir?"

"I will ask the questions here. But for your information,

my young friends, I am Krempe, Inspector Krempe. Police Inspector for this District."

Henry, always the peacemaker, attempts a more conciliatory approach. "Begging your pardon, Inspector. I am Henry Clerval, and this is Miss Elizabeth Lavenza. We have come to this remote location only seeking news of the welfare of our friend. Please, Inspector. You'll have your answers, but I must insist you do not further upset Elizabeth. As it is, we fear the worst."

"Very well then...for the time being, but I warn you both I am not to be trifled with. Do not seek to intrude into official police business."

"We're only here out of concern for my friend and Elizabeth's fiancé. We wouldn't think of intruding into your official duties."

Elizabeth, still seething, realizes that Henry's appeasement, while galling, is effective.

"Thank you for your kind consideration, Inspector I am Victor's fiancée. Henry is Victor's closest friend. We were both concerned as Victor's work seemed to have affected his health of late. I'd thought he was finished with his research project – whatever it was – but recently he once again became distracted. More distant than ever."

"So, you admit to being associates of Baron Victor Frankenstein."

Elizabeth forces a laugh. "Admit, Inspector? Why, of course we do. Henry and I have known Victor since we were all children."

Krempe stares at them with dead eyes. "I beg your pardon Miss Lavenza, Mr. Clerval, but you are no longer children and your admitted friend Victor Frankenstein wasn't involved in some childish game here." Turning his attention to the destroyed laboratory, he adds, "Far from it, I'm afraid."

"That sounds like some sort of an accusation."

The medals on Krempe's coat shine ominously in the still burning rubble. "And if it is?"

"Look here, the truth is, just before we arrived, we heard an awful explosion. You must've heard it too, Inspector. Henry is correct. Victor was obsessed with…" She hesitates, deciding she must keep Krempe in the dark as to her own collaboration with Victor "… whatever he was working on."

She and Victor had long ago discovered that it was simply more efficient in a patriarchal world to have Victor be the representative in all their dealings. In truth, she had been the primary innovator with Victor her willing albeit capable assistant. She would make them pay. She would show them all for underestimating her as a professional and as a woman.

"And just what was the nature of his work?"

Elizabeth looks him straight in the eye and lies. "I only know it kept him away from me for long periods. He was very secretive, even to the point of refusing to see anyone, including me. I missed him so, but he would not be moved."

"Refusing to see anyone including you, his fiancée? Odd

behavior. Wouldn't you agree Mr. Clerval?"

Distracted, Henry replies, "What? Yes. I suppose."

"What do you know of this business Mr. Clerval?"

Henry, nervous now, defers to Elizabeth, "Just what Elizabeth has told you. Nothing more."

"Are you certain of that?"

Henry feels perspiration bead on his upper lip. "Why yes…yes. Of course, I'm certain."

"So, you both claim to know nothing of the specifics of Victor Frankenstein's work. Are you *both* very sure of that?"

Elizabeth, angry now, is through with his attitude. "We've said so Inspector."

"We will set the matter of your truthfulness aside for the moment. As to the matter of Frankenstein himself, his *work,* as you generously put it… it couldn't have turned out any other way. At least based on what I've heard of the goings on here of late."

Henry gathers himself and responds innocently. "Why, Inspector Krempe, whatever do you mean?"

Elizabeth, her anger rising, lashes out at the Inspector. "How dare you make such unfounded accusations. Make yourself clear!"

"Again, I must I beg your pardon Miss Lavenza, Mr. Clerval, but people talk. I make it my business to know what is going on in my district. I find it helps to maintain order. At any rate, certain deliveries were made here. Medical supplies." Elizabeth has had enough and takes a sarcastic tone. "Really? You don't say! Medical supplies delivered to a medical student. You're right! Absolutely scandalous! Your powers of observation do you credit, sir."

Krempe ignores her. "As I was saying…his work is an abomination. He mocks God."

Elizabeth nervously laughs. "Abomination? Mocking God? Really! Inspector, your accusations are completely unfounded

– the result, I'll wager, of paying too much heed to the town gossips."

"Please, Inspector. I beg of you. Consider Elizabeth in all this. I'm sure whatever deliveries were made were nothing more than any physician might require. This is really quite a leap you are making from delivery of a few medical supplies to some abomination. After all, Victor *is* a medical student."

"Nothing of the kind, Mr. Clerval…and I advise you again, nothing but the truth will suffice with me. If you are indeed his good friend, I suspect you know Frankenstein left university months ago to pursue independent research of some kind. That is what I am advised by his former professors."

Elizabeth meets his grim stare with one of her own. "What of it? I don't see where that is any of your concern."

"You implied that the medical supplies he received were nothing out of the ordinary. Far from it. In fact, the greatest majority were quite unusual indeed – power-generating devices, large equipment not at all associated with a standard surgery. Now, enough of your prying into matters that do not concern you. If you truly want to be of service to your friend, then help me search these ruins. He may yet live."

As they begin to search through the rubble, Henry attempts to pry more information from the Inspector. "But Inspector, what about your charge of some sort of abomination as you put it? Of what exactly is Victor accused?"

"None of your concern, of course, but I'm under quite a bit of pressure myself with the locals. My competence has been called into question by the gossips with nothing better to wonder about. There have been a number of missing persons in the last several weeks. I can't say murder, as there have been no bodies discovered. That's in addition to a hanged man being stolen right from the gallows only hours after he was executed. Grisly business!

Now this. Unless I am able to satisfactorily resolve these mysteries, it's only a matter of time until the village leaders… men of consequence… Well, quite frankly, my position is in jeopardy."

Henry tries to pry further. "And I suppose you think Victor is somehow involved."

Krempe isn't having it. "Perhaps…perhaps not."

Elizabeth is only concerned with the task at hand. "Victor is our only priority. Neither petty politics nor your own fortunes with the locals concern us."

Henry scolds her. "Elizabeth! Don't be rude."

Elizabeth snaps back. "We can't just stand idly by while Victor is accused of every mystery in the district. Perhaps the gossips are right to question this fellow's competence."

He glares at her. "Hold your tongue!"

Krempe turns away in anger, then stoops to pick up something in the smoking rubble that has caught his eye. "What have we here?"

He brushes the still glowing embers away and carefully opens the smoking remains of a charred journal. "It is the notes of your dear Victor Frankenstein."

He reads aloud, "'University has nothing more to offer me. My private research into matters of life and death leads me to believe that death can be conquered by man.'"

Krempe snaps the journal shut. "There you have it. He was in league with the devil. There may be no body to recover, but I'm taking these notes as evidence. Good day to you both."

Elizabeth well knows the importance of that journal. She must have it any cost. "Inspector! Surely, you must have misunderstood. Let me see that." Elizabeth reaches for the journal.

Krempe jerks away from her. "You must think me a fool. I am not going to just give over incriminating evidence to Frankenstein's own fiancée. I'd never see you or this journal again."

Henry blocks his path. "Hold on, Inspector. We mean no harm or disrespect. We only want to find the truth."

"If it's the truth you want, then you'll leave me to my work. Now get away before you find yourselves in my jail. I'll not warn you again about meddling in an official inquiry."

As Krempe is leaving Elizabeth calls after him. "Please! Inspector!" Elizabeth turns to Henry. "I must have that journal. It may be the only way to get to the bottom of all this. The Inspector seems to have Victor tried and convicted based solely on gossip he's heard in the village. Henry, you've got to help me convince him. Are you coming or not?"

"Of course."

Retrieving the journal is desirable but not necessary at this point. While tramping around the ruined laboratory, Elizabeth sees some footprints in the burning ash and rubble leading into the forest. Victor is alive! In her excitement, what she fails to note are a trailing set of footprints… larger, much larger, and making a deeper impression than Victor's.

"Come along Henry, the horses have returned. Let's see if we can catch up to that awful Inspector. He can't have gotten too far."

Elizabeth and Henry's carriage did in fact catch up to the inspector's horse in short order. Elizabeth grabs the reins, urging the horses onward until she is able to come abreast of the Inspector. She throws the reins back to Henry and begins to horsewhip the Inspector mercilessly until he falls from his horse.

"Have you lost your mind?" Henry exclaims.

They both get out of the carriage and go to the prone and very still Inspector.

"Dead – must've hit his head on a rock," says Elizabeth with no emotion. She reaches into the dead man's coat and retrieves Victor's journal. "He won't need this."

Together, they move the body off the road, covering it with some nearby foliage.

"You go on ahead. I'm going back. Victor may still be alive."

Henry refuses. "I'm going with you. If there's even a chance…"

"No, it's better if we separate. If I find Victor, we've got to get out of Europe altogether. His reputation is in tatters here. The American South is the place for us. Run by wealthy plantation owners. Plenty of money to fund a new… medical practice."

"Good luck then." Henry moves to embrace her. Elizabeth turns away, heading back up the path on to the smoking ruins, determined.

CHAPTER II
*O NE Y E A R L ATE R

A tavern, located in the notorious Under the Hill area on the Mississippi River in Natchez, Mississippi hosts drunken riverboat men and others not deemed fit for proper society.

Patrons are milling around, standing at the bar, seated at tables talking amongst each other. Mary, a barmaid, is serving drinks and fending off flirtatious advances. Two enslaved women are behind the bar, prepared to clean up or do other low work even the Irish won't be made to do. The women, uncomfortable in the tavern, do their best not to attract unwanted attention. They'll be gone after tonight. A messenger is to come leading them both to the Natchez Trace, otherwise known as The Devil's Backbone. That will begin a treacherous journey north on the underground railroad ending in Canada, or death.

The bartender is oblivious to them. He scolds Mary not to spill any beer and get to work.

Tom, a drunken patron, grabs at her. "Here now, Mary, be nice. Gimme a kiss to go with that beer."

Mary, teasing, pushes him away. "You'd like that wouldn't you?"

Victor enters and sits at a vacant table.

Tom's friend Joe laughs. "I don't think she likes you anymore. It's me she wants."

Mary smirks at that. "You're no better. I deserve a real gentleman."

"I was gentleman enough for you last week."

Mary responds with false modesty, feigning shock, and gives the bully a playful slap on the chest. "Ohhh you…!"

Joe intervenes. "Forget it, Mary. Be a good girl now and

bring us both another round."

Tom is angry now at being rebuffed. "Bitch! Who does she think she is anyway, putting on airs like she's somebody? I guess she'd prefer the likes of the Baron."

"You're wrong on that score. I doubt even Mary's charms would affect him. The Baron's a cold one. I just can't put my finger on exactly what it is, but something's just wrong about him."

"He's strange, all right."

Victor raises his voice over the din. "Landlord!" The bartender sees him and pointedly ignores him. "Landlord... service!"

The bartender reluctantly comes to Victor's table. "Yes, what do *you* want?"

Victor places his order. "I'll have a glass of wine, thank you."

The bartender is in no mood for the foreigner. "I'm a bartender, not a landlord. We serve beer and whiskey. We're very busy here today. Perhaps the Baron would like to take his business elsewhere."

Victor grabs the bartender by his stained shirt. "I prefer the company here which is why I left a bottle of my own wine in your care. You'll bring that wine and leave the bottle."

The bartender growls back. "You heard me. No one wants you here."

"Completely beside the point. Bring the wine. Now!" "All right, but then I want you out of here."

Elizabeth enters the tavern, scanning the faces, looking for…. "Victor! There you are!"

Victor smiles. "Ah. The day is suddenly brighter. I just ordered some wine. Will you join me in a glass?"

Taking a flask from her purse, Elizabeth says, "You know I prefer absinthe. You should have some yourself, Victor. It will clear your mind."

"Go easy with that, Elizabeth. The 'green faery' is as strong as morphine and may cause you to hallucinate."

Laughing, Elizabeth says, "I know that. Why do you think I like it?"

"Don't be foolish. It's a medicinal compound."

"Easy, Victor. It's a harmless pastime…and I'll do without your lecture."

"Sorry. But I do wish you'd take laudanum for your ailments like everyone else. You've had enough anyway. Why don't you let me keep that bottle for now?"

"All right, if it will satisfy you." Elizabeth rolls her eyes. Victor leans in so only Elizabeth can hear. "So, I understand leaving Europe as my family is well known throughout the continent. Our… well, *my* reputation couldn't withstand our staying, but why this backwater? Not only isn't it Europe, it isn't even New York or New Orleans. I can think of a lot better places to practice… medicine."

Elizabeth, deadly serious, responds, "I won't argue the point, but the fact that we are so far underground is entirely your doing."

Victor stares at her, incredulous.

Elizabeth continues. "You'll recall our first medical adventure, shall I say. You wanted a superior brain, an intellect for the creature. I thought it prudent to have a more obedient creation. I let you have your way and the result nearly killed you, and now here we are."

Victor goes silent. She is right.

His creation had escaped, returning several months later. He had learned to speak! A gypsy befriended him in the forest and had taught him language and morality. It was only when she brought him to her family's camp, and they ran him off in fear that the creature realized his loneliness. He returned demanding a mate like himself.

Victor was appalled but reluctantly agreed when the creature threatened harm to Elizabeth.

Through his contacts in the village he procured a suitable body and brought it to life as the creature stood impatiently nearby. A sharp inhale-alive! Once again, he'd done it! The Baron helped her to stand, carefully unwrapping the gauze from her fully bandaged head.

The creature backed away, horrified. "You killed my friend!" he cried.

Victor's source had apparently murdered the creatures' Romany friend rather than go to the charnel house.

Exhausted and frustrated, Victor said, "Fine. If you don't want her..." He grabbed each side of her head and twisted, snapping her neck. She fell to the floor at his feet, lifeless as she'd been only minutes before.

The creature rushed to her, cradling her, willing her back to life. Victor backed silently away. The grief-stricken creature saw Victor. He glared at the Baron with red, swollen eyes. He lunged at Victor. The creature fell into a shelf of highly flammable chemicals which exploded as the shelf hit the stone floor. Fortunately, it created a barrier between Victor and the enraged beast, allowing the Baron time to escape just as the entire laboratory was engulfed in flames, followed quickly by an explosion that destroyed everything.

"Victor?" Elizabeth can see he is lost in thought. She reaches for his hand. "I'm just glad you're alive and that thing is dead."

Victor takes her hand and quickly confirms it. "He is dead. Blown to bits. I barely escaped myself."

"I heard rumors on board ship of a giant man-like beast roaming the forests – a Yeti of some sort. You're certain it's dead?"

Victor whispers to her. "I'd be worried if he somehow survived and was stalking me with thoughts of revenge, but that's impossible. Even if he were alive, he couldn't find us here across the Atlantic. Put it out of your mind. He's food for the wolves back in the old country."

Elizabeth lowers her voice to a whisper, aware she's in a public place. "It's time to begin again, but with more control over our result this time."

Victor scoffs. "I thought we'd learned our lesson. Best leave questions of life and death to the philosophers. Besides which, I don't relish nearly getting blown up."

"Again, your fault. Entirely." She smiles.

"You do not suffer fools gladly, and that's putting it kindly my dear."

Elizabeth laughs. "I consider that a compliment. Look around you." She gestures at the patrons of the tavern. "Speaking of fools…"

The bartender lumbers over with Victor's wine. "Here's your wine." He turns quickly to go without leaving the bottle.

Victor is quick to remind him, "…and just leave that bottle here."

The bartender slams the bottle down on the table and tries to return to his bar, but Victor is not done with him.

"Just a moment, bartender. A glass for the lady."

The bartender has had enough of the insolent Victor.

"Mary! Get off your lazy ass and come wait on these…folks." He finally is allowed to stalk back to the bar.

"All right, all right." she fumes.

Mary is about fed up with the bartender. Just a hot-tempered bully never giving her any credit for all the work she does.

"Can I do anything else for y'all?" "No, thank you, Miss."

"Oooh. You *are* a gentleman, aren't you?" Mary is at once impressed and flirtatious.

Elizabeth is weary at once. "Victor. Please don't encourage her."

Victor smiles. "Just good manners, Elizabeth, nothing more."

Mary returns to the bar. "Let me know if you change your mind." She lets her offer linger as temptingly as she can, pointedly ignoring Elizabeth.

Old Joe loiters near the door, hoping for a handout. He is a vagrant and a drunk. Elizabeth sees him and motions for Mary to come back.

"Come here, girl."

Mary, no longer flirtatious, is cautious now but also deferential, not rude but still suspicious of Elizabeth.

"Yes ma'am?"

Elizabeth gestures to Old Joe. "See that man? Who is he?" "That's just Old Joe, ma'am. You want to steer clear of him. He's no good, just an old drunk."

Elizabeth smiles, attempting to put Mary at ease. "I'm sure you're right, but I'm feeling generous. Here, take this gold coin. I'm buying Joseph a whiskey with it. You may keep the remainder for yourself if you'll send him over to me."

Mary stares at the gold coin in disbelief. "Are you sure, Ma'am?"

"Just send him over."

Old Joe gets his whiskey and then approaches the couple as instructed. "Thank you, Baron. Ma'am." He drinks greedily. The pretense of the Baron in charge continues to work well, so the couple continue the ruse.

Victor says, "You know who we are, then?"

Joe replies, "I expect everyone knows who you are, Baron Frankenstein."

Victor, convivial, smiles. "Pull up a chair and join us. We insist."

Elizabeth smiles. "You're very welcome for the whiskey. There's more where that came from, at least for a man who's not afraid to cut a few corners and bend a few rules."

"Never been much for rules."

"Tell me, Joseph. Have you ever been to the funeral

home…after hours, I mean?"

"Why? What have you heard? I'm not afraid of a few dead bodies, if that's what you're getting at. Dead is dead. That's what I say. Besides, what use have they got for their rings and necklaces? They're dead ain't they? It's not as if they can take it with them."

"A very sensible attitude. They are dead, 'ain't' they, Elizabeth?" She smiles at Victor's private joke.

"The Yella Fever takes a lot of folks around these parts. Lots a folks jes bury their dead at home – can't afford no fancy funeral home. Anyhow, I've been lucky so far. I intend to keep on being lucky."

"Sounds like you're the man we've been looking for. Meet me later at our offices down by the river and we'll tell you exactly what we need."

As Victor and Elizabeth leave, a figure lurking outside the tavern slinks into the shadows…watching.

They live and work Under the Hill in Natchez in a building overlooking the Mississippi River, a few blocks from the taverns and brothels that made the area so notorious and popular with riverboat men, traders, and assorted ne'er-do-wells. It works well for their purposes. Victor and Elizabeth are physicians by day and researchers by night with no one to question their methods. One wall of the office overlooks the river itself and makes a perfect place to dispose of unwanted specimens.

As instructed, Joe meets the pair later at this office, gets his instructions and disappears into the night.

It's after midnight, but Elizabeth and Victor are both up working and planning when there is a knock at the back door.

Elizabeth doesn't want to be bothered. "Go away." The knocking becomes more insistent pounding. Victor tries. "Are you deaf? Go away!"

The knocking is now louder and faster, almost desperate.

Victor stalks to the door. "Very well then!" Victor opens the door to find Old Joe standing there. "Yes, what do you want?"

Joe replies. "I got what you're looking for. I can't be standing outside all night with this. Anyone might walk by."

Elizabeth looks up at him, interested now. "Well, get in here before someone sees you."

Victor is dismissive. "No one is likely to see you at this hour anyhow. Decent people are home in their beds Put your bundle down on this long worktable."

Joe groans as he puts the canvas bag down. "Ahh, that's better. He was a heavy one."

"It better be in good condition if you expect to get paid." Elizabeth, examining the corpse, is suspicious. "It's still warm. Where did you get it? This didn't come from the funeral home."

Joe won't meet her accusing glare. "Never mind that. You said you were in a hurry for it. Just pay me and be quick about it. What do you want it for anyway? What are you doing here? You never said."

Elizabeth is curt. "We never said for a very good reason. It's none of your business."

Joe rankles at this. "No need to be insulting."

Victor consoles Old Joe. "Now, don't mind her. It's just the least you know the better. Let's keep it that way, shall we?"

Joe mumbles. "I guess so."

Elizabeth brightens. "Joe, on second thought, I don't want your visit to be a complete waste of time. Come with me. I have something to show you. I think you'll be surprised. Very surprised, indeed."

Joe ambles over to Elizabeth. "I always wondered what y'all was up to."

Victor is certain he knows the trap Elizabeth is setting for Joe but says nothing.

Elizabeth confides, "You're a curious fellow, Joe. People

don't give you the credit you deserve."

"Well, no, ma'am, I guess they don't."

"Victor and I would be very interested in your opinion."

"All right, but then I gotta be going."

"I assure you; this won't take very long at all."

Elizabeth leads Joe to a glass-fronted cabinet as if to confide in him. She walks slightly behind him, silently grasping a scalpel as they walk. As she raises the scalpel to cut his throat, Joe sees the reflection of the glistening scalpel in the glass cabinet door.

"Wait. No. What are you doing? Are you crazy?" He tries to scream but chokes on his own blood as Elizabeth cuts his throat. Elizabeth is an efficient surgeon. Joe drops to the floor, bleeding out, dying within moments.

Elizabeth looks dispassionately at Joe's dead body. "I needed an obedient, compliant brain this time. So sorry, dear old Joe, but desperate times call for desperate measures, don't they?"

The next hour passes quickly. Elizabeth grabs a saw and takes the top of his head off, removing the brain and placing it in a jar of liquid preservative. She stands back, satisfied.

Victor wraps up Joe's body in canvas. He opens up a trap door in the floor which opens onto the river below. "I'll dump his remains in the river."

Elizabeth is anxious to get started. "Perfect! Now the work begins. Victor! Come! I need you!"

They begin, placing the heart in the chest cavity, sewing up the chest, stitching on the hands, replacing eyes, and placing Joe's brain in the waiting skull. Unwanted organs and limbs are tossed into a waiting bucket at Victor's feet. Copious amounts of blood are in evidence on the body and Elizabeth's hands throughout each surgical procedure.

Finally, the completed creature is lying on the operating table amid bubbling test tubes and humming machinery with flashing lights.

All the while, a shadow watches and waits just outside.

Elizabeth continues to adjust the powerful, life-giving equipment, turning various knobs, levers and switches. Suddenly there is a large crash of life-giving thunder and lightning. The Creature moves!

Elizabeth exults. "I've done it! We've done it Victor. It lives!"

The creature bolts upright from the operating table. With animal-like strength, it snaps the wrist and chest bands restraining it and lurches off the table, growling, angry, and animalistic. There will be no controlling this beast as Elizabeth had planned. It is a monster, pure evil. It is flesh stitched together haphazardly. Two red eyes glow menacingly, patches of hair sprouting randomly like weeds in a garden. The power of the lightning strike broke the thing's teeth into jagged shards.

As it is about to strike, the shadowy figure, abnormally tall but gaunt, with long stringy, hair wearing little more than breeches and a greatcoat, bursts through the heavy door that has been bolted shut. He tosses the ruined door aside as if it is paper. Elizabeth's creation senses the shadowy intruder as a threat and immediately lunges for him. With little effort, the intruder destroys Elizabeth's creation, ruthlessly bashing its head in against the doorframe. A grisly trail of blood, brain and bone follow the dead thing as it slides to the floor.

Elizabeth is furious. "No! What have you done?" The murderous intruder steps into the light.

Victor is stunned. "You!"

Victor and Elizabeth's original creation stalks into the room. Stepping behind Elizabeth, he places his enormous, blood-stained hands on her shoulders.

"Yes. You made me to survive. I was determined to find you after…after you killed my friend. The only chance to end my solitude." His giant hands move slowly toward Elizabeth's fragile neck. "I've been watching, tracking both of you. Your evil must stop. There can be no more like me."

Victor, now knowing why the thing has doggedly tracked them here, begs, "Please leave us be."

Just as Victor had cruelly robbed him of a companion, the creature twists Elizabeth's neck into an unnatural position. She cries out only briefly, her windpipe lacerated. She drops to the floor, dead.

Victor roars in anguish and lunges at the creature. The creature grabs Victor over a massive shoulder, picks up his treasured journal and crashes through a window overlooking the river. He and Victor sink down, down into the muddy Mississippi River.

Murder/suicide is not on Victor's agenda, and he's not certain the beast can even die, so he struggles against the creature's determined strength and the deepening water. The shore recedes and hope fades. The monster trudges on, deeper into the murky depths. Even he, with his great strength can barely move through the thickening mud.

CHAPTER III
*EPILOGUE: PRESENT DAY, NATCHEZ

Since that night of life and death Under the Hill in Natchez, the businesses cater to tourists now. The riverboat men, prostitutes, gamblers, and other rough trade are all long gone.

Today a couple of archeologists are down from the University of Southern Mississippi in Hattiesburg. Gwen and James are on the bank of the river. They're mostly looking for Civil War era bullets, arrowheads and the like. No one expects to find anything particularly earth-shattering in importance. Neither one is tenured, so any find that resulted in a published work will certainly help them both.

All at once, Gwen cries out. "Help me! I've got something. It's big."

James comes, since no one has found a thing. Gwen's in the river about knee deep. It's so muddy neither one of them can see.

"What've you got Gwen?" asks James.

"Not sure, but it's going to take all we've got to ease it up out of the water. It feels like a statue of some kind."

After lots of effort, they finally manage to get it out of the water and up onto the bank. It's a grisly find. A mud-encased statue gripping a skeleton in one arm and cradling a book in the other.

Gwen offers, "The mud man is reminiscent of a Golem – a protector of the community according to legend. There was an active Jewish community here years ago, but this would be something from the old country."

James replies, "True. There is precedent for finds preserved by mud and other certain conditions such as temperature, so this is not completely unheard of. Let's proceed carefully."

"Good. Let's start by very carefully removing the skeleton and the book. We can try to date the skeleton and find out more about the book."

They go to work. Just as the book and skeleton are separated, it began to rain.

Gwen grabs a tarp and covers up the statue. The skeleton and book are put safely in the back of her panel van. As the storm worsens, the pair opt to wait it out inside the back of the van.

Then it happens.

The winds rip the tarp away, and a massive lightning strike seems to strike right at the mud figure. The lightning jolts the figure – yes! It moves. As it struggles to stand, the pouring rain washes away over a century of mud and it – he – becomes recognizable as a man.

A lantern shines deep inside the panel van. The man moves haltingly toward the light. As he draws closer, Gwen and James both can see this is a man – an incredibly large, badly scarred man, but a man, nonetheless. He reaches the van, enters and sits cross-legged on the floor, challenging only the shock absorbers with his weight. Other than his imposing bulk and harsh features, he seems harmless. He eyes the skeleton and the journal.

It was then that he told his tale. He said they were welcome to Frankenstein's remains but not the book. It must never fall into the wrong hands. He takes the book in one of his massive hands.

And with that, he is gone, heading west toward the Louisiana swamps.

Since then, there have been tales of a Yeti, a Bigfoot, or something roaming Honey Island Swamp in south Louisiana.

But that's just a folk tale.
    Isn't it?

Smoke and Mirrors
by Connie Todd Lila

Costermongers hawking their wares blended with the clip-clop rhythm from carriages whose occupants ignored them. This cacophony reached from Piccadilly Circus into Coventry Street and blended with the noise from the small side show glittering there.

"Thus, we quench the flames in hand." Clapping a lid on his dish of fire, the stage magician quickly lifted it again. Two white doves flapped excitedly into the crowd. "And, without so much as an abracadabra, we create beauty on the wing."

He took his applause with a humble nod toward the assortment of viewers. Bright movement drew his attention to the back of the group, where a purple-gowned young woman was tucking something into her ample cleavage. The gent to whom that gold watch belonged never felt it lifted from his pocket as he applauded stageward. The magician stroked his pointed beard and lifted a gull wing brow.

"And, speaking of beauty, perhaps this brightly feathered bird would approach the stage?"

All eyes turned to see where he pointed and rested on the startled red head. Her cheeks colored beneath round eyes and a hand pressed against the black lace at her bodice.

"Yes, my dear, you . . . come forward, if you please."

She stepped forward, darting glances left and right for the authorities. At stageside, she looked up into his dark eyes. With a practiced gesture, he drew from his sleeve the traditional prop, a silk bouquet.

"For the fairest of the fair." While the audience cheered, his arm crossed his waist for an exaggerated bow. Head near hers, he pierced her eyes with a gaze too sharp for his stage smile.

"I saw what you hid in your charming décolleté."

The breath she pulled, louder than his whisper, pressed the stolen watch sharply into her breast. When she reached for the bouquet, he drew her fingers to his lips and grinned,

"I heartily applaud you, my beauty." A tentative smile lifted the paint at the corners of her eyes. He addressed his audience for a final deep bow and flourish of his cape.

"A round of appreciation for this lovely creature, and many thanks for your attention."

He held her with his eyes while the crowd moved on to other carnival attractions and games of chance. Once clear, three long strides brought him to the steps at the side of the stage.

"Manchester the Magnificent, your servant." She accepted his hand, allowed him to draw

her up onto the silent stage. "I believe a sherry is in order." He swept his hand grandly to a fold in the stage curtains.

Backstage, he bade her sit in the only chair, an overstuffed shape long in need of a patch and scrub. He filled two glasses from a bottle that shared a dresser with a kettle, tea canister, two cups, and a half packet of biscuits. She accepted the sherry.

He raised his glass in salute, and, proclaiming, "Here's to crime", drained his glass. When she sipped hers, he sat in the chair beside her, forcing himself close against her. Rouged mouth open in alarm, she pulled a loud gasp.

"Now, none of that. You haven't room for any more breath with a great, gold pocket watch down... here." He put his hand straight down her cleavage and grasped the watch. She aimed a slap at him, which he deflected with the hand lifting the watch.

"So, now what? You call the coppers?" She spoke for the first time, lisping slightly.

"And ruin a perfect working relationship?" Manchester smiled, dangling the watch between them. "While I dazzle them onstage, you'll be relieving them of pickings like these." She struggled to pull her skirts from beneath his legs, but he pressed her fast, flashing that smile that never quite reached his eyes.

"My proposition has to have more appeal than the ones

you've been getting on the corner of Coventry Street." He gestured with his beard toward the west end of the carnival row.

She stopped struggling and sat back, considering.

"I wouldn't know how to do the showy things you pull off."

"Not to worry, my bright bird. It's all done with smoke and mirrors. So, now, what do I call my lovely new business associate?"

She lifted his hand, placed it on her knee, pressing it into the purple silk. Tucking her chin toward her chest, she looked up deliberately through sooty lashes.

"Corinne."

Manchester the Magnificent slid his hand to her waist, then to her bodice.

"Well, Corinne . . . it's showtime."

She smiled and lisped coyly, "Whatever you say, ducks."

Manchester arranged his cape on the brass coatrack and caught Corinne's waist in both hands. The gilded mirror in their sitting room framed her perfectly, tumble of red curls across one shoulder, jewel-encrusted brooch sparkling from the other.

"I've come home with a surprise for you, my bright bird."

Corinne poured two brandies from a cut crystal decanter and offered one to Manchester.

"Is it something to wear in the show again?" A deep sigh plumped her cleavage up above the saffron bodice of her gown.

"Not this time. You will still be dazzling the audience in your satins and jewels, but not in Piccadilly. We are going to America."

Corinne pressed a ring-encrusted hand to her chest, mouth open.

"Manny!"

"We, or should I say, you, my pet, have done so very well these two years past that I have been able to not only keep you like this," indicating their elegant flat with a gesture, "but to put enough by for our passage across the ocean. We leave in a fortnight, sail for a week or so, and put into port in an exciting city with a walk of boards along the ocean, so you'll suffer no sand in your dancing slippers. There are carnivals and ballroom dances inside a grand Pavilion and wealthy people abounding. All of them just waiting for us to... entertain them." Manchester stroked his pointed beard.

Corinne leapt into his arms, covered his face with rouged kisses, then pushed him away and hurried to their boudoir.

"What are you doing, my flighty bird?" Corinne sang joyfully from the other room. "Packing!"

"The people with real money go into that Pavilion. They can pay to see the freak show in them glass boxes... them two-headed snakes and such, babies born stuck together." Corinne pouted strawberry lips, hooking the front of her emerald satin corset. "All I'm taking out in the sawdust is small purses with more snuff than coin."

Manchester tipped her chin to look into eyes that matched her corset.

"You just want to go hear the music in the ballroom again."

"What if I do? I love to go dancin', Manny, and we never do."

'Very well, my jewel. After this next show, we will go dancing." Pulling aside the backstage curtain, he offered Corinne his free hand.

"It's showtime." "Whatever you say, ducks."

Corinne glided up the staircase on Manchester's arm, the

lace flounces of her gown settling over her like feathers. The Pavilion ballroom glittered with lamplight and candle flames reflected from diamonds, sequins, and gold. Manchester swept her into the moving crowd of couples, twirled her so her skirts floated like angel wings, then drew her against him in a lover's waltz.

Twice around the floor, Corinne noticed a small handbag at the edge of a table. Stitched with pearls and jet beads, it lay easily within reach of the dancers. She practiced her gestures, twirling grandly in Manchester's arms. As they passed the table, Corinne scooped up the handbag with a graceful sweep, and wrapped that arm around Manchester's shoulders, the better to drop the bag between their bodies.

"Thief!" The waiter bringing a fresh water pitcher to the table saw Corinne tuck the handbag down between herself and Manchester. He pointed. "Those two!"

Corinne let go of Manchester, clutching the handbag to her chest.

"Manny!"

He jerked her hand toward the grand staircase, already running. Corinne skidded along, running on tiptoes, trying to keep her balance in her slippery dress shoes, Manchester pulling her too fast across the polished floor. He started down the staircase without giving her time to find her balance. The stolen handbag slipped from her hand and bounced down the stairs ahead of them, leaving a wake of snapped pearls and beads. Manchester lost his footing, rolling across them, and pulled Corinne down the crushed marble stairs with him. He landed first, skewed hips twisting the life from his spine. The last sound Corinne heard was her own neck snapping.

"More corn shocks and pumpkins, more!" Professor Mary Haefer assessed the Student Center midway. "A Halloween

Carnival needs to look like one."

Leo Baxter and Greg Schroeder looked up at their advisor. Both gave her a cadet salute at the same time, grinning. Laughing, she shook her head and walked along the midway. The food vendors seemed plentiful, popcorn and cotton candy stands arranged with hot food stands selling nachos, hot dogs, and fried potatoes. The theatre majors outdid themselves creating the "haunted forest walk" with stage flats, fog machines, far too many draping webs, and hidden boom boxes howling, moaning, and groaning. Karen Prescott sat on top of a ladder, dribbling red paint down a broken window in a haunted cabin flat.

"Hi, Professor Haefer." Karen's sunny greeting sat at grisly odds with the decorating task she was finishing. Bloody splatters dappled her blond hair and pink cheeks with gore.

Mary looked up, grinned back at Karen.

"Your backstage magic is very . . . atmospheric." Mary skipped over a spill of red paint.

"Oh, it's theatre. It's all done with smoke and mirrors. If we'd been given permission to set up in the old Pavilion, we could have built on the atmosphere already there."

Mary pressed her lips, gave her head a shake.

"Sorry, Karen, I know. The Historical Society hasn't raised the funding yet to begin the planned renovations. It really is an historical landmark worth saving. Today, however, it is off limits and completely unsafe. Entire floors have fallen in. That grand, old marble staircase to the ballroom has crumbled under its own weight through the decades. Wish I'd seen it back when. Your theatre group's backstage magic will be plenty for the Carnival." Mary admired Karen's gruesome paintwork.

"If you think this is something, walk over and get a look at the Fortune Teller's booth Maria Luisa is working on. She volunteered to be our fortune teller. She's eager to act the part. She had this beloved ancestor in her country who really could tell your fortune. All she had to do was hold your hand."

Across the Student Center, a slender young woman with dark hair draped an aluminum tent support with lengths of exotically patterned cloth, tucking the drapery open to create a cave for a small round table. From somewhere within the tumbling folds of atmosphere came the sound of gypsy violins, souls crying over fortunes gone awry. The effect was perfect. Professor Haefer delivered her jest with a smile of approval.

"Cross your palm with silver for my future, lady?"

Maria peeked out from her curtain cave and grinned enthusiastically.

"Hey, Prof! Well, what do you think? Will anyone want to cross my palm with silver at the Carnival?"

Professor Haefer shook her head and laughed.

"Maria, if anyone could fill their pocket telling fortunes, it would be you, in this very set. You've created an incredible space here. Is that an actual crystal ball?"

Maria smoothed her hand over the sphere in the center of her table.

"Oh, no! This is just glass. Pretty special glass, though. See the bottom? There is a lid that screws off, like a jar lid. This came from an antique shop. It was some kind of old, Victorian rose jar, or flower arrangement jar, for flowers that were saved and dried after someone's funeral."

Maria yielded to a visible shudder.

"Can you imagine? I mean, keeping flowers thrown at you at a wedding is one thing. But grave flowers? Too much connection to the dearly departed, thank you." With that, Maria crawled back beneath the drapery set she was perfecting.

Leo and Greg loaded the extra pumpkins and corn stalks that Professor Haefer wanted. When the wagon was full, they started toward the Student Center. From around a pick-up in the Student Parking Lot swaggered Dax Craig, pit bull demeanor in place. His usual sidekicks, Charlie Theodore and Bill

Rhodes, stood behind him. No one stepped in front of Dax.

Leo tugged the landscape wagon to a halt. Greg stepped from foot to foot a bit, thinking of the switchblades Dax gave his thug friends.

"What up, suck up? Decorating for the ladies now, like fags?"

Dax's cronies howled at this, pointing at Greg and Leo. "Oh, no, Dax, just doing homework. But you wouldn't

know about that, since you never come to class."

Dax lowered his head like a bull ready to charge and glared at Leo, features darkened.

"So, Leo, you still think you'll be taking that tasty blonde home from the Carnival?"

Leo dropped the handle of the cart and stepped up in Dax's face.

"You leave Karen alone, you hear me?"

Dax slid his hand to casually hook a thumb over his side pocket.

"Or . . . what?"

Walking to her car, Professor Haefer saw Leo and Dax facing off in the student lot. Threading carefully, she pulled up as near to Leo as she could and opened her door.

In her most professional, commanding voice, Mary demanded of Dax, "Dexter, what is going on here?"

Charlie bent over, holding his stomach.

"Dexter . . . oh, Dexter, what is going ON here?" He continued to dance about and laugh, pointing at Dax. Dax stood dangerously silent.

Leo stepped between Dax and Professor Haefer and said something that sounded like the students were deciding what attractions to work on for the Carnival. No one else said anything. Mary knew there was more building here but chose to go along with the pseudo-peace all parties silently agreed to. With a final look at Dax, she closed her car door. She knew this was not finished.

The echo that was Manchester ascended the crumbling, dust-covered staircase. Upstairs, in what time had left of the Pavilion Ballroom, floated his Corinne, sighs of sadness lifting the gauzy remnants of drapery like stray breezes. He could just see her, arms gracefully shaping swan-like curves through the air, as she wisped across the dark floor. Sensing his entrance, she spun to face him, arms outstretched in eternal invitation to dance.

Manchester went to her, as he had throughout time, took her in his own spectral arms, and spun her transparent figure out onto the ballroom floor. The breezes that animated the ruined Pavilion coalesced into a likeness of voice, and Manchester whispered to his Corinne.

"The Veil of Time and Shadows grows thinner, my jeweled bird, can you not feel it? The door 'twixt this place and the place of life and dancing is opening. I will see us safely across that threshold, my dear, and you shall waltz in life again."

Corinne lifted her face shape to look into his eyes. Her own, decades old hollows of despair, sparked a dim flash of emerald and then returned to darkness.

He twirled her as he had in life, lifting her layers of time-tattered lace in a semblance of feathers. They spun out over the gap in the center of the fallen ballroom floor, ragged hems of her faded gown shredding away into the darkness below with each pirouette.

Swaggering into the Student Center, Charlie and Bill checked out the food vendors for unsupervised eats. Dax located Karen on her paint-spattered ladder and headed in that direction. Focused on a red detail, she didn't notice his approach until he grabbed the ladder and shook it just enough to make her drop her paintbrush and grab for the stage flat.

"No worries, hot stuff. I would have caught you. Then, you'd be in my arms at last." He grinned an ugly grin, waggling his eyebrows.

Karen's hands came away from the painted flat, dripping red onto her jeans. She glared at Dax, her hands held out to her sides.

"Look what you made me do, you creep!" Tears blurring her vision, Karen backed down the ladder as carefully as possible without touching it, leaning on her forearms. When she reached the floor, Dax seized her, beefy arms clamping both of hers to her sides. She struggled against him, screaming for him to let her go. Several students working nearby looked up and started toward them. Dax let her go, laughing. Karen rounded on him, slapped him hard, and, before he could recover, wiped her hands down the front of his Black Sabbath tee shirt. He jumped back, swore, and gave her one of his dark looks.

"Oh, sweetheart . . . are you ever going to regret you did that." He touched his cheek, drew his hand away red, glared at her again and wheeled away.

Headless horsemen, scarecrows, giant walking pumpkins, and assorted animal-like creatures mingled with cowled figures, dance hall girls, and figures simply draped in sheets with eyeholes. The Student Center atmosphere, redolent with a satisfying blend of scorched sugar and overheated fry oil, tasted like a Carnival.

A sausage-curled blonde in a pale blue Marie Antoinette ball gown waited in the line in front of the Fortune Teller's tent.

Karen linked her arm through Leo's tuxedoed one. With his free hand, he doffed his top hat.

Maria held court in her tent of many colors, hamming it up perfectly to the delight of fellow Carnival-goers. Swirling her hands over and around the glass ball flower vase in front of her, she intoned in a deep, sepulchral voice.

"I see only misery, degradation, and squalor ahead for you, my dear, if you continue to keep company vis dat lazy peeg of a boyfriend who is currently porkink you . . . "

Across the table, her client howled with laughter, while her boyfriend took good-natured shoulder punches in the crowded line. Dressed in vintage, musty, cutaway topcoats, a theatre club Burke and Hare skulked through the line, sneaking up behind people with a tape measure and shovel to consider them for "fit". Friends who could see this either doubled over, giving away the game, or stood straight-faced and let the joke progress.

A new client sat at the table and offered his hands to Maria. She drew a deep, dramatic breath, eyes closed. Laying her own hands palm to palm with the grinning young man, she breathed in again, tilted her head, sniffed. Her eyes flew open, and she pressed the student's hands to her table.

"I see that you vill be detained on your vay home dis evenink by a uniformed indiwidual who vill vant to know vat it vas you added to the punchbowl from your pocket."

More howls of laughter from the line, from him. Karen was next to sit before Maria, who swayed slightly on her cushion, humming an atmospheric tune to the violins crying from the boombox. She poufed and tucked until her skirted crinoline behaved on her chair, then placed her upturned hands on the table.

"Tell me my fortune, oh Madame Mystery." Karen grinned. Maria glanced up at her, suppressed a grin of her own, winked, cleared her throat to sober up for this performance. She placed her palms against Karen's upturned ones, drew a deep breath.

For several moments, no one moved. Maria sat like a statue, breath held. The crowd around the tent shuffled uneasily, not certain if they should laugh and applaud again, or wait for Maria's act to begin.

Maria's palms against Karen's turned ice cold. When Karen jerked hers away, Maria lunged for her, pinioning her wrists in a cold, painful grasp. Her eyelids lifted. Milky, white eyeballs stared blindly at Karen, then rolled back in Maria's head. Karen screamed, pulling helplessly away from that icy grip. Leo jumped forward, tried to lift her from the table. Both of them stared at Maria, who began to speak. On breath like the opening of a thousand graves, words of warning hissed in Karen's direction.

". . . the revenants . . . revenants. . . are waiting . . . waiting . . . do not . . . they yearn . . . they wait . . . you . . . must . . . not . . . "

Boyfriends held their dates; dates held their breath. Unable to move or look away, the Carnival crowd leaned slightly forward, willing Maria to crack another joke and make this okay.

She finally whispered a last word, sending it toward Karen on a dry rasp.

". . . dance . . . ".

Maria's eyelids fell to hide those rheumy, terrifying eyes. Her hands opened and slid forward as she fell across the table. Leo lifted Karen from her chair, pulled her back. Theatre students rushed to Maria, ran for water, for teachers. Shaking, Karen let Leo guide her toward the concession area for a cold drink.

Cup in hand, Karen took small, trembling sips of punch.

She looked up at Leo.

"What was that back there? Was that some of her act? It wasn't funny, Leo. How did she do that with her eyes? Her hands?"

Leo put his arm around her shoulder. "I couldn't tell you, sweetheart."

"Well, now, isn't that a picture worth, oh, say, a dozen words?" Dax slurred. He leaned on the punch table to steady his swaying. When he could stand, he faced Leo and breathed liquor into his face. "How about a real Halloween game, Leo, old boy?"

Karen pressed closer to Leo. He stepped slightly in front of her, facing Dax.

"What the hell are you talking about?"

"Yeah, possibly even that. I'm talking about a little wager, my man. A test of manhood, of just who is strong enough to hold on to your little blue muffin, here."

Leo fisted his right hand just as two teachers and Professor Haefer approached, supporting Maria and questioning her nervously. Pale, shaking, Maria allowed herself to be escorted outside the Center where an ambulance waited. Dax slurred on.

"I will bet you, Leo," Dax challenged, poking Leo in the chest, "that you and your little Karen here can't spend the night, this very Halloween night, up in that old, abandoned Pavilion."

"That's been condemned for years, moron."

"Then one more broken window on the ground floor won't be noticed." Dax stretched puffy lips into a wet grin. "Me and my pals will escort you inside, and we'll be back in the morning to let you out."

"Jerk, we'd just go back out the window after you leave us there.'"

"Not after we board you up inside, you won't, *jerk*," Dax spat. He changed his angry countenance to one of sly cunning. "And, if you be there when the mornin' comes, I swear I will leave this chewy morsel alone forever." His eyes slid over Karen's bodice. "We'll even get a photo of you coming out in daylight with a cell phone time stamp, for proof. What do you say?"

"I say you go to hell and take your stupid ass bet with you."

Charlie and Bill stepped out from behind a wall of hay bales and corn shocks. They came forward to flank Dax.

"In that case, you forfeit your claim to this here lady . . . and my business associates will make sure you watch me spend a little quality time with her." The slurry, foolish expression on Dax's puffy face hardened into a mask of pure evil. Karen whimpered and pressed into Leo's back.

The goons next to Dax palmed their switchblades where only Leo and Karen could see them. Dax gestured toward the parking lot.

"Shall we go to the games?"

Commercial and residential growth over the decades separated the old Pavilion from the normal activities of the city. Most of the vintage glasswork had long yielded to rocks thrown by youngsters daring each other or to bored truants. Bill pulled his van around the circular drive to the darker backside of the building. Dax took his eyes off Leo and Karen long enough to step out the side door and gesture mockingly for them to do the same. Leo never let go of his grip on Karen's arm.

Bill stayed with the van, while Charlie and Dax escorted Leo and Karen up to the building, where a low window, already missing its glass, loomed at them from the dark wall like an empty tooth socket. A sheet of plywood and hammer lay propped beside the window.

"There is already a stack of concrete blocks to step on down there. And, because I am such a swell guy, I even left you flashlights and a couple bottles of water. Can't have you drying up and blowing away before I collect my bet." He directed this to where Karen sniffed back tears, clutching Leo's arm.

"Dax, this is insanely stupid, even for you. Let's just get out of here, okay? Bygones be bygones, go our separate ways."

The hate fire in Dax's eyes burned too hotly for listening to reason.

"One of two things will happen here," he growled. "You're gonna take my wager, or you're gonna watch me take my spoils." His eyes burned into Karen's. Charlie snapped open his switchblade and stepped forward.

Karen sobbed.

"Leo, please. I can do this. We can do this. He's insane, don't push him. We can find a way out after they go."

Arms around Karen, Leo shot one last piercing look at Dax and turned to step down onto the blocks so he could ease her down safely.

When the last of Karen's blue satin skirt whispered across the window frame, Dax and Charlie lifted the plywood into place and nailed it to the old wood.

Dax dropped the hammer, dusted off his hands, and grinned a maniacal grin.

"Trick or treat . . ."

Bill waited in the driver's seat, lights out. Dax and Charlie slid the side door open and stepped up into the van. Dax pulled a sports bag from beneath the front seat and tested its weight.

"You both remember what to do?"

"Yeah, we keep Leo jumping at his own shadow, and lead him away from Karen. What are you gonna do?"

Dax slowly drew a length of rope and a bandana from the bag.

"I'm going to teach that blonde bitch a little lesson."

The ground level casement window Dax jimmied open earlier barely allowed the three of them to squeeze through. Dax distributed the chains, flashlights and loose feathers from the bag.

"Okay. You two lure Leo with rattling chains, whisper his name, go up the stairs and drop feathers on him, anything to get him away from Karen. I'll be creeping low to the floor, watching for my moment to grab and gag her. After I do, I don't care what you do with him. Just don't come looking for me."

Silently, they crept up the stairs to the main gallery. Thick with dust, crumbled bits of fallen plaster, crushed marble and faded flakes of gilded wood, the large space absorbed all sound of footfalls. A flashlight beam reflected, weak and dull, from a glass specimen case still intact. Whatever it once held lay disintegrated at the bottom of the case.

Dax signaled the guys with a finger across his lips, then pointed in the direction he wanted them to go. He hugged the wall, moving in the other direction.

Once by themselves, Charlie and Bill didn't summon much courage. Slowly making their way through the rubble of elegance past, they inched toward an open door. They'd set up their spook show inside that room, calling to Leo, like they were told.

A brief flash of their light showed them where the furniture, faded and rotting, sat in the space. Without speaking, they arranged their chains, knelt on the floor, and began. Bill let loose with a cartoon soundtrack oooo-eee-oooo that rose and fell, echoing in the large hall outside the door. Charlie punched his shoulder, hard. Bill sat back on his heels, scowling. Charlie slid his chain across the floor, giving it a little shake. He tried his voice.

"Leeeeeeooooooo… Leeeeeeeeooooooooo…" Bill grabbed Charlie's shoulder.

"Did you hear that?" "What?"

"I don't know. Sounds. Like wind indoors, or a woman crying."

"You're spooking yourself, idiot. Dax will be pissed off if we mess this up."

At that moment, Bill clutched Charlie's shoulder again.

"Did you see that?"

Even without his flashlight, Charlie could see the whites of Bill's eyes.

"Shut up. See what?"

"I'm telling you, something misty just floated across that floor out there. It headed to that broken staircase."

Charlie ignored him, dragged his chain a little more. He glared at Bill a moment later.

"If you're gonna talk to yourself, you can find another room and tremble on your own."

"I didn't say anything."

Charlie stopped sliding his chain, looked at Bill. "You didn't just whisper to yourself, 'it's showtime'?"

"What the hell does that even mean? Why would I say that?"

At that moment, Charlie's chain slid across the floor on its own. They each felt a cold hand close around their necks from behind. Stumbling against each other trying to stand up, they squinted, hearts hammering. The darkness in the room came alive, gathering into shapes that swelled, shrank, swelled anew into different images, all of them horrible. Dax's temper forgotten, Charlie and Bill clutched each other and ran back to the basement stairs. The squeeze through the window was effortless this time, and they ran to the van.

They sat, breathing heavily, for long, silent moments. Charlie spoke first, wiping his brow and upper lip. Neither one mentioned the reek of urine that filled the van.

"There's something wrong in there, man. It didn't feel right from the start. Dax can do what he wants by himself. We're getting out of here."

Bill just nodded, chest heaving, eyes wide. Starting the engine, Charlie considered their position.

"Dax is going to jump that girl, maybe knife Leo to do it. We are in on this, Billy. Dax won't take the fall by himself. Our fingerprints are all over. We have to report some funny goings on in that place, maybe save someone's life and get our butts out of trouble."

Bill just nodded, staring straight ahead, pulling breath through his open mouth.

Leo tested the flashlights and handed one to Karen. He had to wrap her hands around it and press it there.

"Keep this on and take hold of my shirt and do NOT let go. I don't want to get separated in here. We are looking for another broken window close to the ground floor. I can maybe manage a second-floor window, but I can't get you out that way. Stay with me, honey, we can do this. We'll just give them time to drive away. I can't hear the van in here."

Wide-eyed, Karen clutched Leo's shirttail. They located and

climbed the stairs to the main gallery. Leo swept his light through the room, noting the location of tumbled glass cases and empty stands. He tried not to illuminate the remains of the cases' contents. Together, they reached a wall of windows. Leo moved along the wall, patting for glass that didn't have a sheet of plywood keeping the weather out, Karen matching her steps to his.

Dax made his way across the gallery to check out what might have been a coat room. Rotting threads cobwebbed across the walls that still had hooks. An ancient settee, stuffing burst through the mold-softened fabric, sat against one of the split walls. Smiling, Dax fixed his throne of triumph in his mind, where he would drag Karen, once he had her alone. He crept back through the gallery to crouch in the darkness of the ruined staircase. Straining for sounds of Bill or Charlie doing their spook routine, he thought he heard a woman's voice. A faint odor of smoke, and, maybe, sawdust passed through the room. He hadn't put anything for fire in the sport bag. The guys must be improvising. He scowled. If they set this heap on fire, he was bailing and leaving them to deal with it. He needed to see what they were doing. Testing his flashlight, Dax stepped out into the gallery, cautiously navigating the treacherous obstacle course of deadly shards and foot traps.

Dax's flashlight went out. He shook it, rapped it against his palm a few times. It came back on, and he allowed himself a sigh of relief before he resumed his pace.

Leo paused, opened a bottle of water, and offered Karen a sip. Too scared to let go even one hand from his shirttail, she shook her head. Their wall-patting search for a broken window took them through a hallway and into what looked like a library. A flashlight beam showed them shelves with orderly piles of dust that might have been books. A slow circuit of this room revealed no windows. Karen sobbed softly. Leo tucked his flashlight into his shirt pocket, put his arms around her, and pressed her to his heartbeat. When they parted slightly, he shone his light around the room, located a settee, and led her there. He used the light to show her where to sit back and rest. Her crinoline rustled softly.

"Look, honey, if you want to close your eyes for a minute, I will stand right here. We are going to get out of here."

Karen sniffed and drew a deep sigh. A single tear rolled down her cheek. Leo gently brushed it away with his thumb. She let her chin drop to her chest and closed her eyes.

Leo heard his name. He heard his name coming from the direction of the gallery they'd just quit. Making sure Karen was sleeping, he turned her flashlight on, put it in her lap, and walked back the way they'd come. Back in the gallery, he spread his light beam across the walls, the littered floor. A whisper from the wall across the floor called him.

"Leo . . . Leo . . ."

Slowly, he stepped through glass and decades toward that sound. He came up short against a pillar he hadn't seen in his light beam. It wobbled against him, and a grating sound came from above. Looking up, Leo shone his flashlight on the marble gargoyle that tumbled down, carrying his death in its claws.

Karen tried to turn over in her sleep and snapped awake. She recalled where she was, and why. Leo wasn't anywhere she could see. She clutched her flashlight and softly called his name. Icy hot fear flooded her bowels and she cried out loud for him. The music she heard in response startled her to silence. She stood, clutched her flashlight, and made her way out to the main gallery. Still she heard music – fine, orchestral music, dancing music. It came from above her, from the top of the ruined crushed marble staircase.

"Leo?" She didn't hear her own whisper over the swelling ballroom music above her.

Karen shone her flashlight on the stairs to show her where to climb the broken marble. With each step, the music sounded sweeter, harder to resist. Entranced, she climbed to the top and stepped out into the ballroom.

A blur of feather softness passed by her, through her. She turned to where it paused, pirouetted, then held out arms to her. Little more than a suggestion of arms, a layer of skirt, and sadness where a face should be, the specter beckoned to Karen, reaching gaunt arms out to her, inviting, begging. Karen dropped the hand holding her flashlight and let the light fall to the floor. She stepped forward, holding out her own arms. The floating image took her in a ghostly embrace, pressed her close, then spun her over the shifting marble in graceful time to the music. Round and round they spun, feather layers of spectral skirt ribboning away to float into the void left by the fallen floor. Karen danced, eyes closed, as the spectral form led her out over the ruined opening, where she fell to the first floor below. Shreds of a ballgown long rotted floated down on top of her.

Back pressed to the supporting wall, Dax slid along beneath the staircase. He expected Leo to go looking for a way out. That meant Karen might be alone downstairs. It was worth a look. He took a tentative step away from the staircase wall and his flashlight went out again. Swearing, he slapped it on his palm. It came on, and he moved forward.

The light failed again. Dax shook it hard enough to make

the batteries rattle. This time when the flashlight came on, it shone directly into a face with dark eyes blazing beneath gull wing brows. A cruel grin spread triumphantly above a dark, pointed beard. Dropping the flashlight, Dax backed up a single step before his mouth filled with ice cold smoke, choking him unconscious.

What windowpanes in the Pavilion still endured wore stripes of red and blue light. Charlie and Bill leaned on the squad car, for once doing as they were told by an officer. Two first responders came from the Pavilion doors they'd crowbarred open and set their equipment bags inside the open ambulance.

"One casualty, as far as we could see. Male, around 24. Looks like he ran into a tall decorative post of some kind and the marble statue on top of it crushed his skull when it fell. Damn shame." He filled his mouth from his water bottle, swished, spat. He could still taste dust and death. "Every Halloween, it's something else."

He helped his partner pull a stretcher.

"There are two students inside, male and female. The woman says she fell through the hole in the ballroom floor above her. The pile of debris under that hole came from the ballroom dining floor, and she landed on this pile of old carpets that are all shreds of thread now, but still enough to land on. She'll have a leg cast for a while, but otherwise, she's fine."

The officers chaperoning Charlie and Bill ordered them back in the squad so the survivors of this ill-fated prank could be brought outside. Officer Barnes called after the responders.

"You said there was also a guy inside?"

"Yeah, and there's not a scratch on him. He's inside, sitting with the girl. Looks like they are a couple."

Dax crouched beside Karen on the ruins of carpet that blessed her fall. His flashlight struck one brilliant flash of emerald green from her eyes, and then it was gone. He absently reached to stroke a beard he didn't have, a slow smile growing that didn't quite reach his eyes.

"Well, my jewel, it's showtime."

The woman beside him smiled back and lisped coyly. "Whatever you say, ducks."

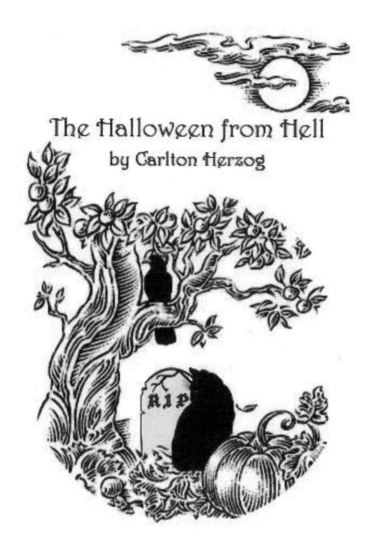

The Halloween from Hell
by Carlton Herzog

In a world dominated by science and technology, it was inevitable the Halloween spirit would go the way of the dinosaur. The world of spirits that it represented simply had lost its relevance in the fast-paced digital age.

Sid Samhain's Little Shop of Horrors did the bulk of its business during the Halloween season. But just as the Halloween spirit waned, so too did Sid's business. Costumes, masks and novelty gifts that used to sell like hot cakes now sat on his shelves collecting dust.

Sid, who used to look at Halloween with eager anticipation, now dreaded its approach. He had reached the tipping point. One more season of losses and he was done.

Two days before Halloween, things took an unusual turn. A diminutive man, no more than four feet tall, dressed in a tuxedo and top hat, strolled into his shop. He had an impish grin and looked as if he had just stepped out of a fairy tale.

"I'm looking for the shop owner, Sid Samhain."

"You're looking at him. What can I do you for? A munchkin or Oompa Loompa costume perhaps?"

"You're a funny guy for somebody with a business heading for the slab."

"I only meant that you probably want something to match your stature."

"I know what you meant. But I'm not here to buy. I'm here to help you move merchandise and get back on your feet. To be a strong presence in the community."

"How do you intend to do that? More importantly, why am I the beneficiary of your largesse?"

"Think of me as your Fairy Godfather. I'm going to bless you with an abundance of Halloween spirits. So many they'll be oozing from every pore."

"You're not making any sense."

"If you read your bible then you would know that after Adam got the boot from the Garden of Eden, he slept around with many a demon. Those unions produced offspring that have been looking for a home ever since."

"Now that's a fairy tale."

"Is it, now? With a name like Samhain which means the lifting of the veil between the natural and the spirit world, I would have thought you a bit more enlightened."

"So far, I've only heard a lot of crazy talk. You'll need to convince me that you're not an escaped lunatic."

"Fine. I propose to imbue your products with those lost spirits. They will use their powers of mind to lure customers into your shop and buy all your merchandise."

"Hogwash. Even if you could do that, what makes you think I'd go for unleashing evil spirits in the world?"

"To sweeten the pot, I will pay you one hundred thousand dollars in cash. That's triple what your merchandise is worth at retail."

"So, in exchange for letting your haunt my goods with your wayward spooks, you'll give me one hundred thousand dollars? Who keeps the profits from the sales?"

"You do, of course."

"What do you get out of this?"

"I am the manufacturer of all your merchandise, sold under various corporate labels. So, I have already made a profit. But there remains the simple joy of helping another person avoid the curse of bankruptcy, for I am a philanthropist. Yours is not the only shop I am rescuing this Halloween."

"How do you propose to call up these spirits and direct them into my goods?"

"Special incantation. The money I spoke of is in this briefcase. See?"

"Well, I'll be. I love the smell of green money." "Here, it's yours now. Do you mind if I begin?" "By all means."

Unclean Spirits of the Netherworld Lonely Ones, Lost Ones,
I summon thee to this haven

That you may find refugee upon the earthly plane. Inhabit that is here.

Let these goods transport you.

In our Dark Father's name Amen.

Sid's merchandise began to glow and vibrate. Wisps of black vapor whirled in the shop, darting here and there as each one found a new home inside a costume, gadget or mask. The possessed merchandise, however, didn't wait for the customers to enter the shop. Instead, they flew off the shelves and out the doors seeking their new owners, willing or not.

Sid didn't care. He was one hundred thousand dollars richer. Whether he got paid for the now-haunted merchandise didn't matter. He had recouped his losses.

When Halloween night arrived, Sid was in his apartment above the shop. He was sipping beer and watching Monday Night Football. Halloween was the furthest thing from his mind. He could care less what his cursed merchandise was up to.

That is, until he started hearing the screams – a few isolated ones at first, then amidst a cacophony of sirens and gun shots and crashes. From his sofa, he heard what sounded like a war zone outside. He was afraid to look out the window.

He knew that he had something to do with all the mayhem, so he thought it best to stay inside and lie low. He barred the door, grabbed his shotgun and pistol, and hunkered down for a long night. He had already closed the blinds a few hours before.

He decided to make himself some coffee, since it was apt to be a long vigil. Then he heard his own car alarm. Then a few more. He peeked through the blinds.

On the street below, he could see several wolf-headed things clawing and tearing at a priest. At first, he thought it was a garden variety robbery fueled by meth or opioid addiction. To get a better look, he ran and got his binoculars. When he trained them on the scene, he saw that the attackers were not wearing masks. They had actual wolf heads. He also saw that some were wearing vestiges of costumes like the ones he had had in his shop. As he looked closer, he could see that two of them still had his store tag dangling from the sleeve.

To fortify his resolve to stay uninvolved, Sid popped open the briefcase to smell the money. But when he did, the briefcase was filled with blank green paper. He had been tricked by a glamour.

That little shitbag. Okay. I've got to make this right. That guy's not dead yet. Maybe I can save him.

He grabbed his gun and ran down the stairs, out the door of his shop and right up to the melee. Two of the three werewolves were eating the victim. The third heard Sid and charged toward him. Sid gave him both barrels and blew off his head. Blood and fur and bones sprayed in all directions.

The two others stopped their feeding. They snarled at Sid as he walked forward with his .357 Magnum raised. They were about to spring when he shot one in the head straight through its eye and out the back. Before the other could react, Sid did the same to him. It never occurred to Sid that his success hinged on the fact that his three adversaries were makeshift rather than made werewolves, so silver bullets were unnecessary.

Sid attended the bleeding priest. He helped him to his apartment. As Sid cleaned the priest's wounds, the priest spoke:

"I was on my way to see you. I wanted to stop you from making a deal with Mister Pixie. Don't feel bad. He put you under his spell. Whatever money he gave you never existed. It was all part of an elaborate glamour. He wanted you to willingly relinquish ownership of the property."

Sid was puzzled: "I don't follow."

The priest said, "You were tricked into turning your merchandise into accursed objects containing the spirits of Adam's demonic progeny. They will seek out those with evil in their hearts, those who have committed great acts of evil or who will. He wants them to seize control of the town and then start reproducing. Right about now, there's a bunch of pregnant women about to give birth to more monsters. We need to act quickly and end this nightmare.

"We're going to fight fire with fire. I intended to imbue your fireman, policeman, nurse and soldier costumes with angelic essences. An army of lesser angels to fight an army of lesser demons, thereby keeping the balance between the dark and the light. But I'm too weak, so you'll need to do the invocation. Here's the incantation you'll need. I'll be fine. Take it downstairs and recite it in your store. The angelic host will do the rest."

"Hold on. You're going to force ordinary citizens to don masks and go fight the hell-spawn possessing the town of Doonesbury?"

"No. The angels don't need to co-opt a human form to have a form. They can whip one up from the molecules in the air. Heaven, you see, is a bit more tech savvy than hell when it comes to these things. Evil beings, whether human or demonic, tend to be a little on the dumb side. Now get cracking before more people get hurt and killed."

Sid went downstairs. When he was satisfied the coast was clear, he began the summoning spell:

I call to thee: Gabriel, Michael, Raphael, and Muriel
Glorious Archangels, Brilliant Seraphim
By the power of the Four Elements of Fire, Air, Water and Earth,
Receive now my Plea:
Unleash thy cherubim, thrones, dominions, powers and
principalities,
Invest them in these hollow objects That they might do thy work
And protect us from the things of darkness That now do harm us
In the Father's name, Amen.

No sooner had Sid done the invocation than a great white light emanated from every remaining costume, mask and gadget in his shop. He watched as figures took shape within each, corresponding to the type of object. The soldier's mask became a soldier, the policeman's costume became a policeman, the Iron Man costumes became Iron Men, the Thor costumes became Thors, the Power Ranger costumes became Power Rangers, and so it went, until Sid's shop was filled with an angelic host ready to fight the forces of darkness spreading through the little town of Doonesbury. The heavenly host didn't give Sid a second look. It marched out of his shop single file and then split into antidemon squads that headed along all four points of the compass. For his part, Sid ran back upstairs to check on the

priest. He was dead.

Sid decided it was time to break out the big guns. He went to his safe and withdrew his bump stock modified AR-15, two hundred rounds of ammunition, and some army surplus grenades he had been saving for the Fourth of July.

I'm responsible for this mess. And I would like nothing better than to put holes in that little creep who induced me to invite a hell horde into my town. He's gonna pay for it. I just need to find his munchkin ass.

He quietly slipped out the door of his shop. He looked up and down the street, which was quiet. That was not unusual since Doonesbury was a small town that shut down at five. Sid figured the action would be in the residential area where all the trick or treating would being going down.

He left Main Street and headed up Canal. He hadn't gone very far when something hit him from behind. He fell face first into the pavement as a cackling witch on a broomstick zoomed by him. He jumped to his feet and watched her come around for another pass, laughing maniacally as she did.

He raised the AR-15 and gave her a short-controlled burst

that shattered the broomstick and sent the green-skinned hag tumbling to the ground. As she tried to get up, Sid let loose another burst that exploded her head. He stood over the body. It was then he realized she was pregnant. Something was moving around in her full belly. A moment later, two talons tore open that same belly and a green-headed goblin baby squeezed through, snapping and snarling at him. He shot it twice, and the tiny nightmare slumped over his mother's bloody body.

No sooner had he killed the monster baby, than Chucky Face, a Pennywise Face and a Frankenstein Face rushed him. He blew them away in a spray of fire.

Now more than ever Sid realized the urgency of what he was about, but he still had no specific plan, nor did he have a clue as to where all the angels had headed. He just kept moving down Canal Street intending to kill any hostile entities he encountered.

Canal Street was long. He had gone several blocks when he came upon two pregnant women walking toward him. From a distance, they looked normal, but as they got closer, he saw that they were very pale. At twenty feet, he could see the tips of their fangs protruding just below their ruby red lips.

That's when they stopped and smiled. Sid watched, mesmerized by the grotesque tableau before him. The two vampires squatted and delivered their monster babies: four baby heads on skittering spider legs that screeched and howled and ran straight at Sid. The two women stood upright smiling but otherwise did nothing except shout encouragement for their hellish offspring.

Sid opened fire, but the spider babies didn't come at him single file. Rather, they encircled him. He hit one even as another bit into his leg. He kicked it off him and shot it. Another jumped and landed on his back, sinking its teeth into his shoulder. Still another charged straight at him and he bashed it with the business end of the AR-15.

The pain from the one biting into his shoulder nearly made him pass out. He had no way to shoot it or reach it. So, he backed into a telephone pole again and again until the thing let go. As it moved dizzily from the repeated impacts, Sid shot it.

He expected the two vampire chicks to jump him next, but they were nowhere to be seen. His shoulder ached and he was bleeding profusely. He did the only thing he could. He ripped off his shirt, found an open patch of dry soil and pressed his back into it in the hope that his blood would clot with the help of the dirt enough for him to press forward.

As he lay there on his back, he could hear footsteps getting closer. He raised his head and saw the two vampire women running toward him.

Those bitches smelled the blood.

Sid played dead and waited until they were nearly on top of him before he sat up and cut them in half with his rifle. He laid back and ground his shoulder into the dirt. Tetanus was the least of his worries tonight.

After he was satisfied that the bleeding was under control, he resumed his mission. He kept wondering where all the other angels and demons were.

As he approached Doonesbury Park, he heard a commotion. Zombies had surrounded a house. Some were trying to force the door, while others were trying to crawl through the windows. A moment later, the door gave. The zombies streamed in and a moment later came out with a family of four as their prisoners.

Sid ran up and picked off the zombies with head shots. Then he questioned the rescued as to what they had seen before the zombies appeared.

"We were all taking a walk down by the park. There was a bunch of people in fright costumes gathered around a very tiny man. He was talking in some foreign language, one I had never heard before. Then the people in the costumes would chant.

The next thing we knew, they all came running toward us and we ran home. I thought for sure they would catch us. At one point, I looked over my shoulder and saw that they were fighting with another group of people dressed as soldiers and policemen. When we reached our house, the dead people saw us and tried to chase us inside. They would have taken us if not for you."

Sid asked, "Which way is the park?"

"Go down a block, turn left, then make your second left and you'll be there."

"Thanks."

Sid headed toward the park. He suspected that's where this mini apocalypse was being resolved. He put a fresh magazine in the rifle, checked the chambers on his hand cannon, and made sure the grenades were all in reach.

Before he got to the park, he came upon a large lawn filled with male themed monsters giving birth to arthropod abominations. There was a Predator and a Pinhead, a Freddy and Jason, a Night King and Trump, all lying on their backs, legs wide open, spewing out baby headed scorpions. Sid didn't hesitate. He tossed a grenade into their midst, then raked them with automatic weapon fire until there was nothing left but writhing bits.

As he got closer to the park, the demon packs got thicker. Pumpkin Heads and Skulls, Slashers, Aliens and Beetle-juices. Sid soldiered on and cut through them like a hot knife through butter.

When he got to the park, he got the surprise of his life. The angel people – mainly in the form of Power Rangers, Iron Men, and Thors – were there sure enough, and they were fighting the demons. But now the demons had somehow fused into one colossal hydra-headed entity. They did so to block the angels' anti-possession spells that would have otherwise liberated those under the demons' thrall.

The angelic ones were not doing well against the behemoth when he arrived. It was laughing at their incantations, swatting some away like flies, and swallowing others whole. Heaven was taking it on the chin, and at the rate things were going, it was just a matter of time before the demons could declare victory and spread their hideous moral cancer unchecked by the light.

Although the gargantuan, poly-headed demon could scoff at angelic magic, it still had to obey the physical laws of the universe it inhabited. Nor did it enjoy any of the mystical protections of its constituent Halloween monsters because their line of descent did not originate with the founders of the vampire, werewolf and zombie line. They were simulacra invoked to house other spirits.

Sid knew nothing of these matters. What he did know was that he had been killing monsters all night and there was no reason he should not be able to kill this one. So, he raised the AR-15 and began popping off the monster's heads, but every time he would shoot one off, two more would take its place.

He realized that the headshots were getting him nowhere, and he didn't have a Medusa's Head to turn the thing to stone.

Then he remembered how Hercules had killed the Hydra. He didn't know if angels could summon fire, but he was out of ideas, so he called to the angels.

"Whenever I shoot off a head, use your angel fire to cauterize the tendons so it can't grow back."

Angels can indeed, as their invocation earlier suggests, manipulate the four elements of fire, water, air, and earth. Thus, one by one, Sid shot off the beast's heads and the angels seared the stumps so the heads could not grow back. It finally fell over dead to the ground.

The collaboration between angel and human seemed a

success. Satisfied that their mission was accomplished, some angels took their leave and ascended back to Heaven. As the ranks thinned, there was a raucous din as wave after wave of broom-stick witches zoomed in, swinging axes as they flew. The hags had the element of surprise. They were able to behead half of the remaining angels, sending their essences back to heaven.

For his part, Sid returned fire. Sid had, for the moment, evened the odds as the shot witches dropped like so many dead birds. Unfortunately, more hell-spawn charged forward from the woods. When they got close enough, Sid obliterated a few with a grenade, but enough got through that a massive hand-to-hand battle between angel and demon ensued.

At some point, Sid spotted Mister Pixie hiding behind a tree situated at the far edge of the park. Sid didn't think he could hit him with a rifle bullet, given the distance and tree coverage. He ducked back into the wooded area and stealthily made his way around the park under cover.

When he reached the spot where the little man had been, Sid could not find him. Then he heard a voice behind him.

"Looking for me? I'm right here."

Sid turned around and there was the little man smiling up at him.

"You didn't seriously think I'd let you get the jump on me, did you?"

Sid's rifle flew out of his hands, followed by his holstered pistol. The little man laughed.

"This is the best Halloween ever. A real Halloween from Hell, if you will."

Sid's mind raced. He needed to buy some time. He played along with Mister Pixie.

"I get it. The forces of darkness have won. What's next?"

Mr. Pixie grinned wide. "Battles like this one are taking place all over the planet. We'll win some, like we did here, and we'll lose some. It's all about the conflict, for we are warriors, not peacemakers. That's why we love it when you humans are tearing at each other's throats."

Now it was Sid's turn to smile. "You haven't won this one yet."

"How so, Samhain?"

Before Mr. Pixie understood Sid's intent, Sid had yanked a grenade from his vest, pulled the pin and slammed it into the ground. The explosion reduced Mister Pixie to green and purple bits. As for Sid, other than being knocked backwards, he didn't have so much as a scratch on him.

He lay there bewildered. *How could I survive a grenade blast, the same one that obliterated that little prick?*

Then then the Archangel Michael emerged from behind a tree. "That was some quick thinking. I almost didn't get a mystical shield around you in time. A second later, and you would be spread all over this field along with that homunculus."

"Now what?"

"Without him to act as the focal point for all that demonic energy, the evil spirits are getting sucked back into hell. At least here, the fight is over, and we've won. Not so in other places. The demons have overrun many cities and towns. We need more soldiers like you."

"I'm the one who opened the door for them."

"Not really. The homunculus was working you with his mind control magic, so you were not acting of your own free will. So, forget the guilt trip and come work for us. I can hook you up with state-of the art firepower."

"I'll pass. One supernatural battle royal is enough for one lifetime. I gotta say, I'll never forget it. This was one Halloween straight out of hell."

SAMHAIN SECRETS

"That it was, my friend. That it was."

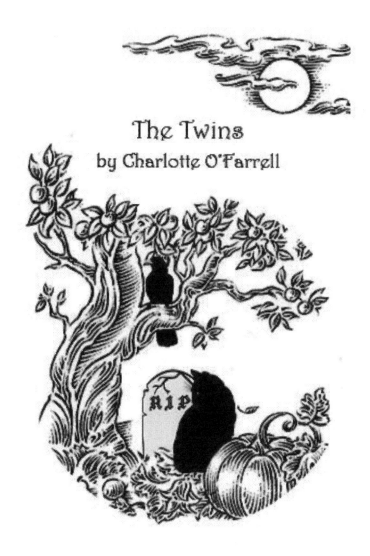

The Twins
by Charlotte O'Farrell

PART I

I wish I hadn't gone for drinks that Friday night in September. I was tired from work and I wasn't in the mood for socializing. The increasingly dark nights had me all lethargic. But I forced it. No point crying about it now, I suppose.

We were old friends, all living in the same city as the university we'd graduated from seven years before. We'd once been a group of seven, but we were down to four – marriages, kids and moves across the country for work had taken the others away, though we met up when we could. As a newly single 28-year-old with a part-time admin job, none of those three issues seemed to be in the cards for me.

We met in the same bar we'd been meeting at every Friday for years. Slightly classier than the places we frequented as students, it had a soothing ambience, with candles on the tables and old-fashioned wooden stools for effect.

"Did you hear about the painting competition at the gallery, Cassie?" my friend Jayne asked. "Looks like it would be right up your alley. They're asking for creepy stuff to display during Halloween. They want local artists to contribute."

We'd met at the university art society all those years ago and painted together a lot, so it made sense for her to ask me. Plus, I'd always been a massive horror fan, especially back then. But I hadn't picked up a paintbrush in years. I shrugged it off, slightly annoyed about Jayne's frequent attempts to "save me" with her little hobby ideas; she suggested something at least once a week. But the idea of the contest didn't leave me for the rest of the night. In fact, I went on the gallery's website on my phone while I was on the toilet to get the details. Making up an excuse, I went home straight after to sketch up some ideas. I hadn't felt this excited about… well, anything, in the longest time.

The creative process had always been a mystery to me. The way ideas drag themselves up from the subconscious is bizarre. Seemingly unrelated aspects of someone's day can weave together to create something totally new, often only making sense to the conscious mind right at the end, when it's ready to make the leap from brain to canvas – or even only after that, when looking at the finished product.

The sketches came out suitably dark. I drew crying clowns with machetes, zombie apocalypse scenes, pumpkins coming to life to bite the arms off those who carved them. But there was one I kept going back to. Marginally more subtle than the others, it showed a pair of young twins holding hands and smiling. A boy and a girl, early school age or so. They looked directly out of the painting into the face of the person looking at it and their grins were unnerving. Behind them, a line of old buildings was on fire, the smoke and flames climbing into the gloomy navy sky.

It would be a lie to say I didn't immediately realize why this sketch resonated with me so strongly. How could it not, given what I'd gone through the year before? But I quickly pushed the link to my own past to one side. There was *more* to it than that. This, unlike the others, was a touching scene. The twins were sticking together through everything – even madness, even murder, even likely death. Despite the horror, it was a love story.

"This is the one," I said to my small, empty apartment.

It was late by then, but I started work immediately. The whole weekend stretched out in front of me, a sea of gloriously empty hours. I could devote it all to starting my masterpiece. Despite not having painted in years, I'd kept my paints and materials up to date, always kidding myself that the reigniting of my hobby was just a day or two away. The sheer joy that flooded me as I got them out, already knowing I was going to complete this painting, was incredible.

The initial stages of the painting went by in a frenzy. I slept and ate and showered, but only when I really needed to. I ignored calls and felt so annoyed by the buzzing of my phone from pointless messages that I switched it off – something I couldn't remember doing in my whole adult life.

Of course, I wasn't working tirelessly. Once my outlines were up on the canvas, easel set up in the middle of my living room, I spent a lot of time just staring at it. I must have spent hours doing that. Something about the twins' eyes captivated me, even at that stage, when they were nothing more than light scratches on the white surface. I could already feel the painting taking a little bit of my soul, drawing me in.

As the hours ticked by, the art took shape. The twins' faces took on structure and nuance, their expressions perfect and by far the most masterful thing I'd ever painted. The flaming background looked bleak and hopeless, just as it did in my mind's eye in the completed version. It was as if years of unused artistic talent and appetite, coiled like a snake inside me, was suddenly striking.

I stopped answering work emails and calls. I now know I had a few calls that week from work, ranging from concern to anger that I wasn't in touch, but they never bothered sending anyone around to check on me.

And just like that, it was done.

I stepped back and took in my painting, all of it, not a single brushstroke or colour out of place. I laid down on the sofa next to it, staying on my side so I could look at my twins directly, and for the first time in days I properly slept.

PART II

I managed to smooth it over with work. I told them I'd been feverish and lost my voice. They didn't ask too many questions. This wasn't a company that valued entry level employees like me; they were just glad to have their assistant back in post.

But I gradually found I couldn't think of anything except the twins in their painting. Whenever I was at home, I sat cross-legged on the floor in front of it, eating takeaways and consumed by it in a kind of trance. I set an alarm to drag myself to work and I resented it every time it went off. I spent each moment outside my flat thinking of the twins.

I called the gallery.

"Um, hello. I've got an entry for your Halloween local painters' contest."

"Ah, splendid," said the young-sounding lady on the other end. "We've had some great ones. Do you want me to book you in? If you handle delivery charges, gallery staff can take it from there. Or if you prefer, you can bring your painting directly and we can do the paperwork -"

"Yeah, that's all great, but do I have to leave the painting with you?"

There was a confused pause.

"I mean, can't I submit a photo or something, and maybe bring it in on the day of the judging?" I felt my voice falter and my cheeks redden.

"The painting will need to be at the gallery, I'm afraid. Rest assured we'll take good care of it and delivery charges back to your home will be paid in full."

I knew this was a bad idea. But two conflicting issues stuck in my head: I knew the twins were destined to win the competition, to stare into the souls of everyone who saw them so the world could know them like I did. But I also couldn't bear to be without them at this point. The idea of going back to my lonely flat filled me with dread.

I thanked the gallery lady. It took all my strength, but when I dropped off my twins with the bemused receptionist the next day, I managed to fill out the entry forms and make it out of the building before I burst into tears.

I spent the next two days with the flat's curtains drawn, lying on the sofa, sobbing at the empty easel. The days until Halloween's judging stretched out in front of me, seemingly endless. I imagined my twins with their soulful, mischievous eyes, the fire warming their backs, looking into the dark gallery and not finding me.

I'd lost track of whether it was day or night by the time the phone call came. It was Glynnis, an old friend who felt like she belonged to a different era of my life. I hadn't heard from her since I split with my ex.

"Sorry to call you out of the blue at this hour," she said, "but I've got some bad news."

She told me my ex, Barry, had been killed in a house fire. I paused for a moment.

"OK," I settled on, finally.

"I'm so sorry. It was on the news, but they haven't named him yet. They're still calling around the family. I just don't know how this could've happened."

"Yeah, that's... quite something. Fire deaths are one of those statistically rare things you never expect to happen to someone you know."

Glynnis went quiet for so long I wondered if the line had broken off.

"So, how are your twins?" I asked her, breezily.

She stuttered something about them being fine, starting to crawl. It was understandable she was shy about them when speaking to me. After all, we'd both got the news we were expecting in the same week. Both had those surprising scans. "Two heartbeats!"

We made awkward small talk for a while longer then I made up an excuse to hang up. Don't get me wrong, I'm not heartless. I wouldn't have wanted Barry to die. But I felt insulted by the idea I had to perform grief. *He* was the one who left *me*, the week after the damn miscarriage. If karma decided he needed to go, why not?

But it wasn't karma deciding, was it? I know that now. It was my canvas twins.

PART III

On the day the gallery opened the competition room in advance of the judging process, I waited outside for hours until opening time. The young staff member who opened the door seemed surprised I was so keen to get in, but he didn't question me.

The twins were behind a rope, on display along with a dozen other Halloween-themed paintings. I sat down cross-legged in front of them, my words echoing through the otherwise empty room, telling them how much I'd missed them. The idea of having them back after the competition was the only thing keeping me going.

But I noticed they looked different. Their hands were locked just that bit tighter. Their eyes were burning with amusement, completely different to the ambiguous look I'd painted them with. Tears fell silently down my cheeks as I noticed a pack of matches in the girl twin's pocket. I hadn't painted that. Suddenly, I understood that my love for them was reciprocated. We would do anything for each other.

"Thank you, thank you," I whispered to them, holding my hands out as if praying.

I'd given them life and they repaid me by avenging me and the twins I'd miscarried. It touched me they cared enough about the problems in my life to intervene.

I spent the whole day there, that first time, just enjoying their company. The guard doing the rounds eyed me suspiciously as he passed through, but I wasn't breaking any rules. When we were alone, I spoke to them. Going home at closing time didn't feel like returning home at all.

As Halloween approached, I was skipping through my

days in giddy anticipation. Win or lose – though they deserved to win, of course – my twins would be back with me again once the contest was over. We'd be a family.

The theme for the Halloween night winners' announcement was orange and black. Luckily, I had an orange work blouse and paired it with straight black trousers. I wanted to look good for my reunion with the twins.

The decorations were spectacular – they caught the spirit of the season without tipping into the tackiness of plastic ghouls and pumpkins. There were streamers and balloons in autumnal colours.

I was served a glass of champagne as I walked in. Everywhere was the hubbub of people chattering, discussing the entries. The whole memory has a dream-like gloss over it now, bright and colorful like the version of summer 1914 in my mind – the beauty and relative calm before hell broke out. I remember the gallery owner, a glamorous woman who made the little black dress she was wearing look like the height of cutting-edge fashion, smiling slightly when I told

her my name.

"Ah, Cassie of 'The Twins' fame. I bet you're looking forward to the announcement!"

That's when I knew my painting had won. My twins. Now the world would love them like I did. I would take them back to my apartment in triumph, knowing that *this time*, I'd given birth to them in the way God intended. This time fate was on my side, rather than determined to rip out my heart and squeeze it dry in front of me.

Everyone gathered for the announcement. There were about fifty of them there – press, patrons, other painters, friends of the gallery. Everyone gripped their champagne flutes and chattered amongst themselves.

The runners-up were good paintings but nothing close to

my twins. One featured a living pumpkin patch devouring a group of trick or treaters. The second-place painting was a surreal take on a killer clown making models out of bones.

"But the winning painting really blew me and the other judges away," said the gallery owner, smiling. I felt my heart thumping in my ears. "It's 'The Twins'! We really liked your dark take on this, Cassie. In fact, we liked it so much that not only have you won the competition and the £300 prize – we've also decided to make it a permanent part of a display here at the gallery!"

My insides turned to stone. My breath caught in my throat. The polite clapping around me, the eyes of everyone on me, swirled into a nightmarish blur.

"Now future visitors to the gallery will be able to enjoy your work, up there with all the greats. Congratulations!"

She was holding out her hand now. The woman who dared to suggest she would take my twins away from me wanted me to shake her hand. I complied, robotically, fighting off sudden furious images of ripping her arm out of its shoulder socket.

£300 to take my children away from me? Who did she think she was?

Her smile wavered slightly at the look on my face.

"Thank you," I choked out, against every impulse in my body. I fled to the next room, feeling the beginnings of a panic attack. I hadn't had one of those since the first time I lost a set of twins.

I heard the gallery owner trying to save the situation, politely saying she understood how news like that could be "overwhelming". A lie the oh-so-polite crowd were only too happy to pretend they believed. What did she know about overwhelming news? How often had she had a grim-faced doctor tell her she wasn't picking up either heartbeat on her ultrasound scan?

I found a refuge: a disabled toilet. I ran into it, locked the door, and curled into a ball on the floor. My breathing was out of control. Every synapse in my brain was throwing off warning signals. Tears jerked out of my tear ducts in furious waves. Every muscle felt tight. I wanted death to free me but that beautiful release didn't come.

"Mummy?"

The little voice stopped the panic attack dead in its tracks. My heart was still racing but my breathing paused. I thought my lungs had locked up.

"Mummy, you won't let them take us, will you?"

Blinking back tears, I turned over on to my back. The twins, in the flesh, were standing over me. Their faces looked fuller and more complete than I could ever have painted. My babies were now a real boy and girl.

"Of course not," I whispered. "You're coming home to live with Mummy forever. I'll never let anyone take you from me." "You're not mad we killed Daddy?" asked the boy twin, blue eyes wide.

"No, no, my darlings. He – deserved it. I'm just so glad you found your way back to me."

The twins sat down cross-legged next to me. I reached out and took one each of their hands in mine. Their palms were so soft, so warm. So real.

"I know what to do, Mummy," said the girl twin. She reached into her pocket and took out the pack of matches. The one I didn't recall painting. "But you'll have to be quick. You'll have to do what I say."

I pulled myself up to my knees. I squeezed their hands again.

"My babies. For you, I'll do anything."

PART IV

At my trial, they accused me of pretending not to remember what happened that fateful Halloween night. They thought I was trying to escape responsibility.

With security camera footage of me starting the fire, I could hardly do that, could I?

But my memory block is real. I recall everything in snippets, snapshots really. I'm no longer sure which are actual memories and which are pieces my brain's put together from the narratives I heard afterwards.

I remember grabbing the painting off the wall. It set off the alarm. The owner's face and those around her looked stunned but they were either too polite or too scared to stop me. I moved towards the door, my twins running unseen at my heels. Nobody acknowledged them – they didn't even know they were there, flesh and blood, jogging along behind their mother. Only I saw them.

I dragged a chair from the gallery's reception to the door we'd just run through. With my twins' help, I pushed it against the handle, jamming it shut. The strength of a couple of people pushing hard against it would have dislodged it, but by the time anyone realized anything was wrong, they probably wouldn't have time to work that out. The smoke inhalation would, all things going to plan, make them too woozy to try it.

We did the same thing with two fire doors on the other side of the room. No-one followed me long enough to see it; they probably just dismissed me as another unstable artist and left me to go back to my life.

"You don't want to kill them, do you, Mummy?" the boy twin asked as we made our way to the other door.

I shook my head.

"Of course not. None of us do. But we need to send a message to anyone who would try to split us up. It's us three against the world."

I'd taken three rolls of toilet paper from the place I'd had my panic attack. We lit them one by one. I threw one in through the other door, tucking the painting the twins lived in under my free arm. I kept it open just long enough to see the burning roll hit a wall of paintings and ignite one – and to hear the first scream – before I slammed it shut.

The other two went through small windows at the rear end of the gallery. Nobody was milling about that end; by the time the fire was big enough to set off the fire alarms, it would be too far gone to do anything about it.

We rushed out of the gallery and down the street. The alarms were going off by then. I heard screams from the windows. All I could do was laugh. I'd freed my twins from the bonds of the painting, and we were together forever. They laughed too, keeping perfect pace with me as I dodged pedestrians and ran along the road.

We killed five, including the gallery owner who had tried to take my twins away. The rest were saved by the gallery's sprinkler system – though I think we destroyed a few paintings in the process. A couple of people ended up in comas and remain there. I sometimes think of sending my twins into whatever fitful dreams they're having and apologizing. It was nothing personal; we did what needed to be done to keep a loving family together.

The police found me around midnight in the children's play park. The reports say I was pushing two empty swings back and forth in the dark, holding a painting and singing to myself. I knew better, of course – I wasn't alone. I never would be again. I smiled at the officers as they handcuffed me and asked what had taken them so long to find me.

Five years on, I see my twins every day. No matter how many drugs they pump me full of in this asylum or how many therapists try to force me to deny their existence, my babies return to me. I feel whole again. I spend all day grinning from ear to ear, waiting for night to fall. They arrive at lights out, perch on the end of my bed, and we sing each other a lullaby. It's bliss.

Rotten Eggs
by Aron Beauregarde

SAMHAIN SECRETS

[EDITOR'S WARNING: ANIMAL ABUSE]

The shovel's pointed tip cut through the damp soil. Max began to dig with the tool, impatiently turning over the dirt until he was about a half foot

down.

"Watch out! Don't go too deep. If you break into them ahead of time, it's gonna smell like death and ruin everything," Teddy scolded.

"I got it. I know what I'm doing. I don't need a freaking babysitter." Max continued recklessly until he saw the brown top of the egg carton. "Bingo."

Mischievous eagerness emanated from the boys. They couldn't wait to make use of the foul dairy. They had buried two dozen eggs in the woods over a week ago, literally laying the groundwork for an important component of their Devil's Night activities.

By that particularly chilly Halloween evening, they knew their eggs would have ripened to a point of ultimate repulsiveness. Anything less would be unacceptable. Teddy and Max had a long night ahead. They'd been plotting the evening for months, now. They didn't see the morbid holiday as a celebration or a night for thoughtful costumes, laughter and harvesting sweets. To them, it something much more serious. Something much darker.

Devil's Night was a long-standing Michigan tradition that found its evil roots in the 1970s. The mischief and crime committed during the annual evening of horror ranged from minor to grave. Everything from vandalism to murder was on record, but what seemed to be the most noteworthy crime was arson. The fires had calmed down in the mid-80s, but the teenage terrors were ready to change that. That night, they'd readied themselves for mayhem, primed to start their first fires and so much more.

They planned to raise hell that night. They planned to do

Satan's work. Much of it was organized and chronological, and they had a schedule to stick to. The blueprint was to scorn and maim efficiently, but if something fell into their lap, they weren't too strict to resist. When Teddy saw the black cat rubbing itself up against the tree, he got an idea.

He carefully handed the two cartons of eggs to Max and unzipped his backpack. "Here kitty, kitty, kitty. Here kitty, you want a treat?" The cat wobbled its way toward him cautiously, purring against Max's shin before meowing mere inches away from Teddy's skeleton-painted face. He wrapped his rough hand around the back of the cat's neck and elevated it off the ground. It flailed manically, swinging its claws through the air.

He pulled a length of coarse, filthy rope from his bag, one end was already in the shape of a noose. "Tighten it around its neck and I'll string up the other end," Teddy instructed. Max did as he was told without question. The measure tightened around the feline's throat. The cat's once enchanting green eyes now bulged, their specific beauty ruined by the cracking bloodiness of the shattered and runny vessels.

Teddy elevated the cat to about shoulder level and tied the rope to the tree trunk for stability. "Give me the bat," he instructed Max. Again, Max remained thoughtless, or maybe he was just on the same wavelength. He held out the tar-toned aluminum stick to his friend. Teddy took hold of it and readied himself like a batter in a baseball stance might.

"This'll be just like a piñata," Teddy laughed before taking his first swing at its ribs. A sickening crunch could be heard, and the sound excited the boys.

"Oh, man! That was sick! I wanna go now!" Max begged. "Don't worry. I'll leave some meat on the bone for you still…"

Teddy ignored his pleas and took his next at bat. This next strike was much more violent. It struck the cat directly in the face and with such force that one of its already popping eyes jumped out completely. Its small jaw was now useless, dangling downward similar to the eye above.

"Top that," Teddy dared. The blood oozing from the cat's head saturated the noose around its windpipe. It was sliding. Max stepped to the side a moment, looking ridiculous as he took a few practice swings in his ghoul attire.

"And Lance Parrish steps up to the plate. After thirty-three homers last year, there's no doubt he has what it takes to put an end to this game," Max joked, doing his best announcer impression. While the deranged pair laughed at Max's impression, they didn't notice the demolished kitty slipping free from the blood-soaked rope.

"Shit Max! See, you were messing around and let it get away! You idiot!"

"Don't get your panties in a bunch, we've got bigger fish to fry tonight anyway. Let's get going. The real fun is next."

Teddy couldn't argue with his sinister grin. The sins they had in queue would be a new extreme. They put a carton of eggs into each of their backpacks and hopped onto their bikes. They had quite a distance to travel; they'd already left the city, but it was a long way to the suburbs.

Normally, the rash of nasty fires were confined to the city, but Teddy and Max were planning to change that. They wanted to bring the inferno that Detroit was forced to deal with out into the boonies and they'd settled on a quiet suburb called Huntington to terrorize.

The streets they made their way down first were swarming with children. They decided that using their eggs on the little ones would make for the most fun. Once the shell exploded on the kids' costumes, Halloween would be over for the brats. It would be impossible to do anything but run home and try and clean off the horrendous stench brought forth by the rancid yolks.

Teddy and Max pelted the now screaming trick-or-treaters, who either began to cry or cursed at them. Their rage depended on their age. The smell was horrid, and even the boys got balance-tilting whiffs as they rode by on their bicycles. One larger boy, maybe a year or two younger than them, had started to freak out. He was dressed as a gorilla, and the fur upon the chest of his suit was now smeared with the fetid bird abortion.

The boy removed his gooey mask and turned back to them. "You ruined it! You assholes ruined my costume! You're gonna pay for this! You'll get yours; I promise you!"

This was a mistake that he couldn't have known he was making. These were not the type of boys that frequented these softer parts, and they were not the type of boys that took a threatening comment in passing. They whipped their bikes around in the other direction, rode up toward him and hopped off.

The handful of other kids around him stepped away. As Teddy walked up to the gorilla boy with his chest puffed out, the other bystanders dispersed. They knew that the vultures of the streets had arrived and that these evil buzzards feasted on both the living and the dead.

"Let me save you the time tough guy." He stretched out his arms waiting for him to make a move. "C'mon, I'm right here. Didn't you say I was gonna pay for it? Go ahead, make me pay, bitch!"

From behind the gorilla-suited boy, a candle-lit pumpkin smashed down on his skull, knocking him to the ground, unconscious. They kicked him in the head multiple times while he lay on the ground. Max cut a head-sized hole in the base of the largest pumpkin near him. He pushed the orange helmet onto the unconscious boy's head while Teddy retrieved a gas canister from the bag.

While Teddy dumped the accelerant onto the boy's face, Max removed a serrated steel blade from the black sheath camouflaged against his thigh. The cuts on the boy's face stung as the gas touched them, drizzling through the areas that had been carved out from the pumpkin. He was beginning to awaken just as Max finished cutting his costume off. He'd been stripped but for the pumpkin covering his skull and his piss-drenched tighty-whities. Max held down one of the boy's wrists with his combat boot and Teddy accounted for the other.

Teddy examined him, lighting the match as the boy's eyes finally reopened entirely. "Let's see if you can keep that promise after this." He dropped the lit match, and flames engulfed the wickedly sharp features of the pumpkin. They covered they boy's entire skull as he let loose a blood-curdling death shriek. As he pleaded for mercy, the demonic duo remained unflinching.

Parents from a nearby house eventually heard the commotion and came out to see what the issue was. All they found was the static burning corpse of their neighbor, his face eaten away down to the bone, still spookily sitting inside a smoldering pumpkin. The screams on the street only grew louder from there.

Teddy and Max were long gone, riding their bikes down the winding backroads that they'd scoured for months in preparation for their rampage. The houses were less close together in the next area, so this was a point of strategy. They had specifically cased a more private location to start the fires, since it would require some time to arrange and build. They didn't want someone sending the fire department before they could get the thing off the ground.

They stood outside the perfect house. Not only was the location ideal, the inhabitants were, as well. This elderly couple wasn't very mobile. The man that lived there got around very sluggishly and the woman they presumed to be his wife required a walker to manage. Their immobility would be the ideal complement for what they wanted to bear witness to that evening.

Watching them burn alive would be like nothing they'd ever

been privy to. Sure, they had just set another boy's head on fire and watched him squirm as the flames eventually revealed his skeleton, but this was different. Watching a mansion-like property be engulfed would create a blaze so big it would ascend to the heavens. They would garner God's attention. They would spread Devil's Night farther than ever before.

It would touch the privileged. It would touch the innocent. It would melt those who believed they were untouchable. Watching the old folks incinerate would be a real treat. How would they react when they awakened to the horror? Teddy looked at Max. It was time to stop wondering and find out.

Max made his way to the thick wires on the side of the house. He'd already played the role of the prowler before breaking in when they'd first cased the structure. He'd made note of which wires served to keep their telephone connected. It didn't take long for Max to relocate the lines, and once he did, he slid the blade into them, severing any chance of outside interference.

They kicked in the basement window and worked their way up. First, they silently inspected the main floor and removed the batteries from both smoke detectors. They ascended the stairs to the second floor, where they assumed the elderly couple would be fast asleep. They doused the rugs outside of the bedroom and then on the rest of the floor with the gas that remained in their primary canister. It was time to begin.

The flames spread quickly. It took a long time for the homeowners to even realize that the fire had started, but eventually it woke them. Teddy and Max watched outside as smoke filled the bedroom. A lamp went flying through the window, shattering the glass and falling at their feet. It helped to filter out some of the smoke that had accumulated inside.

The coughs and shouts began to rush out, and they watched

the old man's head poke out of the window. His face looked like a coalminer's might, covered in filth and ash. He laid over the broken window bordered with shattered glass. The cruel fencing sliced into his flesh as he pushed himself forward. He fell awkwardly from the second story. His back was arched like the letter C, with his head sitting at the base and eventually being the first thing to hit the driveway.

What would be a nauseating crunch to anyone with a conscience was another notch on the belts of the devils that watched. Their masterpiece was reaching its climax, and the sweet cries from inside began to fade. They watched the firestorm rage and the house hollow out, enjoying every moment. They knew they didn't have much time until they would need to move on. No matter how secluded the property was, they knew eventually the smoke would send a signal. They took off down the path toward the end of the road.

There was a small trail they'd discovered that would allow them to reach their final destination quickly. Their last stop was something they'd stumbled upon by happenstance: an old abandoned house, empty and shabby but perfect for one last fire.

They knew the other fires they'd started would undoubtedly be attracting the minimal resources available. If they could get the second one roaring while the firemen were still dealing with the other dilemmas, it had a chance to be big. If this one spread quickly enough, it had a chance to reach the woods and maybe the whole town.

The abandoned house looked beat to hell. The nasty siding was deteriorating, and the windows had been concealed with aged two-by-fours held in place by rusted nails. As they pulled up to the old house, they noticed the previously boarded-up door was unexpectedly ajar. The first thought they had was that some kids had probably broken inside, a concept that excited them. Lighting them on fire would be a bonus.

They quickly found out that wasn't the case when one of the

aged long boards fell from the second story above them. The board hit Max in the head, sending him to the ground. While his friend's incapacitation caught him off guard, to Teddy, the tradeoff above was well worth Max's concussion.

She looked youthful and brandished a curious smile that seemed to be targeting him. Her golden blonde hair glistened in the moonlight as she let loose a playful giggle that captivated. It was hard to tell what she was wearing; he could only see her face until she pushed another board loose. He made sure to dodge this one. Max was still out from the prior hit, but Teddy was anything but concerned for him.

The girl had revealed her outfit to him, or lack of one. Her breasts held firm and round at a perfect height, the nipples hardened by the chill of the autumn air. Her striking exquisiteness left even a modern-day barbarian such as Teddy speechless. She curved her back out toward him flexing her well-endowed figure teasingly.

"Sorry about your friend. I thought this place was abandoned!" she giggled.

"It's cool, don't worry about him." Teddy replied. She could have killed him, and he wouldn't have given a shit.

"So, are you gonna just stand there or come up and have some fun with me?"

Teddy didn't need much time to think about it. He left Max out cold beside him and made his way inside. They'd peered in between some of the boards before but had never been inside the place. The house was a health hazard. The ceiling was covered in black mold and it reeked of piss and feces. But Teddy knew he could tough his way through it to spend a little time with the seductive angel upstairs.

She stood at the top of the stairs to the second floor, awaiting his company. She wasn't wearing pants, either; she was entirely bare from head to toe. With each step Teddy took toward the top of the flight, his smile grew. When they met at the top of the steps, she kissed him. He closed his eyes and passionately returned the favor, intertwining his drooling tongue with hers as any hormone-riddled teen might.

He touched his hand to her soft, smooth breasts and slid his palm down her stomach. This is normally where he might unhook a girl's bra or unbutton her pants, but she'd made it easy for him. He was too randy to even notice, but she had made it *too* easy.

Without warning, many things began to seem different all at once. As Teddy's tongue continued to tangle with the girl's, it no longer felt the same. The wetness in her mouth wasn't quite what it was when they'd begun. It was still moist, but now it was different, with a slight flavor to it. Her jaw cracked, losing any of its tension and her tongue ceased movement, its weight falling dead inside his mouth. The skin his hands groped began to alter in texture. The formerly flawless and smooth surface had wilted, becoming rougher and stretchy.

When he opened his eyes, the girl wasn't a girl at all. She'd aged lifetimes in a matter of seconds into a repellant wench. Her eyeball hung out of her skull inches from his as her bloodied face rained red all over him. Her hair tone flipped hues drastically from a young blond into a dark silver. The sudden transition frightened Teddy, and as he pulled away from his kiss, he tumbled backwards down the staircase. The hag's entire tongue fell off in his mouth and found its way down his windpipe.

She descended the steps slowly, still naked in her now hideous true form. Teddy lay on the ground gagging on the old tongue while it obstructed his air canal. She watched him choke for a few final moments before the life drained out of his eyes. She placed her claw-like hands into his mouth and dragged him outside.

When Max came to, the noose was already around his throat. As the old witch pulled him off the ground, he hung, eyes cracking in his head, beside Teddy. His friend's blue face and dead, blood-spattered expression showed that his spirit had vacated his vessel. As Max struggled pointlessly to escape, he watched the decrepit woman's appearance change.

Her skin sprouted black fur while her hands and feet molded into paw-like shapes. The one eye that remained in her skull turned green as the pupil compressed, shifting from round to vertical. Her body mass decreased to a size that began to look very familiar to Max. It was the same deformed cat from the woods, its eye still dangling while its jaw flapped, yawning horrifically. As Max took in his last breath, he looked over at his dead friend, then back to the black cat. It hissed at him aggressively and ran off into the woods.

Running with the Devil
by Glen Campbell

Procured for him by Earl, his ever-reliable man-mountain bodyguard, Brooke, the blonde groupie with her lips around King Vladimir's erection, was wearing a black sequined domino mask, which Vlad hoped she wouldn't take off before he was through with her. To keep her face a mystery would be so much sexier. It was little turn-ons like this that always made the Halloween show the best gig of the year.

"Hey, King!" shouted a voice from beyond the dressing room door, startling the bobbing head at King Vlad's crotch. It was Earl. "They say you got ten minutes before show time," continued the bodyguard. "Hurry up and bus' that nut."

Evident by the lighthearted timbre of his voice, 'Big' Earl was enjoying Halloween, too. Not surprising, really; at this time of the year Vlad was always more liberal with the impromptu cash bonuses, and right now, for the fine job he did procuring Brooke, the big-man's pockets were teeming with hundred-dollar bills.

Brooke was just the Halloween treat Vlad required. Earl had done well. But then, he always did. Every Halloween, Earl was entrusted with a backstage pass that needed to be given to someone special from among the cattle that were Vlad's fans, someone with a particular attribute, which was neither ample bosoms nor slutty clothes, the usual qualifications for an audience with the King. No, on Halloween, Vlad's needs were more discerning, requiring someone with an attribute that Earl had a unique gift for being able to sniff out.

"The show starts when *I'm* ready, Earl," Vlad shouted back. "Remind everyone of that!"

"Anything you say, boss," Earl replied, his voice diminishing as he retreated from the dressing room to go spread the gospel.

Earl wasn't the type to usually care about Vlad's tardiness.

His concern most likely betrayed his eagerness to get his turn with the naïve groupie who was presently going down on

Vlad's convulsing member.

"Wow," said the groupie, pulling away from Vlad's crotch and wiping her lips. "I can't believe I just gave King Vladimir a BJ."

"I like to make dreams come true for my fans," said Vlad, zipping up the fly of his black leather pants and buckling his bullet-belt. "Well, that was great, but I've got to get ready for the show. Before I go, though, care to join me in a little Halloween tradition I have?"

"Sure," Brooke said as she got up off her knees and watched Vlad pick up a bottle of Jack Daniel's.

Whiskey was poured into two tumblers. "Here."

Vlad handed the blonde a tumbler and then raised his glass in the air. Following his lead, Brooke did the same.

"A toast," said Vlad, "to an absent friend who, on this night, thirty years ago, made all of this possible."

The two tumblers clinked together before being lifted to the mouths of their respective holders. Like a true wannabe party-girl Brooke downed her whiskey in one gulp. Vlad, however, only imbibed half the whiskey in his glass; the other half he poured over the decorative scarification on the back of his left hand.

"What's that?" Brooke asked, pointing at the scar tissue. "It's the sigil of Focalor," answered Vlad.

"Cool," gushed Brooke as if she had understood what he'd said.

"You know, it's true what they say," began Vlad as he opened a drawer in his dressing-table, reached in and pressed two fingers up against the black handle of his *athame*. "Rock n' roll is the Devil's music and if you want to make it, you need to be willing to make a sacrifice."

"Are you sure you have the right item there, darling?"

asked the busty brunette at the checkout as Rory Finch placed what looked like a tiny sickle down on the counter in front of her.

"I think so," answered the young man, clearly uncertain. "What are you going to use it for?" inquired the woman.

"Are you cutting herbs for a potion or," her eyes widened dramatically, "are you making a sacrifice?"

"Um . . . Err . . ." stammered Rory before sheepishly admitting, "It's for a sacrifice."

The woman sitting at the cash register smiled, as if that was the answer she had wanted to hear, and Rory instantly began to feel at ease.

A key figure in Langthorn Valley lore, famous for her bountiful Dolly Parton-esque bust and for, thirteen years ago, selling the infamous Johnny Necro a ceremonial blade, too, Mimi Gribbin had for a long time been someone Rory had wanted to meet. If only he had known she was going to be this pleasant. If he had known before now that her smile would make him feel like a lady killer, Rory would have found a reason to visit her New Age store a long time ago.

"Well, if it's a sacrifice you're doing," said Mimi conspiratorially as she leaned forward, "then you're going to need an *athame*. An *athame* has a straight blade and a black handle. What you got here, honey, is a *boline*, curved blade, white handle."

"Oh," said Rory, already on his way back to the shelves to pick up the correct item. He now remembered the screeched lyric from the third track of Gods N' Monsters' new album, "*With my black-handled blade, I sha" reign in blood*", and quietly admonished himself for his mistake. Luckily, thanks to Mimi's intervention, a potential calamity had been averted.

Moments later, when he emerged from the New Age store, Rory Finch had a spring in his step and a smile on his face. He had his *athame*, and the celebrated Mimi Gribbin had been wearing a low-cut top.

Although it was, arguably, the most important item on his Halloween shopping list, Rory had chosen to procure the *athame* last. Now, with its acquisition, he was ready for tomorrow, the big day. He could hardly wait. Never afraid to use a cliché, Rory reminded himself that tomorrow would be the first day of the rest of his life.

"You're almost there," he muttered to a reflection of himself in the store window. He moistened his chapped lips and grinned.

With everything he needed for Halloween night now accounted for, all Rory needed to do now was kill time. He had decided in advance that a trip to the movies to see *Sorority House Massacre* for the third time would be an entertaining way to kill off some of it.

Putting on his headphones, Rory pushed play on his Walkman and, as he walked off in the direction of the cinema, began to thrash his head as a searing guitar licks thundered along his ear canals.

He had cued up a song especially for this moment, a song that would not only help him celebrate the acquisition of the *athame,* but also give him the fortitude to tolerate each passerby that scowled disapprovingly at the Gods N' Monsters T-shirt he proudly wore beneath his patched-up battle jacket. The song was 'The Heretic's Steel', a relentless fist pumping slab of speed metal, the sixth track from the album *Triumph of Faust* by, of course, Gods N' Monsters, the band fronted by Langthorn Valley native Johnny Necro.

After Sorority House Massacre, which was still awesome even on its third viewing, Rory, headphones on again, head-banged his way over to the record store, hoping his best friend, Del, would show up and join him there.

At Wax Lyrical, Langthorn Valley's only half-way decent record store, Rory loitered among the latest heavy-metal cassettes, vinyl and CDs and took up his record store habit of mentally compiling a top ten list of the best album covers.

Painted covers featuring some kind of badass-looking satanic creature or, failing that, a sexy, scantily clad woman were what usually made Rory's top ten. Iron Angel's latest, *Winds of War*, featuring a nice topless woman shooting lightening from her fingers, made the cut, as did Slayer's *Reign in Blood* and Cirith Ungol's *One Foot in He"*, but, once again, like it had on Rory's last visit, the number one spot for best new release album cover went to Ozzy Osbourne's *Ultimate Sin*. The album itself may have been a bit of a disappointment, but the demonic woman on the cover had an ass worthy of appreciation. The award for worst album cover, however, went to Stryper's *To He" with the Devil* for its depiction of the band with angel wings; Christian metal, *yuck*!

It took about forty minutes of perusing Wax Lyrical's heavy-metal section for the top ten to be finalized. After that, with Del still a no show, Rory finally conceded that his friend wasn't likely to show up, which, really, shouldn't have come as a surprise. Since hooking up with Clara, Del had become a bit of a bore. Music no longer seemed important to him. Fool!

Never mind, reasoned Rory, reminding himself that Del had promised to call round at his place tonight with a pilfered bag of his mom's Acapulco Gold. Content with this prospect and having covertly slipped a cassette of the new Metal Church album into his pocket, Rory left the record store and headed home.

When he walked through the front door of 24 Belle Porte Avenue, the fresh smell of deodorant and hairspray instantly informed Rory that his mom was still home, running late for work as usual.

He heard the familiar clink of glass colliding with glass: the neck of a whiskey bottle striking the rim of a tumbler. The sound resounded down the hallway from the kitchen, which was where his mom usually psyched herself up for another hard night's grind.

Quietly, Rory slunk up to his room. Once there, among the familiar trappings of heavy-metal posters, stacks of vinyl and rows of Stephen King paperbacks, he made a beeline to his stereo, put the needle on the vinyl, grabbed the *Triumph of Faust*'s gatefold sleeve and fell back onto his bed. As he lay down, staring up at the depiction of Hell on the cover artwork, Rory let the music wash over him, transporting him to a heavy-metal world of gods and monsters.

Released earlier in the year, a concept album based around the titular character's deal with the Devil, the *Triumph of Faust* was Gods N' Monster's eighth studio record, and Rory adored it. In his opinion, it was Johnny Necro's finest work to date. Every night since its release, Rory had fallen asleep listening to this superlative heavy-metal opus. It was like nothing else he had ever heard.

Instinctively, from the first listen, Rory had known there was something special about the album. At first, he didn't know what it was, but the mystery enthralled him. Finally, though, after weeks of painstakingly examining every aspect of the record, from its Boschian sleeve to its progressive musical arrangements, Rory realized that, behind the cryptic lyrics and squealing guitar tone, the *Triumph of Faust* was not only a concept album, but also a confession. Like Johann Georg Faust before him, Johnny Necro had made a pact with the Devil.

Tomorrow, Rory would do the same.

There was a knock at the door. Without waiting for a response, Rory's mom pushed the door ajar and poked her head into the bedroom.

"Hey, sweetheart, I'm leaving for work now," she said. "There's pizza in the fridge, which you can have, or there's last night's leftovers."

"Okay," said Rory, eyes still fixed on the vinyl sleeve. "Is Del coming round tonight?"

"Probably," said Rory.

"What are you boys going to be doing?"

Rory shrugged. "Dunno," he answered. "Just hang, I guess. Watch a movie, listen to some music."

"Will Del be bringing his girlfriend with him?" "He better not!"

Faintly, patronizingly, Rory's mom smiled.

"What are you and Del doing for Halloween tomorrow?" she asked.

Rory shrugged. "We'll probably decide on something tonight."

"Mm," murmured Rory's mom, becoming distracted by the wretched state of her son's room.

Dismayed, she shook her head in despair as she looked over the domain of her teenage deviant and saw crusty, dirty socks strewn across the floor, skid-marked underwear, rotting food and, on the walls, a gallery of posters featuring heavy metal bands. Their outrageously coiffured members were all clad in leather and, more often than not, posing in front of a nearly naked model, who, in most of the posters, was playing the role of the band's captive, in chains and manacles or, in some cases, tied to a St Andrew's Cross.

"You know, instead of lying around listening to trashy music all the time, why don't you clean this room up?" Rory's mom suggested, before then pointing to the Johnny Necro poster hanging on the wall, perhaps the most offensive of the collection. "I thought I told you to take that poster down."

"What's the big deal?" protested Rory, despite knowing full well what the 'big deal' was.

"I don't want pictures of that man hanging up in my house." She explained. "He's not someone to be idolized. He's a murderer."

"Really?" challenged Rory, finally putting the record sleeve down to look at his mother. "Then why didn't they arrest him, Mom? Innocent until proven guilty, remember? What, are we living in the Soviet Union now? Jeez."

"You know, you and Del don't do yourselves any favors by walking around town wearing T-shirts supporting that guy. This town doesn't like him, and with good reason. Think of that poor girl's family. The Arnolds still have relatives in this town, you know."

"Fuck this town!"

"I despair of you sometimes, Rory. You need to buck up your ideas. Listening to heavy-metal bands singing about the devil isn't gonna help you get anywhere in life."

Rory stared at her fixedly.

"You're wrong, Mom," he said, "but, if you feel that strongly about it, why don't you join the PMRC, or don't they accept strippers?"

For a moment, mother and son stared at each other with no words passing between them. Rory had hurt her. He could see the pain in her eyes. The silence in the room seemed to be waiting for him to apologize, for him to reflect and remember that she hated her job even more then he did. It was that job that paid for the clothes on his back and the roof over his head.

"Oh, I give up," said Rory's mother, ending the stare-down, "I can't argue with you now; I'm late enough for work already. Take it down!"

With those parting words, Rory's mom exited.

"Fuck this town!" repeated Rory. He then looked up at the offending poster hanging on his wall and added, "Fuck everyone, eh Johnny?"

Throughout Langthorn Valley, it was generally believed that Johnny Necro (real name: Jonathan Walker) killed seventeen-year-old local girl Beth Arnold, probably with the *athame* he had bought from Mimi's New Age store. Johnny was known to have had a thing for Beth. They had even dated once. However, that one date, apparently, was enough to convince the pretty A-grade student that she should have nothing more to do with the long-haired high school dropout who had far-fetched dreams of being a rock star. So, Johnny killed her. Or at least that's what Rory's mom believed, like nearly everybody else in town.

Rory, though, knew better. Johnny killed Beth, that's true, but not just because she rejected him; Johnny had bigger plans than that.

Rory leaned over the edge of his bed and, after brushing aside some dirty socks and Y-fronts, extended his right arm into the darkness beneath it. Moments later, the arm reemerged, now holding Rory's treasured Gods N' Monsters scrapbook.

The scrapbook, a labor of love, contained within its pages everything Rory had been able to dig up on the exploits of Johnny Necro and his Gods N Monsters band mates, before they left Langthorn Valley for better things: high school photos, hand drawn flyers for their early gigs and a ton of newspaper articles on the Beth Arnold murder.

Rory, sitting up on his bed, placed the scrapbook on his lap and opened it to the page that contained Beth Arnold's yearbook headshot.

He smirked as he stared down at the black and white photo of the pretty girl with long dark hair and thick eyebrows.

Though Langthorn Valley had plenty of amateur historians and true crime enthusiasts who would dare to make the same claim, Rory considered himself to be the town's foremost authority on the Beth Arnold murder. His scrapbook told the whole story.

It was when the sheriff 's office released a statement

characterizing Beth's murder as a ritualistic slaying that widespread suspicion fell on Johnny. His fascination with the occult was well known throughout town. Everyone had seen the pentagram tattoo on the back of his left hand. Some had even seen him, as front man of his band, sing songs in the local clubs lauding Satan and other demonic entities. One of his songs, the band's set opener, even described a female sacrifice in lurid detail.

To everyone in town, it was obvious Johnny was the killer. The pieces seemed to fit. The only problem, though, was that there was no concrete evidence against him. The *athame*, the supposed murder weapon, was never found. Johnny claimed it had been stolen from him prior to Beth's murder, and Snot Rocket, the drummer from his band, had given him an alibi to account for his whereabouts at the time of the murder. Johnny was untouchable. A few months later, Johnny and his band left town. They moved to LA and almost instantly signed with a major record label. Gods N' Monsters were on their way to their first gold record, the first of many.

The phone rang.

Rory snatched the receiver from off the neon telephone on his bed side cabinet.

"Hello?" he answered.

"Hey, dude, it's me," said a voice. It was Del.

"Hey, man, what time you coming over?" Rory asked. "Did you get the Acapulco Gold?"

"Nah," Del said, "my mum is hiding her stash someplace new. Anyway, I can't see you tonight."

"Why not?" Rory demanded.

"Clara needs me to help her study," explained Del, after a pause. "She's got a big exam coming up, and she really needs me to help her cram for it."

"So what?" Rory protested. "Fuck that shit, man! I got the new Metal Church album today. You'd really rather study than listen to that?"

"Dude, you know I'd love to hear that album, but this is important. We'll hang tomorrow, though."

"Whatever. Have fun studying."

Rory slammed the receiver back on its cradle. "Dweeb!" he muttered, as a tear escaped his eyes.

Angry at his body for conceding to emotions he was trying hard to repress, Rory roughly wiped the tear away. An emotional barrier, though, had finally been breached and the truth, so swollen, was now leaking out of him. He was scared, Rory realized, as he lay back in his bed; scared that he was losing his only ally in this godforsaken town.

Thirteen years after the death of Beth Arnold, Rory and Del were the only town residents brave enough, stupid enough, and already unpopular enough to walk the streets wearing Gods N Monsters T-shirts. Even though he was a suspected murderer, Johnny Necro was the boys' hero. The fact that he was as unpopular with the townsfolk as they were would have by itself been enough to give him a place in their hearts. The badass bone-crunching heavy-metal music, though, was a nice bonus.

They didn't care that being Gods N Monsters fans made them targets for abuse. They were targets even before they put on the T-shirts and patches that declared their devotion to the band. Overweight, Del was an object for ridicule no matter what he chose to wear. And Rory, pilloried for having a mom that pole-danced at the strip bar on the outskirts of town, had figured that, since every kid in school with a fake ID had seen his mom's 'diamond cut', giving the town something else to taunt him with worked in his favor. Besides, it wouldn't be forever. Johnny Necro had escaped the banal clutches of this hick town, and, like their hero, Rory and Del were going to get out, too.

After graduation, they'd throw their guitars and duffel bags into the back of Del's shitty Lancia Delta and head for LA. Or, rather, that was the plan before Clara Lawson reared her ugly, crimped-haired head. Now all of a sudden, Del was talking about knuckling down to study and maybe even going to college, all that humdrum shit. If Rory and Del were going to realize their dreams, something would have to be done about Clara.

From his bed, Rory reached over to the stereo and turned up the volume. Track three, 'Kill the Bitch', was about to start.

Rory picked up a stone and hurled it at the portly boy wearing the Jason Voorhees hockey mask and Alice Cooper T-shirt. But despite the fact he'd aimed it at the masked boy's head, the stone struck the boy's shoulder, an eye-hand coordination failure that reminded Rory of why Coach Hellwig had cut him from the basketball team. Try as he might, sports just weren't his thing. But still, at least he had hit the boy.

"Ouch," cried the target. "That hurt, asshole!"

Rory seized another stone from the ground. Fearing another hit, the masked boy scampered for safety behind a tree.

"Back off, Del," warned Rory, his stone primed for release. "You shouldn't be running in the woods anyway, fat boy, your flabby thighs rubbing together might ignite a spark and start a forest fire."

"Screw you, dickweed," was the reply from Del, Rory's cowering pursuer.

Ruining the Kiss-like kabuki face paint that had taken him over an hour in front of the mirror to get right, Rory's forehead poured sweat. With Del in hot pursuit, he had been running through the woods, the undergrowth clawing at the heels of his Converse sneakers, for the past twenty minutes. This was not how he would have liked to have spent Halloween night. So long as Del didn't get in his way again, the goal he was working towards would be worth missing some tricks and treats for.

It was an inconvenience, as well as an embarrassment, that his fat friend had caught up with him. Rory consoled himself, though, with the awareness that it never would have happened if he hadn't been hampered by the unconscious girl he was dragging through the woods with him. It was *her* fault he had been caught. Dressed for Halloween in an Elvira costume, like half the females in town, the girl out cold was Del's sweetheart, Clara Lawson, and Rory was planning on killing her.

Looking over his shoulder, Rory could see the Devil's Circle. It was just a little further, a stone's throw away even for him. He picked up Clara's muddy left arm and, dragging the female dead weight behind him, once again began to trudge towards the infamous clearing in the woods where, thirteen years ago almost to the day, the body of Beth Arnold had been found.

"Dude, this isn't funny," protested Del desperately, poking his head out from behind the tree.

"I ain't trying to be funny," Rory yelled back. "This isn't a joke, Del. I'm going to do it, and it's going to work."

Revealing a chubby, ruddy cheeked face beneath a mop of shaggy brown hair, Del removed his hockey mask and surrendered it to the ground.

"But why Clara?" he asked.

"Why not?" answered Rory. "I'm trying to do you a favor, dude. She's only gonna break your heart in the end, and you know it. You really think she's that into you? You told me yourself, she pulls away every time you try anything. She's just playing with you, man. She's getting her jollies from trying to ruin our friendship. Halloween is our night, man, it's always been our night, and she wanted you to spend it with *her*! She's a troublemaker. We're better off without her."

Unceremoniously, Rory dropped Clara's arm. Along with

the rest of her, it slumped down onto a bed of grass and dead leaves. Tired and breathless, he had made it to the center of the Devil's Circle. Now it was time to get bloody. From the back pocket of his faded Levi's, he pulled out his *athame*.

"Dude, this is stupid," pleaded Del, who was standing just outside the Devil's Circle.

Without naming the girl he had designs on sacrificing, Rory had taken Del into his confidence about his diabolic short-cut to fame and fortune a few days earlier. Del, however, had mistaken his friend's talk of satanic sacrifices for dismissible pot chatter. Rory always talked the most amazing nonsense while stoned, like the time when they were toking up while listening to Kiss' *Animalize* and Rory declared that 'Mark St. John was the best guitarist Kiss ever had!' After that little outburst nothing Rory said while holding a joint could be taken seriously. But now, as he brandished his *athame* over the body of the girl he had drugged with a Pepsi spiked with Quaaludes – she didn't 'Taste the Difference' – Rory had finally made Del take him seriously again.

"You don't really think this will work, do you?" "It worked for Johnny Necro," argued Rory.

Despairingly, Del shook his head.

"You're crazy, man. The *Triumph of Faust* is just an album, dude, not a 'how to' guide. If you kill Clara, I'm telling you, dude, you're going to prison, not the Grammys."

"We'll see."

From his shoulders, Rory slipped off his backpack, opened it and pulled out a portable cassette player with a built-in speaker. In the tape deck was a copy of the *Triumph of Faust*, cued up to start playing at the song 'Sacrifice', an eight-minute rock epic. At the beginning of the track, before the screeching guitars entered, there was a lengthy plainsong intro, sung, supposedly, by a congregation of Luciferian monks. According to the album's liner notes, the words the monks sang, taken from the *Grand Grimoire of the Red Dragon*, were an invocation to summon Hell's administrator, Lucifuge Rofocale.

Rory placed the cassette player on the grass and pressed play. A coincidence, maybe, but as the baritone voices of the heretical choir issued out into the night, like spilt ink on paper, the clouds began to blot out the bright October moon. "Forget this, man," Del implored. "Let's go get high and go to Toby Harrington's party."

"You know we're not invited to that motherfucker's party."

"It's a costume party, we'll crash it."

Rory considered the offer for a moment before finally answering, "Nah, this is more important. This is our future right here. A month from now we'll be in LA, with a record deal. We'll be getting blowjobs in limousines and snorting coke off the asses of supermodels. That's our future, man, and, to get it, all I have to do is sacrifice a virgin, and that's this bitch right here."

Muddying his knees, Rory knelt down beside Clara's supine body. He hesitated, and then placed the *athame's* tip at the center of her chest. Through the steel, he could feel her heartbeat. He gripped the handle tighter and drew a deep breath. And then, just as he was about to propel the blade through flesh and bone, Del cried out, "She's not a virgin!"

"Huh!" said Rory, looking up at Del. "You said you and her hadn't . . ."

"We haven't... It-it wasn't me. A few nights ago, she told me... We were on the sofa together watching *Knight Rider*. She likes that Hasselhoff guy so I thought it might be a good time to make a move. I ran my hand up between her legs. But she elbowed me in the ribs, fucking hard! I apologized. She apologized, too, even though *I* was the asshole. She then started to cry and that's when she told me about what her mom's scumbag boyfriend did to her."

"What did he do?" asked Rory.

Del stared back at him incredulously. "What? Did he…"

Del nodded.

"Wow. What an asshole! He's totally fucked up my night."

Removing the *athame's* point from Clara's chest, Rory stood up and kicked a divot into the earth.

"Where am I going to find a virgin now?" He looked at his Casio wristwatch. "I've got only an hour before Halloween is over."

Sensing the threat diminishing, Del stepped into the Devil's Circle and cautiously approached his friend.

"Is this nonsense over now, Rory?" he asked.

"We were going to be rock stars," lamented Rory, staring off into space, that intangible place where he had seen so many of his plans and schemes disintegrate.

"Give me the knife, Rory," said Del, holding out his right hand.

"We were gonna tour with Van Halen." "Rory, give me the knife."

"We were gonna spit roast Lita Ford." "Rory, the knife!"

"It's not a knife," corrected Rory. "It's called an *athame*." "Whatever it is, just give it to me."

Resigning himself to failure with a sigh, Rory handed Del the *athame*.

"Still want to go crash Toby's party?"

"I suppose," said Del flatly. "Would this really have worked?"

Rory shrugged. "Maybe, if the sacrifice was a virgin." "Well let's see."

Thrusting the *athame* forward, Del stuck the ceremonial knife into his friend's chest. In the silence of the woods, the sound of steel puncturing flesh resounded through the night like a thunderclap.

His left lung punctured, Rory gurgled on blood as he tried to speak.

"Judas—" he croaked, clutching the gushing wound in his chest, his eyes wide with shock. Slowly, unsteadily, his bloody right hand then rose up and made devil horns at Del. "— Priest rock!" Rory concluded, before collapsing to the ground.

Blood pouring out of him, Rory died within seconds. However, right before he breathed his last breath, he felt the earth tremble, just like Johnny Necro said it would.

Like a George Lynch solo, murder wasn't easy, but with dedication and practice, one's technique improves and, eventually, it all starts coming together. This was how it was for King Vladimir (real name: Del Jones), who after so many years, so many Halloweens, was now confident with his instrument of choice, his *athame*. Nowadays, there were no discordant squeals or screeches, just a quick, clean execution.

With his weapon concealed at the arch of his back, Vlad approached Brooke. The young woman in the domino mask, who couldn't have been older than nineteen, suspected nothing as Vlad reached out to stroke her long blonde locks.

"You're very pretty," he said. Brooke smiled.

"But you can't see my entire face," she countered, for modesty's sake.

"That's true," Vlad conceded, getting ready to say a line he had uttered countless times before; "but no mask can hide your beauty."

Brooke blushed, and, as if her crimson cheeks were a signal to action, Vlad revealed his *athame* and then plunged its blade into Brooke's breast. As the steel pierced her flesh, to stifle any screams she might have made, Vlad seized the back of her head and forced her face down onto his chest.

He held her there until her struggling ceased and then, when he was sure that every last drop of life had dripped out of her, withdrew his weapon from the deep, bloody cavity it had made in Brooke's upper body.

"That's death metal, babe," quipped Vlad, holding aloft his *athame*, so he could watch Brooke's blood run down from the blade and wash over the sigil on the back of his hand.

Carrying his signature black Gibson Les Paul by its neck, King Vladimir stepped out of his dressing room. With his face painted white, his muscular, bare torso oiled and dappled with blood, he was ready to take the stage.

"Did everything go okay in there, King?" asked Earl, the tracksuit-wearing sentry at the King's door.

"She got the job done," answered Vlad drily. "She's all yours now, Earl. I got her nice and loose for you."

Earl smiled.

"Have a good show tonight, King." "And you have a good time, too, Earl."

Still smiling, Earl entered the dressing room, closing the door behind him.

With his Devil appeased, and another year of rock n' roll excess assured, King Vladimir, platinum selling recording artist and shock rock icon, walked off to bask in the adoration of his screaming fans.

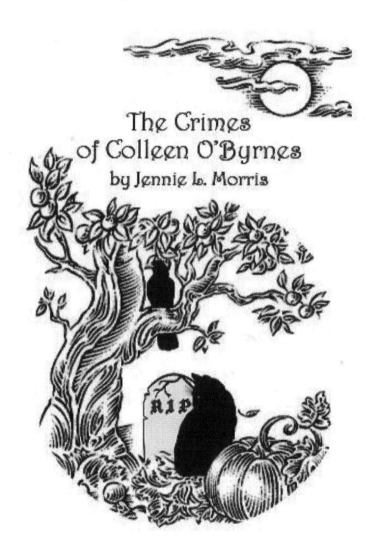

The Crimes
of Colleen O'Byrnes
by Jennie L. Morris

COUNTY WICKLOW, IRELAND, 1880

By lantern, Colleen O'Byrnes walked down the hedge-lined lane toward the village church. Autumn was crisp in the air, and she inhaled the moist,

earthy scent of decay. Harvest season was nearly complete. The last of the crops would soon be put up for winter. Her hands ached from the months of labor, but she was thankful for the work. Her muscles were prepared for the task ahead.

The wee hours of Samhain, the thinning of the veil, kept the old believers inside for fear of meeting ghouls or worse. Colleen, not one to scare, left the others to worry over such meaningless things. The living gave her harm. No spirit ever struck her or pulled her hair, even if her Ma and Pa warned her about fae stealing naughty children or playing tricks on drunkards. It made no difference, and she had to travel the darkened road.

Earlier in the day, the community buried their priest, Father Kinnard Dunleavy. The man, though old, had been spry. His maid found him dead in his bed, peaceful as an angel brought into the Lord's arms.

Colleen, a great-niece to Father Dunleavy, distrusted the holy man. Every Sunday, she attended services, the solemn Catholic liturgy, and received communion. Her parents forced her to give confession every two weeks, though she had little time to do much sinning between helping her Ma, watching her six younger siblings, working in the garden or fields, and mucking out the barn.

Shifting the shovel from one shoulder to the other, she adjusted her patched coat, pulling it close to her. Already, her breath misted in the air, threatening a cold winter season not more than a few weeks away. They worried if the ground would be too hard to dig the grave, as the frost came last week — good thing the village had strong-backed men.

Unafraid of the dark, her Ma and Pa called her an odd child.

THE CRIMES OF COLLEEN O'BYRNES BY JENNIE L. MORRIS

Dark-haired, like a raven's wing, with bright green eyes, Colleen could be considered beautiful at the right angle. On the left side of her face, a deep red birthmark stained her ivory skin. The wine-colored mark touched the end of her eyebrow and wrapped down to her jaw, a jagged crescent moon. When she was not going to the village, she wore her hair pulled back, but in public, she tried her best to cover the mark that so embarrassed her parents.

She used to hate it, staring at her reflection in the cool spring pool by the cottage. Now, nearing twenty years of age, she accepted it as she accepted all things. The Lord gave her the mark, nothing to be done about it, no use in trying all the rank herbal remedies and concoctions brought from well-wishers.

Close to the village, the lane made a Y, the right going into the heart of Droicheaddoire village, while the left went to the Church of Saint Columbanus. She took the left path, cautious of any lurking villagers. This late at night, everyone should be asleep, but she couldn't risk a wandering eye seeing her.

The wrought-iron fence's spiked tops surrounded the graveyard, making it impossible to climb over. Not too long ago, maybe twenty years, people went grave-robbing, and the whole community came together to raise funds for the fence. She crept along the ground, using her body to shield the lantern until she arrived at the gate. It was locked as expected. She pulled out a piece of metal from her pocket. Sliding it into the keyhole, she put her ear to the lock, listening for the spring mechanism.

Odd, as her parents said, she learned this trick from a friend. Often in trouble during church outings or village gatherings, Colleen and Reardon spent hours sitting under a tree as punishment. A year older than her, Reardon's father owned the smithy and was the village's locksmith. Reardon showed her how to unlatch a lock without a key.

It took several minutes before the rusty lock popped

open. She slid her metal tool back into her pocket and inched the squeaky gate open. Once she was inside the graveyard, Colleen replaced the lock, setting it to appear closed.

The fresh grave of Father Dunleavy rested near the back of the graveyard, under the rustling leaves of an ancient oak. A large rock marked the head until the master stonemason could carve a proper headstone. The mound of cold dirt, black and rich, smelled of a newly tilled field.

She set the lantern down on the ground before removing her jacket.

"Forgive me, Lord. I apologize fer disturbing the dead, but Father Dunleavy took something with him ta the grave of which does not belong ta him. Amen." She crossed herself and grabbed the shovel.

Even in the cool air, she began to sweat, digging into the loose earth. At the funeral, she had watched as the men put the casket into a deep hole. She hoped since tomorrow was Sunday, people would stay abed a little longer, with no priest to carry on their weekly sermon.

When she had dug nearly two feet down, she heard a noise. The lantern was turned down low, with her coat obscuring the light from the village. She hunkered down. Someone opened the gate; the distinct *squueeaak* of the hinge filled her ears.

Colleen, cursing her luck, jumped out of the grave and grabbed hold of the shovel, ready to use it as a weapon. The person approached, slow and steady, solid footsteps on the ground. Gripping the wooden handle, she widened her stance, hoping to stun the person and not kill them.

"Colleen," the person whispered. "Colleen O'Byrnes." Lowering the shovel, she moved out of the shadow to find

Reardon McGiffin standing with a shovel over his shoulder. "Why are ye here, Reardon?" she asked, wiping her sweaty hands on her dress.

"Ye know why, Colleen. Tha' old bastard is dead, and he

inna taking what donna belong ta him ta the grave. Besides, I promised ta help ye, given a chance."

She chuckled a sad sound. "Childhood promises, Reardon. Ye have ta think bout yer upcoming nuptials. What will Miss Aisling Mohan and her family think, seeing ye digging up the dead?"

Removing his tailored outer coat, Reardon tossed it over the back of a nearby tombstone. "*Ach*, plenty of willing lasses ta marry in these parts. If it wasn't fer me Ma wanting ta link our businesses, I'd not have looked twice at Miss Aisling Mohan." He jumped into the grave and started digging.

She joined him, the scrape of the shovels against the freshly disturbed dirt soft and muffled. "Why wed her then, Reardon? Ye donna wanna live in a house where ye hate yer spouse. My Ma and Pa, they despise one another, have fer years."

No quick reply. Unlike him. She continued to work, not pressing the issue. Through the years, they remained friends, but at a distance. His was family middle-class, and her family were poor farmers. It was unseemly to see them fraternize beyond a wave or nod.

"Why ye living at home, Colleen? Yer Pa should've found ye a marriage by now, some farmer in the next county maybe?" he asked, wiping his brow. "Ye're too good fer Droicheaddoire."

Moving her hair, she pointed at her face. "Hard ta find a husband when ye've got the mark on ye. Ma needs me. She canna watch all my siblings alone." She stopped and met his gaze in the dark. "I wish I was born a man, no one care then, mark or not. I'd join the navy, sail away, ne'er look back."

They continued to dig, two shovels moving earth far faster than Colleen on her own. Foot by foot, dirt flew up out of the grave, sometimes sprinkling back down on them, causing Colleen to giggle. Even though they were engaged in a serious task, she couldn't help it. She had missed Reardon's company and antics.

With her mud-caked shoe, she prepared to get another shovel full of soil but hit something solid. Several times she tapped the end of her shovel over the thin layer of dirt, confirming they'd reached Father Dunleavy's coffin.

Getting on her knees, she used her hands to wipe away the remaining dirt, revealing the jointed wooden box.

"Let me climb out, ye should be able ta stand at one side," Reardon said. He pushed a shovel into the side of the grave and used it as a step to pull himself out of the deep hole. "I'll get a lantern."

Feeling along the edges of the coffin, Colleen's fingers brushed against its metal hinges. Moving to the other side, she found the three latches holding the coffin's lid closed. Everyone in Droicheaddoire got the same wooden box, nailed shut and put in the ground. A cry went up, as Father Dunleavy was a venerated man, and the carpenter adjusted the coffin for the upstanding village citizen.

Reardon, lying on his stomach, held a lantern over the grave. "Ye ready, Colleen?"

"No," she replied, "but when has that stopped us?"

A small space near the end of the coffin gave her enough room to stand with her feet turned at awkward angles. One at a time, she undid the three metal latches securing the top. Holding her breath, saying a small prayer, she lifted the lid open.

Colleen and Reardon stared into an empty coffin. Confused, Colleen patted the inside of the wood box, sturdy and sound.

"Reardon?" she asked, glancing up. "Where is he?"

Her friend shook his head. "I dunno. We watched them. I saw them close the lid, his body in the coffin. Everyone saw as they lowered it in the ground."

Scared, but not ready to give up, Colleen shut the coffin lid and closed the latches. She used the shovel, like Reardon, and he hoisted her out of the grave. Filthy, cold, and angry, she leaned over the edge and retrieved their other shovel.

"What ta do?" she asked aloud to herself. "Feck, Reardon, Imma dead woman now."

She paced a minute, biting at her nails, tasting the dirt beneath them. Pulling out a small necklace from beneath her collar, she held on to the hand-carved cross on a leather cord. Where would the old man go? He possessed her family's secret. Certainly, he'd take the knowledge to the grave with him, the greedy bastard.

A thought whispered in her ear as if the trees spoke to her. Terrified, the truth of it fitting like a key in a lock, she picked up the lantern and started running.

"Colleen!" shouted Reardon, chasing after her. She paused but a moment at the gate before throwing the lock to the ground and racing down the lane. "Colleen," he repeated.

"He's at the house," she panted. Dropping the lantern, she pushed her legs, running as fast as possible, heaving in deep breaths of air.

Faster, Reardon passed her, grabbing her hand, pulling her along. By the time they reached the cottage, they were both bent over, sweating, grabbing their sides in pain. A light shone in the upper window. The front door hung open, not how she'd left the cottage.

In the yard, she saw the still body of their dog, Rufus. Dashing over the dewy grass, she reached down but saw the dog's wide-eyed stare of death. Reardon joined her, looking at the dead dog.

"Feck," he whispered. "We need weapons."

"Pa has an axe by the shed," Colleen said. She reached down and untied her shoelaces, pulling off her shoes and setting them aside. "We've a butchering knife in the barn. Wait here. I'll get it."

Moving in shadows, low to the ground, she reached the barn. Inside, even in the pitch, she found the long-bladed knife they used for slaughtering the animals. She tucked it against her side, going around the barn to the shed to retrieve the axe. Returning to Reardon, she handed him the axe.

"I can hear someone inside," he said. "I think he's upstairs."

She nodded, almost invisible in the black. "Watch the third step, it squeaks."

Phantoms, they moved across the property to the open door, stopping to listen. Noises, like upturned furniture, sounded from upstairs. Dread solidified in Colleen's stomach. If Father Dunleavy acted brazenly, her family was in a dire way.

Into the house they slipped, Colleen up the stairs first, skipping the third step. Reardon pressed right behind her, the axe held in both hands. Colleen peeked through the railing, trying to discern in which room he clamored.

Then, she saw movement in her parents' bedroom. The littlest, not but two, slept with them in a small bed on the floor. The light, a lantern, shone in her and her sisters' room. Father Dunleavy used a candle to search in the bedroom, muttering to himself, throwing things askew.

Unafraid of the man, she ran to the door, shouting his name.

Startled, the old man dropped the candle. He bent over, fumbling, and lifted it. Colleen saw the horror: the blood on his hands and face, the lifeless bodies of her parents and brother on the bed.

"What have ye done?" she choked on the words. "By the Grace of the Lord, what have ye done?"

"Ye whore, Colleen. Tell me where it is, and I'll spare yer life." He took out a gun, a small pistol from his pocket. "Tell me where it is, Colleen."

She held up her knife and Reardon his axe. "Ye aren't going anywhere, ye murdering bastard," Reardon snarled at him.

"Fecking man of the cloth, ye're nothing but a monster." "I'll shoot ye both afore ye get me," Dunleavy boasted. "Tell me where the damned chest is, Colleen! Where have ye hidden it?"

Hot tears fell down her face. "Fecking bastard. Ye'll never find yer precious chest. Go ahead, shoot me. I donna care, ye killed them all fer nothing."

"Not fer nothing, girl. I'll find those papers. With ye all dead, no one can stop me." He waved the gun at her. "Matter of time is all. Dunleavy is dead. I'm O'Byrnes' last living heir. I'll inherit it all."

Hating him, she changed the grip on the handle of the knife, and flung it at him, hoping to hit a vital organ. Instead, the blade clipped his arm. The gun went off and he shoved past Colleen and Reardon. Dunleavy stumbled down the stairs and right out the door.

The bullet went wide, hitting a beam in the ceiling, raining down plaster. Reardon, half-way down the steps, made to go after Dunleavy. "We can still get him, Colleen, if we hurry."

She fell to her knees, exhausted. "Go home, Reardon.

Change yer clothes, get back in bed. They'll be coming fer me tomorrow."

"Colleen," he stated. "I saw everything, they'll believe us." "*Ach*, they willna believe this, Reardon." She stared up at

him, seeing the despair in his handsome face. "My family is dead, murdered in their beds. I've got the mark on me. I heard it all my life, how I was born under a bad sign. Easy ta follow my tracks from the church ta here." He wanted to argue, but the first tendrils of dawn already snaked over the horizon. "Go now, Reardon. I'll be seeing ye."

After he left her, Colleen went through the house, seeing to the corpses of her family. She put their arms over their chests, fixed their nightclothes, and covered them in blankets. Weeping, she kissed them each on the forehead, praying to the

Lord to welcome them into His Paradise.

Shackled in the village goal, Colleen waited while the constabulary searched the cottage and collected the bodies. They had found her outside, in the wet grass, shoeless, speechless. They tried to force her to speak, even striking her across the face, but she remained silent.

People came by, asking the officer stationed at the tiny, single-celled gaol if everything was true. Instructed not to speak, he did anyway, telling anyone who asked the grisly details of the murders. At some point during the day, she heard Reardon and his father, both trying to stand up for her. After an evening meal of cold soup and water, an officer walked her to a public latrine, where she searched for anything metal to pick the locks. No luck. She went with him

back to the gaol, a model prisoner.

The cell boasted a hard pallet for a bed, and the night guard gave her a straw-stuffed pillow and musty blanket.

Wearing her soiled clothing, she hoped tomorrow someone would be merciful enough to let her put on a new dress.

Colleen climbed into the bed, and it within half an hour, the guard started snoring. She stared up at the cobwebs on the ceiling, swaying with the cool autumn breeze coming in from the small barred window.

"Colleen," she heard someone whisper. She ignored it, until it came again, louder. "Colleen!"

Standing on the bed, Colleen's eyes could reach the window. "Hello?"

"How do ye fare?" Reardon asked.

Silly man, she feared he'd end up in the gaol with her. "Go home, Reardon. Someone will see ye."

"Wait," he said. Colleen heard him fumbling with something, then a little bag flew through the bars, attached to a string. "I'll be waiting at the *Y* in the road. Ye better hurry."

Unable to reply, she heard him leave. Colleen climbed down and sat on the bed. In the little bag was several pieces of metal, some bent at different angles.

Lock-picking tools.

First, she removed her manacles. Easy enough – the pin on the lock to the graveyard was more complex than the manacles. At the door, she reached through and used the angled metal rods to manipulate the mechanism inside. It was a difficult task, since she was unable to see the lock. She relied on her hearing and the tension in the rod.

Colleen's arm tired as she tried to unlock the door. Biting her lip in frustration, she wanted to throw the piece of metal, until she heard the pin move and the door swung outward. Gathering the tools, she put the bag in her pocket and stepped outside the cell.

The guard slept, his head on the small desk, drool rolling down his lip. Begging forgiveness, she picked up his thick wooden billy club and cracked it against the back of his head, hoping to knock him out. She checked his breathing, and it was steady and even.

Using the manacles, she put his arms through the bars of the cell. For good measure, she also attached one of his legs to an iron bar. Taking a clean rag from his pocket, she shoved it in his mouth.

Out the door she ran, wild-eyed from her escape. The mud, cold and wet, squished between her bare toes as she headed for the road out of the village. Slowing the closer she neared the trunk of the *Y*, she clung to the side of the road, holding to the shadows.

Alone, waiting with a small rucksack, Reardon crouched down. He saw her and waved her over. "Colleen, hurry."

She ran to him, breathing heavy. "They'll put ye in the gaol if they find out ye helped me."

"Good thing they'll never find out," he said. "Brought ye some clothes, food, money. Ye've ta get out of Wicklow. Go someplace big, like Dublin or Belfast. Cut yer hair, change yer name."

She grabbed an apple from the bag and took a huge bite. "I've ta get Dunleavy. The bastard, he killed my family."

"He'll kill ye too," warned Reardon.

"Donna matter does it." She gripped his hand. "When I kill him, get the ring. Mayhaps there are other O'Byrnes. If not, the chest and ring are yers, whatever good they'll do fer ye." She slung the bag over her shoulder. "Thank ye, Reardon. Ye may've been my sole friend in Droicheaddoire. I want ye ta have a happy life. Donna marry Aisling Mohan, she inna right fer ye." Sad, she wrapped her arms around him, squeezing him tight. "See they get a proper burial. Lord, a whole family, killed in one night. I canna see the sense in it."

"Me either, Colleen," he said into her hair.

She kissed his cheek, then wiped away her tears. "I love ye, Reardon McGiffin. Keep ye safe."

Off into the dark she went, expecting never to see him again or the village she called home. Colleen headed straight to her family farm, directed there by an ancient ley line to find Father Dunleavy.

She dropped the bag by the barn, grabbing their wood pitchfork, and went to the cottage. Inside, Dunleavy moved about as if the Lord protected him from evil, unafraid of being discovered at the place where he committed such terrible acts.

Enraged, she charged at him, the tines of the fork pinning the man to the wall through the gut. Blood spurted from his mouth, spraying his lower face and clothes. His gun went off, the bullet grazing her left shoulder. She pressed the fork harder with her body.

THE CRIMES OF COLLEEN O'BYRNES BY JENNIE L. MORRIS

"Colleen," he groaned. "look what ye've done." He tried to move the gun to shoot at her again, but she twisted the pitchfork, causing severe pain. Crying out, he shook, dropping the pistol.

Red-black blood dripped down the wall. Colleen let go of the fork, picked up the pistol in her right hand, and held it at him. "Ye ruined my life, Dunleavy, fer nothing. The chest was never here, ye bastard. All this suffering fer yer greed, trying ta get O'Byrnes' titles and land back." She searched around the floor, finding a piece of broken art depicting Jesus at the Last Supper. Pulling it free from the rubbish, she flipped it over, the other side water damaged and stained with age. "Write out yer confession, Priest. Write out ye killed me family."

Trembling hands reached for the weathered canvas. "With what, Colleen?"

"Write yer sins in yer blood, Dunleavy. *I killed the O'Byrnes.*"

As he scrolled the words, dipping his index finger on the blood seeping from his gut, Colleen held the gun to his head.

When he was finished, Dunleavy let the canvas fall aside. "Ye gonna ta get the constable now, Colleen?"

"No," she replied. "I'm going ta kill ye, uncle." She pulled the trigger. The bullet entered the front of his forehead. He fell limp and slid sideways down the wall.

Unconcerned, she searched his pockets, finding his money. She tucked it away for later. The signet ring, the key to opening the box hidden at Reardon's house, was on a chain around his neck. She broke the chain, removed the ring, and put it on the leather cord along with her wooden cross.

As a child, playing in the fields, she had found the ring and brought it to her uncle. When she was older, Colleen heard the story of how the O'Byrnes heir lost the deeds to the land in a game of cards while drunk, turning them from landed gentry into poor farmers. When cleaning out the attic, Colleen discovered the old chest and recognized the lock, a perfect match to the ring.

Being a curious sort, she asked her uncle whatever happened to the ring, and he told her never to speak of it. Such a precious thing could never be found by such a dirty farm girl, and they'd throw her in the gaol for thievery.

Strange as she may be, Colleen wasn't a fool. As a prudent precaution, she asked Reardon to hide the small chest. Unfortunately, all her misgivings turned out to be correct. *Fecking Dunleavy, greedy bastard, may the Devil take him.*

She pulled his body outside and pinned his confession to his coat.

Tired of being filthy, she grabbed an enamel bowl, a hard bar of soap, and a towel from the upturned kitchen and went outside to the water pump. Priming the pump, she pulled on the clanking handle until cold, clean water ran from the spout. She dunked her head under it, scrubbing out the crusted dirt and blood, before filling the bowl. Stripping off the ruined clothing, shivering in the chill, she washed and rinsed away the traces of the past two days.

Inside the wreckage of the cottage, she managed to find clean clothes. Putting on layers, she grabbed her mother's wool coat and her best shoes. In her parents' bedroom, she moved one of the floorboards and found the small stash of money they had secreted away for an emergency. Packing a small haversack and suitcase, she went out into the night, glancing one last time at her family home, before heading off down the road toward the west.

BOSTON, MASSACHUSETTS, UNITED STATES OF AMERICA, 1890

The Sisters of the Eternal Flame Sanatorium welcomed all those suffering from the great scourge of humankind called by many names, but here they referred to it as tuberculosis. Colleen O'Byrnes, re-christened Kathy Collins, worked as an aid, caring for patients in all stages of the disease.

Right off the boat from Ireland, she had wandered the streets of Boston for two days before running into an advertisement for the posting. She showed up to the interview with no references, no education, but with a willingness and eagerness the other prospects lacked. She asked for no pay, instead requesting room and board along with basic education afforded at grammar school. The nuns and doctors at the facility gave her a six-month trial, but she stayed on for ten years, with pay.

One of her first patients, an elderly woman, helped her write a letter to Reardon. Using a false name, Mr. C. Barnum, Colleen provided him with the details of her new life and sent back the signet ring. Perhaps one day he'd be able to use it and the documents.

About a month later, she received a letter from Ms. R. Miller. For the next decade, Colleen and Reardon wrote back and forth, using the pseudonyms. She kept every letter in a box beneath her bed, on lonely nights rereading them to chase away the melancholy.

In her pressed white dress, sensible black shoes, and cap, Colleen helped feed one of the sickly patients a rich broth of beef stock. He'd turned for the worse last week, a young man withered away to skin and bones, coughing up red spittle.

The patients enjoyed her accent, still thick after years away from home. When the nuns and nurses left her alone, she told them old Irish folk tales to pass the time or read the latest installment of their favorite dime store serial. The work, physically caring for the ill, was hard. She found the emotional bonds she formed with the patients to be the harsher of the two components. Colleen lost dozens of friends to the disease. Their names were etched on her heart.

"Kathy," called one of the younger nuns. "You've visitors.

I'll finish here."

Dabbing Mr. Wilson's chin, she wished him a good afternoon before handing over the bowl to the sister.

"They're in the family luncheon room," the nun said.

Quickly, Colleen stopped by her room to change into a clean dress and reapply her lipstick. She never received visitors, not one. Glancing in the small mirror, she reached up and caressed the streak of white in her black hair. It started growing out not long after leaving Droicheaddoire, a permanent reminder of her past. She pinned back her cap and smoothed out her fresh dress, ready to meet her mystery guests.

The luncheon room, a bright, cheery space decorated with floral arrangements and plenty of depictions of holy Catholic scenes, was the main area families and patients visited in colder weather, or if the patient was too ill to stroll in the small gardens. She spent plenty of time here over the years, in the background, helping patients if needed while they spent time with family and friends. Once, she even served as a witness in a marriage.

Going through the double door entrance, Colleen glanced around the room, noting a few visitors today. She spotted a man wearing a bowler and a young woman sitting alone by a window. She watched for a moment as the young woman stared out at the street below. Colleen grabbed hold of the doorframe. Her mother. It was her mother's profile she saw in the young woman.

Weak-kneed, she approached, afraid and hopeful all at once. "Tha' canna be Reardon McGiffin, come across the great ocean to America."

The man glanced up as his face brightened. He'd grown more handsome with age on him. "Kathy, did we surprise ye?" Unable to help herself, she threw her arms around him. "Reardon, Lord above, I thought I'd die without seeing yer face again. I prayed fer this, every night," she whispered into his ear. "I've missed ye."

"Colleen," he whispered back, stroking her back. "Will be alright, lass. Been a long time coming, but I promised ye, dinna I?"

She chuckled, pressing her face into his shoulder. "Tha' ye did, Ms. Miller." Releasing him, she stepped back, letting her eyes feast upon him. He was broad, with the same dark coloring as before. No wondered he married soon after she left. "And who is yer pretty little companion?"

"Do ye not recognize me, Colleen?" the young lady said, her voice sweet and innocent.

Grabbing the young lady's hand, Colleen stared at her. Dark black hair, with their mother's nose and pale blue eyes.

Same as her dead sister, Ina, six years old when Father Dunleavy stole everything from her.

"I canna believe it, so I willna say," Colleen glanced at Reardon. "Baby Ida?"

"No longer a babe, but this is Ina, yer sister. Seems, she was a fighter like her big sister." Reardon nodded at Ida. The girl pulled down her collar, showing an old scar on her neck. "The doctor fixed her up after realizing she was alive."

Pulling Ina in her arms, Colleen held her in amazement. "Why dinna ye tell me?"

"I asked him to wait, Colleen," Ina said. "Even with the confession of tha' man, the coppers thought ye did it. Ye're still wanted fer murder. The McGiffin family raised me, sent me ta school, said I was their godchild. I was safe. If ye came back, they'd have hung ye fer murder and escaping from the goal."

Brushing away tears, Colleen kissed her sister on the cheek. "*Ach*, look at ye, near a grown woman. Ye've the look of Ma on ye, a great beauty. Going ta school, a proper education... I owe ye, Reardon. Dinna ye bring yer wife?"

Ida began laughing. "He's not married, Colleen. Mr. and

Mrs. McGiffin invite every lady over ta the house in hopes he'll pick a bride. I think he's smitten."

A small clearing of a throat interrupted their conversation. Dr. Carlston, the head physician at The Sisters of the Eternal Flame Sanatorium and Colleen's friend, waited for an introduction.

"Dr. Carlston, may I introduce my old friend and his cousin from Ireland, Mr. Reardon McGiffin and Miss Ida McGiffin. Dr. Carlston runs the facility. He is a brilliant doctor," Colleen rushed.

A handsome man, in his mid-thirties, Dr. Gregory Carlston had worked at the sanatorium a year longer than Colleen. He'd spent numerous nights teaching her how to read and write. "Kathy, I didn't know you were expecting guests. A true pleasure. Kathy is one of our favorite faces here. The patients adore her. She's been a true blessing." He placed his hand on her shoulder, a friendly gesture.

"I'm as surprised as ye, Dr. Carlston. Would ye like ta join us fer tea and coffee?" Colleen asked out of politeness.

He smiled, showing off his perfect white teeth. "I wish I could, but I've a meeting with a potential patient and his family. Someone of importance in social circles, very secretive." He shook Reardon's and Ida's hands. "A true pleasure to meet you both. If you are in Boston for a few days, I would love to invite you all out for dinner. Kathy is a book of secrets, speaks little of her life back in Ireland."

"We'll certainly entertain the idea, Dr. Carlston," Reardon said with a nod. "A pleasure. We donna want ta keep ye waiting. Ye seem ta be an important man."

"I admit, your accents are particularly charming," Carlston added, before walking away.

Colleen instructed Ida and Reardon to sit while she went to the small kitchen. Collecting tea, coffee, and an assortment of desserts, she carried a tray back to their table and poured a cup of hot coffee for herself.

"Is he yer intended, Colleen?" Ida asked, pouring a cup of tea. "He is a handsome and friendly man, appears ta think highly of ye."

Setting her coffee down, Colleen put her hands in her lap. "No, Ida. Dr. Carlston is a nice gentleman, but not my intended. We started working here bout the same time. He taught me ta read and write. We became friends. The sisters, though courteous, tend ta keep ta themselves.

"Enough bout me and this place, tell me of home. Tell me of Ireland, and yer growing up, and yer life? I canna get over how ye resemble Ma. Our parents would be proud, an O'Byrnes educated. I'm proud of ye, Ida."

"Tell her, Reardon," Ida ordered, shoving a cookie into her mouth.

Wiping his hands on a napkin, Reardon then rubbed his chin. "We went ta the courts with the documents in the chest. Is what took us so long ta visit, waiting on an answer. The magistrate, deliberating and viewing county records, ruled in our favor. They restored yer title and lands, plus a hefty sum of money, a sort of tax revenue owed. Ida, as she is considered the sole living heiress, is granted the use of the title Viscountess Donharbor, and the right ta pass this on ta her children."

"Viscountess Donharbor," Colleen repeated, the words pleasing. "A proper lady, ye are, Ida. Use the money wisely, and donna go wasting it on fashion. Buy a good house, marry a good man, and keep the money away from him, ye hear me. 'Tis yer money, family money, ye save it fer yer children."

Ida grabbed another cookie. "We've got a house, Colleen. A big manor house, tha' right, Reardon. It reverted with the title. Was being lent ta a family, the land farmed and taxes collected, no debts ta pay. We saw it on our way here. Reardon hired a respectable woman ta run the manor while we're away and got ahold of a trustworthy man ta oversee the land. County Cork if I recall."

Stunned, Colleen leaned back in the chair. "Well Ida O'Byrnes, my wealthy sister, remember where ye come from, and ye'll be alright. Yer Ma and Pa, potato and turnip farmers, simple folk with much love fer their children. Someone like Reardon helping ye, I've no doubts ye'll flourish.

"I hate ta cut this short, but I've ta get back ta work. Tell me ye'll be in Boston fer a few days. I canna go my whole life seeing ye fer thirty minutes."

Ida and Reardon got up from the table and hugged Colleen.

"We'll be back tomorrow. Reardon has something ta discuss with ye. I love ye, Colleen." Ida reached up and traced her moon-shaped birthmark. "I remember ye telling me stories, lying in bed, and me asking how the moon gotta be on yer face."

Taking her hand, Colleen kissed it. "Ye did, little one. Go on now, see some of the city. I'll be here tomorrow, waiting on ye."

Watching them leave was the hardest thing Colleen had witnessed since the death of her family. She held her breath, counted to ten, and returned to work, putting her nervous energy to good use. The rest of the day flew by, and before she realized, her shift ended. She needed to go to the main kitchen for her supper.

Changed into a simple blue dress and sweater, with her long black hair braided down her back, Colleen went to the workers' dining hall. It was a small room with five tables. She brought with her a book as usual. Accustomed to eating meals alone, she carried her meal of roasted beef and vegetables over to her vacant spot and began reading.

She had fallen in love with books, a distraction from life. Consuming them with a ferocious appetite, she read anything available in the sanatorium's library. Currently, she read a biography on a Roman Emperor, a tormented man with a terrible childhood.

"Kathy?"

She closed the book and looked up. Before her stood Dr.

Carlston, plate in hand. "Please, join me."

He pulled out the chair next to her. "What are you reading tonight?"

"A biography on Nero, the Roman Emperor." She showed him the weathered book. "Difficult ta read, but almost like a penny-dreadful."

Laughing, he agreed. "You have to be the most well-read person in this place."

"Passes the time," she replied, tucking the book on her lap. "I like ta imagine far-off places. It helps ta swallow the pain here. I listen ta these peoples' stories, and at times they're great tragedies. Lives ended ta soon, parents stolen from their children, poor folk from the streets never knowing a kind word. I do little ta ease their suffering."

"You do important work here, Kathy. Not one day have I seen you fail to give everything to help our patients." He put his hand over her hand. "It is commendable what you sacrifice to be here. Your friends, they must be dear, travelling from Ireland to visit."

She nodded her head. "I still canna believe it. Like a dream, seeing them again."

Sighing, he gripped her hand. "I have no right to ask you this, but I think we've been friends for a long time. Are you going back to Ireland, Kathy?"

"I dunno, Gregory," she answered. "There are things I've not told ye. Things tha' will change how ye perceive me. I'm unwelcome back in Ireland, at least part of Ireland."

"You can tell me anything."

She searched his expression. Open and honest, he always treated her with dignity. Disclosing a secret, like betraying a friend, was hard after a decade. With a rambling start, she glossed over the gritty details but told him the basics of her sordid past. "Tha' was my sister. I long thought her dead, and he was my best friend who's watched after her all these years."

"Kathy—Colleen, I'm speechless. What a horrible, terrible thing to happen. I understand your reason for being quiet about such a history, especially around the nuns." He gave a soft sigh. "Your uncle was a monster. How could they believe you would do such a thing to your own family?"

Turning her head, she pushed her hair aside, showing her birthmark. "In Ireland, small villages have superstitious people. When I was born, the women said I was cursed, born under an ill-omen. In a way, they were right. Priests are sacred beings, the Lord's vessels on earth. Ta think of him harming his relatives – no one would believe me. The villagers still believe I murdered my family. Ireland is dangerous, but ta live without my sister, my last flesh and blood. A hard question ta answer, Gregory."

"Does Mr. McGiffin weigh in on your decision? It appears he has feelings for you, Colleen," he added.

"He's a good friend. I willna lie, in my youth, I thought perhaps I loved him. But it was an irrational love, as it was unrealistic. My family, poor farmers, and his being well-off, not a match." She sipped her cold tea. "Does it matter, Gregory? Ye're a handsome doctor. I imagine ye've women lined up ta go on social occasions with ye. Some of Boston's finest young ladies waiting fer yer attention."

Laughing, he shook his head. "I spend too much time here to be social. It matters, well, because I've been a fool, and should have asked you years ago, out to dinner. I like you, Colleen. I've liked you for a long time. Ever since you walked into the interview, filled with fire to get the position here. For all my academic and professional accolades, I'm afraid I'm rather a nervous person when it comes to personal affairs."

THE CRIMES OF COLLEEN O'BYRNES BY JENNIE L. MORRIS

Flattered, she blushed. Through her work, Colleen grew accustomed to men paying her absurd compliments from their sick beds. She liked to jest with them, but everyone realized it was in fun. Gregory's intentions were not flirtations, but the words of a sincere man.

"Ta be honest, Gregory, I'm surprised," she replied in an intentionally light tone. "Ye're a good man, a wonderful friend. Since arriving in America, I imagined my life spent as a spinster. Paying penance here, helping the sick, when I failed in helping my own family. Imma soured woman, Gregory. I've hate in my heart, and no amount of praying will take it away. I'll always hate my uncle." She stared at the table, ashamed of her past, even if she'd kill Father Dunleavy again. "Ye deserve a better person than me — a pretty, innocent lady, refined and elegant. I'm a rough Irish lass, better at picking potatoes than fitting inta society. What will yer colleagues think, courting the Irish trash?"

Bold, he laced his fingers with her. "Before you make your choice, please think about my offer. I can't compete with a past now returned to you, but I ask for you to consider my proposal. When have I ever cared for society? My colleagues hide mistresses or are lushes. Not all physicians are reputable people." He kissed the back of her hand. "I'll see you tomorrow, Colleen O'Byrnes."

The next afternoon, Colleen was given leave for several hours to explore the city with her visitors. Ida and Reardon brought her to a fine eatery not far from their hotel, where they shared a bottle of wine in honor of reunions.

Bursting with joy, Colleen listened to their stories of Ireland. She heard of Ida's childhood in the McGiffin home, and of her time spent at a school for girls, where she completed a degree in teaching at such a young age. Reardon shared the antics of a youthful and rebellious Ida, a wild girl much like her older sister.

With the backing of the McGiffins, no one in Droicheaddoire or County Wicklow taunted Ida about what happened to her family and her murderess sister, Colleen the Crazed. Of course, they whispered it behind her back, Ida said, but the gossip died down until it was hardly mentioned, and then in a sort of tragic way. Each year, a small gathering placed flowers on the family tombstone, each of their names carved on a large pillar of granite in the Church of Saint Columbanus' graveyard.

"Good ta hear they pay respects ta the family," Colleen said, dabbing at her eyes. "I feared they bury them in paupers' graves, thinking them unfit."

Reardon shook his head. "My father demanded a proper burial fer them all, and no one argued. Even took up a collection ta donate money towards the tombstone."

"I'll be back," Ida announced, sliding out of her chair. She headed towards the lavatories.

Reardon rolled his eyes. "She's not subtle, yer sister. I might as well ask ye, fer if I donna ask ye now, she'll hound me all day. Come back ta Ireland with us, Colleen. Come back and live at this manor house. No one will recognize ye in County Cork. We can start anew. We're still young."

"Are ye asking fer Ida or fer ye, Reardon?"

"Both," he said with a shy smile. "Ye said those words ta me, then left, without waiting fer a reply. I've loved ye, Colleen since ye was ten years old, and we sat under the oak tree. I dinna see it as punishment, spending time with the prettiest girl." He cleared his throat. "Everything went wrong. It shouldna happened how it did, and I lost ye over it."

First, she thought he meant her family's tragedy, but a heaviness weighed on him. "Ye've got a secret, Reardon McGiffin. I see it on ye, like a bag of brick 'round yer neck."

He paled, shaking his head. "Forget it, Colleen. It matters not. We're here now, together. We can be together again."

"Tell me, Reardon, or I walk out tha' door, and ye'll never see me again. God help me, I will." She glared at him, gripping her hands.

Covering his eyes, they teared up. "Colleen, I dinna know what he was gonna do. I swear on the Holy Bible I'd have told him no. We thought it was a jest, a game he wanted ta play on the villagers bout sinning. Dug a small tunnel, rigged the casket, and like a miracle he'd be walking the earth again. Father Dunleavy killed the other two tha' helped him, found their bodies two days later in the lake. I dinna know, I swear, tha' he intended ta hurt yer family."

Silent for a moment, she waited, unable to look at her best friend and believe him. Ida returned, the smile dying on her lips.

"Ye're not going back ta Ireland with us, Colleen?" she asked, sorrowful.

Hiding her betrayal, Colleen forced a smile at Ida. "I've not decided yet, sister. Reardon made a strong case in favor of it, which I'll consider. Fer now, my dearest one, I've ta get back. This afternoon has been a rare delight. I promise ye'll not have ta wait long fer my answer." She kissed Ida on the cheek. "I love ye, Ida. My beautiful, intelligent sister."

She walked over and kissed Reardon on his stubbled cheek. "Meet me tonight, at the sanatorium. We've more ta discuss." Stepping back, she thanked them for a lovely afternoon and looked forward to tomorrow.

On her walk back to the sanatorium, she seethed. Colleen, engrossed in her thoughts, passed the steps leading up to the front door. She went straight to her room, changed into her uniform, and started work, all the time thinking of her folly.

After the evening meal, the ambulatory patients liked to play games or dance in the main recreation hall. Colleen supervised, helped change the music, and occasionally served as a dance partner. She played games with cards and dice, and she was usually a threat to the competition, but her heart wasn't in it tonight. When refreshments of lemonade and small snacks arrived on a cart, she dished them out, trying to maintain light conversation with the patients.

One of the best remedies she'd found was hope, not giving up on life, but to celebrate and continue forward. Those who tried to act normal, interacting with their fellow patients and staff, tended to live longer and stave off the advanced stages of the infection for far longer than those who gave up as soon as they walked in the doors.

Near ten o'clock, curfew for patients to be abed, Colleen went to the front doors and saw Reardon sitting on the steps, waiting. She opened the door and invited him in.

"Would ye like tea or coffee, Reardon?" she asked, heading up to her private quarters.

"No. I'm fine, Colleen."

In her room, she shut the door and locked it. "Snooping nuns," she said, setting the key on her dressing table. She offered him the wooden chair at her desk while she perched on the edge of her bed.

"Does Ida know, Reardon?" Colleen asked, unpinning her white cap.

He shook his head. "No one knows. I tried telling my Pa when they put ye in the gaol, but he was busy trying ta get ye released he dinna have time ta listen."

"Ten years, Reardon. Hundreds of letters. A simple confession, but ye held on ta it." More tears. It pained her, seeing him cry, but a cold core of loss dampened her emotions. "I donna think I can forgive ye, Reardon."

Falling to the floor, he knelt before her. His head bent on her knee. "I'm tormented, Colleen. Every day, I hate myself fer what I did ta ye and yer family. Do ye think I'd purposely hurt ye? God smite me if ye think tha' be true. I was a foolish boy, listening ta a tricky fecking bastard. He wormed his way inta my head. I believed it was a lesson he was teaching the village. How could I've realized he meant ta harm yer family?" Removing his bowler, she ran her hand through his hair, comforting him like a child. "He tricked ye, Reardon. Dunleavy, a terrible man." With her other hand, she worked out the straight razor shaving knife from her pocket. "All will be well, Reardon. Debts and payments rendered." When he glanced up, she ran the straight razor across his neck, opening the skin, a gush of red flowing.

Unbelieving, he reached up with his hands, trying to stop the bleeding.

"Quiet, Reardon," she said, sliding to the floor, holding him in her arms. "I love ye, Reardon. I always have, and I always will."

COUNTY CORK, IRELAND, 1893

Colleen held her swollen belly, while Ida ran in the succulent gardens of Groomsnora Manor, collecting butterflies for her studies. The verdant land stretched out before Colleen, soft rolling hills, dotted by their sheep and cattle herds. Their prized horses were in the paddock, the farrier affixing new shoes.

"What is my stunning wife doing this morning?" Gregory asked, bringing her a cup of tea with a slice of lemon. He wrapped his hands around her, enjoying the transformation of her body as their child grew.

"What is my handsome husband doing this morning?" she returned the question, kissing him on the cheek. "Off ta visit patients, I think."

He rested his head close to her cheek. "Perhaps, but it's a gorgeous day. We should take the carriage and go for a picnic by the little spring. What do you think?"

How he enjoyed spoiling her. "Dr. Carlston? Shirking yer duties?"

He kissed her neck, and she tilted her head, providing him access to the tender spot. "If you keep this up, Mrs. Carlston, we won't leave the house at all today."

"I'm fine with tha'," she teased. "A'course, I'm as big as a house."

"Maybe I like my women big as houses," he nipped at her ear. She giggled and slapped at his arm. "Let me get dressed,

ye devilish man. Tell Ida of our plan. She loves a good picnic." He kissed her again before heading down the hall. She watched him leave, rubbing her belly. That man would do anything for her, as he already proved.

At the sanatorium, he hauled Reardon's body to the basement for cremation. Helped her clean up the mess in her room. He conjured the lie to tell Ida about Reardon's sudden departure. He even left Boston, turning in his notice and training a replacement. Six months after Colleen brought Ida back to Groomsnora Manor, Gregory showed up with a bouquet of flowers and a wedding ring.

At first, Colleen felt obligated to marry him. Over time, however, she found in Gregory Carlston a partner. His lust for life and love of Ireland brought back a joy long missing in her heart. The return of her sister Ida, Colleen, finally had a perfect family. Sins of the past no longer woke her in the night; she slept dreamless and content.

THE CRIMES OF COLLEEN O'BYRNES BY JENNIE L. MORRIS

As a self-proclaimed Anglophile and research geek, it's no wonder that Jennie L. Morris writes Romance and Historical Fiction with a flair for realism. Her love for learning led her to obtain degrees in Anthropology and Biology, which she often relies on during her writing process. Coming from NE Ohio, and raised on a small beef cattle farm, life was anything but ordinary growing up.

Jennie now resides in rural Kentucky, among the bluegrass and dazzling horse farms, with her amazing husband and their boxer Archie. When she isn't reading or writing, she is feeding her tea obsession or perfume addiction, letting the scents and flavors fuel her creative fires.

When Sith Arrives
by Douglas Ford

WHEN SITH ARRIVES BY DOUGLAS FORD

[EDITOR'S WARNING: ANIMAL ABUSE]

They said they planned to drown the kitten, the old lady and the little girl, but not if I took it home with me. Just a little kitten, I saw, almost full black,

just a small map of white on its chest, and all ears.

I knew my mother would say no, but what could I do? I had my arms full of the books I just checked out, and I could think only about what I would do with those when I saw the empty burlap sack sitting near the old woman's feet. They could hold my books—storybooks, mostly, including the stories about Brer Rabbit I asked the librarians to find for me, the one that had the retellings by Julius Lester I wanted because they didn't have that ignorant-sounding plantation talk that Mama like to criticize. I wanted to show her that not all books made us sound like that, even with the old stories. She disapproved of a lot of things, like old books. And cats.

"You can take it," the old woman said, referring to the kitten. "Bad luck to kill a cat, especially this close to Halloween, so I'd prefer you go on and just do that—take it."

The girl, perhaps her granddaughter, held the kitten to her chest, like she didn't want it to get away.

"Distemper," continued the old woman. "Nothing else to do but put it out of its misery. Drowning's the best way I know." They sat on a porch attached to one of the ramshackle houses that lined the street leading to the library. She looked at my books and seemed to read my mind. She indicated the burlap sack. "I was going to use that to drown the cat. Good bag. I'll let it go for a dollar. Throw in the cat for free. You got money, girl?"

Next to them was a crudely carved pumpkin, already rotting in the heat despite Halloween being still several days away. I reached into my pocket, feeling for the change I saved for lunches. I counted out a dollar. I gestured toward a dish of milk sitting on the stoop.

"Can I take that, too?"

"That's for Sith," said the woman. "Halloween's coming, and you got to be ready for Sith in case he comes calling early."

I figured Sith to be another cat of theirs, but I saw no sign of it.

That's how I got the cat.

I didn't know what distemper was, but Mamaw knew.

"You stupid girl," she said. She wouldn't touch the kitten, and she told my brother, Marcus, not to go near it either. She spoke to me from the other side of the screen door, barring the way inside of the house.

"They were going to drown it," I said. "*Drown it.*"

"That's what you do to a cat with distemper," said my mother, and from where he watched over her shoulder, Marcus laughed. Night approached, and from the other side of the screen door I could smell the pork chops she'd prepared for dinner. My stomach rumbled.

"What in the sack?" said Marcus.

"Books," I said, "but don't worry, they're not for you." Though almost twenty-one, Marcus didn't read much and preferred magazines with naked ladies in them. I knew where he hid those magazines and almost said something so Mama would know, too. I thought about what he'd do to me later, so I bit my tongue.

Mama said, "Take out those books and have that bag ready. Looks like we're going to the swamp." She turned without acknowledging what I heard: somewhere, back of me, what sounded like a witch's cackle, and momentarily I imagined that the old woman and her granddaughter were watching from the shadows beginning to pool in the street and surrounding houses. Just a Halloween decoration, I corrected myself, though commemorations of the coming holiday remained sparse on our block. In the distance, something did duck behind a hedge, and though it looked like a little girl, I paid it no mind.

From inside the house I heard my mother command Marcus to find the car keys. He complained about dinner going cold, but she yelled something back that put this complaint to rest. Again, my stomach rumbled. In my arms, the kitten cried. Its sound blended with the memory of the name spoken by the old woman, as if repeated over and over, an incantation for protection. *Sith, Sith, Sith.*

But we certainly wouldn't need it. I never believed my mother would drown this kitten. She just wanted to scare me from bringing home any more animals. Unmoving, I faced the screen door, doing my best to look repentant. Mom got no chance to see it though because Marcus appeared in the door first and plowed me out of the way to make room for our mother, who swung her purse and directed us to the old car that barely even ran anymore.

"You drive, Marcus, and you," pointing to me with her crooked index finger, "grab that sack."

I followed, feeling helpless and having nowhere to run, and I held the kitten and the bag with my books all in one hand as I opened the rear door. Instead of getting in the front seat with Marcus, Mom sat in the rear seat opposite me.

The streetlights that actually worked began to flicker and glow with yellow, not doing much to cut through the settling darkness.

"You didn't empty the sack like I told you," said Mom, regarding the mound on the seat between us. The kitten squirmed in my arms, and when I made no move to empty the bag's contents, she picked it up herself, and the books spilled out onto the seat.

Normally, she showed a lack of curiosity about the books I checked out of the library, but for some reason she picked up the top title—the one by Julius Lester—and she regarded it in the flickering yellow light that passed by the car window. "More talking animals." She spoke these words with

judgment.

"Not just any talking animals," I said. "These are ancestral stories."

"Ancestral stories," she repeated.

From the driver's seat, Marcus laughed, and Mom hit him the back of the head with the book.

"Just drive," she said. "Wait. Take the next turn."

"I thought we were going to the swamp," said Marcus. "We are. I just decided we're going a different way." So

Marcus turned down a road I never even noticed before, one I wouldn't imagine leading anywhere good.

"I'll tell you an ancestral story," said Mom. "It even has talking animals. Who gave you that cat, anyway?" I noted that she refused to even look at the kitten. It pawed at my shirt and teased out a loose thread.

"I don't know. Some old white lady."

"Some old white lady. There you go. Marcus, there's another road coming up. You see it?"

"I see it. It looks like pig trail."

"Well, you turn on it. We're taking a different direction tonight. Going to show the two of you something. How old you think that lady was? The one who gave you a sick cat?"

I didn't know how to answer. I considered myself well-read for my age, but that didn't make me an authority on people's ages. "Sixty?" I said, using a number I thought cast the widest net amongst the elderly.

"Okay, sixty. That would make this story older than even her. Don't miss the next turn, Marcus. Road's going to run out if you do."

"Nothing marked out here, Mama." He hunched over the wheel as he struggled to make out shapes in the darkness.

"Turn on the brights, then. So, before this old white woman was even a baby, people were telling the story I'm about to tell you, and you wouldn't find it in any library. Not that anyone with a complexion like ours would even be allowed in the library. You think you're treated differently now, you wouldn't even recognize that world. If one of us folks even looked at a white person the wrong way, along comes trouble of the worst sort. And that's what happened in this story—a feckless young man in a general store forgets to look down in the presence of a white woman who came with a craving for pickles and sardines. You know the circumstances I'm talking about?"

I nodded.

"I can't see you, so you better answer me," she said. "Pregnant," I said, using a word I knew she didn't like.

But no rebuke came. "That's right, and for whatever reason, she worried her daddy would throw a fit, make her marry someone she didn't love, maybe kill the one she did love. I don't know. I just know she pointed at that young man who didn't know where to direct his gaze, and she screamed that word."

"He rape her?" said Marcus. For whatever reason, I didn't want to share this story with him. And something about him saying *rape* made my skin crawl.

"That's what she said, only it wasn't true. And that stupid man didn't know much, but he knew enough to run like hell out there. Get a head-start before they could organize a manhunt and track him down. But where does an ignorant man like that go, one who lived here all his life?"

As if she planned it to happen, the car began to slow. Marcus leaned further over the wheel. I felt the cat purr. "Road's running out," said Marcus.

"Turn the wheel left," Mama said, and when Marcus did, the headlights illuminated a portion of a white structure, what I soon recognized as not just a house, but a mansion— an old mansion, run-down, but once majestic, with tall columns framing its front door and kudzu running up its decaying walls. I had no idea we lived anywhere near such an edifice. Seeing it sent a chill down my back.

"People live there?" said Marcus.

"No—not for over a hundred years. That's the old Rosemount house, gone to rot. Used to run the wheels of commerce around here, mostly the turpentine business. The family had its hands in other dealings, depending on who told the story. Some of it unsavory, mostly dealing with the slaves they kept. Black magic, voodoo. Anyway, that man in my story? Probably just a generation or two from being a slave on this land. Even so, probably got his hands dirty forging turpentine for the railroad to take north. Thankless enough work that he felt like a slave."

From outside came the sound of frogs and crickets, along with other creatures of the swamp. The kitten in my arms suddenly hissed and swiped at the car window, as if striking at the mansion. "You said your story had talking animals," I said. "I'm getting to that. This hapless man accused of rape started making his way through the swamp, and he decides he won't get too far before a boat of white men come along and pick him up. On dry land, the dogs'll sniff him out and rip him to shreds. If they don't get him, the gators would—he knew that for sure. That's when he came across that manse

you see out there, sinking like an old forgotten locomotive. "He didn't just invite himself in, and though he knew it to

be abandoned, he watched for lights in the windows. When he saw none, he pressed his face against the windowpane and looked for signs of life. Just shadows inside, but he could make out what looked like a big, comfy smoking chair right near a big old fireplace. He couldn't think of anything better than a crackling fire so he could dry his soaking clothes. So, he went inside."

From outside the car, the night pressed in upon us. The cat

relaxed again and went back to purring. The mansion looked like a thing crouching and waiting to pounce. Even Marcus kept his mouth shut and waited for Mama to continue.

"Didn't take much to get inside. No lock on the door, and no problem finding kindling for the fire. He found himself too tired and weak to care about anyone seeing smoke rise from the chimney. Soon enough he plunked himself down in the chair and wondered how long he should take before moving on. Probably as long as he could stand the smell of mold that filled that old room.

"By and by, he heard something in the foyer behind him. He ducked down in the chair—the back of it faced the door —and brought his knees up close to his chest to keep hidden. Maybe someone on the hunt might take a quick look inside, and when they didn't see him, they'd figure he moved on. He stayed still, dreading the sound of an approach.

"Something approached, all right, but not a man. It was a cat, a black one as big as a dog. As the animal pawed its way to the fireplace, he relaxed a bit, though the size of it gave him some pause. Not enough to begrudge a fellow creature in need some of the fire he built, so long as it kept a fair distance. Some of his unease came back when he saw what the creature did: that cat went up to the fire and plucked out a burning coal with its mouth. Then it stretched itself out and began sucking on it.

"That man didn't care much for such an animal in his presence, but not enough to give up his chair, nor that fire, so he uttered a quick prayer and settled back. Just as he got comfortable again, he heard more commotion behind him. 'This is it,' he thought, and once more, he pulled his knees up.

"What came along wasn't a human, but another black cat, this one even bigger than the first. The size of a bear cub this time. That cat gave him a quick look that said it didn't think much of him, and then it walked past his feet and sidled up next to the smaller one. In like manner, it plucked out a coal from the fire and began sucking. Then it spoke."

Here it comes, I thought, listening, barely breathing. With the animal noises outside, I heard a cackle like before, but neither Marcus nor Mama seemed to notice. Mama continued:

"It said, 'Have preparations been met?' The fugitive just sat there, not sure if he should reply. What preparations? But he didn't have to say nothing. Instead, the first cat answered. It said, 'We have to wait for Seth.'"

Hearing that name woke something inside me. I thought of the name used by the old woman when talking about that dish of milk. I wanted to ask her to repeat the name, but smartly, I kept quiet and waited for more.

"That poor man said nothing, but he did a lot more praying in that head of his. He didn't know what he did to deserve any of this. Woke up that morning, just expecting an average day, but you know what I taught you. Marcus, you remember anything I taught you?"

"Not to expect nothing," Marcus said.

"That's right. Good boy. And let this story serve as a reminder, because there was more strangeness to come. Just a few more minutes pass with the fugitive shivering in his chair, the cats watching him while sucking on their coals, and then he hears another round of commotion behind him, even louder than before, like something breaking in. This time, along comes an even bigger, blacker cat than the other two combined, this one as big as a pony. That man thinks maybe Seth has shown up. But this cat, it walks over to the fire and beds itself down in the flames, like he just found the most comfortable mattress in the world. He looks at the man and blinks his big red eyes real slow and says, 'What are we going to do with him?' The first cat, the smallest one, answers: 'Nothing 'til Seth arrives.'"

My mother fell silent, as if listening to the sounds outside.

At first, I thought she might have heard the cackle. I silently waited for her to say something.

"That the end?" Marcus said. "What happened?"

"What do you *think* happened?" Mama said, her voice suddenly strained. We jumped, both Marcus and me. The realization that something nagged my mother set in, and for the first time, I sensed that she hated me for making her go out here. The story, I thought, only served to buy her time to think, and I felt sure that she would now tell us we could go home and bring the cat with us.

No such luck though.

Instead, she suddenly snatched the kitten from my arms with one hand while with the other she shook the burlap sack open. Before I could protest, she had the kitten stuffed inside it and held it across the seat for Marcus to take.

The story served as a diversion, alright—a diversion for me so she could take the kitten when I least expected it. I hollered, but Mama spoke louder and told Marcus to get out of the car. "Straight ahead—there's the water's edge. You can see it in the headlights. Watch where you walk and don't fall in like a fool."

My mother held me in the seat—not to comfort me, but to keep me from running out after Marcus. I fought her, but she proved stronger, and in a state of struggle, we watched Marcus take the burlap bag to the water's edge. In the headlights we saw him throw the bag with all his might. In the distance, we saw a splash.

I let out a wail, and Marcus smiled triumphantly in the headlights.

But as he began walking back, something caused him to trip.

It was the kitten. Somehow, it made it out of the bag, and it swam back to shore. Probably ran on the water, justifiably terrified. Swearing, Marcus grabbed it by the scruff and held it up for Mama to see.

"Throw it back in," she yelled, "harder!"

Marcus nodded, and I took up my screaming again.

Holding it by the scruff, Marcus hoisted it back and threw it toward the water. Again, a faint splash. Again, Marcus smiled. And again, something got caught up between his feet when he started walking back.

The kitten had done it again.

"Do it again," Mama said, and the whole terrible process started once more. Again, the same results, and so he tried again and again. By then, I stopped my wailing and crying, and I heard myself laughing, practically cackling like a witch.

"You can't do it, he won't let you," I sang, positively joyful, and for no certain reason, that name came back, not the way my mother said it, but the way the old woman had. "Sith won't let you. Sith won't die." This flustered both my mother and Marcus, so on the last try, Marcus threw him further than before, and this time, he turned and ran back to the car. In the headlights, I saw a little black shape appear at the water's edge, but by then, Marcus had found his way back behind the wheel.

And I couldn't have heard what I heard then—Mama shouting, "Drive over it, Marcus," because she would never say such a cruel thing. But Marcus said, "Alright, you little shit," and he put the car into gear.

I felt the bump. We all felt it. Then I began screaming all over again. And I kept screaming as Marcus put the car into reverse, rolling back until we felt the bump again. I began pleading then---please, please, let me get out of the car to see if it's alright—but Mama held me, and Marcus shifted the gears so that we could roll forward again. Once again, that bump.

I fell silent, watching that abandoned mansion disappear into the darkness as Marcus returned us to the road that took us here.

The silence in the car broke when Marcus asked a question.

"So, what happened after the third cat came in?"

"What?" Mama said. Her hold on me hadn't relaxed, as if she feared I'd open the door and jump out into the road.

"The story with the cats," Marcus said. He looked at us in the rear-view mirror, his stupid face smiling.

"What do you think happened?" Mama said.

The smile wavered for a moment, as usually happened when you asked Marcus to think.

"I wish Sith had shown up," I whispered, but neither reacted to my words.

"Wasn't a true story," Marcus said. "I only like true stories. Not that made up shit."

"It was plenty true," said Mama. "And I'll tell you what happened. The fugitive ran off after the horse-sized cat came in."

"And that was the end?" said Marcus, squinting like a true skeptic.

"No," said my mother. "The end is that the lynch mob caught him. They hung him to a tree until he was half-dead, and then they burnt him to a crisp. After that, they celebrated. And that's a true story."

"He should've waited for Sith," I whispered.

My mother just looked at me like I'd spoken in French.

Nobody spoke of the kitten in the days that followed, Mama acting like none of it happened. I spent more time in the library, and it came to light that Marcus had a girlfriend, as unlikely as that seemed.

On evenings he made it home, Mama quizzed him, and

eventually it came to light that this girlfriend either lived with a man or—even worse—was married.

Mama called him a fool.

"You start messing with married women, trouble follows. It always does," she said over dinner.

"He can't do nothing to me," Marcus said, as if that would allow the whole subject to drop. But Mama kept asking questions, and eventually she got the other man's name out of him.

Sid. Only I heard it different.

"Like the cat's name," I said, and they both looked at me, Marcus chewing in that loud way of his.

"What'd you say?" Mama said. "What cat?"

"The one in that story you told us," I said. "Seth. 'Wait 'til Seth arrives.'"

"That wasn't the name. It was Martin. 'Wait 'til Martin arrives.' You don't listen."

"I heard you just fine. You called the one the cats were waiting on Seth."

In truth, I'd spent my time at the library trying to uncover the source of the story Mama told us and had come up with nothing. I even had the librarians helping me, and all I succeeded in doing was frustrate them. I even asked them for factual accounts of fugitives running from lynch mobs in local histories, but they said no such thing ever happened in our neck of the woods. When I asked about the old mansion, they hadn't heard of that either.

"You hear Mama call the cat Martin?" I asked Marcus. He told me to shut up and let him eat.

The next day at the library I tried again, this time using the name Martin. Still no luck. Then I tried a different name —Sith.

The librarians huffed at me, but one of them came back with something from the Halloween display: a book about superstitions. In its pages, I finally found something useful. Some people believed in a large black cat, the Queen of Cats, one that the descendants of the Celts called Sith. She prowled about on Samhain, what we now call Halloween, and if you didn't want her messing in your business, you needed to put out a saucer of milk in front of your house.

I thought of the old woman and her granddaughter.

I made sure to pass their house on the way home, and sure enough, I saw the two of them waiting on the porch, as if they expected me to come calling. In place of the old pumpkin sat a new one, carved with a grinning jack-o-lantern face.

"You still got the kitten?" said the old woman, calling to me from where they sat.

"Yes, I do," I said. Then I added to the lie just to see what she'd say. "I named it Sith."

"Bad luck to name a cat like that," she said. "That's a witch's name." Her granddaughter fidgeted, and the old woman held her still. Briefly I got the impression that the girl looked different, and for an instant, she looked like a prisoner. *Did you eat the last one*? I almost said, but I decided I ought not. Instead, my attention shifted to the saucer of milk still sitting where I'd seen it last.

"You get a new cat?" I said.

"I told you what that was for," she said, noticing where my eyes shifted. "You get on home. You putting on a bedsheet and going out for tricks and treats?"

I'd forgotten all about Halloween falling on a Saturday, this very day in fact. I lied and said that I planned to dress up, just nothing with a white sheet.

"You best get on home then. Sith'll be waiting for you," she said.

At home, I thought about putting a dish of milk outside

our door. Our house contained no decorations— Mama didn't want strangers coming to her door—but I knew she wouldn't let me waste anything from her refrigerator, especially not for a Halloween superstition. As I settled in, I felt good about not doing so. If Sith would come, I would welcome it. That night, I dreamed of kittens as big as horses.

In the morning, I awoke to screaming. Mama screaming.

Something got in during the night, though you couldn't tell by the way the windows remained intact and the way the furniture stayed orderly and in place.

Everywhere, that is, except Marcus' room.

His body lay in the middle of the floor, amongst the chaos of toppled drawers and shredded sheets and magazine pages.

Something had ripped into his body, too, though neither Mama nor I had heard fighting or any kind of commotion. Along with the smaller cuts on his body, the cut on his throat went deeper and longer than all the rest, nearly removing his head from the rest of his body. We heard no yelling, no screaming in the middle of the night though.

Police explained that by what covered his head. A burlap sack.

I never told anyone what I suspected: that this was the same sack we used when trying to drown the kitten.

If I said what I suspected—no, what I *knew*—Mama would just accuse me of lying. Or once she stopped blaming Sid, or whatever name that other man went by, she would blame me of something worse. Like complicity. Would she be all that wrong?

Before the police closed the case as unsolvable, they collected alibis from everyone.

But Mama went on talking about Sid. She still talks about how that man got off scot-free.

And me, I know about another explanation.

WHEN SITH ARRIVES BY DOUGLAS FORD

And I always keep a saucer of milk outside my door.

Author's Note: The story used by the mother in the story to distract her daughter has appeared in various forms, particularly in African American folklore. I am indebted to this tradition for providing an important component to this story. For readers interested in a more undiluted form of the story, I recommend the version called "Better Wait Till Martin Comes," which appears in *The People Could Fly: American Black Folktales told by Virginia Hamilton.*

Hugging Red Maggie
by J. J. Smith

HUGGING RED MAGGIE BY J.J. SMITH

[EDITOR'S WARNING: SEXUAL ASSAULT]

Yule Clary, husband, teacher and now event organizer, listened as his wife and another woman, the woman who was responsible for the nightmare that the school sponsored Corn Maze of Fear had become, spoke behind him, as if he weren't there.

"It's simple. You'll do as you agreed and give your husband 15 lashes," Evin Zinnert said to Yule's wife Autumn. Yule could hear Autumn sobbing as she picked up the cat-o-nine tails that lay on the platform. Tightly gripping his fists, clenching his jaw, and pushing his shoulders up against the cross beam of the stocks, he readied himself to be whipped. How the maze—which started as three-and-a-half acres of a fun fund-raiser for the high school where Yule and Autumn taught—became ground zero for the diabolic, he didn't know...

Only a week earlier, Yule was marveling at the dried-out stalks swaying in the cool October breeze. It was a beautiful sight, one he never would have witnessed if he hadn't come up with the idea of a Halloween-themed attraction as a fund-raiser. The stalks were the cherry on top of the full cake the evening had become. He thought of it that way because it was the first night of the maze—which wasn't a maze at all but rather a course that visitors, mostly youths, were willing to pay to pass through to get a quick, safe scare from the several frightening scenes that dotted the course.

It was a huge success, which made Yule seem smarter to the school's staff, parents and volunteers. He was the one who'd proposed the idea that they could attract enough visitors willing to pay $15 per head to walk among the stalks to justify the effort. Proving him right, on opening night the corn maze attracted 152, and with the sales of hot dogs, cold drinks, and tee-shirts, more than $2,200 was earned for the school's sports and extra-curricular activities programs.

During the week that led up to opening night, Yule had experienced a few fears of his own, but those fears disappeared because the first night's take had more than justified all the work expended by staff and students alike. Most of the school was involved with this project in one way or another.

Why a course and not an actual maze? Well, no one would get lost in a course as they could in a maze, thereby allowing the visitors to enjoy the attractions, which were scary but not too scary. The scenes were designed to give teens and young adults a quick fright, not induce trauma.

Near the entrance was the first scene: a sinister "scarecrow" who stood on a platform surrounded by corn stalks, and whose arms were spread wide on a post and lintel like a traditional scarecrow. He would step off the platform to welcome the guests and give them a quick rundown of what to expect. The scarecrow was played by a member of the school drama club. He would end the greeting by stepping back onto the platform and resume being a scarecrow.

The other scenes included more spookiness. Witches were stirring a cauldron that had rubber hands and feet floating in the soup, and they said they needed "more meat". An evil clown named Pogo had some boys tied to posts, and he would taunt the boys, who acted scared and said they "wanted to go home".

A farmer named Ed wore a disguise that had been cut from a mask portraying a former president so that it looked like he was wearing someone's face. Ed would ask the crowd if they liked his mask. He'd follow up with, "I took it off a trick-or-treater." Those parts were played by drama club members and adult volunteers, many of whom were alumni, which was a testament to the club's faculty advisor Mr. Gould. As soon as the scenes were decided upon, Mr. Gould organized auditions that attracted a plethora of participants.

That was followed by rehearsals the level of which had casual observers believing Mr. Gould was preparing the players for the Shakespeare Festival and not the corn maze. But the students loved it; they even took to calling themselves "Mr. Gould's Ghouls". On opening night, the course was peppered with not only Gould's Ghouls but also ghosties and senior class beasties, the latter of which lurked in the stalks waiting to go bump in the night with the visitors, especially nervous freshmen.

So why did they call it a maze when it wasn't one? Marketing, that's why, because who would want to go to the "Corn Course of Fear"? Admittedly, a course misidentified as a maze wasn't very educational, but so what? He was proud of what he'd produced, and there were eight more nights to go until Halloween. The first two nights and the last two were weekends.

They could expect to sell more tee-shirts, which featured the sinister scarecrow between two corn stalks, beckoning guests to enter under a shockingly lettered sign that said, "Corn Maze of Fear". The money collected from the first night's admissions and concessions strengthened Yule's belief that the fund raiser would surpass its goal of $8,000. It didn't look bad for the teacher who'd organized the whole thing.

That very relieved teacher spent the last few hours supervising the volunteers, overseeing ticket and concession sales, and dealing with problems as they arose. One such problem was that eight visitors hadn't yet completed their tour through the course, which was now closed for the evening. *What a weird way to end the night*, Yule thought as he started his search at the end of the course, but he just shrugged and smiled. *Well, it is almost Halloween.*

Yule passed three of the scenes, and as he did, he directed the students staffing those scenes to sit tight because a few more visitors had to pass through the maze, and he was going to hurry them along. At the next scene, he was surprised, and relieved, to find all eight missing guests.

Most of those guests did not enter the maze together, much less as a single group, so he didn't expect to find them all at the Red Maggie Whipping Post scene. "Red Maggie" was the name given to the town's whipping post. It had been used in the 17th and early 18th centuries to punish thieves, swindlers, gossips, perjurers, blasphemers, and practitioners of witchcraft, in many cases before they were executed.

While it was called a whipping post, Red Maggie actually was a single column that held a pillory in a lowercase "T" design, enabling the stocks to hold the hands and heads of two prisoners, thereby leaving their backs exposed and putting them in the perfect position for a flogging.

Those placed in that position were said to be "Hugging Red Maggie," which, according to the town historical society, was so named because it was painted red to disguise the blood that was left behind. The historical society had the actual Red Maggie in its collection, and the curator graciously allowed carpentry students to take measurements and photos of the pillory, which time had dulled to a muddy red, so they could produce the scarlet replica that was now the focus of a handful of visitors watching "Noira the Witch"—as played by school alumna Evin Zinnert—receive a flogging for "trafficking in spirits"

Yule watched as another drama club member read the charges against Noira, but it was a parent from the PTA who proceeded with the flogging because the school board deemed it too intense to have a student conduct the whipping, although students could watch. For the scourging, they used a cat-o-nine-tails, and with each bite of the whip into the red-streaked, flesh-colored plastic that covered Ms. Zinnert's back, she let out a yelp. She had started the night with shrieks – screams were also deemed too intense – but as more and more floggings occurred, reenactment fatigue set in, affecting her performance. Nonetheless, she followed the script and when 40 lashes were reached, she fell to the platform so that her plastic covered back faced the crowd.

When that happened, Yule took it as his cue. He stepped onto the platform and said, "The Corn Maze of Fear is closing for the night and there are still a few scenes for you to experience, so we would appreciate it if everyone would please continue through the maze. Thank you, and the Corn Maze of Fear is open every night from 7-9 until Halloween, so be sure to tell your friends."

After a few moments, Ms. Zinnert asked, "Are they gone?" "Yeah."

She held up her hand, and Yule helped her to her feet. As she stood, the sounds from the next scene could be heard. She looked at Yule, smiled and said, "So a lot of visitors tonight?"

"It was a good turnout. I hope it keeps up."

Once Ms. Zinnert gathered herself, she moved in the direction away from the visitors. Yule followed and walked with her. He was married to Autumn, his high school sweetheart, and he loved his wife, but he found Evin Zinnert attractive and he enjoyed those moments he could talk or flirt with her.

"I saw the end of your scene. You're good. I understand you did some fund-raising for the school when you were a student here."

"I graduated a couple of years after you…when I was a senior, I ran some fund raisers, mostly for the class trip to Washington. Enough money was raised that year for all the seniors to go on the trip."

"That's right…did you know my wife Autumn? Ah…she was Autumn Benedict back then."

"I knew her. She was on the student council, and I had to deal with the council to organize the fund raisers."

"We got married after she graduated from college…well, it was after I got my master's in education. She's working on her masters now. Back when we were students, we couldn't wait to get out of here, but now we're back and likely for good."

"I also moved away right after graduation. Now I'm back, but I don't expect to stay."

"Well, I'm glad you came back. We don't get a lot of alumni participation in fund-raising activities like this. Oh, they donate money and supplies, but not their time. I think a lot more people would like to get involved the way you did, but they just don't know how. Thank you for volunteering to help with this project."

"I saw the opportunity and took it. It was that simple."

"I wish more alumni were like you," he said as they reached the entrance. "You probably want to head out, and I've got to shut down the concession stands. You know, ensure all the money is accounted for and that these kids get home."

"Have a good rest of the night," she said before turning to the parking lot.

It took another hour to shut everything down and ensure the money was safe until it could be deposited in the bank on Monday. As Yule did all that, Evin kept flashing though his thoughts, and she was the last thing he thought of when he laid down next to Autumn.

The next day was Sunday, and Yule proudly told Autumn how well the maze had performed. She hadn't been able to attend the first night, but they had planned for her to oversee ticket sales that evening and for the rest of the week. Once at the maze, Autumn's management skills asserted themselves, and she organized the students who staffed the ticket table, and she was on hand when the scene actors entered the maze. That's when she saw Evin, who was looking straight at Autumn as she passed.

The look in Evin's eyes unnerved Autumn, who then sought out Yule. "Who was that woman, the one dressed like a pilgrim with a bloody back?"

"Evin Zinnert. She was in your class. She's in the whipping post scene. She's playing the witch who gets whipped."

"Oh, I thought I recognized her." "Did you know her?"

"No! I didn't know her at all. I mean I recognized her face, but I never hung with her or anything."

Yule shrugged and returned to supervising the concessions tables while Autumn returned to the ticket table. Once 8:30 arrived, he found Autumn and asked, "How many tickets did we sell tonight?"

"Eighty-two."

He then moved to the counters at the exit where he was told 69 visitors had exited the maze. *Again,* he thought. *Well, there's school tomorrow. This must shut down so these kids can head home, so I'm going to move those people along. Who'd have thought I'd have to do that two nights in a row?* While it was a bother to have to search for the visitors, Yule was happy to have sold all those tickets, which tallied to another $1,200, and raking in that much money stoked Yule's feelings of pride and satisfaction – mostly pride.

However, the giddy feeling that filled him transformed into genuine surprise when he turned a corner on the course to find the 13 missing visitors were at the Red Maggie scene. Just as the night before, Yule waited until the drama was finished before stepping on the platform and instructing the visitors to proceed through the rest of the course. Like the night before, he exited through the entrance with Ms. Zinnert (who said for Yule to call her Evin), and this time Autumn was waiting.

"The money from the ticket sales is ready," she said.

"Thanks, honey. Do you remember Evin Zinnert?"

Autumn looked at both and brusquely answered, "Not really. I'll bring the money to you." She then moved off.

"Okay," he replied, drawing it out. Surprised by Autumn's response and actions, he tried to keep the good feelings going. He turned to Evin, smiled and said, "Thanks for tonight."

"I'm having fun," she said. "See you tomorrow." "You bet."

Shutting the maze down and seeing that everything was secured went quicker than the first night, and Yule and Autumn were soon in their car pulling out of the parking lot. She then surprised him further by saying, "I can't help with the maze tomorrow night."

"What? Really?"

"Yeah, I've got things to do to prepare for Tuesday's classes, so I'll have to stay home Monday night."

"Okay, but I thought you had that under control."

"I thought I did, but I was wrong," she said, and that ended the discussion.

There were more surprises for Yule on Monday, for that was when he really started to pay attention to the faces of the visitors who entered the maze. At the end of the night when he went to search for another 22 visitors who were still in the maze, he headed straight to the whipping post scene.

Before announcing that the maze was closing for the evening, he took long looks at the visitors' faces and realized that some of them not only were among the first to enter the maze that evening, they also had been to the maze before. He wondered what it was that so captivated these people that they were glued to the spot for nearly two hours to watch the same scene over and over. He mentioned it to Evin, who said, "It's obvious. Those are the assholes that get off on seeing a woman whipped."

By Tuesday, what at first had been surprisingly weird to

Yule had become routine, for he not only began to expect that visitors would cluster at the Red Maggie scene, it became such the norm that he decided to wait 20 minutes after the last group of visitors entered the corn maze before he followed to announce the closing of the attraction. However, by the time Halloween arrived, Yule was swamped with overseeing the rest of the event, and Autumn had rejoined the corn maze staff.

"Are you sure you can break away from grading papers?" asked Yule.

"It's the last night of your big fund-raising project. I'm not going to miss the event that's going to get my husband noticed and promoted to the head of the department, so even if I have to stay late tomorrow to catch up, I'll live." Since Autumn was the only one Yule truly trusted, he posted her to oversee ticket sales. It was a wise move, because the cash box was overflowing. Yule said he needed to get the cash from the tickets and the concessions in the school safe, but he also needed to call the night. Autumn volunteered to do that, and Yule nodded agreement, and picked up the cash box.

When he returned from securing the money, he saw the scarecrow standing with a group of teen girls, and Pogo, Ed and the witches were peppered among Mr. Gould's Ghouls. But there was no Autumn, and the kids stationed at the maze's exit were still on duty. He approached them and asked, "Has Mrs. Clary come out?"

"No, I haven't seen her," said the senior student who was put in charge of monitoring the exit. The two other students with him repeated the same.

"Okay," Yule said. "When she comes out ask her to wait for me here because I'm going to the entrance and walking through." The students mumbled and nodded in the affirmative, and, satisfied they would do as directed, Yule walked into the maze and followed the trail. Soon he was turning the corner to the clearing that featured Red Maggie, where he was greeted by expected and unexpected activities. The expected was that there was a group of about 50 visitors standing mesmerized by the scene. The unexpected was that Evin was not at the whipping post being flogged, or even in her witch costume. Rather, she was nude and dancing around the group.

Yule gasped as he took in her undeniable beauty. Her curvy body, flowing hair, and all-around sexiness made him recall Botticelli's *The Birth of Venus*. While he was enamored by her gorgeousness, the rational part of Yule realized that if her nude dancing got out, or worse still, if some students should witness this, it would bring holy hell down on the school, and likely end his career. To forestall that, he had to act, which led him to utter a pathetic, "What the hell is going on here?!"

Evin then sharply turned her attention to Yule, smiled, and in a flash, she was dancing around him. At first, she danced in a circle, but just as quickly she was rubbing up against him, planting little kisses on his face and shoulders and filling him with desire. As strange as that was, it was made stranger by the slippage of time that, from Yule's point of view, seemed to cause events to occur in flashes, for in a blink they went from standing on the trail, to standing on the platform that held Red Maggie, to his head and hands being held firm in the stocks. From that position, his head was being held up and forward, so he looked out at the crowd, the members of which had their collective backs turned to Yule.

Beyond the crowd was Evin, who continued to dance with the ease and grace of a ballerina. She also moved in a manner that suggested she was enticing the crowd into…action? Yule didn't know why, but that was the word that came to mind.

Beyond Evin was the cornfield, from which emanated a strange light. The light wasn't bright and steady as it would be from a vehicle's headlamp or any other electrical source; rather, it was wild and erratic, for it twisted and pulsated like the light from a fire. The glow spread all through the cornfield, suggesting that in this case, the fire was a bonfire, and that possibility filled Yule with panic.

Yule wanted to yell out to Evin, or to any of the crowd, but he found he not only couldn't speak, he couldn't even open his mouth. All he could do was watch as Evin danced around the group one more time before heading into the field and disappearing among the stalks. She was quickly followed by the crowd, and within a couple of minutes they were all gone. Yule again tried to pull free from the stocks, but he was held just as firmly as before. Not long after the last crowd member disappeared into the field, Yule felt someone slap him on the buttocks. He still couldn't turn his head, but he didn't have to wait long to find out who it was.

"Because you helped me achieve this, I think you deserve to know what's going on and why, and to really see these fuckers for what they are."

Just as suddenly as he was made mute, Yule could again speak, and he said, "Helped you?! What the fuck are you talking about?! Get me out of here now!"

"In time. First I'm going to tell you a story."

Confusion flooded through Yule, but he also realized he needed to let her speak in order to get free.

"It goes like this…When I was a student, I was involved in all sorts of extra-curricular activities, and most of those involved some sort of fund raising. During my freshman and sophomore years, I was content to be in a supporting role, but during my junior year, I assumed leadership roles, the pinnacle of which was fund-raising for the senior class trip to Washington. During a Junior Class Officers meeting, it was made clear that some students wouldn't be able to go on the trip because their families just couldn't afford the full price, but that if we raised enough money, the cost of the trip would be reduced with the goal being to make it affordable for everyone.

Because I thought it unfair that some students wouldn't be able to go, I became committed to changing that. I organized and held bake sales and car washes, operated the ticket booth at the student-teacher basketball game, and ran raffles during the games. I even sold candy bars door-to-door. I'll have you know I sold the most candy bars, and it worked. I helped raise enough money so the entire senior class could go. No one was left behind. I was very proud of that, but on the second night of the trip, there was a secret party in a room at our hotel.

"Some of the seniors pooled their money and rented another room, but on a different floor away from the chaperones. Invitation to the party was by word of mouth. Of course, I was invited, and not long after arriving one of my classmates named Tony Fulmar -do you know him? Never mind. He brought a cup of punch. I could smell the alcohol, but I thought, 'one won't do any harm'.

What I didn't know was Tony put something in the drink that caused me to black out, and they…took turns. And Tony, good old Tony, that bastard raped me twice. After he raped me the first time, he must have liked it so much that as soon as everyone else had a turn, he had to come back for seconds. Apparently, after he saw me at the corn maze, he's been bragging about balling me, and his wife Giselle overheard him, now she thinks that I was her dickhead husband's high school girlfriend, and that I'm here to get him back. Isn't that a hoot?

"Getting back to that night, I don't actually know how many raped me, but I do know that more than a dozen classmates — 'classmates,' what a joke — more than a dozen of those motherfuckers watched it happen and did nothing to stop it. That included several girls…including Autumn."

Yule was stunned by her words, and he yelled, "Not Autumn! Not my Autumn!"

"Shut up!" she commanded, and when he was quiet, she continued. "These were people who I had gone to school with for years, yet no one called a teacher or lifted a finger to stop it. I don't know if it was cowardliness, or pure meanness, but they let it happen.

Then later, out of shame or guilt, they put the blame on me. I was the one held responsible for what was done to me, not the boys who raped me. But it wasn't enough that I was designated the school slut. They weren't done with me yet. They decided to give Evin Zinnert a nickname, one that would brand me as an 'easy' fuck, and that I'd never be able to shake off.

They started calling me 'E-Zee', and I later found out that E-Zee's home phone number was on the wall in all the boys' bathrooms. I found that one out just by answering the phone. Even though I was embarrassed and ashamed of it all, I couldn't ask my parents to change the number because they'd want to know why, so I stopped answering the phone, until...there were times when I had no choice.

That's when I heard all the things those motherfuckers wanted to do to me...Funny, don't you think? For the rest of the school year I was something to be whispered about and laughed at. It didn't matter if it was during homeroom, in the cafeteria during lunch, or in gym class, there was always a small group of my classmates who would look at me and giggle.

I coped the only way I could, and for the rest of the school year I dropped my head in such a way so that my hair would hang over my face, that way I wouldn't have to look at them laughing... I pretended I didn't hear the remarks and catcalls, and of course I didn't go to the prom or even graduation. I couldn't wait to get to college and be free of them, but I wasn't free, because I grew to hate them so much that I never really left, or they never left me. I wanted to get back at them. I wanted them to feel what I felt. I wanted them to hurt.

"It was in college that I first found Wicca, and through that I learned of 'the Left-Hand Path.' Wicca is white magic, and conversely, the Left-Hand Path is dark magic. I saw that as my opportunity to get revenge. But summoning dark spirits and controlling them are two different things. It turned out they would do what I asked, but in their way.

"You were right to wonder why some of the visitors kept coming back to see me get whipped. I used the Left-Hand Path to put a spell on the advertising for your corn maze. That's why the maze was such a success. It attracted those assholes…those upstanding men and women who secretly salivate at the thought of a victim getting whipped…even if they knew it was fake. I did it because I knew some of those assholes would be the same assholes who watched me get raped, but to get the Left-Hand Path spirits to hold them, I mean *really* hold them, I had to pay the spirits with blood… my blood, and that meant really getting whipped. Josh—the parent from the PTA who read the charges and whipped me

—at this point he'll do anything for me. Anyway, back to me. I held tight onto the whipping post. I hugged it like a lover, and I did love it. I loved it because I knew what would happen. Halloween is when the spirits are at their most powerful, and with my pain and blood and love, the spirits had what they needed to open a portal to the spirit realm. All that was left was to lead those assholes into the cornfield, and you saw how that went.

"Your ignorance was bliss…it's unfortunate for you that… well, you'll know soon enough." Suddenly, figures emerged from the cornfield. It was the missing group, and they quickly and silently headed for the exit. "Now that it's begun, you'll soon understand," Evin said.

Yule watched as a parade of visitors stepped out of the cornfield and followed the path out of the maze… that is, all but one. A single visitor ran toward the platform, and Yule recognized the figure as his wife. Her face radiated fear, and when she reached the platform she said, "The things going on in there…I can't believe it…we saw what they'll do to us if we don't do what you tell us to," she said, her voice frantic. Yule realized she was talking to Evin. "Please, I'll do anything you want."

That's when he spoke up. "Autumn, get me out of this!" At that point she did move to a position behind him, but she didn't release the stocks. Again, he said, "Autumn, get me out of here!" This time his voice was uneasy, almost frantic.

"I…don't know what to do," Autumn said.

"It's simple, you'll do as you agreed and give your husband 40 lashes," Evin commanded.

"What!" Yule yelled.

"Your wife agreed to give you a whipping while I watch. The alternative is…well, I don't even know exactly what's in that cornfield, but I do know it's hell on earth courtesy of the Left-Hand Path. Since she's so good at watching, Autumn got to see some of it, and it's locked in her brain, but now she has a choice. Live with the memory or inflict 40 lashes on you and it will be washed from her mind. She chooses the scourging." Evin then turned to Autumn and said, "You better make it a real effort. I'll know if you don't. Now start!"

"I'm sorry," she whispered, and brought the cat-o-nine tails down on Yule's bare back, eliciting a scream.

"Again!" Evin demanded, and Autumn complied. The pain grew in intensity and Yule's scream was louder. "Again!" the witch said, and again Autumn brought down the whip on Yule. "More," said Evin, and with each strike of the whip, the witch increased her demands, and each strike grew in strength so that eventually one continuous scream escaped from Yule's lips. But then, just as quickly as it began, it was over.

"I can't do it anymore. It's too much!" Autumn said. "You're only halfway there. If you end it now, you'll suffer."

"But he hasn't hurt anyone."

"If that's what you want," said Evin, and Yule, semiconscious from the pain, heard a scuffle occurring behind him. There was the rustle of the corn stalks, and then it was quiet. He passed out and didn't come to until a pair of strong hands removed him from his confinement and dragged him a few feet from the platform, where he was dropped. He fell back into unconsciousness. He woke to scores of police and EMTs tending to the shocked and bleeding victims and victimizers. Anger and hatred engulfed family members, with those who suffered under the lash asking why their spouses subjected them to such cruelty. But not all the flogging victims were able to articulate their questions. Giselle Fulmar looked near death, as Tony tried to explain what had happened.

There were plenty of arrests, and newspaper photographers and television camera operators shooting video, as well as dozens of onlookers. As he was loaded onto an ambulance, Yule scanned the crowd, but there was no Autumn. Stranger still, he struggled to recall her face. *Was forgetting what she looked like her part of the penance?* he wondered, frightened that he would forget her forever. *No! I won't let that happen.*

The school district was scandalized by the eruption of sadomasochism, and the board had the corn maze quickly cut down, revealing that there was nothing hidden in the field. The board also fired Yule but said nothing of Autumn, and while Yule was persona non grata at the school, no one complained when he showed up to retrieve his and Autumn's personal property. No one there seemed to have any idea about who he was talking about when he mentioned Autumn. The items he said were hers had been relegated to the Lost and Found, and there wasn't any opposition to him taking them. That wouldn't be the only item for which there was no opposition to Yule eventually carting away.

With Autumn gone, Yule lived like a monk. In addition, in order to keep the home, he had shared with her, he needed a job and the income it supplied. Because of his level of education, he quickly found employment enabling him to keep both the house and Autumn's memory alive. However, once the work problem was solved, depression set in, causing Yule to go to the basement and remove his shirt. On the nights he did that, he would feel the scars on his back throb, making him feel as if she was with him. Eventually what he needed to do next came to him.

It was the day after Thanksgiving when he drove to the back of the high school to find the Red Maggie post, as well as bundles of dried corn stalks, next to the garbage dumpster. Yule had no problem helping himself to the whipping post and as many of the bundles as he could load into his car. Once at his house, he found that the stalks fit into a corner of his basement. It took a little time, but he was able to get them to stand straight like they had in the cornfield, and he organized them into a small path. Obtaining the rest of what he needed wasn't as easy.

In January, he had to travel to the city, where he cruised crime-riddled neighborhoods in search of a prostitute. When he found one, she had him drive to a remote alley. However, rather than have sex, he knocked her unconscious, handcuffed her, and covered her head with a plastic bag. He was driving so he didn't see when she frantically tried to take her last breath. Once her got her into his garage, he cut her up her body and froze the parts.

Two more months passed before he felt confident enough to search for more of what he needed, and when he came up short, he decided to volunteer at a homeless shelter. By doing so he was able to identify homeless who really didn't have any family, and he made friends with them. Over several months he identified two more women, both mentally ill and alone in the world, and he was able to lure them into his car and his home, where he put a plastic bag over the head of one, while the other he kept captive for Halloween.

When October 31st arrived, he set the dead women up near a dummy of Pogo, the evil clown. He made Pogo using a clown costume stuffed with newspaper and topped it with a bag that he put the clown mask over. He did the same with a witch costume that he used to create a Left-Hand Path witch he named Evin, and he positioned it next to a cauldron. He filled the kettle with water and the prostitute's body parts. The remaining victim was alive when he locked her into Red Maggie.

The front of Yule's home was decorated to the nines in all types of Halloween decorations, including those that produced screams, shrieks, and music. Yule dressed himself up as farmer Ed, complete with a mask made from the cut-off face of a human mask, and he distributed candy to the neighborhood children. The town had set 9 p.m. as the curfew for trick-or-treat, but Yule let the noise-making decorations run until late into the night. No one complained, because after all, it was once a year.

When 9 o'clock arrived, farmer Ed withdrew to the basement to scourge the remaining captive. However, unlike at the corn maze a year ago, Yule didn't stop at 40. He continued well past that number to 50, 75 then 100 lashes. Blood not only ran down the victim's back, it covered the whipping post— truly making Maggie "red". It splattered onto the ceiling and onto the stalks that Yule had arranged around the basement to resemble a cornfield. With each lash of the whip, one thought filled Yule's head.

Maybe if I finish what Autumn couldn't, they'll let her come home.

He continued well past midnight, which was long after the

victim had slumped lifeless, only being held up by the stocks. At that point Yule halted and took a deep breath. He then turned to the stalks and waited, but nothing happened. That's the way it remained up until the light of sunrise glowed beyond the basement's covered windows. The stress and realization that he had failed caused tears to stream down his face, but then he heard a voice. It was soft but urging and came from the stalks.

The voice said, *"Next Halloween...until then, keep the path wet."*

Made in the USA
Middletown, DE
21 July 2021

44189408R00298